BLOOD
OF THE
MAZZAROTH

BY ERIC T. EICHINGER

CASTLE BRIDGE MEDIA
DENVER, COLORADO, USA

CASTLE BRIDGE MEDIA
Denver, Colorado

Cover art by Chikovnaya/Shutterstock and r2dpr/Shutterstock.
These images have been modified.

This book is a work of fiction. Names, characters, business, events, and incidents are the products of the author's imagination. Any resemblance to actual persons, living or dead or actual events is purely coincidental.

BLOOD OF THE MAZZAROTH
2026© Eric T. Eichinger
All rights reserved.

ISBN: 979-8-9940410-2-4

No part of this book may be reproduced, stored in a retrieval system, or transmitted in any form or by any means, electronic, mechanical, photocopying, recording, or otherwise, without the prior written permission of the author, except as provided by U.S.A. copyright law.

For Robert Wilson
Who didn't balk when I said, "I have a crazy idea..."
and encouraged me to keep writing.

Prologue

Los Angeles, California
Thursday, August 22nd
11:56 P.M.

THE GIRL HAD BEEN DEAD long enough, and the waiting was almost over. A filthy skeletal white van skulked through the City of Angels. The deathly pale vehicle's low hum hardly stirred the slumbering tent-city dwellers as it meandered through its desired snakelike path.

"You've arrived at your destination," the GPS navigation blurted.

Wolfgang Manteuffel, a white, well-chiseled man, compressed the brake pad and slowly squeaked to a stop. Experience seeped through every crack of his middle-aged alabaster face. He opened his tinted window for a clearer view of St. Mary's Catholic Church across the street and confirmed the address. He switched off the navigation system of his cell phone and tapped the numbers on the dial pad. A dark demanding voice answered. "Are you in the *exact* location I said?"

"Yeah, no one's here, and I'm out of view of the cameras," Manteuffel said.

"Perfect," said the voice.

The thin green digital clock in the dashboard hit 12:00 a.m.

"Are you ready?" the voice asked urgently.

"Semper fi," Manteuffel said.

"That's my man. The scroll has been opened. So, it begins. Remember, be *precise*." *Click.*

Manteuffel donned a surgical mask and gloves, as he crammed his San Francisco Giants ball cap over his head and snuck back to the rear of the van compartment. He looked over his deceased passenger. A result of his skilled hands. The cakey quality of the innocent girl's young blood was already causing her bright blonde hair to stick to the clear plastic sheet beneath her.

The back doors creaked open piercing all the quiet that the 400 block of St. Louis Street had to offer. Manteuffel stepped out in a faded brown leather jacket. He looked both ways down the road. No life of any kind was around.

The tall strong figure tugged the plastic sheet with the girl's body toward him. He quickly but gently picked her up and laid her back down on the sidewalk. He stood over her, spreading her feet and legs carefully about a foot apart, and placed her right arm almost straight out angled slightly up toward her head. He stood back, pulled out a small slip of paper, cross-referenced the image on it against the body, and surveyed the streets one more time.

He gingerly straightened her left arm out, but at a lower angle than her right. *Good enough.* He scrambled into the back of the van and slammed the doors. The digital clock changed over to 12:02 a.m. as he shifted the van into drive. The van sped off, leaving the girl's body unnoticed. This would not last long. The first day of school for the new year would begin at dawn.

Chapter 1

Los Angeles, California
Monday, January 6th

IT WAS A TYPICAL STAR-CROSSED day during an otherwise atypical ill-omened year when Chase Fischer first heard of the prophecy. His clarion showed up in the form of an intrusive detective. Never in a trillion years would Fischer have believed what was foretold, or that *that* morning he would have needed to utter one of the more terrifying phrases he could imagine.

"I'm sorry, am... am I a person of *interest*?"

Those words sounded much more innocent in his head before he said them, Fischer thought. The lightning hot endorphin rush which fires at the back of the neck when tension surfaces in conversation sparked immediately for Fischer. It was a sensation he hated yet was reluctantly all too familiar with recently. Fischer swallowed with difficulty as he was escorted to an LAPD squad car.

Detective George Greppin stood 6'4" and possessed a strong commanding presence with his powerfully built African American frame. Greppin owned a mere four-inch height advantage over Fischer's svelte 6'0" figure, yet seemingly dwarfed him, as Greppin held the backseat door of his squad car open for Fischer to enter. Fischer's rose-gold spun hair waved in the breeze, seemingly saying goodbye to freedom.

How did I get in this situation? Chase Fischer examined his thoughts…

Not ten minutes before Fischer had cavalierly roared down the road toward his office on his candy-apple red Triumph Bonneville motorcycle, with his formidable German Shepherd, Luther, riding in the sidecar. It was a much-needed fresh new year he looked forward to. He'd waltzed in beaming with pride wearing his new black motorcycle jacket with red vertical racing stripe. He knew he'd never reach Steve McQueen coolness status, but it didn't hurt to try from time to time. Fischer had expected to see what the week's plans beheld over coffee and office pleasantries with his secretary Jeannie. But this morning the tone in her voice was off. He regrettably remembered at her urgent prompting that coffee would have to wait as there was an LAPD officer waiting to see him.

The police squad car hit a speed bump pulling out of the parking lot of Church of the Epiphany, calling deeper attention to this budding fact. Fischer wondered, had he done or said something wrong? His emerging caffeine headache didn't help matters.

As they cruised along, Fischer closed his eyes and retraced his steps leading up to his encounter with officer Greppin. He did his best to ignore the suffocating sensation of riding in the back of a police squad car for the first time. *Focus…*

Fischer had heeded Jeannie's urging, left Luther with her at the front office, and quickly walked down the hall into the cozy conference room where Detective Greppin awaited him. Jeannie had always said that room, full of bookshelves, a pair of leather couches and a wall mounted electric fireplace 'rounded out the ambience.' However, with an intimidating police officer grilling him in there, that space was decidedly less warm.

Fischer continued probing his mind. *What went wrong?* Fischer replayed the conversation they'd just had and pondered what might have led to his current predicament.

"Morning, officer," Fischer had said. "Can I help you?"

"Rev. Doctor Chase Fischer? What do I call you?"

"Yes, uh, Pastor is fine. Or Doctor. Either is fine. I hear both about the same interchangeably."

Greppin sized him up with a once over of his eyes. "There're a few sides to you, aren't there? Don't you guys usually wear a black and white clerical collar?"

"I save that for when I preach in the pulpit."

"I see. I'm Detective George Greppin of the Los Angeles Police Department. Is this your business card?" Detective Greppin showed Chase his business card which read:

Rev. Dr. Chase L. Fischer
Sr. Pastor: Church of the Epiphany
Professor of Ancient History: Christus Veritas University
Los Angeles, California

"And your contact info on the back?" Greppin said, flipping the card over.

"Yes, that's me."

"Can we talk?" Greppin asked.

"Sure."

"Please, have a seat," Greppin offered with a directness that didn't feel like he was asking. The detective pulled out a photograph and presented it. "Do you recognize this person?"

The young woman in the photograph was a gorgeous young blond, probably college aged, with striking features, wearing a fitted female UCLA t-shirt and skin-tight jeans.

Fischer held the picture and studied it up close for a few seconds. "Can't say I do, officer."

"Detective," Greppin said tersely. "Are you sure you've never met her before?"

Fischer thought for a moment longer, more intently this time.

"I think I'd remember meeting a girl like *that*. Is she missing or something?"

"Or something. She's *dead*, Pastor Fischer," Greppin said, slowly leaning in. "And what you say is rather interesting because I have reason to believe that you *have* met her before. And as a matter of fact, your business card was found in her possession when we made the discovery of the body.

Mind if we continue this conversation downtown?"

Fischer opened his eyes, reborn from his private memory horror trance and gazed at the LAPD precinct office. *Downtown. Great.* In no time Detective Greppin ushered Fischer into his next 'first' of the day—a police interrogation room, accompanied with his very own set of Miranda rights read to him.

Fischer had only seen these kinds of places on television or in the movies. The small table, a few hard-seated chairs, in an uncomfortably small room, and of course the classic two-way mirror which he could only assume had more LAPD eyes observing through the other side. What the cinema never conveyed was the pungent smell of old body odor lingering in rooms like this. *Honestly, how often do they clean this place?*

Fischer knew he was innocent. He figured a simple explanation to the top brass would soon clear the matter up. He unzipped his jacket as he caught his own reflection in the mirror. A preppy buttoned-up shirt and yet another one of his vintage characteristic argyle-patterned ties. Few people if any had looked as dapper as he had that morning, Fischer mused with the smallest crack of a grin. Fischer's smirk didn't last long.

Detective Greppin entered the room with a laptop and a smile. Fischer was about to make a smart comment about the importance of Lysol and inquire who the superior officer might be when Greppin pressed play on the video.

The footage showed the sanctuary of the Church of the Epiphany, and Fischer leading worship with a packed house.

"What *is* this?" Fischer asked skeptically.

"Just wait," Greppin said, fast-forwarding and then pausing on a frame. He pointed with a long finger, "That is you, and *that* is the girl from the photograph I showed you earlier." She stood in worship near what appeared to be friends of hers. Greppin zipped through a bit more of the footage to the post-worship receiving line.

"*And* that is you shaking her hand and talking to her."

Fischer rolled his eyes. "Officer, honestly, this is very explainable."

The door opened and another officer walked in with a steaming cup of coffee. He was athletically stocky with sandy blond hair. "Dr. Fischer, I'm homicide detective Justin Praider. We're listening."

Fischer recoiled. "You can't be *serious*. This is a recording of Easter Sunday." Fischer could easily tell from the video it was indeed the high holy day of the resurrection of Christ. The white vestments and annual decorative Easter lilies were a dead giveaway. "Do you have any idea how many people pass through the doors on any given Sunday, let alone Easter Sunday? You're expecting me to know and remember every face? It's January. That was last March, the 31st if I'm not mistaken."

Detective Praider brushed his slightly long flowing hair in need of a cut from his brow, loudly slurped his drink, and jotted down some notes. Then he threw a curveball.

"Do you ever shoot archery?"

"Huh? What about the girl?" Fischer asked.

"Oh, we'll get back to the girl, Dr. Fischer," Praider said curtly. "Just answer the question. It's a simple question."

"Archery? Sure. I used to shoot a little while growing up with my dad. At a range. A few deer hunting attempts. We lived in the Midwest, Wisconsin. It's what you do."

"What kind of bow?" Greppin asked.

"Compound," Fischer said awkwardly.

"Ever have much hunting success?" Praider asked.

"No... *No*." Fischer said, feeling the magnitude of the situation increase with each new question. Greppin continued what was now clearly an interrogation.

"The only deer we ever *killed* was one we hit with the car. I remember, we had to get out and field dress it right then and there on the side of the road," Fischer said.

"With a knife?" Greppin said.

"Well, since I had just trimmed my nails—*yes*, a knife."

"Sarcasm won't help you, Dr. Fischer. And how might she have acquired your business card?"

Fischer recalculated for a second. "Ah, I see we're back to the girl. I usually leave my cards out near the receiving line at church. They're easily accessible for anyone with remote interest."

"You know, it's funny. I took the liberty of checking that out this morning before you arrived. I didn't see any available," Greppin said, flashing intensity through his eyes. Fischer's dull caffeine headache was brewing stronger.

"You have a lot of answers, Dr. Fischer." Praider said irritated. "Do you have an answer for how *this* happened?" Praider tossed a photo across the table. It was the body of the blond girl, bloody and dead on the side of a road. Fischer torqued to his side so as not to have the image seared into his mind. *Too late.*

"Her name was Shelly Davidson. Say her name Dr. Fischer. *Say her name.*"

"I… I'm…" Fischer choked up.

"She's got a lot of unusual knife cuts all over her body, you wanna tell us about those? Or how about this one," Greppin said. He flicked out another photograph. This one of a dead woman impaled with arrows. The victim was older, middle-aged, and brunette. Fischer began to feel nauseated.

"I'm sorry…"

"Sorry for what, Dr. Fischer? For *what*?" Greppin asked, standing and leaning over him as his voice elevated in powerful authority.

"I'm sorry, I can't look at this." Fischer said. "I didn't do this if that's what you think. I didn't do *any* of this."

"Are you sure, because I assume you're pretty well versed in *this* subject matter too, pastor," Praider yelled as he emphatically threw down a final photo as if he'd triumphantly won a poker tournament.

Fischer could barely bring himself to look at the third photo and quickly wished he hadn't.

Chapter 2

THE CRUCIFIXION OF CHRIST IS referenced every Sunday around the globe, by any good minister worth his salt. St. Paul exhorted 'Christ crucified' be preached without ceasing. Ever since the dawn of Christendom, preachers have been well versed at describing the crucifixion of Jesus, in physically graphic detail, if need be, in sermons, Bible studies, or conversation. The scourging, the cross carrying through the *Via Dolorosa* toward the peak of Calvary's hill, the thorned crown jammed on Jesus' head, the pierced hands and feet, the chest cavity asphyxiation, and his taunted final death right down to the spear plunged into his side, all gruesome necessity for God in the flesh to die, in order to rise, and triumphantly defeat death—for the sins of the world.

The Rev. Dr. Chase Fischer had studied, taught, and preached Christ crucified for many years. He had believed it as far back as he could remember. As familiar as the topic was to him, it was no less disturbing to examine a photograph of a present-day man crucified in downtown LA. The dark-haired male victim looked possibly mid-thirties and slightly emaciated, though from the photo it was hard to tell. What was unmistakable was the fact he was literally nailed to the wooden cross and wearing a crown. *Odd it's a fake plastic looking crown. If someone went to this much trouble, why not a crown of thorns?* Fischer thought.

"A college student, a stay-at-home mom, and a John Doe from one of the tent villages around the city," Greppin said.

Fischer's earlier seed of a caffeine headache had fully bloomed into a migraine. "Could I have some water, please?" Fischer asked as his head began to throb.

"I'll look into that for you," Praider said chidingly as he slurped another sip of his own coffee. "Do you feel like another movie, George?" Praider asked.

"You know, I think I could be up for just one more, Justin."

They began cuing up another segment on the laptop. Fischer wondered for a brief second how they got all this, but ever since the COVID 19 pandemic he and all his preacher friends essentially became overnight televangelists streaming live services *ad infinitum* throughout the farthest crevices of the internet. Fischer stared directly at what he believed to be a two-way mirror. His frustration level heated toward boiling as his head began to pulsate.

"Are we about done yet?"

Through the looking glass stood a young twenty-something cutesy female officer, with brown hair and platinum blond high-lighted streaks, just long enough to be tied back into the shortest of ponytails. She indiscreetly shook off her nerves, hoping the elderly white-whiskered cop next to her didn't notice.

"Chief, I've seen enough," she said.

"You think you're ready for this, Jade?" the Chief asked, with Tom Izzo coach-like questioning in his gruff speech.

Officer Jade opened the door of the interrogation room which brought the conversation to a halt. "Alright, guys, clear the room. It's my turn," she said.

Fischer's eyes swung over to her immediately. She wore her fitted uniform very well over her muscularly toned petite figure. All three men in the room couldn't help appreciating. Jade appeared mostly Caucasian, but her brown eyes and naturally tan skin suggested an unidentifiable sliver of Hispanic, Asian or perhaps Arabian trait in her heritage. Her aura somehow conveyed a half-Disney princess and half Amazon Warrior effect.

Praider and Greppin reluctantly walked out.

Fischer sighed as if an angel descended into the room for him and him alone, ending the siege against him. He could only imagine what heavenly language she might bespeak next.

"Coffee, Pastor Fischer?" She asked politely.

Unbelievable.

"Uh, *yeah*. I'd love some."

She caught Praider just in time.

"Praider, could you bring him a cup?"

Praider grimaced. "Sure thing, GJ."

"Dr. Fischer, I'm Detective Jade, pleased to meet you."

"Oh, you're the Gospel," Fischer said.

"What's that, now?"

"Sorry, in my line of work we speak of 'Law and Gospel,'" Fischer said. "It's a delicate interplay of knowing when to apply which approach to any given situation, like spiritual triage. Sort of your version of 'good cop, bad cop,' I suppose."

"Law and Gospel, huh? We like to think we're all good cops here, Dr. Fischer."

"Right, I was just s—"

"Listen, you're in a bit of a hole here, but I think you can help yourself and all of us out by answering a few more questions for us, and we'll get you home to your family soon enough."

"Huh? Oh, no family. I live alone."

"I see," Jade said.

Praider returned with the hot coffee and set it down in front of Fischer and exited quickly. *Awesome.*

"What do you know about the zodiac?" GJ asked.

"The zodiac? A lot, I guess. The twelve constellations, their various meanings, origins. What do you want?" Fischer asked.

"The killer. The Zodiac *killer*," Detective Jade said shortly.

Of course, Fischer recalled. He remembered seeing a recent headline referencing some title like, "Is the Zodiac Back?" It harkened back to the 1960's Zodiac murders that haunted San Francisco Bay. But he hadn't paid it much mind. It's hard to know which media to believe these days. Then again, considering the circumstances, perhaps he should have paid more attention.

"Detective, I can assure you I have nothing to do with a new sort of copycat Zodiac killing spree, if that's how you think these deaths are related." Fischer felt unheard as Detective Jade pressed play again on the laptop video. This one depicted Fischer preaching in the pulpit. Detective Jade turned up the volume at just the right moment.

"Is God telling us something in the stars? Does He have a message for us embedded in the constellations of the zodiac?" Fischer declared in his recorded sermon on screen. He looked at Detective Jade and started laughing.

"Is something funny, Dr. Fischer?" She asked. "The original Zodiac killer loved toying with the cops and sending messages. Don't you think with all the other circumstantial evidence it's odd you're publicly referencing the zodiac *in a sermon*? It seems that's the exact type of flaunting a copycat Zodiac killer might do to mess with us," Jade said.

"It's just, well, today is Epiphany, you know, after the twelve days of Christmas, January 6th *Epiphany*."

"Enlighten me."

Fischer snickered. "Again, ironic choice of words. *Epiphany* literally means 'the light shining out.' This clip was from yesterday's sermon where I referenced transitioning from the season of Christmas to Epiphany. Yes, I posed the question, 'Is God telling us something in the stars?' My church is literally named Epiphany, Jesus is the true Star, the Light, you know, "I was blind but now I see.""

Jade blushed as Fischer continued. "Correct me if I'm wrong, but the original Zodiac killer didn't actually follow the zodiac constellations as a source guide. He just called himself that, right?"

"That is accurate," Jade said.

"Were any of these murders during the end of November?"

"As a matter of fact, yes. This one." She pointed to the photo of the woman impaled with arrows. "She was killed on November 24."

Fischer pulled out his cell phone from his pocket and clicked open his email app.

"Ok. There you go. I was out of town for almost two weeks at the end of November, on recreation in Florida."

Fischer scrolled through his archives until he paused with a smile. "Here, this is my flight itinerary, the departure and return dates bookend November 24 by a wide margin. *And...*" Fischer quickly opened the link to his photos catalogue. "I have multiple sources with time-stamped photos to corroborate that fact." He slowly swiped through the photos. "Here's my parents, who live there, and here are some other friends. Here are their phone numbers, would you like to call them to verify the facts?" Fischer asked in a snarky checkmate fashion.

"No, I'm sure it checks out."

"Now, where is all this coming from anyway?" Fischer asked incredulously.

Detective Jade looked into the glass mirror and back to Chase with an astonished expression of defeat.

"We received a tip," Jade said.

"A *tip?*"

"Independent of your business card being found in the pocket of one of the victims, someone pointed us in your direction with the videos. Remember, it has been in some of the minor tabloid press. It was enough to make us want to dig deeper. Our informant didn't give us a name but sounded like he was a former student of yours and provided us with a direct link to your specific sermon, referencing the zodiac. After a little digging there seemed to be enough worth investigating."

Dr. Fischer had a pretty good hunch that his former student might want to smear him in this way and portray him in as negative a light as possible: Nate Maddix, an obnoxious elitist punk of a kid. Probably one of the sharpest knives in the academic drawer, and the snot-nosed kid knew it. Fischer had never known someone so desperate to be a leader, sans the followers. Fischer had given him an A- in his Ancient History course and had never heard the end of it.

"That's not all the correspondence we've had," Detective Jade continued. "We also received *this* last week." She showed Fischer a small stationery card revealing nothing more than a symbol drawn in simple pen ink. "Does this look familiar?"

Fischer's heart sank. He immediately recognized the symbolic signature, and the evil it represented.

Chapter 3

WOLFGANG MANTEUFFEL DROVE HIS WHITE van up a winding remote dirt road near the San Gabriel Mountains. Few vehicles drove this far up past the main trailheads. The rocky unleveled path deterred most other recreational drivers from going this deep past the foothills.

Manteuffel backed his van into the bramble brush and a couple trees with low hanging foliage. The thin wood branches scraped along the side of the van frame like nails across a chalkboard. He shut off the engine and went to the rear of the van compartment.

A large goat head mask lay crumpled up on the floor. Manteuffel picked it up and smoothed it out. He laid it back down and grabbed a pair of binoculars and a bag of trail mix. He returned to the driver's seat and scanned the trail, munching on his snack. He didn't bother looking down the trail. He only concerned himself further up the mountain. His next victim would be more tired near the end of their hike, so they'd be headed down the mountain.

A fiftyish man rounded the bend high up the trail and came into frame of Manteuffel's binoculars.

"Right on cue. Seems like old times," Manteuffel said quietly to himself.

# # #

The LAPD Chief continued to watch the interrogation concealed behind the viewing mirror separating the two rooms. Detective Jade hovered over Fischer waiting for his next words. Fischer finally spoke. "I could be mistaken, but this symbol of a circle with a cross through it looks like the signature of the original Zodiac killer, his imprimatur if you will."

The Chief spit out the mouthful of coffee he was about ready to swallow, hitting Greppin's shoes standing next to him. "*Damn* it. I didn't authorize her to share that information. I don't want that to get out to the public. I didn't even know she had that with her. George, did you?"

"Chief," Greppin said. "It's a rookie mistake. It's her first time at this, and you just appointed her."

The Chief rolled his eyes. "Damn." And headed for the door.

Fischer's eyes popped up as Detective Greppin and an older distinguished looking man barged into the interrogation room. Jade raised one eyebrow and quickly turned around.

Greppin's deep voice took control of the room. "Dr. Fischer, this is the Chief of Police, Chief Tatum. Thank you for your time. I think this was a big misunderstanding. Sorry for any inconvenience." They shook hands with Fischer.

Chief Tatum chimed in. "The original Zodiac killer was a long time ago. Most people don't remember or have any common knowledge of it. I'm not sure if this is officially a copycat, if they're related at all, or what the hell is going on, but we did receive this piece of correspondence this week. Although tell me, how did you recognize it as the Zodiac's?"

"Mostly from pop-culture pulp fiction trivia, I guess," Fischer said.

"That's a pretty old tidbit of information to remember," Praider said.

Fischer smiled. "I am a professor of ancient history. My mind tends to hold on to details like that. "Chief Tatum," Fischer collected himself, "is this real, is this actually happening, again?"

Chief Tatum took a long deep breath in contemplation then sharply exhaled through his nostrils. "We don't know what's going on just yet," he said. "The original Zodiac killer was never caught. *Technically* it's still an open case. He would be extremely old right now to be messing around with us. So, I highly *highly* doubt it could be him. Plus, that was all essentially in the northern California area, this is LA. Is it a copycat? Or just some random idiot with nothing better to do? We don't know. But there are thousands of people doing thousands of horrible things, every day, and we did have this sent to us, to mess with us apparently. You're oddly associated with some of it, but, well, who isn't at this point…" The Chief flailed a frustrated wave of his hand into the air and stormed out. His voice rattled through the hall corridor. "Somebody get this man home. Clearly this is not our guy."

Greppin shook Fischer's hand a second time. "Again, Rev. Dr. Fischer, sorry we wasted your morning."

"Does that mean I'm no longer a person of interest?" Fischer asked.

"Not at this time," Greppin stated in a cryptic manner. "If you think of anything more, let us know."

Fischer surveyed the photographs on the table one more time. *This can't be happening.* He picked them up and shuffled through one last time.

"This one. Shelly…"

"Davidson," Jade said.

"Shelly Davidson." I guess I evidently crossed paths with her a while back? Awful. Still…" *There is something familiar about this, but I can't place it.*

Greppin raised his eyebrows.

"Nothing definitive comes to mind, detectives," Fischer said. He shook his head in fatigue, set down the photos, picked up his empty coffee cup and motioned toward the door. "Can I get a refill here?"

"He's all yours, GJ," Greppin said with a smirk. "Oh, and I wouldn't say you have egg on your face, GJ… but maybe a small omelet. You heard the Chief. Get the man home."

Fischer was pretty sure Detective Jade sighed in annoyance after that comment, but he didn't mind. Something warmed his heart at the thought of getting to spend a little more time with her.

Chapter 4

DRIVING IN LA TRAFFIC IS never fun or easy, but it's an altogether different view through the backseat window of an LAPD squad car, Fischer thought. *If Dante had conceived an eighth layer of hell this might be it. Still, it's certainly better riding back here when not viewed as a suspect.*

Fischer sat diagonal from Detective Jade as he reflected through the events of the morning and took it all into consideration. People die everywhere, every day. People even get killed every day in large cities. In a broad region like SoCal, that's well over 25 million people. Statistics are always much higher in highly populated places like this, *always*. Fischer reasoned. *Are those violent murders all connected? How could they genuinely suspect he had anything to do with it? Crazy.*

The car was quiet as they rolled down the highway until the Police radio squawk-box blared out a traffic accident on the 405. Detective Jade reached over and turned the volume down slightly. Fischer noticed a tattoo on her right forearm that peeked out slightly when she extended. It was letters spelling a word, but Fischer couldn't make out what it said.

"Tell me about your ink," he said.

Jade embarrassingly covered it with a quick effort to roll down her shirt sleeve but shook her head acknowledging it was too late.

"I'm supposed to keep that covered up when in uniform, per department policy," Jade sighed. "Sometimes it sneaks out." She pulled it back further so he could see. The tattooed word was spelled in a bubbly colored balloon style writing. It was tricky to read normally, particularly from Fischer's angle. He began trying to decipher it aloud.

"Cap… Capri?"

"Capricorn. It's my sign," Jade said whimsically. "It was kind of a big thing for me in college.

"Tell me you don't believe in all that stuff," Fischer said.

"Oh, I definitely think there's something to it. I mean, at least a little bit… The stars you were born under and all that. It's powerful."

Fischer shook his head. "Only as powerful as you make it in your mind. Tell me you don't read the *horror-scope* daily, do you?"

"Not anymore," Jade said. "I used to, now it's just kind of an occasional thing, I guess. For fun. What's your sign, Dr. Fischer?"

"Fun?" Fischer asked. "Nope, not playing."

"Oh, come on," Jade said.

"I don't want to feed into your enthusiasm any more than I have to, or have you judge me by some predetermined stereotype standard… *Again*. People already do that plenty because of what I do for a living."

"So, tell me more about the thing with God and the stars." She adjusted the rear-view mirror slightly and made eye contact.

"Oh, right, 'Is God telling us something in the stars' from my sermon." Fischer knew he had to be careful in how he phrased what he said next. He'd seen some people take things way too far with the concept. "Well, there's astronomy, and then there's astrology. I take it you know the difference?"

"Sure," Jade said. "Astronomy is the studying of the stars in the galaxy, scientifically, and astrology is more or less attempting to interpret them with meaning into our lives."

"Right," Fischer said. "However sometimes we forget we've come so far in our advances of scientific study, that we lose sight of where we came from and how it all started, particularly in the field of astronomy."

"Such as?" Jade's interest was piqued.

"Well, our modern world has incredibly powerful telescopes that can take us into deep space, and we can learn and observe things our ancient ancestors couldn't, and that's great and awesome, but we mustn't forget the lessons from medieval astronomy, or really, I should say, primaeval astronomy, that still carry over to us today.

"Like?" Jade asked.

"Like our entire workweek still flows and is influenced by it. The ancient astronomers could only see seven planets, or wandering stars, as they thought of them. Pretty much everyone knows Sunday and Monday got their names from the sun and the moon. And Saturday is the next easiest one.

"Saturn?"

"Right. And Jupiter is the kingly planet and has long been associated with similar attributes of Thor from Norse mythology. So, when the Anglo-Saxons adopted the Roman calendar—boom—the fifth day of the week became known as—"

"*Thursday?*" Jade asked with growing confidence.

"You're an A student so far," Fischer said. "Mars is Tuesday and still faintly connects to Mardi Gras. The other planets; Mercury, and Venus round out Wednesday and Friday respectively. Their names don't sound the same through the languages, lost in translation from the early Germanics to Latin, and so on."

Fischer loved illuminating listeners with historical information, particularly when theological in nature. It was exhilarating to him. However today he had trouble identifying if the source of exhilaration came from the topic of discussion or Jade's sweet almond eyes that seemed captivating to him, particularly the way only one of her eyebrows crinkled when she seemed intrigued.

"Interesting," Jade said. "But how is God involved in all that?"

"Well, it's all right there in Genesis 1, detective."

"I grew up Catholic. Sunday school, weekly mass, but I find it hard to believe all that as literal," Jade said.

"You and most people, I suppose," said Fischer. "And yet so willing to believe in so many other, hokier things… like astrology, say?" Fischer asked risking a playful comeback.

Detective Jade shook her head with a smile. "Oh, no you *didn't*. And I thought we were going to be friends."

"What's more interesting," Fischer continued, "is that we've deliberately stuck with the number seven for our weekly pattern—as if God created us that way with a day of rest in mind—and humanity has fought to keep it that way with leap days and leap years, through math and newly discovered science, despite transitioning from the Roman calendar to the Julian calendar, and the Gregorian calendar we use today. *That's* interesting."

Jade took an exit and the squad car bumped over an uneven patch in the road, jolting Fischer back to reality that he was in fact riding in the back of a police car. They careened down the exit ramp nearing his church, but still a bit of a ways off. She stopped at a red light.

"Listen," Jade said, as she shifted awkwardly in her seat. "I want to hear more, and I feel bad we detained you all morning and didn't provide any food for you. Do you like In-N-Out Burger?"

Fischer briefly considered the opportunity. *The experience at that place is insufferable, particularly the long lines... The long lines.*

"I *love* In-N-Out Burger," he fibbed.

Chapter 5

FISCHER LOATHED THE OPTICS OF sitting in the back of a police car inching through a fast-food drive-through, even if it was a cuisine hot spot for native Angelenos. He did his best to pretend he was in the back of a limo being chauffeured around like some Hollywood elite film or rap star, but to no success. *This is ridiculous.* He was just happy he wasn't wearing his clerical now.

Detective Jade turned her head back. "I'm not going to have anything, but let me get you something, it's on me, Dr. Fischer, it's the least I can do after this morning."

"Um… Okay, I guess I'll go with the Double Double combo—Animal style, and a Coke."

Jade snickered briefly.

"What's so funny?" Fischer asked.

"Yeah, no, it's just, I usually order Animal style as well," she said.

"I see," Fischer smiled in mild amusement. He looked out his window and saw a young boy in the car next to them. He waved and smiled more, but the mother of the child shot him the stink eye and promptly barked instructions to her son to look away. *Police car. Right. This is fun.*

"Ok, God and the stars," Jade said.

Fischer refocused. "In the book of Genesis, there is a particularly intriguing verse, 1:14, written in the direct context of day four of creation, when the sun, moon, and stars were spoken into existence. It says, 'Let there be lights in the expanse of the heavens to separate the day from the night. And let them be for signs, and for seasons, and for days, and years.' Three of those four qualifiers serve as time measurables for us: days, years, and seasons. The fourth however—"

"Signs," Jade said.

"Signs make the whole thing all the more enthralling, particularly when you read the whole passage in context. So, detective, what 'signs' might that refer to?"

"The constellations?" Jade said as she inched up in line. "Wait a minute, the *zodiac*?" She turned her head all the way back and made direct eye contact with Fischer.

"*Exactly*. Remember, we have electricity lighting up all our towns and cities, it's really challenging to get a vivid unadulterated view of the night sky today and fully appreciate just how bright they shine at night. Or frankly, to get people off their technology for a hot blessed second and just look up to appreciate what's above them. But, for the early patriarchs of humanity, every night was a primitive laser light show, enveloped by a celestial nocturnal OMNI-max screen canvas which moved in annual rhythm. It's comically ironic that our manmade technology and harnessed electricity, while illuminating our lives down here, simultaneously makes our view of the heavens that much dimmer."

"I don't get it," Jade said. "What signs in the constellations would God use? I thought the early Greeks and Romans assigned all the meaning to the constellations, from mythology, and such."

"You're getting behind, detective."

"Really? Don't you mean getting ahead of you? I think I've been tracking what you're saying."

"No," Fischer pointed in front of them, "You're falling behind in the car line."

Jade slunk in her seat and self-consciously pulled forward.

"Certainly, the Greeks and Romans projected their gods and stories into the stars, and our culture today retains a lot of that, but they didn't come up with all of it on their own. They often borrowed, quite liberally I would add, from other sources."

"Such as?" Jade asked.

Fischer cleared his throat. "Stories from a very primitive public domain of oral sources, specifically the Hebrews. Think of it, Adam lived all the way until the generation immediately before Noah. That's almost a millennium of perpetual first-hand knowledge echoed down of God, creation, the fall of mankind, the serpent, *and* the protoevangelium."

"What?"

Chase Fischer's mind was always racing ahead of itself, lost in deep thought at parties and seemingly disconnected in conversations. People frequently miscalculated him to be aloof, or 'distant,' but the truth of the matter was he was usually thinking on a deeper level. When random 'celebrations of nothingness' topics invariably arose, Fischer knew it wouldn't take long for his eyes to glass over. Fischer's headspace all too often felt like a boxer sitting in the corner, eager for the next bell ring, signaling him to pugil forward with the next theological connection point. Most of the time it was a debate, but every once in a sweet while it became a sparring dance. Fischer much preferred the dance and was currently enjoying this particular waltz with Jade.

"Sorry," Fischer said. "The protoevangelium, commonly referred to as the *first Gospel*, occurs all the way back in Genesis 3. God promised to send a seed of the woman, a prophesied champion, whose heel will be bitten by the serpent, yet that very heel will crush the serpent's head. Christianity obviously understands that to be none other than Jesus Christ."

"Double Double combo—Animal style, and a Coke," Jade ordered. Her eyes refocused on Fischer in the rearview mirror. "So, you're saying those early stories were around previously, and the Greeks and Romans pulled from them?"

"Yes, and heavily added to them for their own stories. Only the best artists can steal from others before them and pass it off as their own."

"Don't I know that," Detective Jade agreed.

Fischer continued, "The theory is there was a shared language until there wasn't."

"Ah, the Tower of Babel."

"You *did* go to Sunday school, didn't you?" Fischer said with delight. "After that language scrambling episode, the people groups naturally went in different directions, but they took their knowledge of some of those earliest stories of how man sought to be reconciled with God. There's a great book on the subject, *Lord of Legends*, written by some German priest."

"Interesting," Jade said, as she slid the small, perforated plastic door compartment between them open and passed Fischer his bag of food. "But I still don't understand how any of this has to do with the stars in the zodiac."

"Well, let's start with Virgo," Fischer forced out while chewing his burger. He sipped his Coke. "Why is the constellation Virgo known as 'Virgo' and not something else?"

"I don't know, that's what they assigned it," Jade said.

"Yes, but what does Virgo mean?"

"It's a woman."

"Right, but what kind of woman? What does it sound like?"

"Virgo… *virgin*?" Jade asked.

"Bingo. A virgin woman, and one of the other smaller constellations closest to her is Coma, and there are some interesting interpretations on it being a seed, the desired one, or… more specifically, an *infant*. Now what would a specifically virgin woman be doing with an infant?" Fischer gobbled down some of his fries and took another long sip of Coke. "I would think a virgin with child would sound familiar, *especially* to a Catholic."

"That is interesting, but a bit far-fetched. You're saying God *designed* the stars that way?" Jade processed as she pulled out of the drive-through and accelerated down the road.

"I'm saying humanity speaks of certain star constellations in similar descriptors of how Christ is referenced in the Bible. The question is, why? And there are many more examples. Some stronger than others, remember our days of the week, some are apparent, others we must dig through the translation to uncover the deeper root meanings. Regardless, God created the stars, they are set in patterns that circle around us, illumined by the sun no less, as if they are repeating an annual story—perhaps the glory story of a savior to come, and man references these stars."

Jade pulled into The Church of the Epiphany parking lot and shifted into park.

"All very fascinating Dr. Fischer," Jade said hesitantly.

Fischer could tell she wasn't quite buying it. "I think it is fascinating, particularly when one re-examines passages like the language in the Psalms, 'The heavens declare the glory of God, and the sky above proclaims his handiwork,' now *this* is where it starts to get really good."

Jade's eyes lit up as the police radio began squawking orders.

"All units report, we have 10-65 in progress. All units report."

"Armed robbery, gotta go," Jade said abruptly.

Detective Jade exited the vehicle, rounded the car and opened the door for Fischer. "This was good information. Thank you. I may be in touch," she said with a cryptic smile, hopped back in the driver's seat and zoomed off.

Fischer stood in the parking lot reflecting for a moment. He faintly heard the police siren turn on as Detective Jade sped away. It had been quite the exhilarating day to say the least. *It was a fun waltz while it lasted. What did she mean by that? 'I may be in touch.'* Fischer wanted to delve further into that topic for a moment but turned and saw Nancy, the elderly matriarch of church gossip, standing nearby with her mouth agape.

"Pastor, was that *you* getting released from a police car?"

Great...

Chapter 6

PASTOR FISCHER POLITELY PARRIED THROUGH a tricky chat with Nancy, explaining the misunderstanding, his innocence, all the while pretending to understand her point of view of how the optics 'might' look to the neighborhood, or others who eventually heard about his episode with the police. *Only if you tell them, Nancy. Only if you tell them.* Nancy sped away momentarily pacified. Fischer unconvincingly hoped for the best.

Fischer caught his breath admiring his Triumph Bonneville sparkling in the sun for the briefest instance before he swiveled back toward the other end of the parking lot. There stood The Church of the Epiphany. The majestic stone gothic architecture and stained glass always inspired Fischer to aim toward reverent excellence in everything he did. And the eyesore of cosmetic issues and general state of disrepair of the roof reminded him that all of God's people are works in progress, himself included. Fischer checked the time on his cellphone. 1:47 P.M.

What a wasted morning, but maybe not.

Fischer made his way up the walk to the church door, noticing the gait in his stride was a smidge shorter as he moved with stone stiff legs. The adrenaline of the morning events finally wore off revealing a soreness in its wake. *Probably shouldn't have agreed to two days in a row of rock climbing over the weekend. The effects are catching up.* Fischer opened the squeaky brass door handle of his church full of hope and intrigue in the new year.

"Mor—afternoon, Jeannie. I guess it's still 'Magic Monday,' where *anything* can happen." Luther, Fischer's beautiful German Shepherd, recognized his master's voice and came bounding around the corner with his regal look and customary black and tan coloring. Fischer indulged two jump-hugs from Luther, before he snapped his fingers relaxing Luther contently at his side. He sheepishly looked at Jeannie.

"Insane day already, as you well know, I'll fill you in on all the details later about 'Joe Friday,' but I'm already incredibly behind on my plans for the day," Fischer said.

"And I'll bet, Nancy, 'Queen of the gadflies,' will only make it all the more fun for you," Jeannie said.

Fischer rolled his eyes. "I'm sure she has a busy afternoon of Facebook ahead of her." Fischer was eager to change subjects. "I was planning to ask you this *morning*, but did you like the Deadpool chia head I got you for Christmas?" *How many church secretaries appreciate Deadpool?*

Jeannie sparked a big grin. "Yes. It was awesome, thank you. Coffee is still here, but it's cold. Warm it up for you?"

"No thanks, I'm good."

"Ok, well, it's 'Magic Monday' alright," Jeannie said. Her 60ish frame slowly rose from her desk with her list ready to go. The robust opera trained Scandinavian vocalist and coffee addict matched Chase wits for wits in office repartee. Jeannie had been a secretary for a Navy admiral, packed her own heat, possessed a memory recall more reliable than Google, *and* was a fan of the MCU. And somehow, she packaged all this in a zany Sandra Bullockesque personality. Fischer hit the jackpot in the office administration sweepstakes, and he knew it.

"Lay it on me," Fischer said, tapping his fingers across the desk counter.

"Your earlier appointment left becau—"

"Yup. I know. Have to reschedule."

Jeannie looked directly into Fischer's eyes. "Pastor, she can, but she was less than thrilled. It's never good to upset the women's missionary league."

"I know. God loves everybody. Please don't remind me." Fischer started down the hall toward his office.

"*Wait*, Pastor—I have a few more quick notes for you." Jeannie lifted her pad and raised up her 1950's framed glasses that usually hung around her neck. "I finally received a return call from our previous attempts. The National Church presidium has yet to decide about your pastoral status because of, well, you know."

"Yeah. I thought we'd have heard something conclusive by now," Fischer said. "Not the news I wanted."

"Also, the Fergusons are requesting a release from our membership rolls. I'm sure it's not related," Jeannie said.

"You are kind," said Fischer. "The dad is the park ranger guy, right?"

"Uh-huh. Charlie and Benita. Hardly ever here anyway, but their daughter Chelsea you know."

"Yeah. Chelsea, sweet kid. She's been involved with the church for so long, and I even had her for a class last year at the university. Seems she's been flaking away for a bit. I reached out with some concern a while back, but was assured 'all was fine.' Figures," Fischer said with a tinge of disapproval.

Jeannie nodded. "Yup. She'll find her way back hopefully, might take a while. And lastly, the Chiparros want you to do a home blessing for them. Michael and Vicki said they had a break-in over the holidays, freaked them out."

"A home blessing request after a burglary? Cool. Although, they just adopted that cute little two-year old last year—"

"Three-year old, he just turned four," Jeannie said.

"Right," Fischer thought. "Chris? Christopher?"

"Christian," Jeannie said. "A break in must have been a scary episode for a little kid."

Fischer and Luther headed to his office for the briefest of workdays. He outlined the week ahead, sermon ideas, correspondence follow ups, prayer lists, and meeting agenda notes. He stopped suddenly. Fischer scribbled furiously then tossed his pen across the room, hitting the wall. *Can't block out those photo images those detectives showed me.* He stood, desperately in need to clear his head from the overwhelming information he'd been exposed to. Luther cowered on the floor wincing an anxious high-pitched whine.

"Come on, Luther, I think it's been a day."

They headed out to the parking lot and the Triumph. Most dogs merely hope to have their head poke out of an occasional moving car, but Luther indulged every open canopy ride in the Bonnie sidecar. It was only a short two block drive to the house, but it was the only time Luther's watch dog looks were comically muted by the wind blowing back his flimsy ears.

Fischer collapsed at home into his cozy leather recliner. It had been a splurge, but a guilty pleasure worth every penny. His two-story cape house, a parsonage owned by the church, was way more than he needed as a single man. The four-bed/two-bath home stood out as the only cape for blocks, with bright green shudders and a fading yellow trim. Fischer enjoyed this as the paint job gently harkened of his beloved Green Bay Packers and Midwestern roots.

Luther ran in with a slobbery wet tennis ball. "Oh, yeah. Is it time, old boy?" Fischer popped up and out the door with his best friend. The faint half-light of the day still just barely illuminated the backyard enough for a brief session of their daily fetch ritual. Fischer had wisely invested in a handled scoop and ball thrower as to avoid Luther's saliva-soaked ball.

Fischer spent the rest of the day following up on this to-do list tasks. He concluded by jumping up onto his rock-climbing hangboard mounted above the doorframe between the kitchen and the living room. The plank shaft board with various narrow slits and crevices was designed to strengthen finger grips for climbing. Fischer would routinely free hang as long as he could at the end of most days, and meditate on creative homiletical ideas, or mentally catalogue his tasks accomplished; *set up the Chipparo's home blessing appointment? Check. Reach out to the Fergusons, and Chelsea? Dead-end. At least I tried. New sermon illustration material acquired? Double check.*

Fischer dropped down achieving a new personal record, a twenty-seven-minute free hang. *Not bad.* He walked outside and looked up at the stars in deeper thought as he gently massaged his fingers back to feeling normal. A *Zodiac copycat? Unbelievable.* He couldn't resist temptation. Fischer pulled out his iPhone and scrolled through the app store, resting on a star constellation app. He pondered a moment, then clicked it.

BLOOD OF THE MAZZAROTH

Downloading...

"Come on Luther, let's get some grub." They went back inside to the kitchen. Reheated left-over Chinese wasn't the worst meal. It steamed in the microwave as he poured Luther his kibble. Fischer scarfed his steaming pork and noodles down, missing the companionship he'd enjoyed through previous years. *Don't think about her, Chase, don't think about what happened.* He had to do this alone now. He glanced at Luther, ever hopeful for a scrap from his master's plate. "At least you never complain about my cooking, Luther."

Luther's ears perked up. Fischer knew his canine assumed a morsel would come, and he'd better deliver. No sooner did Fischer flick a chunk of Mongolian BBQ into the air did Luther snarf it down. The tasty bite never had a chance of hitting the floor.

Fischer's mind wandered to Detective Jade. *She was intriguing, but easy fella.* Fischer hadn't felt that kind of excitement chatting with a woman in quite a while, even if it was under bizarre circumstances. Still, all things considered, she seemed to have... Fischer tried to think through the appropriate words... *An arresting quality.* He quietly snort-chuckled to himself, amused by his own puny joke. He'd probably never cross paths with her again anyway.

Fischer walked past his makeshift wet bar on a shelving unit and easily justified pouring himself a healthy dram of whisky into his small glass snifter, Jameson Black Barrel Irish—neat. Above him hung some of his accolades: a Big Ten Track & Field Championship plaque from the University of Wisconsin, and a curl-warped photograph of him and his old teammates. A Master of Divinity diploma from Concordia Seminary, St. Louis prominently stood out in its dark wood frame. The composite portrait of roughly one hundred male graduates wearing clericals gazed back at him. Over the years, Fischer had softly ex-ed out faces in pencil of fellow classmates who no longer served in the ministry, for various reasons. There were about twenty faces marked, guys who quit, wore out, moral failure, and two who unfortunately died. *Will I be next?* He air-toasted the remaining faces and scanned over to his last diploma which read:

The University of Basel, Switzerland.

Chase L. Fischer

ERIC T. EICHINGER

Ancient World History
PH. D *Summa Cum Laude*

Good times, Fischer reflected with a devilish grin. He savored another sip and checked his phone as it dinged.

Download complete.

Fischer gleefully tapped open the screen unlocking the astronomy app and delighted in the star universe that surrounded him. As he moved the iPhone around the house, the screen displayed in real time the stars and constellations surrounding earth, with breathtaking precision to longitude and latitude coordinates in connection to the position of the phone.

"Let's check this outside, Luther."

Outside, the stars sparkled as Fischer played with his new toy. *Technology is amazing at times.* Fischer raised his phone as the circle in the center of the screen highlighted the stars and constellations in view. The app lit up Scorpio, naming each star, and filled in a soft illustration of the body of each constellation, and then faded away as Fischer continued moving it. There was Cassiopeia… Orion, Draco, Virgo… Leo… Fischer had fun zooming in and out, hovering over each new constellation. *Extraordinary.*

"Wait a minute…" Fischer scrolled back to Virgo and zoomed in further. The body of the Virgo constellation filled in around the stars designated. Fischer put his hand up to his mouth in horror.

"*Shelly.*"

Chapter 7

THE MOON SHONE OVER VENICE Beach. The drum circle group finished beating out their routine bohemian sunsetting ritual some time ago. They packed up as the local drifters, grifters, and junkies were transiting into partying away the night. Per usual, they patronized the local drinking establishments while other extra-curricular narcotic activities ensued.

Wolfgang Manteuffel sat in the driver's seat of his white van wearing dark sunglasses and his Giants Ballcap. The night was dark enough to reduce visibility. And the dwindling beach crowd was more than inebriated enough to care. He went to the back of the van compartment.

The 50ish hiker man's body was already quite cold. He hadn't put up much of a struggle. The mountain had done most of the work wearing him out sufficiently. Wolfgang tore off the sweat-chilled T-shirt the body had on, no scrapes, cuts, or bleeding. The strangulation marks around the body's neck would only intensify as more time passed, and tattle to authorities about the kind of death he experienced.

Near Wolfgang's side was the large goat head mask staring him back in the face. He paused a moment staring into its eyes. "You about ready, buddy?" He took off the hiking boots and socks and studied the victim for a moment. He scratched a short message on a yellow Post-it note paper slip and crumpled it up.

Wolfgang looked down at the small cooler on the floor. He took the lid off to check on the contents. About a dozen fish drifted around listlessly. Mostly halibut and white croakers. He tapped at the fish a few times to liven them up.

"White croaker. Fitting." Manteuffel mused to himself with a chilly hollow laugh.

Chapter 8

January 7ᵗʰ

"YOU'RE TELLING ME, YOU BELIEVE the positioning of the body of victim, Shelly Davidson, matches the positioning of the Virgo constellation?" Chief Tatum's eyes bored into Fischer with an intensity he'd never quite experienced before. The two previous generations of Tatum's family police ancestry mounted on the wall behind his large oak desk intensified the magnitude of the situation. Tatum held a paper of the Virgo constellation Fischer printed out that morning.

Fischer's head sank. Admittedly, his idea sounded much more concrete in his own thoughts last night after a glass of whisky than when spoken aloud in a critical tone from the chief of police in the LAPD Hollywood precinct headquarters.

"I appreciate your enthusiasm," Tatum said. "We see this all the time, from civilians who watch too many television shows, and think they've figured out everything. One guy recently, obsessed with CSI, was convinced we should be able to use cameras to detect the reflection off the eyeball of a victim to reveal the image and identity of a perpetrator—no such technology exists. Pastor, with all due respect, I'd like to encourage you to stay in your lane and let us do our job."

"Chief Tatum," Fischer said. "I really think this might be connected to—"

Tatum stood up quickly. "To the *Zodiac*? A lot of people, good people, law enforcement people, detectives, for years chased after that madness. And this one's supposed to be different? I hate to tell you, pastor, but a lot of these cases go unsolved. We don't always have the manpower to assign to these incidents. And it's not like there aren't plenty of other shenanigans going on in this city we need to turn our attention toward. But I'll indulge you for one more moment. If what you say is true, and you *could* be on to something, what about the other two victims? How do they allegedly connect, if they connect at all, and what should we do with your theoretical information?"

Fischer sat back discouraged, but the moment passed quickly. Detective Greppin entered the Chief's office.

"Here's that file you wanted, Chief." Greppin said, handing the folder to the Chief. Tatum opened it and compared the image of Shelly Davidson's body next to Fischer's Virgo printout.

Fischer rose and snuck around the side of Tatum's desk to see the two images side by side for himself. The positioning was a spot-on match just as he thought he'd remembered from his brief view of the graphic photo he'd seen of Shelly Davidson. *I knew I was right.*

Chief Tatum cleared his throat. "It's interesting Dr. Fischer, but I'm afraid that's all it is right now."

Their heads popped up, and all attention turned to a quick knock at the door. Detective Jade walked in. Fischer's heart leapt.

"Chief, Grep," she said, "there's a new development. That body found on Venice beach Praider got called in on…" She noticed Fischer. "Oh, hi there." She perked up with an awkward smile.

"Another drunk tourist that fell off a boat and washed up?" Greppin asked.

"No. You wish," Jade said grimly. "It's another unusual homicide scene."

Chief Tatum slammed the file down on his desk. "*Damn.*"

"What are the details?" Greppin asked.

"Disturbing again… um, should I?" Jade glanced at Fischer and back to the Chief, as if asking permission.

Fischer walked back to the center of the office in closer proximity to

Jade. *How does she smell like that? Do cops wear perfume? Easy Tiger, you hardly even know her.*

"Go ahead," Chief Tatum said. "After all, he *may* be on to something."

Fischer could almost see the laced sarcasm dripping from each of Chief Tatum's words.

"Is that right?" Jade asked, quickly looking Fischer up and down. She continued with her report. "The victim is male, middle-aged, Caucasian, and was found with a large goat head mask over his head. Creepy. No clothes other than his ripped pants, and some fish nearby."

"Fish?" Greppin asked.

"Is that strange? It's on a beach," the Chief said.

"The positioning of them seemed intentional. That's what Praider reported." Jade paused for a moment and ventured in a direction that blew Fischer away. "Chief, permission sir?"

"What is it?" Tatum asked.

"If I may sir, I think I'd like to have Dr. Fischer accompany me on an interview I've set up. I have a source about the Zodiac, an old source, retired from the force, and Dr. Fischer has demonstrated a reasonable amount of knowledgeable about the topic when I escorted him home yesterday, particularly if you think he 'may be on to something.'"

Fischer surveyed the group to see how her pitch landed. Greppin rolled his eyes. Chief Tatum cringed, lifting his right hand up to massage his temples briefly, then quickly straightened up in a snap.

"This is police business," Tatum said. "He's not part of this investigation; he's not even a chaplain for our department."

"Maybe we could make him an honorary chaplain, sir?" Jade asked.

Fischer had no idea where this was going, but he liked the sound of every word. It wasn't every day a pastor/professor of ancient history got to assist a police officer, and a cute one at that, in an active investigation, and interview a special witness about a potential serial killer. Before Fischer's fantasy carried him away too far, he caught a sliver of Jade's tattoo on her forearm and then it hit him. *Sea goat.*

Chief Tatum stammered as if in negotiation with himself, cop hunches versus sage experience. "I don't care for this sort of thing, you've got to be kidding me, GJ," Tatum said.

"Chief?" Fischer asked. "Shelly Davidson was killed in late *August*, wasn't she?"

The room went silent. Greppin picked up the file and shuffled through it. He showed Tatum.

"How the *hell* did you know that?" Tatum asked, as they all looked perplexingly at Dr. Fischer.

Fischer sensed he somehow achieved authority in the room. "Virgo begins in August," Fischer said. "And then enters September. Detective Jade, this is your month this time, isn't it?"

"*Excuse* me?" Jade stepped back as if shot in the shoulder.

"Whoa." Greppin mumbled under his breath.

For the second time that morning, Fischer cringed at hearing his own thoughts spoken aloud. "Your sign, detective, your *zodiac sign*, you're a Capricorn, this is your month, *January*, right?" Fischer said.

"Uh, yeah, it is," Jade said awkwardly, blushing with confusion.

"Nice save," Greppin said under his breath.

"And what's the sign for Capricorn?" Fischer asked in his typical Socratic teaching method of asking questions.

"It's something like a goat with a fish tail," Jade said.

"Exactly," Fischer said. "Capricorn, a figure with the head of a goat and the tail of a fish, is right now, this month. And I'll bet a fist full of fifties that the fish near the goat-head victim were 'intentionally placed' around his *feet*?"

Jade's jaw slowly dropped in surprise.

"Now that you say it, I think they *were* at his feet," she said.

Fischer and Detective Jade both looked at Chief Tatum, then to Greppin, and back to the Chief.

"I'm sorry, how does *he* know you're a Capricorn?" Greppin asked confusedly.

"Oh, for heaven's sake," Tatum grumbled. "Fine, *honorary* chaplain it is. You have forty-eight hours. But you're not riding together in a squad car. Let's keep some semblance of policy. He's on his own dime."

Chapter 9

FORENSIC PATHOLOGIST, CHAD BOSTIC, EXAMINED the body of the goat-head victim at the LAPD morgue. He scratched his short beard that matched his freshly cut silver fox hair. He paid close attention to the contusions from strangulation markings around his neck. Bostic set his frameless eyeglasses in position and typed notes on his laptop as Detective Justin Praider walked in.

"I'm here for the goat head mask," Praider said.

Bostic motioned to a side table. "It's right over there."

Praider picked it up, causing a crumpled yellow Post-it note to fall out. He unfolded it. "Hey, Bostic. Check this out. What do you make of *this*?"

# # #

The only thing more exhilarating than riding down an LA freeway on a motorcycle is doing so speeding, completely in the right, following a police officer with no fear of being pulled over. Detective Jade's squad car weaved through traffic effortlessly. Fischer's Triumph Bonneville zoomed along as shadow. *Man, Luther would love this.*

Jade had told Fischer they would be interviewing an old source, some elder statesman of policing that had some knowledge of the original Zodiac case. *I just hope I can be helpful.* They pulled up to a small, but nicely maintained, single-story home in the foothills of San Bernardino, the outer rim of greater Los Angeles.

Fischer waited for Jade to exit her vehicle. He could tell she was in mid conversation. He admired the curb-appeal of the home while anticipating their entrance. A light coffee exterior, trimmed in blacks and some whites really made the home pop, finished off with an adorable brick driveway and immaculate landscaping. She jotted some notes, ended the call, and quickly convened in the driveway with Fischer.

"I just got word from Detective Praider. Apparently, the goat-head mask coughed up some evidence. Possibly more communication from the Zodiac. The chief wanted us to have it before we had the conversation here today. It was a small slip of paper crumpled up inside the mouth of the mask with three words." Jade showed her note pad to Fischer.

A Moth Zzar

"Does that mean anything to you, Dr. Fischer?"

A Moth Zzar? "No idea," Fischer said. "'Zzar' isn't even a real word. Did you transcribe the message correctly?"

"Positive. I *triple* checked,"

"Maybe it's supposed to be some type of anagram or something?" Fischer asked. "I hate anagrams. They're so silly."

"Maybe," Jade said, shake-fidgeting with her pen. "Praider is of the mind, and it sounds like the Chief is too, that this isn't really zodiac stuff, at least 'The Zodiac Killer' *exclusively.*

"What do they think?" Fischer asked.

Jade hesitated, clicking her pen push button fast in and out. "That maybe this is more the actions of some disturbed Hollywood fanatic, obsessed with movies. There're tons of bozos like that out here, you know.

"Movies?" Fischer asked.

"Remember in *Silence of the Lambs...* a moth is found in the mouth of one of the victims. Maybe this could be some sort of weird wink to that."

Fischer stepped back in thought. "That's a pretty random bit of film history, even for a movie buff. But what about all the other zodiac connections?"

Jade grinned. "The *alleged* zodiac connections, Praider was quick to point out. The Zodiac Killer was also made into its own movie. And perhaps all the talk of stars is more like 'Hollywood' stars."

Fischer shook his head in disbelief as they walked up to the door.

Jade rapped the small dusty iron doorknocker three times. "Well, let's see what we glean here. This is a very old acquaintance of my father's. I've already prepped him with some of the information as to why we're coming."

"GJ," the voice greeted them at the door. "Great to see you. Come in." A short Asian looking man welcomed them into his home as the door swung wide. He was plump and balding, roughly in his 70's by Fischer's estimation. He wore charcoal dress pants and the classic white 'wife-beater' undershirt, but quickly put on a button up shirt, though didn't bother buttoning it up, Fischer noticed.

He looked at Fischer, smacked his hands together and rubbed them. "So, you want to talk about the Zodiac killer…"

"You got it. Joe, this is Rev. Dr. Chase Fischer. Yes, we have a few questions," Jade said.

"Reverend, eh? Very nice. I am Zhou Ming," they shook hands. "Everyone just calls me 'Joe,' though." He looked them over back and forth a few times and smiled in delight. "Tea?"

In no time Joe seated them in his modestly decorated living room, on a faded floral-patterned couch. He quickly served them hot green tea on the Chinese standard hollowed wooden tray. Fischer took a sip of the hot tea, never understanding why the Chinese allow the leaves to float throughout the cup. He spit a tiny leaf shred or two back into the tea and set the finger burning cup down on the clear glass coffee table.

Joe began to speak. "So, you think you have a new Zodiac killer on the prowl? For the record, I strongly believe that this current episode is not the same as the old Zodiac killer."

"You're sure?" Jade asked. "I know he would be very old now, but couldn't it be possible he'd still be able to give orders through some young sick enthusiast pupil?"

Joe sipped his tea and swallowed. "I think that is too far-fetched. No, I wouldn't assert the actual Zodiac would do that. I was there. I was new to the department in San Francisco at the time and was only around towards the tail end of the matter. They didn't give me much to do on the assignment of the Zodiac, but I knew enough that it drove everyone crazy."

"What can you tell us?" Jade asked, as she jotted down notes.

"I remember… That guy, whoever he was, just seemed to want attention. Cat and mouse pride games with the cops. Pride is a big motivator for a typical serial killer, you know. Your guy doesn't seem typical."

"Why do you say that?" Jade asked.

"Well, with the details you shared earlier, this guy seems like he's trying to say something, something big. Yes, he wants everyone to know *what* he's doing, but there seems to be a bigger *why* to his methodology. This has nothing to do with the original Zodiac killer, and this is no copycat, in my opinion. This is something much larger, methodically coordinated and, well… I think much more sinister."

"*More* sinister than slaying random people and terrorizing a city?" Fischer asked.

"*This* 'Zodiac' killer, your man, has a different face than the Zodiac of the past." Joe said, as he poured more tea into their tiny Chinese teacups.

The three pleasantly concluded their conversation over a few more sips. It was fascinating for Fischer to be part of an active investigation while getting a deeper reveal into Detective Jade's background. *Where might all this be going?* Fischer considered as he grabbed his tea one last time. Fischer politely took a one last minuscule sip. He couldn't bear to ingest the whole bitter beverage. Joe escorted them to the door, shook Fischer's hand, hugged Jade, and kissed her on the cheek. "It is good to see you again, GJ. Any time. seriously. Bye-bye for now."

Fischer and Jade walked back to their vehicles, but not before Fischer sparked an idea.

"You know, detective, something occurred to me. I'm pretty sure 'J' stands for Jade, but I don't know what the 'G' stands for in 'GJ.'"

"Nope, not playing," Jade teased with a smile. "I wouldn't want to lend to your enthusiasm."

Fischer smiled back for a moment. *C'mon Fischer, quite flirting, she's probably not pastor's wife material for you anyway, though for all I know I might not be a pastor for much longer. She certainly is more than just a pretty face...* Fischer's smile melted away lost in thought, paused. His mind tracked back to what Joe said *...A different face...* Fischer's demeanor became serious. GJ opened her driver's side door but stopped herself from entering the car and stared over the top of the roof at Fischer and his motorcycle.

"Where are you?" Jade asked.

"Joe said, this Zodiac killer has 'a different face.'"

"So?"

"So, it got me thinking about the *faces* of the zodiac. The zodiac does actually have different faces—*decans*."

"Huh?"

Fischer turned his serious lost-in-thought look directly at her which seemed oddly intimate in the moment.

"I can explain it better if you take me to the location of the crucified man."

Chapter 10

FISCHER TAILED JADE'S SQUAD CAR to a small, forested area in the Huntington Park neighborhood of Los Angeles. Traffic was much worse than earlier. Rush hour was starting to heat up. Rush hour in Los Angeles… *Ugh,* Fischer thought. Rush 'hour' was twice a day for generally three hours at a time. *What a farce.*

They stopped near a sign which read:

Salt Lake Park
Department of Parks and Recreation

The high soaring trees canvassed a lovely walking trail, and plenty of youth activity sites; small playgrounds, exercise stations, and the premier feature—a large skateboard park. Activity buzzed about them.

Fischer looked around quizzically. "Why would the killer impale a man on a cross here? It's incredibly sad with all these youth around. It must have been completely disturbing for the community."

Jade surveyed the area. "I've been thinking through everything you've said. Sagittarius is the end of November and most of December… Sagittarius is the *archer*. That would potentially explain the woman shot to death with arrows. It happened right before Thanksgiving; I remember."

"I thought the same thing," Fischer said feeling a sense of seriousness come over him.

Jade motioned toward a small cluster of trees. "The man on the cross was over there." They walked near them.

"Alright, Doctor. You made me bring you all the way here. What's your theory with these 'decan' things?"

"Decan," Fischer began, "is rooted from an old Semitic word, *dek*, the word used to describe the smaller constellations, their 'parts,' or 'faces.' It still carries over into English a bit, like why we call the 'deck' of a ship its 'face.' Anyhow, each of the twelve zodiac signs have three decans, thirty-six in total. Think of them like a smaller family unit that accompanies the larger more prominent signs through the zodiac belt along the meridian line."

"*And?*" Jade asked with a twinge of annoyance.

"Remember our earlier discussion about Coma being near Virgo and how their positional relationship enhances the story in the stars? Well, the crucified victim was stumping me for the longest time, particularly with Libra, until I remembered that one of Libra's decans is the Southern Cross. I had to look up the other two…"

"Oh, for the *love*… Chase, are you really going to make me ask what they are?" Jade said with a scowl.

"Libra's three decans are the Southern Cross, the *pierced victim* of Centaur, and the North Crown. Sound familiar?" Fischer said, sensing his pulse picking up in pace.

"But why here?" Jade asked.

Fischer looked around for any sort of clue, but only half his mind was focused on the task. The other half of his brain was reflecting on the fact that Detective Jade just called him 'Chase' for the first time. *Interesting.*

"Hold on a second," Jade said opening her phone. She began scrolling through a search.

Fischer crossed his arms. He proudly clung to his Gen X mindset, having experienced the last sniff of the old world of genuinely talking with people without constant technology interruptions, and actually looking in the eyes during conversation using real social skills. The incessant checking of data on smartphones was more than bothersome, but evidently a necessary evil for younger Millennials and Gen Z types.

"Chase, check this out. When I was using Google maps on our way here, something caught my eye." She held up her phone for Fischer to see as she spread her fingers on the screen to zoom in. There was Salt Lake Park where they currently stood. The street grid surrounded and filled in around the edges as Jade zoomed further in.

"Look," she said. "Just down the block from here, a very interesting business establishment, wouldn't you say?"

Fischer was almost in shock, but there it was in plain writing. A little 'mom and pop' business entitled: Libra Scales Co. "Unbelievable."

"I'm calling this in; this is *huge*. Dialing now…" Jade said.

"Tell them, I want to see the wounds of Shelly Davidson, too," Fischer said, turning to his side and entering deep thought mode.

Jade jolted up in surprise. "What? Why?"

A voice answered Jade's phone. "Praider, here." Jade clicked the speaker option for Fischer to hear.

"Praider? GJ. I'm with Dr. Fischer at the site of the crucifixion guy."

"What are you doing there? I thought you w—"

"Never mind. Long story. We're coming in to debrief. In the meantime, pull the Shelly Davidson file. We want to see *all* the photographs."

"Again?"

Fischer leaned in toward the phone. "Detective Praider, Dr. Fischer here. You said that Davidson's wounds were unusual. I think I might know why. And that's not all…"

Jade looked up in curiosity.

Fischer took a deep breath. "I think I know what 'A Moth Zzar' means."

Chapter 11

CHAD BOSTIC CUED UP THE postmortem photographs on the large screen monitor in the LAPD conference room. Except for Chief Tatum's office, this was the nicest room Fischer had seen at the LAPD headquarters, yet. The long, smooth, USB port-infused redwood table with twelve surrounding black leather swivel chairs set a serious tone. The wall-mounted cabinetry tech-equipment signaled that no expense had been spared for this room in the building. *I guess some California tax dollars have been justifiably spent.* The space was quiet as Bostic, Praider, Greppin, Jade, and Fischer awaited Tatum's arrival. *Don't screw this up.*

Fischer coached Praider typing in search commands on the department computer system, securing constellation images for comparable side to side imaging. The last one started to load when Tatum entered, displaying what Fischer surmised was his typical foul mood.

"Alright, Dr. Fischer. You have my attention. *Again*," Chief Tatum said.

Fischer took a deep breath and sipped his disposable tiny paper cup of water. "As you've been prepped by Detective Jade, we believe there are some strong connections of constellations to the killings. Working backwards, the Capricorn man and the goat head…"

Fischer clicked the split-frames together of the victim and an image of the Capricorn sign of the sea goat. "And the woman shot to death with arrows matches themes consistent with Sagittarius, the archer."

He clicked another side by side of the images. "We just came from the site of the crucified victim, noting the acute proximity to a business entitled 'Libra Scales,' and it seems the three smaller decans of the Libra sign are all represented on the victim."

Fischer pointed a red laser pen at the screen. "The Crown constellation, the impaled victim of Centaurus, and of course, the Southern Cross are all duly evident with the victim. Earlier I posited that only the body positioning of Shelly Davidson, the Virgo victim, matched the positioning of the Virgo constellation. I now believe there's even more continuity."

Fischer pulled up the graphic puncture wounds of the Davidson girl and had to pause. *Don't lose your lunch, Chase.* He took another sip. "My hunch seems to be correct. The decan constellations appear consistent to her wound patterns. Coma Berenices has fourteen stars in its grouping, and the top of her torso has fourteen slashes, patterned very similarly. Centaurus is next with eleven stars pairing to eleven deep cuts in her abdomen." Fischer kept clicking through the photos, each one worse than the prior. "And Bootes, or 'Arcturus' has fifteen named stars." He clicked to Shelly Davidson's mangled back photograph with fifteen lacerations. Fischer noted even Jade quivered with a disturbed chill.

Greppin rubbed his temple and spoke first. "I don't understand. There are millions of stars, how are these particular constellations set apart? How can any sense of pattern be made out of all that by the average person?"

"This is no *average* person," Jade said. "This killer is extremely calculated."

"Okay, fair enough. He's an aficionado on the subject, but still," Greppin said.

"To your question," Fischer said. "There are forty-eight original constellations, dating back to Ptolemy in mid first century A.D. He wrote the *Almagest* which includes a star catalogue containing these forty-eight 'original' constellations. It has stood the test of time and essentially served as the foundation of astronomy for nearly the last two millenniums."

"But why does his opinion matter so much?" Greppin asked. "Don't we know more about the vastness of the universe now with modern science?"

"That's the point," Chad Bostic said assertively. "Today modern astronomy knows we live in a heliocentric solar system. Everything revolves around the sun, hence the 'solar system.' But Ptolemy's theory of a geocentric universe was revolutionary and reigned supreme and virtually unchallenged for fourteen centuries. Not until Copernicus, Kepler, and Galileo would global thinking begin to make that shift toward how we think today. What Pastor Fischer is saying is that this same thinking has been in place and developed for a very long time, compounded over a thousand years; only until recently can humanity poke holes in it."

Fischer enjoyed when his Ancient History muscles could be flexed, and particularly in tandem with another historical mind. *Forensic pathologist Bostic knows his stuff.*

Fischer drove the discussion forward. "If you want further corroboration, an even earlier manuscript was discovered in 2022, which directly links to one of the best astronomers of antiquity, and the father of trigonometry—Hipparchus. Ptolemy had always referenced his original star catalogue map, from a century and a half before Christ, but all copies were lost to history, until recently. A palimpsest was discovered by archivists, a manuscript with multiple layers underneath. Ancient texts etched away and written over on the same vellum, like old school recycling."

"I saw that article, too," Bostic said. "Their use of multispectral imaging technology is fascinating, and Hipparchus' measurements were found to be even *more* accurate than Ptolemy's."

Well done, Bostic. Impressive.

"Exactly," Fischer said. "Again, the original forty-eight are based only on what the naked eye can see... What God created for man to see naturally and what was evident to him."

"God?" Tatum squinted his darting eyes. "What does God have to do with this?"

Fischer sighed in dumbfounded frustration. He cradled his right elbow into his left hand, pinching his thumb and index finger together where his nose and forehead met to ward off a potential tension headache. "Everything." Fischer said. "This is important to keep in mind for what I have to say next... *Mazzaroth.*"

Fischer's grand reveal evidently fell flat. Searching eyes from the collection of officers in the room exchanged confused glances all around like high schoolers who'd stayed up too late partying the night before a final.

"I believe 'A Moth Zzar' is an anagram for Mazzaroth."

"So, you trade some mumbo jumbo for different mumbo jumbo?" Praider asked.

"'*Mazzaroth*' isn't English. It's Hebrew. An ancient Hebrew word in fact, that some speculate could refer to the pattern of constellations in the heavens, that God gave a message in the stars, and I think some lunatic is—"

"Stop. *Enough*." Chief Tatum sighed raising his arm in a halting fashion. "Okay, I've heard all I need to at this point. I know pastors like to preach, but you do know not everyone believes in God, including in this room, and I'm not interested in listening to all this speculation. You do my job long enough, you'll easily understand why." He twisted gently in his chair uncomfortably absorbing the discussion. "We're deep enough into this and I don't want to get sidetracked further into the weeds with Biblical cosmic God theories and guesswork. I'm looking for facts."

Fischer exhaled in disappointment.

Tatum doubled down. "The mind sees what it wants to see, God included. If you want to force an interpretation or make these events connect, you can justify and explain away most anything. But, if what you're saying is true, and this presumed serial killer loves showing off with some sort of zodiacal pattern… then where's the Scorpio victim?"

Fischer and Jade cross-examined their eyes in bewilderment.

"Virgo, Libra, *Scorpio*, Sagittarius, Capricorn and so on. If what you say is true, there should be another victim for Scorpio, shouldn't there? I do my homework too, *Pastor* Fischer," he said with a glint in his eye that suggested he hadn't failed upward into the office of the Chief of Police. He had earned it through years of sleuthing out fact from fiction. "This is again, all very entertainingly compelling, pastor, but we still don't know *who* is doing this, *why*, or more importantly, the first thing in how to stop him in the future. If you're so sure, where's the Scorpio victim? Find it. I'll even extend you honorary chaplaincy another week."

Find a Scorpio victim? Who has time for this? I have my actual responsibilities to tend to. I... Fischer tried to negotiate with himself out of committing any further or investing more of his time. But something inside him was brewing. A compelling force to speak the truth, no matter what. That and Fischer had learned over the years, anytime he attempted to negotiate with himself, he usually lost.

"Chief Tatum, I'm no detective, but I—"

"You got *that* right."

"Chief," Jade said, "Dr. Fisher is an expert in his f—"

"It seems you've done enough by filling his head with too much information to begin with. An assist on an interview was one thing, against my better judgement after you exposed sensitive information, and *then* you took him to a crime scene? Ill-advised, if you want to know the truth. In my day, *police* did police work. You'd be wise to remember that, *detective*. I wouldn't want to demote you," he said in no other way to interpret but as a threat.

"Chief Tatum," Fischer said surprising himself as he stood in slight hesitation, having seized back attention in the room. *I'm gonna sound like a weenie... sigh. I have to say it ...* "Sir, sometimes it's easier not to speak the truth... But as Chaplain, even if only honorary and temporarily, I'm telling you; like it or not, God *is* real. That means the devil is real as well, working through most of the people the LAPD has to deal with I might add, and I strongly suggest specifically including whoever's doing this. You can choose not to believe in the bigger divine picture here, but I'm telling you, there is a deeper darkness to this whole thing, *darker* than any of us can possibly fathom. This killer you're looking for... If I were a betting man, I'd say he believes this is some sort of celestial prophecy from God for him to carry out to fruition. And if it's facts you're looking for, you'd be well off to know that the manuscript discovered by archivists took place at the Museum of the Bible of all places. It's *all* historical information, even if you choose to deny it. You wanna mock me? Fine. You know what, I'm done."

Fischer flung his hands in the air, turned, and walked out resolutely slamming the door shut.

Chapter 12

THE PROPHET LAY IN WAIT, focused on his target. His long sniper rifle rested perfectly still as he peered through his scope. A small breeze blew past him. A fly landed on his forehead. He clicked two rotations to the left and adjusted range. The sun bore down in the remote desert outskirts of Antelope Valley.

BANG.

Two hundred yards away, a Mojave ground squirrel exploded off its raised rock perch.

Manteuffel, standing safely behind him, lowered his binoculars. "You still got it."

The Prophet stood up with his 5'10" stout middle-aged frame and a grin of satisfaction. He giggled through his long Arabian-like brown beard. "I still remember my first kill," he said.

"You never forget," Manteuffel agreed.

The Prophet finished sucking down his supersized Coke through a straw and threw it indiscriminately to the ground. "Sometimes I miss the war."

"You mean Iraq. *The War* is everywhere, remember." Manteuffel said.

"Of course. Come on, let's get out of the heat."

The two loaded up their gear into the Prophet's black hummer and rolled away. The Prophet's white American 'apple pie' looks had faded away some time ago by his long and unruly facial hair, accenting a subtle Islamic quality about him. He took off his large sun-protective brimmed hat and donned his trademark rectangular-framed black sunglasses. "The progressions are going well, Wolf. The Scroll continues to reveal its truth."

"The Way is working its wonder," Manteuffel said.

"Yes, its glory is perfect as it is exquisite. Many will see and fear. Just as I told you." The Prophet pointed to the glove compartment. "Before I forget, your next installment is there."

Manteuffel opened the compartment and found his envelope. He quickly counted the hundreds inside. He sneered. "You're a thousand short."

"Ah, but what of the child?" The Prophet asked.

"Now that we've found him, it's only a matter of time."

"You said that before," The Prophet said slightly irritated.

"I sinned and you forgave me," Manteuffel said.

"My well is only so deep, Wolf. So is the message, so is the Way."

A long pause hung in the air as the two sped down the highway. Dusk was rapidly approaching as the sky lit up in a glorious shade of tangerine. The Prophet inserted a piece of spearmint gum in his mouth and began to chew. "I have no doubt you will be successful, my friend." The Prophet laughed and slapped Manteuffel's knee. "It is all to be," The Prophet concluded, and cackled some more.

# # #

Tuesday, January 14th

Chase Fischer typed away in his study at home. He couldn't believe a full week had gone by since his crazy interactions with the Los Angeles Police Department. As thrilling as it was, truth be told, he was relieved. One more thrill crossed off his bucket list, and some unique experiences. Besides, all his recent extra-curricular activities were causing a backlog of action steps on his usual routine and tasks. There was the weekly sermon writing, a Bible study prep, a lecture at the university, not to mention an inundation of emails, but no relieving news from the national church body praesidium, or the district office for that matter about the determination of his ecclesial future. Fortunately, there were plenty of other things for Fischer to preoccupy his time over. *Hopefully no funerals sneak up this week.* The time crunch was real.

Fischer finished his correspondence notes on his laptop and walked over to his makeshift wet bar, an old wooden 1940 era Philco radio. He hovered over his options for a nightcap before adding meat to the bones of his sermon outline for the weekend. *I think it's a scotch night.* He debated between Glenlivet and Lagavulin 16 before pouring. The Glenlivet won.

Fischer's email *pinged* as he relished his first taste. He checked his inbox as he held the strong burn on his pallet. Another concerned member worried about him possibly being 'arrested' at the church, and how that would affect the Church of the Epiphany's public image. *Thanks, Nancy.*

Luther perked up from his lazy slumber by his master's feet. His ears stiffened. His brief muted bark only meant one thing. Someone was approaching the door of the house. The doorbell rang liberating Luther to do what German Shepherds do best—loudly intimidate a would-be demonic ninja-assailant, but usually just the hapless mailman.

Fischer peeked out his window at his modest porch with peeling ivory paint, but something was different. Detective Jade stood there, wearing civilian clothes; navy blue high-top Converse shoes, flared stonewashed jeans with just the tiniest rip over her right mid-thigh. Her ensemble came together, save the top button, of her fitted long sleeve light brown Henley which accentuated her dark eyes.

"Quiet, Luther." *What in the world?* "Well, Boy, this is certainly an interesting development."

Fischer opened the door and greeted her, holding Luther back by his collar. "Hi, sorry. He's usually fine in public. It's the homestead he gets a little wound up protecting."

Jade extended her hand for a sniff. "Good dog," she said, stepping in as Luther relaxed. "I thought you said you 'lived alone?'" Jade asked.

"I, uh, yeah, I do. Is, is everything ok?" Fischer tried to fill the void of the awkward pause, but his efforts only accentuated the oddity of the moment.

"Uh, yeah," Jade said clumsily. "Sorry for intruding like this. I just figured I owed you an apology for how last week played out."

"Oh, not at all. I usually get treated much worse on a routine basis. Par for the course in my line of work," Fischer assured her. "I'm sure it's nothing compared to what the average policeman faces, particularly in the current political climate."

"Right, um… Anyhow, the gang usually gathers at this local pub, and tonight's our night. I thought I'd repay you with a drink on me?"

Fischer introspected for a split second. *I've really got to be careful here. I don't want to lead her on. Are you ready for this yet, Chase? C'mon, it's just a friendly drink, not a date.*

Fischer lost track of time as he debated, and the silence gave way to a full-fledged tongue-tied pause, which Jade addressed.

"It's, you know, just a great place," Jade fumbled out dropping her eyes down to the floor.

Fischer looked out from his front porch at Jade's pearl white 1965 Ford Mustang sitting in the driveway. "Are we going in *that*?" he asked excitedly.

"That was the plan."

"Cool," Fischer said, smiling at her. *This is totally a date. Is she even suited for me? Open mind, Chase, keep an open mind, for now…* "And the guys won't mind me encroaching on their hangout turf?"

"I'm sure they'll think it's kind of funny, with the whole temporary honorary Chaplain thing. Sort of round off and wrap up the whole experience for you."

Jade offered an unforgettable look—an inviting smile in such a penetrating, yet comforting way. Fischer wasn't sure to trust her with his wounded heart but was too afraid not to.

Jade stepped out on the porch. "It'll be fine."

Chapter 13

"HEY, GJ. WHAT'S *HE* DOING here?" Fischer heard Praider's gruff voice blurt out as they walked into the pub. *Funny, right.* Fischer sighed.

"Shut it, Praider," Jade barked back.

She certainly knows how to handle herself and not take crap from anyone, that's for sure.

Boardner's by La Belle had a respectable sage vibe to it. Live music played in one section, while a quieter more elegant segment awaited them off to another side. There were several off-duty cops, probably twenty or more, Fischer reckoned, as Jade waved to several parties while they walked past them. None were in uniform, all of them dressed in civilian clothes. The jocular conversation topics signaled their expertise as they enjoyed themselves blowing off steam. Fischer caught wind of various wild arrest anecdotes as they walked past them along a beautifully polished wooden bar. The long bar had long brass extended rail which curved and wrapped around the end. Jade guided them to the curved corner, and the open spot it presented. Praider, Greppin, Bostic, and another guy with short red hair and freckles were in a booth across and diagonal from them. The red head was waving them over to join them.

"I recognize the others, but who's the guy waving us over?" Fischer asked.

Jade looked over nonchalantly. "Oh, that would be Squirrel," Jade said flatly. A quick roll of the eyes revealed her level of conflicted admiration about him. "We'll get our drinks and scootch in with them for a bit, I guess." She flagged down the bartender. "I'll have a cabernet… *and*?" She looked at Fischer.

"Ah… I'll go with, let's see, the Spatan Dunkel on tap." The bartender headed off on assignment. "*Squirrel*? Does he cover Disneyland?" Fischer asked with a snicker.

Jade chuckled. "Most officers have a calm and coolness to their demeanor in the field. They are trained to deescalate any given situation. You can usually expect and trust a certain level of professionalism with whoever you may be working with. But every once in a while, there's someone that behaves a bit more erratically than expected. We call those rare special breeds, 'squirrels.' Every department usually has one, and he's all ours," Jade said with an embarrassed grin.

The drinks arrived, and after their first gratifying sips, they headed to the booth.

"Should I bring a bowl of nuts, for Squirrel?" Fischer asked.

Jade shot a sly look from the side of her half-slit eyes "Be nice."

They sat down after a mild shifting of the present company. The cozy plump green and white striped padded booth screeched as they settled in and rested their drinks on the center oak tabletop. Greppin's height and frame commandeered their carved-out corner of cop chatter. From left to right sat Fischer, Jade, Praider, Bostic, Greppin, and Squirrel. Greppin and Praider both drank light beers, as Squirrel reveled in himself with an appletini. Bostic looked like he was about ready to ingest a science experiment. A flaming cube of sugar burned over a perforated spoon suspended across the rim of a clear glass containing a dark green liquid. Bostic then poured a small amount of water over it and into the elegant looking elixir, stirring the concoction with the spoon. By all appearances it was the quintessential drink one might expect a forensic pathologist to enjoy. Jade asked the question Fischer was dying to. "What's *that*?"

"Absinthe," Bostic said wryly. "It's an eccentrically classic invention from France."

"This is the spiritualist guy, right?" Squirrel asked, shifting focus to Fischer.

"*Pastor*. Evening," Fischer said, raising his pint for an informal "air-toast." Fischer looked Squirrel over. His tiny five-pointed star earring in his left ear sealed the deal. He'd never seen a more punchable face.

"Okay, so, I've gotta say, what was with that whole 'Mazel tov' thing? Greppin asked.

"*Mazzaroth*," Fischer said, with distinct pronunciation.

"'Mazzaroth,' all right. You really believe that's true? Cause I'm gonna tell you, people don't just walk out on the Chief like that. You pull something like that, you better be right."

Fischer sensed the table was all ears waiting for what he said next. The background music of the pub oddly transitioned at that precise moment from a louder upbeat song to a lower ballad, adding an eerily melodramatic effect, which didn't help matters. *Come on, Fischer, it's homerun time. Your credibility is on the line.* He took a deep breath and one more sip of Spatan before answering.

"The zodiac signs we know today, people assume mostly come from the Greeks and Roman mythology stories, invented, and assigned to convenient star groupings reinforcing their character narratives. This automatically paints a picture of foolish fantasy in the minds of many today. The ridiculous astrological association built off this only further compounds the silliness of the whole concept, and preys on the naivety of the young, the innocent, or those seeking some sort of extra meaning in life."

Jade self-consciously slouched back and crossed her arms.

"It's easy enough to do," Fischer said understandably and offered a discreet wink at Jade. "However, I'm more interested in where the Greco-Romans got their ideas *from*. One could argue they adopted and twisted an elaborately detailed story that was already associated with them, a message in the stars from God, if you will."

"The Mazzaroth," said Greppin.

"Bingo," Fischer said, dinging a spoon on the rim of his beer. "The Hebrew vision of the stars, from the earliest days, which tells the glory story of the Messiah to come and save humanity."

"The Hebrew Zodiac," Bostic said solemnly.

"Not *exactly*," Fischer corrected. "'Zodiac's' etymological root is 'animal,' where we get *zoo*, or *zoology* from, hence the representation of animals in the secular zodiac, or even the Chinese zodiac for that matter."

"If *Mazzaroth* doesn't mean it's the Hebrew zodiac, then what *does* it mean?" Squirrel asked.

"Great question. 'Mazzaroth' is a *hapax legomenon*, a word only used once in a language, or in this case the body of the Biblical text. One usage greatly complicates our ability to say much about it with confidence from a scholarly perspective, but 'the Way' might be a better translation, as in the way the twelve signs repeat themselves annually in season, repeating a story."

"And Jesus once referred to himself as 'the Way' right?" Jade asked rhetorically.

"Exactly," Fischer said.

"Oh, come on." Praider said. "I'm familiar enough with the Bible and the church to know that constellation interpretations aren't part of it. If God has a 'message in the stars,' it would seem the Bible might talk about them."

"He did," Fischer said. "And it does. Job is one of if not the oldest of Biblical writings. It says, in the greater context of God speaking to Job about creation, and more specifically the acute context of other named stars and constellations, 'Can you lead forth the Mazzaroth in their season, or can you guide the Bear with its children?'"

"Ursa Major and Ursa Minor, Polaris," Bostic said, chiming in.

Fischer grinned wide with his Hollywood smile. "*Right*. Pleiades and Orion are specifically identified as well. Listen, believe it or not, Job is not allegorical, he was a historical figure of great renown that studied the constellations but couldn't comprehend or articulate the workings of heaven through the laws of the universe—which modern science has no answer for, mind you. But Job was being forcefully reminded that the firmament is the creation of God, who was the one questioning him."

Fischer couldn't help noticing Praider shaking his head with a smirk.

"You're right, Praider, in that it's not discussed much as a major point of emphasis in the church, and I'm well aware many people don't think Job actually lived, but there is a lot more in the Scriptures than people realize."

"For instance?" Praider asked.

Fischer took another deep breath, chased it with a taste more of Spatan, and summoned the best of his memory recall ability. *Nope.* He opened his Bible app on his phone.

"The first chapter in Genesis for starters. Indulge me for but a minute…"

"Too late," Squirrel said.

Fischer ignored him as he cued up his app. "Listen to the opening section of Psalm 19. A cursory reading makes it sound like King David is just talking about creation in general, but when considering the possibility that God may have written a message in the stars to reinforce for His people, it's compelling." Fischer read from his phone's small screen.

> "The heavens declare the glory of God;
> And the firmament sheweth his handywork.
> Day unto day uttereth speech,
> And night unto night sheweth knowledge.
> There is no speech nor language,
> Where their voice is not heard.
> Their line is gone out through all the earth,
> And their words to the end of the world.
> In them hath he set a tabernacle for the sun,
> Which is a bridegroom coming out of his champer,
> And rejoiceth as a strong man to run a race.
> His going forth is from the end of the heaven,
> And his circuit unto the ends of it:
> And there is nothing hid from the heat thereof.
> The law of the Lord is perfect, converting the soul:
> The testimony of the Lord is sure, making wise the simple."

Fischer shifted to memory. "Link that to Romans 1:20, 'For the invisible things of him from the creation of the world are clearly seen, being understood by the things that are made, even his eternal power and Godhead; so that they are without excuse.'"

Fischer lowered his phone recognizing he had seized everyone's complete attention and concluded his thoughts. "I think it's all very enthralling."

"Interesting," Greppin said. "So, how is this 'story of God' supposed to go, if all we've got to go on are the secular zodiacal signs?"

Fischer was thankful for a softball pitch question. "The CliffsNotes version would essentially be Creation, the Fall of mankind, the promised Messiah to come and crush the head of Satan the Old Serpent, who bites his heel in the process, but is ultimately defeated, and mankind is eventually restored through the cross of Christ."

"That's it?" Greppin asked.

"Well, the grand story is certainly much more elaborate and blurred from the secular Hellenization over thousands of years, but according to the Hebrew calendar, and their understanding of a six-thousand-year-old earth, a rough count back makes logical sense to begin with Virgo, the *virgin*. Is that fair?" Fischer asked, looking at Bostic.

"I'm an old earth guy, but yes, according to your *theory*, the math checks out," Bostic said.

Fischer swallowed another few swigs and continued. "Christ Jesus, being born from a virgin, is the promised seed. This woman, *Virgo*, is surrounded by three other associate constellations; *Coma*, a male infant underscored as 'the Desired One,' *Centaurus*, a dual natured being emphasizing the dual nature of Jesus, God and man, and *Arcturus*, the Great Shepherd, the 'Coming One' with a sickle to harvest."

Jade finished her wine and emphatically slammed it on the table enthusiastically. "Oh, please, let me do *Libra*."

Fischer grinned at her. "The floor is yours, Madam."

"Libra is the Scales," Jade began, and like the victim we studied, the three decans are the Cross, a slain victim, and the Crown, all of which make allusions to the crucified Christ." Jade beamed a delighted self-satisfying smile.

"What do the 'scales' mean?" Squirrel asked.

Jade's face quickly faded to the classic 'deer in the headlights' expression.

"The weighing scales," Fischer said in quick-save fashion, "are the Bibles' lock and step metaphor for judgment, as in to be weighed, measured, *and found wanting*, as Libra's balance is uneven. This is how all will stand before God on the last day, but only through the price paid of Christ crucified can we be saved."

Greppin started giggling in his deep baritone voice. "I'll give it to ya, Pastor, you're good." Greppin said before turning serious. "So, you think that some weird psycho killer Christian is following this pattern, to make a point?"

"To be emphatically clear," Fischer cleared his throat, "A *true* clear-thinking Christian would never do something like this. Like with everything, something pure and unadulterated has been corrupted and twisted for evil purposes. But yes, I believe some twisted demented soul is behind this, and seemingly following a mangled version of this, from my professional opinion."

"But it doesn't matter if we don't find the Scorpio murder," Jade said.

"And for an illustrative murder venue, I don't think a *Scorpions* concert has been in LA for a long time. Okay, I'll bite. Do the thing with Scorpio," Praider said, as if throwing an olive branch upon the table of discussion.

"It's funny," Fischer said. "The scorpion stings, but the serpent does indeed *bite*."

"Same difference," Praider said.

Fischer thought for a moment, treasuring another taste of his Dunkel, as he mulled the irony of incessant data checking on smartphones in public as he opened his astronomy app again to examine. "You might be right, Detective Praider."

"Huh?"

Fischer dove in. "The three decans in Scorpio all have to do with a serpent contending with a Christ-like heroic suffering servant. The first is a serpent struggling with Ophiuchus, *the healer*. The next is Ophiuchus wrestling with the Serpent, stung in one heel by the Scorpion, and crushing it with the other. And the third is Hercules, *a dual-natured god/man hero*, who is wounded in his heel, with the other foot over the Dragon's head."

"I thought you said they all had to do with serpents?" Greppin asked.

"They're all inter-related. Check this out." Fischer scrolled through his Bible app. "Revelation 20:1-2, 'And I saw an angel come down from heaven, having the key of the bottomless pit and a great chain in his hand. And he laid hold on the dragon, that old serpent, which is the Devil, and Satan, and bound him a thousand years.'"

"Maybe we shouldn't be looking for a scorpion connection so much as we should be looking for a serpent," Jade said.

"Holy crap," Squirrel said, coughing down a sip of appletini down the wrong pipe and gaining the attention of all present. "You guys are looking for a murdered victim connected to a snake? ...I remember I got a weird dispatch request a while back from an erratic 911 call-in about some old guy dying at *the Viper Room*. She wasn't on the line very long, details were sketchy. I checked it out, no one knew anything. Loud band that night, but nothing out of the ordinary for one of West Hollywood's most notorious nightclubs. Dead end. We never heard anymore."

"Squirrel, think hard, was that in *November*?" Jade asked.

"Coulda been."

"Did you check the hidden whisky bar in the basement?" Fischer asked. All eyes were back to him, their faces perplexed that he knew such a thing existed. Fischer liked to fancy himself as a low-grade whisky buff, who every once in a while, liked to splurge. The clandestine Viper Room whisky lounge was one of those nights. Fischer always hedged his potential alcoholic tendencies against drinking only expensive whisky, as to limit his quantity, frequency, and diminish addictions. *Work in progress*.

"The Viper Room has an incredible hidden high-end whisky bar in the basement. It's just past the cashier, you kinda have to know it's there to find it," Fischer said guiltily.

Jade began thinking aloud. "High end A-listers like to pop in there from time to time. They'd have hidden cameras in a place like that, surveillance footage," she said excitedly while searching Greppin's eyes.

The table grew quiet for a moment until Greppin took charge. "Anyone feel like bar hopping tonight?"

Chapter 14

JADE DROVE HER MUSTANG WITH Fischer riding shotgun in search of a lucky parking spot on the Sunset Strip. Squirrel had hopped in the backseat, all but ruining the evening with his annoying third-wheel presence and chatter, Fischer thought.

Jade mercifully struck parking gold, jolted to a stop, shifted into reverse and flawlessly parallel parked in lightning fashion. The three got out. Jade lit a cigarette and puffed quickly as they made their way toward the Viper Room's thin glowing neon lights in the distance. Fischer did his best to hide his disdain for cigarette smoke. The three arrived at the entrance finding Greppin, Praider, and Bostic already waiting for them. Jade, over halfway done with her cigarette, tapped it out underfoot and the group walked in.

The Viper Room had metamorphosed through many names, owners, and identities through the years. It had been a jazz bar, a gangster gambling den, a club, and most recently an A-list Hollywood hot spot. Its reputation infamously came back on the map in the early 1990's on an unfortunate Halloween night when rising star actor, River Phoenix, met his unfortunate early demise from a drug overdose on the premises. It's well-known Hollywood lore that owner, Johnny Depp, still closes The Viper Room every October 31st for that reason.

Fischer entered the notorious club considering its ominous past and speculated what lengths an establishment like this might go to in order to conceal more negative attention. The rock band of the night blared reverberations through the place as the group of six passed through the stairwell doorway and descended toward the basement. Fischer was the caboose in their train line. By the time he arrived at the clandestine location, conversation had already begun with Praider leading the charge, and Greppin asking questions.

The blond bartender, dressed smartly in a flamboyant colored jacket which oddly accented his well-groomed slicked back ponytail, bristled, and began talking. "Eye in the sky? I know someone faking to be an off-duty cop when I see one," He lisped out his next demand. "Look boys, no drinks, no answers. And I like big tips."

Fischer's cell phone vibrated in his pocket. A new text message registered, but the present conversation was too intriguing to bother looking just yet.

"Fine," Praider said. "Give me a whisky I guess."

"What kind, pretty boy?" the bartender said with a wink.

"I don't know, Jack Daniels, whatever." Praider slapped down a twenty.

"Sure thing," the bartender said, pouring with swift professionalism. "So, what do you want to know?"

"I want to know about an emergency call from this location about someone dying, which possibly took place in November."

"Listen, there mighta been a guy," the bartender grinned. "But it looks like there are five more in your party. No money, no honey."

The group collectively rolled their eyes and reluctantly coughed up cash.

"A lot of cheap dates here," the bartender said.

"Oh, for crying out loud," Fischer slammed down a hundred-dollar bill. "Make mine a *Lagavulin*."

"Finally. A man who knows what he wants," the bartender smiled, grabbing the requested top-shelf bottle. The drinks flowed as did his words. "There mighta been a guy, old guy, long white hair, and his group, not the kinda people that usually get down here, if ya know what I mean. Tent people. You can tell. I think it was his birthday or something. He had a silly fake birthday hat thing on, and his group was sorta dragging him around like a *Weekend at Bernie's* type of thing.

"A weekend at what?" Jade asked.

"We'll watch it later," Fischer said tapping his elbow against her arm. "You're sure he wasn't just passed out?"

"I've seen a lot of people pass out in my days," the bartender smiled with confidence. "This looked different."

"So, how'd the night end?" Praider asked.

"His group carried him out."

"They carried him out? And that didn't stand out as odd to you?" Jade asked.

"I've seen a lot of people carried out of this place over the years, but again, this seemed unique. His color, the birthday celebratory festiveness of it mixed with some frantic activity."

"How frantic?" Greppin asked.

"The phone call. The woman was a bit hysterical."

"You heard the 911 call?" Jade asked.

"Again," the bartender sighed, "A hysterical woman, in a night club, in Los Angeles, with live bands and famous people making cameos. Any given night here has those elements. It's just, the old man stood out. He was memorable, and something about it looked off."

"I don't suppose you know which tent city they took him back to?" Greppin asked.

"I might," the bartender devilishly smiled. "You guys still thirsty?"

Squirrel barked out, "You son of a—"

"Easy, Sweety. No need to get ugly. Tell ya what, let me tend to that table over there, and I'll get right back with you all when you decide what you want. Remember, this *is* a business establishment after all."

The bartender promenaded off as Jade, Praider, Greppin and Bostic conferred. Squirrel sipped his drink and examined the art decorating the walls, dialing his phone. Fischer stole a moment and checked his text. He recognized the number of his Bishop, Mike Walton. He opened the message:

"Chase, Urgent. The president of our
church body will be in my office tomorrow

*morning, first thing. He's requesting your
presence. It doesn't sound good. As you
know, we're still dealing w your ecclesial
charges... Sorry for the last-minute nature,
but I think you know your whole career is
on the line here. —Imperative for your future"
Please be here. 8am sharp. MW"*

Fischer's heart sank. He'd been waiting to hear something regarding this matter for a while, exoneration, understanding, reconciliation, anything positive, but no. This didn't sound good. *Lovely.* He somberly turned back toward the group just as they were showering the bartender with cash for the next round. Fischer dropped his last fifty-dollar bill on top of the pot.

"They might have said they were from the tent village about a quarter mile west from here."

"Excellent. We'll check it out," Greppin said.

"In the meantime," Praider slapped down his LAPD badge. "We'll be taking that 'eye in the sky' camera footage you've got."

The bartender slouched in disbelief.

"Right about now, *Pretty Boy*," Praider said with a massive smile.

"Gotta go," Squirrel said, clicking off his phone.

The guys began escorting the bartender up the stairs.

"Who was that?" Praider asked Squirrel.

"Huh? No one."

Jade turned to Fischer. "And I thought New York was the city that never sleeps. I guess this crazy night keeps getting crazier, you up for the tent village next?"

"Actually," Fischer said, "I think I have to call it a night."

"Oh. Really?" Jade said a bit deflated.

"Sorry, something's come up. Another matter I have to tend to with my job."

"I see. You want me to give you a ride back?" Jade asked.

"I wouldn't want to slow down your progress of the night with the others. It's okay. I can catch an Uber. Besides, I probably need to think alone on this one for a while to prepare."

"Suit yourself," Jade said, heading toward the staircase. She looked up the stairwell then back at Fischer. "Hey, Fischer, great job leading us here tonight. That's good detective work. You know, for an *honorary* chaplain."

Jade winked and headed up.

"Thanks." Fischer smiled as he watched her ascend the steps and out of sight. He turned back and caught his reflection in the mirror. It was a painful slap in the face back to the reality of his life with its pressing unsettled issues. He summoned his ride through the Uber app and savored the last of his second Lagavulin of the night. *What am I doing here? I'm no detective. This fantasy has been fun for a while, but it's over now. I've got bigger career problems. And after tomorrow it might all be over. Sobering. No. Steady there, Ace. It's not like he actually has anything on you.*

Fischer thumbed through old photos on his phone and stopped on one of a bombshell young red-headed woman. *Rosalynn.* He sighed and scrolled to another picture, a selfie of him and Rosalynn together, her kissing his cheek, and him grinning ear to ear. *Well, maybe he does... Maybe.*

Fischer closed his phone with a frustrated click, lapped up his last libation, and trudged up the steps seeking his mystery driver of the night. He wasn't looking forward to the lion's den that awaited him in the morning, and for good reason. Church politics could make Chicago politics blush. Fischer was keenly aware church politics was a uniquely diabolic gift, personally purchased, wrapped, and bow-tied by Satan himself.

Chapter 15

DETECTIVE JADE ZOOMED BACK TO LAPD headquarters ignoring every speed limit sign along the way. She entered the video department. Praider and Bostic were already queuing up the newly acquired footage.

"There she is," Praider said. "The show's about to begin."

"Popcorn?" Bostic said, dryly.

"No thanks... *Seriously?*" Jade asked in a twinge of surprise.

Bostic pulled out a large stash of boxed Cracker Jacks from his black duffel bag.

"Well, all right." Jade delightedly sat down as if they were snugly settling in for a special pre-screening invitation of a soon to be released Hollywood blockbuster. Jade's chair shrilled into quiet as Praider began the tape.

"A lot of different nights to choose from in November. Here we go," Praider said.

# # #

Wednesday, January 15th
9:17 A.M.

Bishop Michael Walton's office was located in a beautiful section of

Orange County, just across the southern border of LA County. The office's warm living room setting with plush leather couches and chairs overlooked a small park with a fountain at its center. Fischer gazed out the window spying some birds in an aerial dogfight until his attention reverted to his cell phone's clock.

"This is ridiculous. I thought you said eight *sharp*," Fischer said with a snap at Walton.

Fischer turned to see his Bishop seated comfortably in one of the chairs, sifting through papers on the coffee table. Walton was as tall as he was soothing in demeanor. He was a stoically seasoned churchman with the seemingly appropriate silver hair and glasses accenting his features. His typical black suit completed his ensemble.

"I can't say I haven't seen President Schumacher do this type of thing before," Walton said. "Would you like another coffee?"

"No, I'm fine. It's an unnecessary power play. He's trying to send me a message," Fischer said with grizzled annoyance. "He's still bitter."

"Can you blame him? After how things played out."

"I guess I expect a higher standard from the president of our church body," Fischer said.

"I suppose he might say the same of you?" Bishop Walton said, in a gentle mentoring tone.

"Fair," Fischer said. "But this whole situation is ludicrous."

"Yes," Walton said. "But the presidium is methodically thorough if anything. And if I may strenuously suggest, you must be extremely careful here, and I caution you never to say—"

"Gentlemen," President Harold Schumacher said barging into the room. "Good to see you. Sorry, I must have lost track of time."

The disingenuous tone was palpable, Fischer thought. *How could someone held in such high esteem by so many come across that insincerely?*

President Schumacher possessed a powerful bear-like presence, rounded out with a bit of a belly, brownish-gray hair, and a mangy beard all but begging for a good trim. He wore the pious full circled white clerical collar around the top of his neckline, and charcoal suit. His whole wardrobe including shoes escalated into the several thousand-dollar range, Fischer figured.

"Michael, good to see you, good to see you brother," Schumacher said as they shook hands and embraced. "Too bad our visits are usually over ugly situations like these." Schumacher turned toward Fischer. "And here's our shooting, I mean, sorry, rising star." President Schumacher extended his arm to greet Fischer.

Fischer reached out, to match the political theater diplomacy he was observing, feeling like he was dipping his hand into a piranha bowl. Schumacher's powerful hands clamped with pinching grip, much more forceful than necessary, Fischer assessed, as he adjusted to match strength. *To think, this was almost my father-in-law.*

# # #

9:37 A.M.

Jade's eyes were struggling as she downed another cup of coffee. Bostic and Praider were in no better condition, squinting toward the flickering light in the small, darkened room.

"Stop right there, Praider," Jade said. "That guy right there, right there, heading into the men's room, with the ballcap on."

Praider squinted. "What *is* that? A Detroit Tiger's hat?"

"Giants," Jade said. "San Fran."

Praider sped back through the frames summarizing as he clicked. "Here's our birthday guy, the one I'm pretty sure the bartender was describing. Old guy with long white disheveled hair and the crown. Looks like he's having a good time with his, ah, girlfriends around him. Looking okay. Heads to the restroom. And immediately this guy with the hat heads in after him. Fast forward. About five minutes later, ballcap guy comes out. And not for another twelve minutes does the Party Grandpa come out."

"And he looks worse, much worse," Jade said. "Zoom in on their faces and print."

"Greppin and Squirrel should be coming back in on their shift soon," Praider said. "Let's give them the image of this Party Grampa and see if they can ferret out anything from that tent city near the Sunset strip."

\# \# \#

"So, to be clear, Chase," Schumacher said with a stroke of his beard, "when dealing with ecclesial charges of this nature, to retain your pastorate, you'll need over a seventy-five percent majority vote in order to stay on the ministry roster, or you will be defrocked. As you know, there are thirty-five district presidents, with an additional five vice presidents on the presidium, rounding out to forty, and myself which serves as tie breaker. It's incredibly steep. And I know of a few guys that won't even bother listening, considering the subject matter. To them, divorce is tantamount to the end of the ministry. Anything else you have to say?"

Schumacher's smugness hung in the air for a brief moment as Fischer calculated his next move of verbal chess.

"*Divorce* is a term reserved for those who have actually been married. Rosalynn and I were only engaged. It's *impossibly* unfair to compare calling off a wedding to divorce."

"You left her at the altar!" Schumacher yelled back.

"That is hyperbole at best," Fischer fired back.

Schumacher smiled through his scraggily beard as he scratched it, more out of habit than anything. "I'm sure Mary would have been *just* as understanding had Joseph done the same. Church would look very different at Christmas time, and beyond, wouldn't you agree?"

"Oh, come *on*," Fischer said restraining himself.

"In my day that just wasn't done. Considering your four-year relationship and build up to marriage, it's humiliating and inexcusable."

"Harry, I—"

"Don't call me 'Harry,' Chase. Not now. And of course, your actions are only symptomatic of the bigger problem at front and center. Your fornication tendencies which might as well be termed adulterous in light of the fact that engagement is essentially considered a legally binding estate in the church."

"Only by a rare few," Bishop Walton said with measured reverence.

"Thanks, Michael," President Schumacher said through a glance of gentle annoyance.

"Oh, that's just great," Fischer said sarcastically. "That is libel in nature, and you're supposed to be my president, intercessor, and advocate?"

"Father-confessor, and I call it like I see it," Schumacher said.

"Let's review one more time," Fischer said. "Yes, it's true, I broke the 'Billy Graham elevator rule' *once*, in an apparently gross miscalculation on my part counseling a female co-ed student behind closed doors. NOTHING HAPPENED!" Fischer roared. "You and I both know this is a witch-hunt, compounded by the extremely unfortunate consequences of her lie of an accusation, and you're allowing it to spill over and make it personal. Honestly, I was trying to do the mercifully right thing, and counsel a seemingly hurting soul. How was I to know that girl was struggling with mental illness, not thinking clearly, and had nefarious intentions?"

"Sally, a daughter of Christ," Schumacher said, with humanizing effect in a trial lawyer-like tone.

"Sure, fine," Fischer said turning his tone down. "Sweet Sally *fabricated* the whole thing. Why, I do not know."

Bishop Walton cleared his throat, as a coach grabbing attention of his team. "The '#Me Too' phenomenon, for right or wrong, was all the rage then, sir."

President Schumacher rolled his eyes.

"Sir," Fischer said calmingly. "With all due respect, when that news went public, there was no evidence presented, because there was none to present. The allegation went unfounded, and my congregation believed me."

"Not *all* of them," Schumacher said. "And I'm thinking of one in particular."

"True, and I'm thinking of a few more than one." Walton said.

Fischer paced briefly in calculating fashion. "The devil is good at what he does, isn't he? Deception. It's painful that some people left the church over a lie and gossip. It's painful still that Rosalynn didn't believe me. And incredibly more painful that she, um…" *Be respectful, Chase, this is her father*. "Acted in retaliation."

"Retaliation?" Schumacher asked.

"I loved your daughter, sir. Part of me always will. Indeed, I wanted to marry her. But it's been over a year now. I've moved on. And Rosalynn has too, earlier than… Well, humbly speaking, maybe there was a reason I had to back out of the wedding. It might be good of you to consider that maybe I was wounded too. Maybe everyone you think is innocent in all this, isn't actually as innocent as you think."

"In my opinion," Bishop Walton said, stealing a hesitant glance at Schumacher's reddening face. "Much of this revolves around the topic of forgiveness."

"Chase," Schumacher said. "You need to learn to be less demanding. You need to watch what you say." Schumacher shot a look at Bishop Walton, and then back to Fischer.

"Sounds like you have one vote in your favor, Chase. But it remains to be seen if you'll have enough when all is said and done. Remember, you don't only have one major cloud swirling over you, you have two. And they're about to get tornadic."

Chapter 16

11:21 A.M.

GREPPIN AND SQUIRREL MEANDERED THROUGH a tent village near the Sunset Strip showing a picture of the old man Party Grandpa to anyone who cared. The homeless population was only increasing with no end in sight. Southern California's ideal weather all but ensured the swelling of this long-term problem. Any solutions only seemed to further enable the homeless.

"I feel like we're Hansel and Gretel wandering through the woods here," Squirrel said in exhausted despair.

"As long as I'm Hansel," Greppin said, offering a rare moment of humor. The two officers approached the next tent.

"Knock knock," Squirrel said.

A woman peeked out, looking much older than she probably was with her meth skin, smoke-yellow teeth, and unkempt graying hair.

"Have you seen this man before, know who he is?" Squirrel asked.

The woman squinted at the picture. "Oh, yeah, Johnny. He's over there. He's been sleeping for a long time. I hope he gets up soon; he owes me some money. Do you have ten dollars?"

"Over where, ma'am?" Greppin asked.

She pointed back to a half-propped tent about thirty yards diagonally behind her. "That's his place, but he smelled bad, you know, hadn't taken a shower in a while, so they covered him up."

"In blankets?" Greppin asked.

Squirrel began heading toward what remained of Johnny's tattered green tent, ripped with a few holes and one bent pole.

"No, silly. The dirt," she said.

"You covered him in dirt; you buried him because he smelled?" Greppin asked.

"No, I didn't. His friends, but he's only been sleeping. He'll probably be up soon. He owes me money, ya know."

"*Grep*," Squirrel yelled. "You better get over here. We're gonna need forensics."

# # #

3:57 P.M.

Fischer's Triumph Bonneville inched through traffic on the freeway, navigating through the occasional honking cars until he slowed to a halt. The attached sidecar prevented him from weaving through traffic, an illegal move to be sure, but tempting in situations like this. He stole a glance at his GPS. The long red line through the coordinates to home clarified the reason. *Accident ahead, great.*

Post meeting brunch plans with Bishop Walton had turned into late lunch plans, and a long lunch at that. Debriefing, discussing, and praying through the ramifications of the session with President Schumacher was much needed and appreciated. Bishop Walton was a salt of the earth man of God, and a salvific harbor in the tempest that was Fischer's life in the last year.

Fischer looked at his watch. *Rush hour already? Can nothing go right? I'm gonna be late for my home blessing appointment with the Chiparros.* The thought of having to perform a 'home blessing' after the morning's tongue-lashing session was divinely poetic. God's timing often amused Fischer, pondering a potential deeper divine personal lesson to be learned for him. Fischer looked at his watch again and sighed with a shake of his head.

# # #

5:35 P.M.

Bostic examined the body of Party Grampa Johnny, and methodically typed notes into his computer. Significant decomposition had set in owing to the amount of time the body had decayed exposed in the elements, but the severe blackened discoloration signaled something out of the ordinary.

Detective Jade popped through the doorway with a swift knock at the door.

"Evening, GJ," Bostic said.

"Just coming back on duty. I heard they found a body. *The* body? Anything yet?" Jade asked with a sparkle of anticipation.

Bostic took off his glasses in fatigue, briefly pinch-massaged the top of his nose where they'd rested. "Well, I'm obviously not done with my examination and tests, but so far, yeah, there's a lot going on here." He twisted slightly back and forth on his swivel chair loosening his leg muscles. "You're not gonna believe it, GJ. Are you ready for *this*?"

Chapter 17

FISCHER DESPISED UNPUNCTUALITY, BUT A quick stop at home was necessary before the Chipparo home-blessing. Luther needed a run, the email inbox required a few responses, and Jeannie needed a couple of detail specific questions answered before the weekend services, delivered in Fischer's all too familiar apologetic accent when tardiness got the best of him. Fischer zipped through his tasks before he donned his clerical collar, grabbed his ceremonies book agenda for special services, and hopped on the Triumph.

"*Luther.*"

Luther jumped into his usual sidecar spot. They zoomed down the highway. Fischer stole a quick glance at Luther. If German Shepherds could smile, Luther did every time he was beckoned to join Fischer for a sidecar ride in the Bonnie. Fischer loved every second of it.

The home-blessing had become more of an antiquated event over the past generation. Fischer rarely received the invitation to perform one but loved the concept and the theological implications of it. *If anything, this world needs more home blessings after what I've seen.* Fischer drew near to the Chiparro residence. It was a brick four-bedroom one level home in a charming Pasadena neighborhood that would make most other zip code residents blush with tax appraisal assessments. Each house along the street was more unique and larger than the next. The perfectly manicured lawns, sculpted trees, and landscapes never ceased to marvel Fischer. *How do these people pay for all of this?* The Chiparro's long-extended driveway had just enough space left for Fischer's Bonneville.

No sooner had he cut the engine did he begin salivating. Michael and Vicki Chipparo had successfully enticed Fischer earlier in the week with tales of serving a Jamon Iberico, a Spanish ham impaled on a spike and board with a special long blade to carve the thinnest slices of succulent meat shavings, easily elevating any dinner party into the highest stratosphere of charcuterie enjoyment as a conversation piece. *I can't wait.*

Fischer waltzed up to the front door noticing it ajar, seemingly waiting for his entrance. The big band jazz radiated an inviting ambience. The tipped over lamp was Fischer's first clue—something was awry. Fischer knocked loud on the opened door.

"Hello? Michael? Vicki?" Nothing. *Something's not right.*

Luther respectfully crept in tailing Fischer's trepidatious steps. Fischer performed a quick scan of the front living room space and hallways. A cockeyed picture on the wall, and a few broken chachka pieces on the floor, a thin wooden chair tipped on its side, near the downed lamp. *Looks like a struggle took place, maybe?* He could see the kitchen countertop island from where he stood. There was the Jamon and charcuterie platter, and a bottle of Justin red wine waiting to be poured. *What happened?* Another scan to his left answered his question with horror. On the floor over the other side of the leather couch lay Vicki Chipparo on her back, eyes half-opened. A small pool of blood was beginning to stain the carpet.

Fischer scrambled over to her and assessed as best he could with limited medical training. He checked her pulse as Luther sniffed her with his wet black nostrils. *She's weak.* It was tricky as Fischer's own pulse began to race. He could still hear her breathing. *Okay, good... Did Michael do this? What is going on?*

"Michael?" Fischer yelled. *Dear, Lord,* Fischer had another terrorized thought as he wiped his hand away from his mouth. "Christian?" No answer. Luther began to growl in low intensity.

Fischer tip-toed into the kitchen which provided vantage points to other connected rooms. Down the dim hallway to the right Fischer could make out

Michael's body laying half in the hallway and half into a side bedroom. Fischer pulled out his cellphone and called 911. A dark figure darted out of the bedroom at the end of the hall toward another room at the back of the house. *Holy cats. Someone else is here...* Fischer dropped the phone in panic. *Was it ringing yet?*

"Luther." Luther knew his cue and raced after the assailant. Fischer looked around, starting to tremble. *Get a hold of yourself, Chase.* The long Jamon ham blade was right next to him on the kitchen island countertop. Fischer picked it up, feeling less like a samurai swordsman, and more like a frightened hobbit holding 'Sting' for the first time. A flimsy weapon to be sure, but its length looked intimidating. *It's go time.*

Fischer retrieved his cellphone from the floor, dialed 911 again, and cautiously inched down the hallway toward Michael. A glance revealed he was still breathing too. Fischer peered into the next room. Luther frantically nosed around the room but hadn't found his target yet. Fischer dashed over to a back door and opened it.

"911, what's your emergency?" No sooner had the sentence blurted out than a fist hit Fischer squarely in the face. Fischer staggered back, flailing his arm across him, spun around, dropping the blade and phone as he tended to his nose. Luther pounced into rageful pursuit. The unavoidable eye-watering effect overcame Fischer's vision, but not before he caught a glimpse of the man, in a dark jacket and ballcap, streaking to the far corner fence gate of the backyard, with what looked like Christian slung over his shoulder. *Christian, no.*

Fischer picked up his phone again and barked commands. "This is Pastor Chase Fischer. I need help. I'm visiting a home of some friends at their house in Pasadena. An attacker's here. He's *hurt* them."

"What's the address? Where are you sir?"

"I don't *know*, we're off of Michigan Avenue," Fischer managed in frustration as he jogged over to the fence gate in time to see Luther biting the lower leg of the man.

"Hold on," Fischer said. "*Get* him, Luther."

Luther's teeth clenched deep with the zeal of a rare full release command from his master. The man screamed in agony crashing onto the sidecar of Fischer's motorcycle. Christian fell to the ground like a lifeless ragdoll. The man rolled over offering Fischer a clean look at his squarely chiseled middle-aged white face, with slightly greying hair.

The man's left arm went up to block Luther's jaws, freeing his right arm to whirl around and pummel Luther's ribcage and head. He pulled out a small screwdriver from his pocket and swiped Luther good. Luther crept back howling from the wound, as a little blood began to ooze. The obviously skilled man got up and carefully scooped Christian up off the ground. He screamed again in agonizing pain severely limping toward a dingy white van parked in the street. Luther's jaws had done some significant damage.

The man took the body of the unconscious child in through the driver's cab, started the engine and peeled out. Fischer darted to Luther and examined him. It was a little scrape. Not too bad. *Thank goodness.* Fischer bounded up to his motorcycle and assessed the scene in shock. *I can't let him get away with the boy.*

"Sir," his cellphone beckoned. "Sir, can you tell me what's going on?" Fischer glanced at the mailbox, read back the exact street address to the 911 operator, and amazed himself as he listened to his next words fall from his mouth. "A man's abducted their child, and I'm in pursuit."

Fischer put the phone in his pocket, careful to leave it on. He was no expert in tracking coordinates but figured it couldn't hurt. In a panic he figured somehow someone might be able to track them, wherever they might end up. Luther gingerly hopped in the sidecar, and they sped off.

A couple neighborhood hairpin turns later Fischer could see the white van taking the onramp towards the 210 West. *Gotcha.* Fischer zoomed after in pursuit, zipping carefully through a red light, noting the camera flash for a future traffic violation ticket. *Best money I'll ever spend.* Fischer raced up the onramp and began weaving through traffic to catch up. The miles quickly passed by as Fischer slowly closed in on the white van which was swerving oddly.

The van took an exit, slowed, and turned right. Fischer aimed to follow but squeezed the brakes almost flying over the handlebars as another car nearly slammed into them. A steady line of four more cars stuck Fischer there in agony. *Come on, come on.* Fischer could barely see ahead where the white van turned left down another road. Finally, Fischer made it there and turned, following down toward the exit. *I know this road. It leads to the one and only Jet Propulsion Lab… And a massive hiking trail.*

Fischer careened down the curving roads into a park-like atmosphere, carefully avoiding joggers, and frisbee golfers. In the distance of one of the parking lots Fischer spied the parked white van. Fischer rolled to a stop and assessed the situation. The man was standing next to the opened passenger door getting Christian out. He stopped when he saw Fischer.

Fischer popped up his helmet visor. Their eyes locked. Fischer thundered his Triumph engine in neutral. The man grimaced in frustration and staggered off into the nearby brushy woods. Fischer drove up to the van and barely dismounted before he cut the engine, popping off his helmet in the process.

"Christian?" Fischer was almost afraid to look in the passenger seat. There was Christian, sleeping, completely out. *Unbelievable.* Luther stood resolute looking out into the woods. His low growling signaled his readiness for his master's next order if need be.

Fischer picked up Christian. *Wait a minute, where is all this blood from? Maybe Luther bled more than I thought?* Fischer looked around. Christian wasn't bleeding. Fischer finally felt pain on his inside right arm. He pulled back his sleeve a bit and saw the huge red slash. *Must have been from that blade somehow when that guy punched me.* As Fischer's adrenaline lowered his pain increased. A sensation of lightheadedness began to set in. *Not good.* Fischer carried Christian toward a frisbee golf goal and in blurred vision thought he saw a small group of players approaching. "*Help.* I need hel—" Fischer collapsed with Christian to the ground.

# # #

A black hummer stopped on a dirty road along the far side of the wooded brush. The doors clicked to unlock. Wolfgang Manteuffel emerged from the thicket with his injured leg and climbed into the vehicle. The hummer pulled out before the door even shut.

"You failed me again, Wolf," the Prophet said.

Wolfgang shot a piercing look back at the familiar voice.

"I'd watch that attitude of your body language if I were you, Wolf."

"Sorry," Wolfgang said.

"Were there any casualties?" The Prophet asked.

"I don't think so. At least, I tried not to," Wolfgang said dryly. "Could have been. The woman put up more of a struggle than I expected, it got rough. And the guy, well, I hit his head pretty hard against the corner of the door frame. I missed on the tranq with him, and I had to move fast. She was screaming. I slipped into autopilot," Wolfgang said.

"Enough of them. The kid. I want the *kid*. I need the kid. We all need him…" The Prophet said.

"I know, I know, but then this Good Samaritan showed up."

"Good Samaritan?" The Prophet asked.

"This pastor and his dog."

"A *holy* man, really?"

"Yeah," Wolfgang said nursing his calf muscle in pain. "I heard the couple talking about it before I engaged with them. I wanted to deal with the matter before anyone else arrived." He pulled up the pant leg revealing the deep bite marks and blood.

"We'll get that looked at soon. We need you healthy and strong. There's still a lot more work to do," The Prophet said demonically with a guttural voice that sounded as if another deal with the devil had just been made. "First, tell me more about this Good Samaritan."

Chapter 18

Thursday, January 16th

CHASE FISCHER'S BODY STIRRED HALF-AWAKE in a hospital bed. He began to come to. His mind started firing into gear, though his eyes hadn't opened yet. *Ugh...Sore... Where am I?* The sounds of the machines hooked up to him triggered a clue. *Am I in the hospital? What hap—Christian...*

A woman's soft distorted voice began to speak, but Fischer couldn't register the identity. *Who is that?* Fischer's groggy mind flashed through possible candidates with a gradual melancholy descent, *Mother? Rosalynn? Nancy? Vickie? Shelly Davidson?* But then a warm intriguing thought passed over him as he sensed another hand holding his. *Jade?* Fischer's eyes eagerly flickered open and came into focus.

Jeannie sat bedside with a soothing smile. "Text and theme? Do you have a text and theme for your sermon this week, Pastor?" Fischer recognized this was one of Jeannie's go-to lines of humor any time she wanted to tease him with a little added pressure. He usually took his sweet time crafting his sermon throughout the week, but Jeannie often got him to chuckle first thing on Monday mornings by invoking the phrase with fake urgency. Fischer smiled and laughed. He was back.

Fischer sat up, and Jeannie adjusted the automated bed backing to assist. "What happened?"

"You lost a lot of blood, Pastor. A lot," Jeannie said. "But the doctors said it was only a matter of time until your strength would return."

Fischer looked down at his right arm. His forearm was almost entirely bandaged.

"They stitched it up. Luther's fine, too," Jeannie said.

Fischer began to piece together the memories of what happened. *The Jamon blade, the attacker, and the Chipparos.* "How are the Chipparos?" Fischer asked.

Jeannie's face dropped with tears forming in her eyes and took a couple breaths. "Vickie was brought to the hospital but died in the ambulance on the way. And Michael has blunt force trauma to the back of the head. There's been significant swelling. He's in a coma."

Fischer absorbed the news with deep stings like he was getting punched and slashed all over again. "What about Christian?"

"He's okay, physically at least. Considering he was adopted recently they have him in the protective custody of the DCFS. He was apparently in that window, so all the legalities checked out, and at the moment seems to be the best option."

"There's no other family?" Fischer asked.

"No," Jeannie said. "They're obviously hoping it's just temporary and that Michael will recover soon."

Fischer shook his head. "Good grief. Absolutely tragic."

Jeannie tried her best to make sense of the situation. "I mean, it's LA. They live in one of the best parts of town, which can attract the have-nots who want to take from the haves. Very odd they would have *two* break-ins so close together though, especially in that neighborhood."

Fischer thought about the Chipparo's previous break-in, and the whole reason for a request of a home blessing in the first place. But this didn't seem like a break-in. This seemed personally specific. *Why?* Before Fischer could formulate his thoughts into words they were interrupted by a knock at the door.

"LAPD... Freeze, don't move," Detective Jade said comically, seeing Fischer sitting up and well.

Fischer lit up inside and was pretty sure he didn't hide it well. "Detective Jade. Have I got a *story* for you," Fischer said.

"And I've got a story for you."

"Oh, so *this* is the detective I've heard so much about," Jeannie said.

Jade crossed her arms with an interested smirk and raised eyebrow at Fischer. "Heard so much about, eh?"

"Well, I…" Fischer felt a blush arising in a rare moment of embarrassment.

"Detective…" Jeannie squinted towards Jade's hospital sticker badge, reading the words printed aloud. "Gemma Jade."

"*Gemma?*" Fischer said with delight.

Jade covered her hospital sticker badge red-handedly and then gave up.

"Gemma Jade… *GJ*," Fischer said, looking her over as if filling in a little more of her identity. "Fitting. Cool name. I like it."

Jade attempted to recover into a miniscule semblance of professionalism. "Thank you. Well, Dr. Fischer, we do have some things to discuss if you're up for it."

Jeannie rose from her chair. "I think I'll let you two catch up." She looked Gemma up and down. "I can see you're in good hands, Pastor," Jeannie delivered her line with an atypical accent of maternal approval as she winked at Fischer out of view of Jade and made her exit.

Jade looked into Fischer's eyes and turned serious. "I'm very sorry about your friends."

"Uh, yeah," Fischer said sinking back into the dire moment at hand.

"I listened to your 911 tape. What you did was incredibly stupid," Jade said as she gently pinched his toe under the blanket.

"I suppose so," Fischer said. He reluctantly raised his wounded right arm.

Jade reached out and grasped Fischer's hand. "But equally valiant."

"Thanks. I couldn't let the kid be taken. He seemed lifelessly dead during the ordeal. I'm glad he's ok."

Jade sat down in the empty chair. "He was tranquilized. They found a syringe with residue at the home."

"*Tranquilized?*" Fischer asked. "That's odd. *Very* odd for a break-in, don't you think?"

A grim look came over Jade's face. "Child abductions are a dime a dozen these days, especially here, and I have to tell you, sadly, I've seen stranger things in Los Angeles than I'd care to tell you about."

Fischer believed her words with a slow melancholy nod. "I can only imagine. What happened after the Viper Room?"

"We checked the footage, and found the old guy the bartender was describing, and a man we identified as the probable suspect who poisoned him. Wasn't the best footage, and he had a ballcap on shadowing his face."

Fischer snapped up his head with a stiffened spine. "Really? But what about the Scorpio connection?"

"Squirrel and Greppin found the guy's body near the tent-village. He was poisoned with a cocktail of powerful toxins, and among them was the venom of a scorpion."

"I don't believe it. No way," Fischer said.

"Way. Bostic, our top forensic specialist, said that his blood contained traces of the Arizona Bark Scorpion, which is indigenous to the area, and possesses venom that can be fatal. It would have needed to be a lot to kill a grown man, hence the extra toxins, Bostic suspects. But get this, you wanna guess where the wound site was on the tent-dweller man's body?" Jade asked.

Fischer didn't have to think long. "His... heel?"

"Yup."

"Unbelievable," Fischer said in lowly pomp. "We were *right*. Does the Chief th—"

"The Chief feels this is sufficient evidence to move forward with a more aggressive investigation and provide more resources. You have his full support."

"Unreal," Fischer said in disgust. "*Who* would do this?"

"I don't know," Jade said, "But we've got an even bigger problem on our hands. The clock is ticking until January nineteen."

Fischer cocked his head immediately. "Aquarius. Presumably the next murder."

Jade smiled with vindication. "You're an A-student so far, Dr. Fischer. So, heal up quicker, cowboy. That's five days from now. And I think you've got one more overnight here until they can release you."

"That's not much time. I'm not sure where to begin," Fischer said.

Detective Gemma Jade stared at Fischer with a glint in her eye. "I actually do have an idea, but you're not going to like it. In fact, I'm pretty sure you're gonna hate it."

Chapter 19

Friday, January 17th

FISCHER WALKED WITH DETECTIVE JADE back into the LAPD conference room. Squirrel, Greppin, and Praider greeted them.

"What are you two, *partners* now?" Praider asked with a silly grin on his face.

Fischer sensed his face reddening a bit but squashed it with good reasoning. "I'm not supposed to drive for another twenty-four hours, and besides, you guys impounded my bike, so I needed a ride here anyway."

Greppin stood with his arms crossed and a big smile on his face. "Yeah, our resident pastor vigilante is in the house. We can't and don't usually pursue people in car chases, so what you did was—"

"*Cool*," Squirrel blurted out.

"I was going to say, *illegal*," Greppin said. "But, yeah, if I'm being fair, pretty noble. Also, very sorry to hear about your friends."

"Thank you." Fischer shook hands with the three of them, and quickly tended to his tender arm, checking on the stitches. *Pain. That reminds me, I've got a funeral to prep for this week, and not an easy one.* Fischer's thoughts began to descend into despair of how Vickie's loved ones would deal with the tragic loss of her life, but his thoughts didn't go too deep before

Chief Tatum walked into the room.

"Dr. Fischer," Tatum said, "we have the upper hand for the time being. As far as we know this new Zodiac killer, or whatever he is, doesn't know we're on to him. But we don't have much time. We all know Aquarius is the next constellation in the murder pattern that seems to be emerging. I took the liberty of looking up the decans. The Southern Fish, Pegasus, and Cygnus the Swan are all in relation to Aquarius. What sense can you make of this? You have the floor."

Fischer sat down, calculating how to convey his words best. "Remember, the common understanding of the zodiacal star constellations we know today are based on the ancient Greco-Roman mythology stories, but like many stories, they were based on a borrowing of an even more ancient understanding. This is important, because whoever is doing these crimes is basing their thinking off of the Hebrew Mazzaroth 'zodiac,' not the commonly understood secular one."

Fischer surveyed the faces in the room making sure everyone was tracking him. The affirming nods and focused attention gave him his answer as he prepared to go further.

"Biblically speaking, water has always been a purifying source of life for God's people."

"Baptism," Praider said. "But that doesn't show up until the New Testament, pretty late for this subject matter."

"Yes," Fischer said, "but there's tons of Old Testament typology, er, let's call it, Biblical foreshadow." Fischer attempted unsuccessfully to motion with his hands to express the idea. "God preparing his people for the concept of baptism."

"Say what?" Greppin asked.

Fischer rubbed his forehead with his hands over his eyes trying to unpack everything as simply as he could for the team. "In Genesis at creation most translations say something like 'the Spirit of God *hovered* over the water.' Water was obviously present at the flood, renewing the planet, and a white dove *hovering* over it, and again, the water of the Red Sea for Moses to lead God's people through it to a promised land, even at Jesus baptism, the Holy Spirit appears in the form of another white dove *hovering* over him standing in water. Sorry, I could go on and on. There are many examples."

"Is there a point coming sometime soon?" Chief Tatum asked. "What difference does all this make?"

Fischer considered for a moment diving deep into thought as he paced around the present company seated at the table. "This killer, he's looking at the zodiac differently, perhaps uniquely. He's looking at it through a skewed theological prism."

"Meaning what?" Greppin asked.

"Meaning, he thinks God, or at least his version of a god, is telling him something through this, and he's acting on it. That means we must begin looking at it the way he does, if we have any chance of figuring out what his messaging might be."

"And ultimately stopping him," Jade said.

Tatum motioned with his hand to Fischer. "Go on."

"Cygnus, the Swan, might not have originally been a swan. It's a white bird to be sure, but most probably linked to the dove of the Holy Spirit. In conjunction with the Southern Fish, one of the more ancient symbols of God's people, the Ichthus."

"*Ichthus*?" Greppin whispered in a stealing glance at Praider.

"It's all Greek to me. Forget it he's rolling," Praider said quietly.

Fischer returned from the inner recess of his mind to the present in swelling momentum.

"He sees Aquarius as some type of divine water bearer, bringing salvation upon God's people. Baptismal language often involves a death, by *drowning*, at least of the sinful 'Old Adam' of an individual. I'm thinking… Oh, God. I'm thinking it would make a lot of sense if the next victim were attempted to be killed by drowning."

"And Pegasus?" Jade asked.

Fischer continued, "Actually the oldest fables involving Bellerophon and Perseus find Pegasus' origin near the peaceful ocean pool *waters* where the King Father of gods resides. He's essentially a chiefly heavenly horse delivering messages with celestially swift speed. He might represent the expediting action of God's work from above to his people below."

"Well, that's just great," Tatum said. "Peaceful waters? Considering the fact that we are literally on the coastline of the *Pacific* Ocean, which is larger than all of earth's landmasses put together. The next murder could pretty much be anywhere. Thanks for narrowing things down for us, Dr. Fischer."

"Or even swimming pools, ponds, or water parks, for that matter," Greppin said.

Praider sighed in defeated exasperation. "Water slide parks? *Great.* Should we be concerned about a kid as the next victim?"

"After what I witnessed this week, I'd say we can't rule out anything," Fischer said.

"Yeah, let's put out an A.P.B. for anyone who ever gave their kid an aquarium," Squirrel said, souring the mood further.

Greppin stood up snapping his finger. "*Squirrel.* That... actually makes a lot of sense."

"Really?" Squirrel asked surprised.

"Kind of. Squirrel, I want you to do a run-down of all the major aquariums in the SoCal area. See if anything stands out for the dates we're talking about."

"Gotcha, all right. On it." Squirrel headed out with his marching orders.

"Praider, do a cross analysis of all the other major water themed venues, look for anything..."

"*Fishy*? Sorry, I couldn't resist," Praider said, excusing himself quickly.

"*Go*," Greppin said. "Chief, I think if you put in a call to the Coast Guard, that would be a good proactive move."

"Consider it done," Tatum said. "Meanwhile, I'll be working through the past data, birthdates of the victims, locations, exact dates of the murders, and see if it tells us anything on a broader scale. And GJ, did you tell Dr. Fischer your idea yet?"

Fischer turned toward Jade. "Oh, right, an idea I will apparently *hate*?"

Detective Gemma Jade smiled devilishly at Fischer with a couple quick raises of her eyebrows and a quick Samantha Stevens *Bewitched*-like crinkle of her nose. "We're going to attempt to get into the mind of the killer's 'skewed theological prism.'"

Fischer pondered her comment for a moment. "And how are we supposed to do that?"

Chapter 20

JADE DROVE HER LAPD SQUAD car with Fischer riding in the front passenger seat. Fischer had never actually ridden shotgun in a car with a literal shotgun loaded to the ready and resting near his left kneecap. *Not sure how comfortable I am with this. Still, it's better than riding in the back of this car.* Jade rolled to a stop somewhere in West Hollywood, parking curbside near a street front store. The store's swinging wooden sign read:

Astrology & More
Emporium

"Are you ready, Chase? Come on, what's your sign?" Jade asked in mock passion.

"This is a bad idea," Fischer said. "Tell me this wasn't one of your old haunts."

"Was that a pun?"

"Unintended," Fischer said, "but, if the broom fits."

"Honestly, you're too hesitant. It's like you're superstitious about superstition. Seriously. Is there some law against this or something?" Jade asked pointedly.

"As a matter of fact, there *is*." Fischer seized the moment as if on cue in one of his university classes. "It falls under the category of 'Thou shall not misuse the name of the Lord.' Sound familiar?"

Jade slouched back in her seat in defeat, crossing her arms.

"A sixteenth century monk brilliantly expounded on that this way, 'we should fear and love God so that we do not curse, swear, use satanic arts, lie, or deceive by His name, but call upon it in every trouble, pray, praise, and give thanks.' This whole astrology world is in the category of the occult. It's a form of divination. The Scriptures clearly speak against this in several places as an abomination to the Lord. God is real, and therefore so is the devil." Fischer looked out his window at the establishment, which fired him up even more. "This garbage entices people, unaware of real dark spiritual forces at work, in a 'just for the fun of it' kind of innocence but it dangerously introduces the deception that our lives are steered by unseen forces in the star patterns or worse. It's not harmless."

Fischer noted the silence in the car, feeling convicted he'd lectured too long. He looked over at Gemma appearing to sleep peacefully with her eyes closed. She broke the awkward silence with a humorous fake snoring sound. "Huughhh… Shhhh…"

"Terribly clever," Fischer said with an annoyed chuckle and headshake.

Jade sat up sighing with a deep breath and smirked. "Wow, you must have a lot of friends." She grabbed his arm, careful to avoid his stitches. "Look, I *may* have had my palm read here a time or two back in the day. It's just amusing now mostly. Admittedly this is a gamble, but if it helps us get inside the mind of the killer, and figure this whole thing out, that's a net positive, right?"

Fischer couldn't argue with that. "Fine."

The two of them exited the vehicle and walked into the store. A small bell over the door jingled as they began to look around. The room was ensconced in tarot card imagery, jewelry, and zodiacal sign star charts. The overpowering incense smell almost knocked Fischer down. He noted the apparel section with capes, hooded cloaks, hats, scarf-shawls, staffs, and more.

"No opportunity of merchandise exploitation has been spared," Fischer said cuttingly.

Jade rolled her eyes.

"Hello," a cryptic voice greeted them.

Fischer looked across the room and saw a short plump older woman with silver hair, dressed in mostly black, wearing a necklace full of colored marble sized stones, miniature skulls, and metal charms, all held together in a cord of colored yarn string.

"I'm Maren. Can I help you?"

"I don't think so," Fischer instinctively blurted out.

"Don't listen to my friend," Jade said, "We're here to learn more about Aquarius."

"Ah," Maren said clasping her hands together. "Your world becomes clear once you understand how the universe influences it. Yes. Let us unpack this mystery together this day. Please sit."

The three of them sat at a small wooden table near the far back quiet corner of the shop. Maren lit a candle resting on the tabletop. "First, I must see your hand," Maren said to Jade.

Jade comfortably offered her right hand without hesitation, palm up. Maren's wrinkled hands gripped it as she closed her eyes.

Milking it for all the worth, Fischer insufferably thought, fuming in annoyance.

Maren opened her eyes and traced her index finger around Jade's palm lines.

"Yes, *Ah-ha*. I see love in your future. Yes, love."

Jade blushed, "Oh, really. That's interesting." She looked at Fischer.

"Are you actually falling for this?" Fischer asked. "A male/female couple walks in, and she hints at budding generic romantic tension. I'm blown away."

"Anything regarding Aquarius? I'm an Aquarius," Jade asked.

"Hmmmm," Maren thought. "It's unclear."

"I'll bet," Fischer leaked under his breath.

"I need to see your hand too," Maren asked Fischer.

"Come on, Fischer," Jade said.

Fischer extended his hand. "Oh, for heaven's sake."

Maren held both of their hands in hers. Her thumb rubbed over a small silver ring Fischer wore, marked with a faint Christian cross. "Yes, it's becoming clearer now. Yes. The full moon of Aquarius will rise with power and emotion, in general and for you both personally. You must avoid making impulsive decisions..." Maren faded off in silence.

"Anything else?" Jade asked.

"Yes." She squeezed Jade's hand. "You are *not* an Aquarius, and... Oh my." Maren homed in on Fischer's hand, "Oh. Oh, dear. Yes. Oh. You." Maren opened her eyes looking straight into Fischer's. "You," she continued, "You're going the wrong way. You're going to *hell*."

"*Okay*," Fischer said with a snap, pulling back his hand. "And we're *done*." Fischer stood looking back at Detective Jade. "This was *so* helpful, thanks." Fischer couldn't help himself as sarcasm oozed with every word. "I don't believe in the stars cosmically controlling our fate or directing our steps."

Maren stood. "I can tell you are a learned spiritual man, not used to listening to someone of the likes of me. But I wager you do believe in some of it. I know you believe in another book of words, and a story of stars directing otherwise men's steps, some two thousand years ago to the birth of a special child?"

Fischer had headed toward the door but stopped in his tracks.

Jade spouted up from her chair.

"Oh yeah, Fischer, the *Wise Men*. Ohh, that is interesting."

Fischer stood facing away from both of them with his hands in his pockets, deep in thought. *Maren makes an interesting point, somehow... Diabolical.* He lifted his head and turned toward them both. "Maren," he walked back over and extended his hand again, but this time for a professional shake. "Thank you. You've given me an idea."

"Words of thanks are lovely, but cash is lovelier," Maren said.

Jade opened her wallet and covered the transaction. Fischer waited for Jade at the door and accompanied her out.

"So, Dr. Fischer, let me get this straight, the soothsayer gave you an idea?" Jade said in playful tease as they returned to the squad car.

"Yes," Fischer said humbly, "and as a matter of fact, you're going to *love* it."

Chapter 21

JADE'S SQUAD CAR DROVE THE two of them up the meandering hill country toward Griffith Observatory. They parked and began the long walk toward the majestic architecture which blurred the lines between various iconic buildings around the globe. It presents in stately Taj Mahal fashion, while offering a white exterior Washington D.C. feel, yet crowned with a mosque like dome. The Observatory's summit commanded a regal vista over different directions of the Downtown Los Angeles Basin, Hollywood sign, and the Pacific. The golden sunset from there was more than enough to get Fischer excited but paled in comparison to the observatory's best appeal. LA's Griffith Observatory owned the exclusive ability to peer into the deepest regions of space with some of the most powerful telescopes in the world, for free.

"I do think that this place is awesome," Jade said. "My dad used to take me here from time to time when I was a kid. So, what's the big idea 'Magic Maren' gave you?"

"Not magic," Fischer said. "Magi, which *is* etymologically linked to the word *magician*. The magi followed a star, the Star of Bethlehem, to Christ. It's still a bit of a mystery as to how they knew to do that, but the fact remains, they relied on the stars for a divine revelation. What if our guy—"

"The killer?" Jade said, somewhat comically. "Just checking who 'our guy' is."

"Yes," Fischer said, surprised at his own cavalier comfort with the topic, "Our guy, the *killer*, is also relying on a specific messaging. I know they have weekly star reports. It might be well worth our time checking with some of the experts here on recent activity."

Jade began to snicker.

"What?" Fischer asked.

She began to softly sing as they walked, "We three kings of orient are; bearing gifts we traverse afar…"

Fischer smiled. "You know, it annoys me that I love that hymn so much."

"Why annoyed?"

Fischer sighed reluctantly. "Well, there are three theological errors in that first line alone." Fischer could tell Jade had an 'oh brother, here we go again' look on her face, but pressed on anyway. "According to Biblical *and* secular history, they weren't kings, they weren't from the orient, and we don't even know if there were three of them. Three is plausible because of the number of gifts; gold, frankincense, and myrrh. Still. It's a beautiful song, and I *love* the message it conveys."

"Westward leading, still proceeding…" Jade continued singing.

"Guide us to thy perfect light," Fischer harmonized with Gemma for the last line. The two of them walked past a small gathering of people offering fliers.

"Are you looking for a cool new church?" a voice asked.

A girl shoved a tract into Jade's unassuming hand, who politely, but promptly, folded it and put it in her jacket pocket.

"Thank you," Jade said, insincerely.

The small group pressed Fischer. "And you, sir?"

"No, thanks. I've got a good one." *Odd place to be soliciting for new church members. Gotta love Cali. The land of fruits and nuts, indeed.*

Fischer and Jade arrived at the entrance and walked into the expansive facility. After a quick orientation of the room, they made their way toward the information booth.

A young college-aged attendant perked up as they approached. "Can I help you?"

"Hello, yes," Fischer said. "Look, I know this place's ethos is big into 'old earth' theory, macroevolution, proving the possibility of intelligent life on other planets, hoping to colonize Mars, and similar interest points, but I'd like to chat with someone here that might know a thing or two about vast interstellar patterns, and how one might interpret them."

"I can help you, sir. What would you like to know?" The attendant asked.

The young girl's purple-dyed hair and apparent gum-chewing habit somehow signaled to Fischer that he wasn't yet chatting with the expert he was seeking. "No," Fischer said, "I'm more thinking of someone possibly versed in astronomy, history, *and* the theory of a potential divine message in cosmology."

"Um, do you want to take a tour?"

"No, I…" Fischer lowered his head, floundered in frustration.

"Are there any astronomy experts here that also believe God created the universe?" Jade asked poignantly. "We have a few questions."

"Oh, got it. Wait. You think *God* made the universe?" the purple-headed girl asked confusedly.

"Right," Fischer said.

"Oh." The girl thought for a second. "Yeah, there's this old volunteer guy we've had forever, Jesse. He's probably your best bet for, ya know, science fiction talks like that."

"That'll be great," Fischer said, facetiously. "Get us Jesse."

The attendant girl escorted Fischer and Jade over to a large window near a telescope and instructed them to wait. "Feel free to check out the scope before Jesse arrives," the girl said as she somehow seemed to gallop off.

Fischer looked at Jade. "I swear, I think some part of her believes she's a unicorn."

With a few moments to kill, Fischer leaned forward to peer into the scope, not paying attention to Jade leaning in from the other side. They bumped heads in an odd intimate exchange.

"*Ouch*. Ohhh, I can't believe we just did that," Jade said.

Fischer bowed and extended his arm. "Sorry. Please, ladies first."

Detective Gemma Jade shook her head in a brief chuckle, winked at Fischer in slow dramatic fashion as she held her eyelid down, bowing forward and gazed into the powerful telescope. "*Wow*. It's even more brilliant than I remember. It's been a while since I've done this. Amazing." She came up and offered Fischer a turn. He leaned in.

"Extraordinary... Truly."

"Gotta say, that's a win for science and technology, eh, pastor-professor?" Jade asked.

"And here I was thinking God is the great architect through this view," Fischer said without flinching or looking up.

A wheezy sage voice began to speak from behind them joining the conversation. "Science and technology think they're winning now, but the true victory has already been decided, only yet to be revealed."

Fischer straightened himself away from the telescope and turned in amazement to see the man standing before him.

Chapter 22

FISCHER AND JADE WERE GREETED BY a portly old man with the wildest white lambchop sideburns Fischer had ever laid eyes on. Small beads of sweat adorned his widow's peak.

"Jesse Sophis. Pleased to meet you. I got here as quick as I could. I don't always get these kinds of requests."

The wrinkled stocky man who could have been anyone's favorite grandpa, shook both their hands. *This guy could give Santa Claus a run for his money.*

"Mr. Sophis, thank you, yes. I'm Rev. Dr. Chase Fischer, and this is—"

"You're a Reverend? Are you with the Church of the True Nativity?" Jesse said with some concern in his slightly out of breath voice.

"*True* Nativity? No," Fischer said, quickly giving Jesse his card.

Jesse briefly examined Fischer's business card. "I see. Okay, good. And this is your wife?" Jesse looked over Jade with a bright smile.

"Uh, no, uh," Fischer said, exchanging a self-conscious look with Jade.

"I'm Detective Jade, LAPD. Dr. Fischer is my associate in an ongoing investigation," Jade said recovering.

Get a grip, Chase. "I understand you are a man of science and a man of faith, is that right?" Fischer asked.

"I love astronomy," Jesse said cagily. "The firmament is God's canvas indeed, but the primitive view of it tells us much much more. More than modern science ever will."

Jesse motioned to the observatory around them and then started fidgeting with his hands. "You said 'investigation.' Does this have anything to do with the Zodiac attacks?"

Fischer and Jade shared a look of elation with each other. "You're *exactly* who we want to talk with," Jade blurted out. "What might you know about that?"

Jesse sighed a deep breath. "Only what I've read in the news, mostly tabloid websites." He sucked in a deep breath. "How can I help you?"

"I was wondering," Fischer began. "The original wise men, the magi, followed a star to the Christ child. I know there are certain theories as to how that happened…"

"Yes," Jesse confirmed. "Go on."

"Somehow, they trusted, believed, and acted on some idea of a divine message leading them to the Messiah. But how exactly? In other words, what ideology could they have followed paired with an astronomical phenomenon?"

"What do you mean? It was some rare bright star, right?" Jade asked innocently.

Jesse Sophis took a step back in deep thought. "That is the simplest suggestion that most people know, and most skeptics laugh at," Jesse lamented, as he took out a handkerchief and dabbed his head. "A true star, vouchsafed to the magi alone, perhaps. Or others say it could have been a meteor or comet, mistaken for a star."

Fischer chimed in with delight. "It also could have been an unidentified supernatural light, similar to the angels 'great light' observed by the shepherds, upon news of the birth of Christ."

Jesse volleyed back another rapid response. "There is of course Balaam's prophecy of a star appearing, and Daniel's prophecies, held captive in Babylon, and the influences of the teachings floated down amongst the learned men."

"Yes," Fischer said in countering fashion, "but I tend to settle on the bright spectacle of the conjunction of the planets, Saturn and Jupiter."

Jade's head swiveled back and forth as the two men impressively tossed out theory after theory.

"Jupiter," Jesse smiled. "The kingly planet. Fitting for an infant king, but I hold on to something better than that."

Fischer balked. "*Better* than the conjunction of Jupiter and Saturn which happened around Christ's birth? And perhaps more importantly that phenomenon is paired with the most trusted ancient historians, Tacitus, Suetonius, Josephus, and others testifying there was generally around that time a widespread expectation for a Prince to arrive in the East."

"Yes, though too indefinite I think, particularly for wisemen clearly demonstrating definite respect for the Messiah's birth," Jesse said. "I'm more interested in Virgo," he calmly stated.

"*Virgo?*" Fischer and Jade both exclaimed in surprised unison.

Jesse looked out the window, bouncing slightly on the balls of his feet, obviously savoring the rare moment when people appreciated his specialized knowledge and interest.

"It is an astronomic fact, independent of all hypotheses, that at the precise hour of midnight, at the winter solstice, the last week of December, in the period in which Christ was born, the sign of Virgo was rising on the eastern horizon. Another astronomic fact is the spring equinox, just nine months prior of that same year, was on the meridian, with the line running precisely across her bosom. And it is further astronomic fact that at the same date, at midnight, the star of the little constellation, Coma, was directly on the meridian."

"The virgin mother, and her kingly infant son," Jade said in disbelief.

Jesse's eyes popped wide at Jade and back to Fischer. Fischer could tell Jesse was thrilled and amazed they appreciated what he was talking about, and where the conversation was going. "Yes, that's right," he said. "These signs are, in my humble opinion, remarkable indications of where the facts and signs coincide." Jesse gripped his left arm, mildly massaging it.

Jade stepped closer in excitement. "And Jupiter and Saturn converged right around the same time? How often does that happen?" She asked.

"It's exceedingly rare," Fischer said.

"Technically," Jesse said, "it's about once every twenty years, however, they don't always converge the same distance apart. Sometimes they are much further apart than others, and sometimes they are not visible from the naked eye. The times they do converge close enough to appear like one massively bright star, *and* visible from the naked eye, is roughly only once every seven hundred years, and yes, as Dr. Fischer so aptly put it—*exceedingly* rare."

"And that conjunction was evident when Christ was born?" Jade asked.

"Yes," Jesse said as a shiver came over him. "Is it cold in here?"

Fischer played with his ruddy-gold five-o'clock shadow stubble in thought for a moment. "I seem to recall Kepler had an interesting theory concerning the rarity of these conjunctions. He opined that such conjunctions coincided with the birth of prominent human affairs; Adam and creation, Enoch, Noah and the flood, Moses and the Exodus, Cyrus, Christ, Charlamagne, and Martin Luther and the Reformation."

"It's certainly a fascinating topic to consider, isn't it?" Jesse said with twinkles in his eyes. "That, corresponding to the Old Testament star prophecies, corroborated by extra-Biblical historians, and the ability for the Magi to assemble this knowledge, and utilize the primitive 'well-reflection' method to tell if a star was directly above them, specifically in Bethlehem, say, offers three strong conclusions. Are you ready?" Jesse asked.

"Lay it on me, Jesse," Jade said humoring him, yet somehow laced with genuine fascination, as she kept jotting down notes.

Jesse grabbed a nearby chair, sat down, and cleared his throat. "Let me sit for a second and catch my breath."

"Are you all right, Mr. Sophis?" Jade asked.

"Yes. I'm all right," Jesse got out after an awkward pause. "First, that a star reading of this rare conjunction of Saturn and Jupiter betokened the birth of a great virtuous, princely, operator among men, and the beginning of a new order of things. Second, the sign in which it was born, Pisces, indicated the people among whom the child was to be born, and third, the children of Israel were already at that early period associated with the sign of Pisces."

Fischer snapped his finger. "Giving way to the fish ichthus symbol, of course. Interesting. I've not heard the Pisces connection at the birth of Christ before."

Fischer took a deep breath. "So, I guess my ultimate million-dollar question, sir, is this… Is there any current major interstellar activity going on right now in the star charts, that someone learned about this subject matter, but not necessarily of the right mind, might draw conclusions from?" Fischer looked back toward Jesse, and just then noticed the sweat soaking through Jesse's shirt.

Jesse looked up, with an ashen paling face. "There's always… I suppose… things people can gather and take too far… There was that September 23, of 2017, 'Sign of the Son of Man' fascination that captivated several church influencers, but that was some time ago. Actually, there is one *major* phenomenon fairly recently… I'm surprised you haven't thought of yet… considering this topic… Actually, the more I think about it… very interesting… I… um…"

"We're losing him, Chase. He's having a heart attack," Jade said.

Fischer scanned the oblong shaped room looking for, *there she is*. He yelled to the purple pony-tailed girl at the attendant desk. "It's Jesse. Get an ambulance, *quick*."

Chapter 23

THE AMBULANCE DOORS CLOSED, AND the emergency workers rushed Jesse Sophis away from Griffith Observatory as quickly as they'd arrived. Fischer and Jade could only watch as it sped away with lights flashing and siren blaring.

"Well, that was unexpected," Fischer said in disbelief.

Jade's cell phone buzzed. "I sure hope he's all right," she said before answering her call.

"It's Greppin." She swiped open her green answer tab. "Hey George. What have you got?"

Fischer could hear Greppin's deep voice radiate through the phone like a smooth Motown DJ. "We've been researching, crunching all the data, and cross-referencing everything as much as we can. We've been able to compile a list of potential scenarios, and we think we've identified a likely venue for a possible January nineteenth incident. Before I get into it any further, where are you? Did you manage to turn anything up with the good Dr. Fischer?"

"Long story, we're here at the Griffith Observatory. No real leads yet, nothing solid. What's your idea?" she asked.

Greppin continued. "There happens to be a gala event at the Aquarium of the Pacific on the evening of the nineteenth. It's a Sunday. Some big fundraiser of some sort. And get this, the keynote is speaking on the moon's gravitational pull in conjunction with the ocean tides."

Jade looked up at Fischer rocking her head to the side and back with a 'that's not bad' look on her face.

"That's where I'd be, if I were the killer," Fischer said loud enough for Greppin to hear, but equally in earshot of a family with small children walking by that moment. A shameful cringe later Fischer returned focus to Greppin's instructions.

"You better come back in," Greppin said. "We've got some *major* planning to do before that and not much time to do it. If we're right about this, obviously we don't want to signal a strong police presence to the killer. So, we'll have to be there under the radar, dressed as civilians. It's a black-tie event, GJ, so you better get your high heels ready. The Chief's secured two tickets."

Jade looked up at Fischer. "Well, what say you, Fischer? Wanna be my plus one?"

Fischer was still learning how to decipher Detective Jade's personality. *Did she mean that in jest or not?*

The call ended and they drove back to the precinct headquarters. Jade put a call in to Praider and they discussed surveillance vans, a disguised security presence, talking points, Fischer's potential role, protocol and procedure. As their conversation meandered through the details, Fischer's mind wandered through the insanity that was his life lately, and back to Jesse Sophis, the Magi star trek, celestial interpretation, and what it all meant in the big picture with a killer on the loose. That and what Miss Gemma Jade might look like in an evening gown.

After a long debrief in the LAPD conference room with Chief Tatum, Greppin, Praider, Squirrel, and Jade, they adjourned for the night. Jade escorted Fischer to the impound lot to retrieve his motorcycle. "You sure you feel up for driving?" Jade asked.

"Why thank you officer, I believe I am of sound mind and body now," Fischer said, extending his opened palm for the keys.

She dropped them in his hands. "All right. I'll see you on the nineteenth and hope we're right."

"Yes. Have a good night. We'll get him," Fischer said confidently as he mounted his bike, donned his helmet, turned on the engine, headlight, and zipped out the gate. Traffic wasn't bad on his ride home as he weaved through the darkened streets. Fischer's stressed thoughts kept racing. *I've got a funeral to plan, Michael to check on in the hospital, meetings to prep for, a sermon to write... or maybe it all comes to an abrupt end. When will the Presidium meet and decide my fate? I just need resolution on something in my life right now.*

Fischer pulled into his old garage, shut off the engine and then he noticed an oddity in his sidecar. *That's weird.* Fischer leaned down and retrieved a baseball cap in the bottom of his sidecar floor. He picked it up. "San Francisco Giants? How did you get in here?"

He strolled into his house and tossed the hat on a table after a brief examination of it. Luther was overdue for attention. The next hour went quickly with kibble, walking, and throwing the tennis ball around, multitasked with email responses and text exchanges from church members and their various needs. Fischer came in, heated up a frozen dinner in the microwave, scarfed it in minutes, and sat down at his table with a solid dram of scotch. He stared across the table at the hat. *Where did you come from?*

Fischer sipped and thought through the last sequences with his Bonneville. The Chipparo home. *Hmmmm.* "Luther, here, Boy." He showed Luther the hat.

Luther sniffed the cap. "Grrrrr."

"Really?"

Fischer reflected. *Baseball cap... Here's an idea out of left field.* He scrolled through his phone contacts. Gemma Jade. *Facetime? Why not? Here goes.* He dialed.

"Chase?" GJ answered on camera. She exhaled some cigarette smoke and dabbed it out, swatting away the vapor in the air.

"Gemma, hi, yes. Sorry, it's me."

Fischer adjusted his framing for her. "Listen, random question. I remember you said the guy in the Viper Room wore a ballcap, right?"

"Yeah. Why?"

Fischer's eyes bore into the hat sitting on the table facing him. "Any chance it was a San Francisco Giants ball cap?"

She thought for a second. "Actually, yeah, it was. How'd you know that?"

"What if I told you I found one in the sidecar of my bike tonight?" He turned his phone so she could see it.

"What? How?"

Fischer looked down at his bandaged arm and thought about chasing after the man at the Chipparo home. The punch to the face, the sliced arm. Luther's pursuit. Biting him. Falling onto the side of the Triumph Bonneville. He turned the phone camera back to him.

"Gemma, Luther was with me that night, he chased the guy, bit him good, and when he bit him, he fell onto my bike. It *must* have fallen during their scuffle. Do you think it's the same guy?"

Gemma was quiet on the other end for a moment processing. "If the guy we observed at the Viper Room is this new 'Zodiac Killer' or whatever, and it was the same guy at your friend's house that night, the big question would be why?"

Fischer reflected for a moment. "He didn't seem to want to kill them, like the other victims."

"He was methodical. He had tranquilizers, remember," Gemma said, adjusting her camera angle.

"Gemma, if it's the one and the same killer, he wanted something else that night, something different." Fischer shuddered to think through the reasoning of the killer and barely eked out the words. "He wanted the boy."

Chapter 24

Sunday, January 19*th*
7:17 P.M.
100 Aquarium Way, Long Beach

PACIFIC OCEAN WAVES CRASHED QUIETLY in the distance as guests walked up toward the magnificent aquatic building. Its undulating design and brilliant blue glass exterior were enhanced all the more as the exterior lights turned on, offering an extra bioluminescent appearance of the aquarium. Little did the gala guests realize the activity taking place in a nearby unmarked van.

Fischer, Jade, and Squirrel sat in the back of a surveillance van in a designated parking area near the Aquarium of the Pacific. Squirrel ran through the monitors and tampered with a few dials before handing earpieces to Jade and Fischer. Fischer watched Jade, wrapped up in her navy LAPD jacket, put hers in and immediately followed suit. He was impressed with how tiny the high-tech earpieces were. *Virtually undetectable, amazing.*

Squirrel held the earpieces in front of Fischer. "Be careful with these. I know it's an aquarium but try not to get them wet. They're really expensive," Squirrel said. "Let's do a quick sound check. Greppin and Praider are already inside in their security positions. Say something, GJ."

"Evening fellas, how's the water tonight?"

Fischer heard Jade's voice whisper in his ear. Then the others chimed in.

"Real funny, GJ. Praider here."

"Greppin, here."

"Dr. Fischer, it's your turn," Squirrel said.

"Fischer here, testing, one, two, three." Jade gave him a thumbs up.

"Praider, check."

"Dr. Fischer," Greppin's voice came through. "Remember, you are still essentially a civilian. We're using your expert eyes only. If you see anything that triggers your mind with all of this, let us know. If anything happens, you do *not* engage. You talk to us. Got it?"

"Understood, GG," Fischer said.

Jade lowered her head, hand to brow, in mortification as Squirrel jerked back as if someone hit him. Jade silently breathed the words Fischer presumed was now obvious to all.

"He *hates* that," she said, cracking a smile.

"Coast is clear," Squirrel said. "Let's go."

Fischer opened the back of the van and hopped out. He stood tall in his full 6'0" frame, dressed smartly in his classic black luxe Express suit, with silver flared tie. He held out his hand and helped Jade out, who gladly accepted his chivalrous offering. Gemma Jade gingerly took off her jacket and stepped out into the evening air. The half-light of the sunset hit her solid chartreuse dress and freshly pixie cut hair with highlights. Her strapless top hugged her shape hand to glove, and a racy long slit of the left leg didn't make anyone's imagination work too hard.

"*Wow*. That's an Audrey Hepburn movie," Fischer said.

Jade smiled with an elegance he hadn't seen in a long while. "And that's a *Jerry Maguire* quote," she said smartly.

"Touché. I suppose they're both classics now."

Detective Gemma Jade twirled in the Hollywood 'magic hour' that is dusk. "Are there any creases?"

"Only in all the right places," Fischer said without thinking. *It's amazing she has a gun hidden in there somewhere.*

Jade stared stunned for a moment, broken mercifully by a giggle as

Squirrel spoke into their ears, "Laying it on a little thick there aren't we, Doctor?"

"Oh, right, everyone's listening. I was merely answering her question," Fischer said in a flustery cracked voice, and extended his left arm toward her. "Shall we?"

Jade softly closed the van door, but it didn't click all the way shut. She tried a second time, to no avail. After a third frustrated attempt of being discreet, Jade comically swung the door wide and back again slamming it closed as hard as she could and linked her arm with Fischer's. "Let's," she said.

They casually sauntered through the parking lot and mingled with gala members lined up at the entrance, eventually making their way inside toward the hors d'oeuvres table. *Shrimp, really? Figures* Fischer thought. Jade took two drinks from an attendant and offered one to Fischer who cheerily accepted.

"Remember," Jade said, "if we're right about this, he could be anywhere; he could be anyone. Let's split up and see if something jumps out at us." She floated away into the sea of people.

Jade's sobering words jogged Fischer back to the serious point at hand. He surveyed the incredibly cavernous room. The white walls only made the enormous model sperm whale that hung above them stand out that much more, which didn't need much help to do so in the first place. A tuxedo-dressed string quartet played Vivaldi which filled the expansive hall. At the far end was a gigantic glass walled aquarium, about two and half stories high, with three vertical panels of glass top to bottom. Fish of all kinds swam within it. It was an incredible backdrop for the presentation of the evening, which would be starting soon. Some two hundred seats were slowly filling up as an attendant set a water bottle by the podium.

Fischer scanned the room again only to bitterly pause on a familiar face in the crowd. Nate Maddix, the acrimonious college student who all but made an intramural sport out of slandering his good name last year, was merely a few yards away. He noticed Fischer and began making his way toward him. *Just forgive him Chase, he's only an over-privileged kid who doesn't know any better. You've got bigger fish to fry tonight.*

"*Mr.* Fischer," Nate said cuttingly through his bleached-white teeth perched within his freckled face. "Well, look what the cat coughed up. Are you still teaching?"

"Sure, why wouldn't I be, Nathan?"

"Only several reasons I suppose... People talk, you know. You may remember my date, one of your *former* church members. We most assuredly won't be popping by any time soon. She's got a new church, a much *better* one."

Fischer recognized in horror, Chelsea Ferguson. *No wonder she's not been back to Epiphany, and her parents wanted a transfer... hanging around this bozo. Lord only knows what he's said about me.*

"Is that so? Good evening, Chelsea." Fischer extended his hand to greet but was not met in kind. "You know, you can't believe everything you hear, guys." *Grace, Chase... Grace. Just forgive and move on.*

"Even if it's half right, that's too much for us," Nate said snidely.

"Particularly if what you hear originates from the pit of ineptitude that rests between your ears, *Mr.* salutatorian." *Too late.*

"I *knew* it," Nate fired back. "You see, Chelsea, a real class act we have here for a university professor. You *will* be history when the board of regents hears about your prejudice versus favoritism grading methods."

"No. You earned every grade you 'worked' for in my class, especially the one you had your Daddy Warbucks try to buy for you."

Nathan's face went scarlet. He couldn't hold himself back any longer and flung his drink at Fischer. "*Screw* you, Fischer."

"*Ahhhh*," Fischer reacted in disgust. The beverage hit a glancing blow across Fischer's face, his ear with tech piece took the brunt of the splash which created a high-pitched squeal in his ear. Fischer winced in pain and looked up in time to see Greppin prepping to escort Nate Maddix out of the building. *At least the live music didn't stop for the classic awkward pause.*

"Excuse me, sir, right this way," Greppin said.

"Hey, I paid a lot of mon—"

"Your night is *over*, sir."

The unfortunate episode was over almost as quickly as it had begun. Fischer walked to the restroom, dabbed down his clothes, and adjusted his hair. *Decent I suppose.* He was alone. "Check, check. Guys? Anyone hear me?" He took the earpiece out. *Fried dead. Great.*

Fischer walked back out just in time to see the keynote speaker being introduced to a standing ovation. Everyone sat quickly and the lecture began. Fischer could see Greppin, still outside the glass door arguing with Nate Maddix. *Give it to him, Grep.*

Jade sat toward the rear of the audience to keep eyes on as many as possible. Fischer walked up the back right side of the audience trying to present himself as casually as possible. He scanned around and rested his eyes back on the speaker. Fischer quickly became mesmerized by the beautiful colored fish of various sizes serving as a live backdrop in perhaps the largest aquarium he'd ever seen. Fischer calmed down and tried to think through the moment with what he knew. *Aquarius. Check. Southern Fish decan. Check. Cygnus the Swan? No birds anywhere. Pegasus? No. Some type of holy flood... Hovering over the water. Cygnus has wings... Hovering over the water... and Pegasus too, hovering over the water... Look up.*

Fischer discreetly inched closer to the front. He gazed through the aquarium glass toward the top. The top was open air. *Let's get up there.* He glanced back at Jade who was obviously trapped in conversation by some guy hitting on her. *Can't blame him... I'd better check up there before it's too late. No time to alert anyone, even if I could. Gad.* Fischer saw a stairwell exit chamber and casually entered. He darted to the top and out onto a patio area looking over the massive aquarium tank beneath him.

He looked up. *Nothing there.* He heard a little scuffling. *What's that sound?* Fischer quickly looked around. An old portable storage locker was near the edge of the aquarium tank. The closer Fischer walked toward it the louder the sound grew. Fischer flung the door open in shock.

A gagged middle-aged woman was affixed to some large iron wing shaped hunk of metal. Plastic adjustable zip-ties secured each of her four limbs to the horror contraption.

"Oh, my *word*." He pulled down her mouth-gag.

"Help me," she said weakly through tears.

"Oh, it's the Chaplain again," a voice said from the blindside of the locker door.

Before Fischer could turn, he was sucker-punched and shoved down and out of the way.

Fischer looked up to see what looked like the same man at the Chipparo home drag forward the bound woman teetering on the aquarium water's edge.

"You almost closed the scroll," he said with a nasty sneer.

"What?" Fischer said, rising incredulously to his feet.

The man tipped the woman toward the water. All she could do was beg. "No. Please don't. NOOOOO—"

Splash.

Chapter 25

THE KEYNOTE SPEAKER, IMPECCABLY DRESSED in a black suit with a subtle Honolulu Blue handkerchief, was in the middle of an epic delivery of a speech he'd given dozens of times, but he'd never forget this evening's dissertation. As he spoke to the crowd, the people before him began rising, screaming, and pointing at him. He turned about and was the last to see what everyone else was reacting to.

A bound woman sank to the bottom of the aquarium immediately behind him in full view of the stately crowd of some two hundred people. The bound woman plunged fast hitting the floor of the tank and tipping in such a way that propped her up cock-eyed diagonal against a rock facing the crowd.

Atop the aquarium tank Fischer panicked in terror as the man scurried away. Fischer took one look down into the tank, ripped off his jacket, and dove in after the woman. The tank water was as frigid as it was deep. Fischer had been at the bottom of enough ten-foot-deep swimming pools in his day to know that around that depth the water pressure became noticeably impactful upon the head. Twenty to thirty feet of water on top would become a problem fast. This tank seemed a bit deeper than that. Fischer kept swimming down. He pinched his nose blowing out a smidge of air from his inner ear's eustachian tubes, which relieved some of the pressure. He got down to the frantic woman. *Not much time before we both run out of air.*

Inside the tank, Fischer yanked at the binding, but it was too tight and too sharp. The fish had cleared out and oddly seemed to respectfully stay away. Fischer tried freeing all four of her limbs, but nothing worked. He looked up through the blurring water toward the window. Jade's chartreuse dress was unmistakable through the other side. *Is that her gun? Pointed in my direction? Oh my—*

BANG.

Jade shot her firearm straight at the glass. *BANG. BANG. BANG.*

The glass chipped a little powder dust but was so thick it was virtually impenetrable for her caliber of gun. Jade ran toward the glass, putting up her hands as a lens and peered in as best as she could, making eye contact with Fischer.

"Get up. *Hurry*," she mouthed to him.

Fischer knew he couldn't go up for air and come back to save the woman, she wouldn't make it. He kept fidgeting. *Keys.* Fischer grabbed his keys from his pocket and began scratching one of the plastic binds. *Come on, this is taking too long.*

SNAP.

Yes. Fischer went to the next limb but was beginning to freak out. His head was throbbing to a painful beat he'd never experienced before. *I'm not gonna make it.* Fischer felt a large fish descending upon him. He turned to face his most unique end only to see Praider handing him a breath from a scuba tube. Fischer stole a quick breath, knowing the woman needed some too. They looked at her face. Her ghostlike face told them they were too late. She had clearly already breathed in water. Praider took out a small knife and instantly cut away the remaining zip-ties. Together Praider and Fischer raced her back to the surface.

Fischer breathed in sweet oxygen as his lungs heaved for a number of rich breaths before slowly relaxing again. He didn't dare imagine what the lifeless woman was experiencing.

"Here. Take her," Praider said.

Greppin's big mitt of a hand seized the woman and hauled her up onto the deck, positioned her and began resuscitation.

Fischer swam to the edge and pulled himself out of the water beside

Praider. They watched as Greppin gently did the work. Jade entered Fischer's periphery vision crouching over the woman, but all his focus remained on the victim. *Come on, Lord. Please. Bring her back...*

Suddenly the woman convulsed and vomited up water.

"Help me," Greppin said to Praider. They turned her over on her side. She coughed more and gasped for air. A collective sigh of relief began to break over the small crowd gathered around her. Fischer was about to turn toward Jade, when she beat him to the punch.

Jade grabbed Fischer's tie and yanked him up. "What were you *thinking*? You weren't supposed to get involved."

"My earpiece got disabled. I couldn't get anyone's attention. I had to act quick," Fischer said. He turned toward Greppin. "Did you get the guy?"

"What guy?"

"The guy, the man who did this. He pushed this woman in."

"No, I didn't see anyone," Greppin said.

"Me neither," Praider said.

All eyes fell to Jade.

"Unfortunately, no," Jade said flicking her arms in the air briefly and resting them on her hips.

"Squirrel, anything on your end? What did you see?" Greppin asked.

Fischer looked around and recounted his experience. "I'm not positive, it all happened so fast, the man hit me from my periphery, but I think it was the *same* man I encountered in the house earlier this week."

"*Squirrel*? Squirrel, come in," Greppin asked again. "What is going on?"

The woman sat up with some help from Praider. "There *was* a man," she said, breathing heavily. "A horrible man. He did this to me. Thank you for saving me. I don't know what I would have done, I—" She began to break down and sob.

Downstairs in the observation hall The Prophet sat comfortably in his chair. He had enjoyed watching the pandemonium unfold. He stood in his black Armani suit and pink tie with his hair slicked back in a ponytail. His phone chimed prompting him to check his texts.

In the car. Where are you?

The Prophet serpentined through the crowd, dialing the number from the text. He blended seamlessly in with everyone else walking here and there, making calls, and reacting in frantic conversations from the night's event. His phone call was received on the other end.

"Hello, Wolf. Hang on. I'm heading out now."

"Did it end well?" Wolf's voice echoed back.

"I'm afraid not. I watched the whole thing. She only breathed water in just for an instant before they freed her and got her out. I expect she'll survive."

"Seriously? What does that mean for us? For the Scroll, if they all are not sacrificed, does that mean we fail?"

"No. There are contingences. Our god is a merciful god, to an extent. There will be blood to be paid, a lot, in addition to the eye for an eye that must be made up now. How, I haven't yet decided."

"It was that *guy* again. The one from the house. I'm telling you, he's on to us," Manteuffel said. "And those were cops, or FBI, or something. I'm pretty sure there was an undercover agent with a gun that tried to save the day."

"She was LAPD," The Prophet said definitively.

"Are you sure?"

"Absolute. Let's just say I have it on *good* authority." The Prophet sauntered past a few LAPD police officers rushing into the aquarium as he strolled out into the parking lot. "We've got their attention, which is part of the task at hand."

"Unless they stop the whole thing," Manteuffel cautioned.

"Leave that to me. I have a little insurance policy, a *couple* actually," The Prophet said coldly, ending the call. He opened the door to his black hummer, seeing Manteuffel keeping a low profile in the backseat.

"The agent in the greenish dress with the gun, she yelled, *Fischer* before she fired, and I think in a tone of concern. That makes me wonder…" The Prophet mulled as he started up the engine and put it in drive.

"About what?" Manteuffel asked.

"If she and this Fischer aren't a *pair*. If it's the same man you said, let's see if we can't track down this 'Pastor Fischer' Samaritan and pay him a visit. You may have just helped me make my decision." They drove out the Aquarium of the Pacific's parking lot exit.

At the other end of the lot Fischer, Greppin, Praider and Jade walked up to their unmarked van. Praider put into words what they were all hoping. "Squirrel better have something more for us to go on."

Jade opened the back of the van in astonishment. It was empty. Squirrel was gone, nowhere to be found.

Chapter 26

Monday, January 20th
1:33 P.M.
LA Downtown Medical Center

FISCHER SAT WEARING HIS BLACK clerical suit in a hospital room looking over Michael Chipparo and spoke somberly. "We buried her today. She's with the Lord, now, Michael."

Michael was still unconscious, in a coma and connected to machines monitoring his vitals, as well as a steady stream of oxygen through his nostrils.

"You should know it was one of the more difficult tasks I've ever had to do, Mike. Big turn out too…"

Michael was unresponsive. Fischer knew to keep talking. He read from the Psalms, said a prayer, and sang a hymn. Having visited thousands of people in the hospital during his ministry, he had always heard one never knows what registers in the mind when spoken to in this state. *For all we know this could do some real good.*

Fischer grabbed Michael's hand and kept talking. "Your son is safe in protective custody and being looked after… until you get out of here. And you're *going* to get out of here. I've been working with detectives through the Los Angeles Police Department. We're gonna track down and catch this guy who did this to you. I've actually got to go to a debriefing this afternoon."

Fischer's phone buzzed breaking up the estranged awkwardness of the visitation. It was an unfamiliar number. He exhaled. *I'll bite.* "Hello?"

The voice on the other line was faintly familiar. "Hello? Pastor Fischer?"

"Yes."

"Jesse Sophis."

"Oh my. Yes, Jesse, how *are* you?"

Jesse laughed. "I've been better. I'm still in the hospital. The LA Medical Center, downtown. I had surgery and—"

"You're *kidding*. I'm here right now visiting a friend. What room are you in?"

Fischer got the particulars and within moments knocked on the doorpost of Jesse's room, discreetly pulling back the drawn partition. "Jesse?"

Jesse smiled when he saw Pastor Fischer standing in front of him. He laid back in his bed which slightly elevated his top torso. The stitches in his chest were visible at the top through his loose-fitting hospital gown. "They have me up and about walking the halls right away, a few times a day. It's more exercise than I've had in years. Good to see you, Pastor."

"You gave us quite a scare the other day," Fischer said. "Glad to see you're doing all right,"

"Thank you. Yes, a surprise, Or maybe not. What can I say, I like my bacon and brie sandwiches," he said guiltily. "Anyhow, I was enjoying our conversation very much. Tell me, did you figure it out?"

"Well, we didn't catch who we're looking for, if that's what you mean." Fischer said.

"No, you were asking about recent astronomical signs that potentially could be interpreted in a skewed way…"

"Yeah?" Fischer said intrigued.

"Considering the line of your questioning, I wanted to share that December 21st, 2020, might be intriguing to someone like you described."

Fischer thought for a moment, briefly puzzled. "That date does ring a bell."

"We discussed the extreme rarity of the conjunction of Jupiter and Saturn, every seven hundred years or so. December 21st of 2020 was the last such instance, and a very significant astronomical event of recent, I think."

"Of course. The Christmas Star." *How could I forget.* Fischer remembered reading numerous theological articles and hearing mentions of the phenomenon that year leading up to Advent and Christmas celebrations. COVID 19 all but squelched any deserving attention on it, stealing the focus and sucking all the joy out of the season, and the people out of worship due to quarantine. "That *is* interesting."

"You remember we discussed the peculiar birth of a prominent person around the appearance of such a rare celestial event? I might think that would fall into your criteria of interest. Someone born at that time w—"

"Would have just turned four," Fischer said, jolting back a realization. "Jesse, I've got to run, but thank you, you've given me a lot to think about." Fischer spoke a brief prayer of healing over Jesse, and darted out the room, heading to his Triumph Bonneville, never more thankful of the close proximity for a hospital clergy designated parking spot.

He mounted his bike and fired it up but sent a quick text before speeding off to his LAPD debriefing.

Jeannie, pull the Chiparro file. I need to know Christian's birth date…

Chapter 27

LAPD Headquarters conference room.
3:07 P.M.

FISCHER DASHED INTO THE CONFERENCE situation room, feeling tardy for school.

Greppin, Praider, and Jade all sat as Chief Tatum pontificated over them. "This is a disaster. It's *ridiculous*. How could this happen? Where is he, huh? Just what tree did Squirrel climb up into?"

"Not for Clare Nelson-Frost," Praider said.

"Hmm?" Tatum turned.

"Clare," Praider said. "The woman whose life we *saved*. I'd like to point out it wasn't an entire disaster. We at least spoiled that event from happening."

"Yes," Tatum said calmly, "and that is certainly commendable, but as Greppin's interview with her confirmed, unfortunately she didn't have any new information helpful to catching the person who put her in that position."

Tatum flopped a copy of the *LA Times* on the table. The front page said:

LAPD Thwarts Zodiac Attack

"And now *everyone* knows it," Tatum said. "We've lost the element of surprise. Before, the killer didn't necessarily know we were on to him, but going all in like we did, we've gone and shown our hand. How did we *not* get that guy? With all the boots on the ground we had there, all the tech issues, all the *civilian* interaction." Tatum sneered at Fischer. "And now one of our own officers conveniently goes missing with nary any evidence to share from the entire audio/visual surveillance system the whole night." Tatum slammed down his file of the report.

Jade fidgeted uncomfortably for a moment in her seat. "Sir, I'm sorry, are… are you suggesting Squirrel's a traitor?"

Chief Tatum looked across at Greppin causing him to weigh in.

"All the evidence seems to point to that," Greppin said. "It's too convenient otherwise, that all the recording devices are empty, and this is beginning to seem like a bigger organized event than one person could pull off."

Fischer stood lost in thought for a moment, recalling an odd bit of detailed information that seemed quite significant all of a sudden. "Chaplain."

All eyes looked at Fischer. "The man who pushed the woman in the water called me 'Chaplain.' And I'm fairly certain it was the same man I ran into at the Chipparo home. How would he know I'm a Chaplain? If Squirrel is working both sides that would explain it."

"No," Praider said. "No way, Squirrel, a turncoat? I just don't see it. Is he weird? Yes. But working both sides?" He shook his head. "I dunno. What do I know? I don't really know the guy all that well, I guess. Anything's possible."

Fischer cautiously waded deeper into the conversation. "If he *was* somehow involved with this, on whatever level, the killer would have been a step or two ahead of us this whole time, right?"

Praider reflected more. "Wasn't Squirrel the one who thought of the Viper Room connection for the Scorpio murder?"

Detective Greppin's eyes went large. "Man, you're right. He led us right there. It always seemed like a bit of a jump for me."

"That's right. He all but told us to look there, didn't he," Praider said.

Tatum tapped his finger over his mouth, pinching his chin. "That would be consistent with the killer bragging to us like with the other messages sent, flaunting information, right in front of our eyes."

Jade crossed her arms, disgusted emphatically. "He's one of our own, guys. This isn't right. No benefit of the doubt? *Honestly?*"

"We're just processing all the information, GJ," Greppin said gently.

"I hear more trial, judge, and jury talk," Jade said unimpressed.

"You said yourself he behaves unpredictably. It's certainly plausible, isn't it?" Fischer asked.

Tatum stood up and ruled with a gavel-like voice. "Obviously we hope he turns up. But until we know otherwise, considering the circumstances, and what we know, we *must* assume it's possible he's been compromised… on whatever level. And we have to move forward."

Jade exhaled in sharp exasperation. "I'm *appalled* you would all turn on him so quickly." She stormed out.

"So, what next?" Praider asked. "I can work with Bostic in forensics on that winged contraption he strapped the woman to. It looks like it was custom designed. Maybe forensics can get some evidence off it, samples, something…anything."

Greppin stood. "I'm acquiring a list of all the donors of the gala. I want to see who is giving what kind of money. Considering the lecture topic, it seems our man might be so inclined."

Fischer's phone pinged. He checked his text message feed. It was Jeannie. *Christian Chipparo, 12/21/20*

Fischer's heart started pumping like a jackhammer as a chill ran from the top of his spine throughout his body ending in an uncomfortable startled shiver.

"What just happened? Fischer, you okay?" Greppin asked.

"Guys," Fischer could barely get the words out, I think I might be on to something. And I think we need to check in with children's protective services…"

# # #

Detective Jade approached her locker in a huff. She opened it and flung her bag to the bottom. She caught her reflection in the small mirror on the door and paused for a moment. A few small photographs were magnetized to the frame. She studied one of the pics of her, Squirrel, Praider, and Greppin, smiling hoisting drinks in a toast. She slammed the locker door making a loud rattling sound.

"This is so messed up. *Where* are you, Squirrel?" She asked to the universe.

Jade laid her arm over the locker and rested her forehead against it, composing herself. She calmed down, caught her breath and opened the locker again.

"Keys, where'd you go?"

She looked in the top of the locker, then a small lock box compartment, and another small ledge box on the inner locker door. She looked at her jacket hanging in front of her, and through its pockets. Jade pulled out a slip of paper.

"What are you? Oh yeah." It was the Church of the True Nativity pamphlet.

Detective Jade stared at the pamphlet for a moment. She zeroed in on the website domain at the bottom of the handout: Truenativity.com

Jade studied it a bit more. "Let's check you out a little bit, shall we?"

Chapter 28

FISCHER RODE SHOTGUN WITH PRAIDER in his squad car. They pulled into the large parking lot of the Los Angeles Department of Children and Family Services. Praider found a spot and began parking.

"So, let me get this straight," Praider said unbuckling his belt. "You were at a home blessing, that you were performing for a family in your church. And when you arrived there was an active break-in in progress, and the guy you believe abducted their child, an adopted son, mind you, is the same guy caught on camera from the Viper Room?"

"Because of the hat," Fischer said, getting out of the car.

"A San Francisco Giants hat you found in your sidecar?"

"Right."

"And you believe this is also the *same* guy behind the aquarium attack?"

"Yes," Fischer said. They began walking toward the building.

"But what's the whole thing with the star again?" Praider asked.

"There's this theory, arguably the best theory, about what the actual nativity star was. The very star the original wise men followed at the time of Christ's birth. It very well might have been an extremely rare convergence of the planets Jupiter and Saturn, appearing in the night sky like one bright star. This rare conjunction only happens once every seven hundred years or so, and it happened fairly recently."

"December 21, 2020," Praider said, processing everything.

"Yes. And there's another, less appreciated observation I guess, that whenever this particular star phenomenon happens, an incredibly prominent person in human history is born, sort of a game-changing figure."

"And this kid is *that* special?" Praider asked.

"Our guy may think so at least. Whoever's behind all this is apparently watching the stars for signs, interpreting ancient signs, and presumably acting on perceived instructions. All I'm saying is 'this kid' was born on that specific date, and 'this killer' seems to want him badly."

"But why?" Praider asked holding the door for Fischer.

Fischer stopped and looked directly at Praider unsurely. "I'm a little thin on the why part just yet."

They approached the front desk in the loud and busy lobby area full of industrial couches, chairs, and various people ranging through children, youth, and adults. Fischer's heart hurt for the wide array of emotions he saw across the faces in the crowd. *Thank God places like this exist.* Praider's police uniform cut through the sea of people with ease. The heavy set greying haired lady at the reception desk greeted them with a half-smile. "Can I help you?"

"We are looking for a young boy, about four years old. His name is Christian Chipparo," Praider said.

"That sounds familiar," she said looking through a clipboard of apparent old notes. "What is this regarding?"

"We want to make sure he's safe," Fischer said.

"And *you* are?" the woman asked defensively.

"His pastor."

"I see," she said, now scrolling through the computer database. She paused for a second. "I can assure you he is safe, he was placed actually, earlier this morning."

"*Where?*" Praider asked.

"With whom?" Fischer followed up like lightning.

"Could you hold on," she said uncomfortably, "let me get my supervisor." She stood and walked back to a side office door and tapped on the frame. "Jayanne?" She walked in. After a few moments a slender professional middle-aged brunette walked out to greet them.

"Hello, Jayanne Richardson," she said politely to Fischer. "Officer," she said noddingly to Praider. "Christian Chiparro was successfully returned to his father this morning."

"Christian Chiparro's father is in a medical coma in the hospital right now. I saw him this morning." Fischer said desperately.

"His *actual* father?" Jayanne asked.

"His legal adoptive father, but I would think that would be *actual* according to DCFS standards," Fischer said.

"It usually is, but I don't understand. His blood father was here this morning. He had all the legal documents, birth certificate, and blood match verification. Everything."

"Is there an address? Contact information?" Praider asked.

"We usually don't give that information out," Jayanne said.

Praider leaned over the counter. "This *isn't* usual."

"Well," Jayanne said uneasily. "Glendale. It was in the mountains. Beautiful view overlooking the city. I went there personally for the in-home inspection earlier this week."

"What did the father look like?" Fischer asked.

"He was well-kept, had a beard, nice suit. Longer hair but pulled back. He was very well spoken, extremely so I would say," she said.

Fischer's heart sank as he leaned over with both hands propping him in place against the counter.

"Don't worry, Pastor," Praider said. "Warrants like the one we're going to need are usually expedited in lightspeed fashion for juvenile situations like this."

Praider took charge with dagger eyes back to Mrs. Richardson.

"I'm going to need that Glendale address, right now. And any file you have on Christian, *pronto*."

Chapter 29

JADE SAT IN A SMALL quiet LAPD office room at a computer desk. She took a savory sip of Peets, French Roast blend. She was delighted the department splurged for some quality coffee for a change, and on a day she really needed it. She typed in the web address for TrueNativity.com and began scrolling through and clicking links.

The banner across the top of the page had a shirtless Arabian looking man with his head covered by a holy shawl cloth with gold and blue trim. The background depicted a type of holy temple, with a large gate, surrounded by clouds and decorated in Hebrew lettering.

The website screamed low budget, with busy text and messy visuals, giving the feel it was designed by someone who thought they knew what they were doing, but clearly did not. Complete disregard for modern visual aesthetics was obvious.

Jade searched through vast listings of book titles offered for sale, sermon series videos, study videos, links to written articles, and blog posts. The various links read like a disorganized prophecy manifesto, with titles such as The Real Kingdom The True Covenant The Anti-Messiah The Ultimate Revelation and endless more. Jade clicked on one that said The Secret Language. And began reading:

Holy writ has been encoded in a "secret." Yeshua has hidden Himself in His Word. Only the Selected Few, whom He has given His Lifeforce vision, and taught them this <u>celestial language</u> can discern the Truth. These men then have the responsibility to teach the rest of The Selected Ones. I am El Nachash. So speaketh the Prophet.

"What in the world *is* this?" Jade asked incredulously to herself. She noticed the phrase <u>celestial language</u> was hyper-linked and clicked on it guiding her into another whole wormhole of delusions. She kept skimming through the material.

The original language is not Hebrew, it is that of the stars... the star chart, found within the Mazzaroth—the Heavenly Scroll of Elohim. It is a language of physical to spiritual parallels. All mentions in the Bible of Heaven refers to the Mazzaroth. Alas, The Scroll has been corrupted!

The pagan world, delusional by pride and greed has been conditioned and programmed to worship the creature, the false image of the Messiah— Jesus of Nazareth. Jesus is the false Messiah, The Fallen Star. Christianity is the great deception which has veiled the eyes of the real star gazers of the true Nativity!

"No way... You've *got* to be kidding me." Jade said, putting her hand over her mouth and kept scrolling and reading. "Who *is* this guy?" Her eyes lit up when she found the link: <u>About El Nachash</u>.

Click.

I, El Nachash, have been anointed and commissioned by The Most High to restore all things. My truth credentials for this task, are my life experiential training, the divine commissioning of Elohim, and His anointing. In past translations, Biblical "scholars" have failed. I am tasked by the celestial assignment to make right the heavenly scroll, in the living fulfillment of its message.

My charged endeavor to restore the truth from the deceitful pen of scribes is prophesied at the turn of the Ages (Pisces to Aquarius) as The New Son of Man is prophesied to overcome The Interstellar Dragon. We have entered the transition of the ages and that restoration has begun...

In so doing I expose the false prophets, lie teachers, and useless shepherds who claim to be "anointed" by The Dragon, (Jesus of Nazareth) not The Creator, my Father.

Jade took her last sip of coffee and thought for a moment, rubbing her forehead.

"This is some serious 'One Flew Over the Cuckoo's Nest' stuff," she muttered aloud before she clicked one last button: Print screen.

# # #

Fischer coasted home on his motorcycle and safely shut off the engine and headlight. He took off his helmet, unzipped his jacket and just thought for a moment as dusk set in. His garage was safe, old, and dirty, but satisfyingly comforting. *I can't believe it was a dead end at the Glendale house. It was like no one lived there. When Michael wakes up, what are we going to say?* He shook his head and went inside to let Luther out. After a quick bite of reheated pizza and an apple, Fischer went outside.

"Wanna go for a walk, boy? I've got a little more work to do..." Fischer clicked the leash clamp sound and Luther came running toward him. They walked a few blocks, a familiar path the two had moseyed many times before to the Church of the Epiphany. They rounded the parking lot and Fischer noticed Jeannie's navy-blue van still there. He glanced at his phone clock. 6:17 P.M.

Fischer entered the office and saw Jeannie still working, running copies, and polishing the bell choir bells.

"Still burning the midnight oil, are we Jeannie?"

"Hi, Pastor, the copy machine has been on the fritz, and I had a couple medical appointments this week. Just juggling time and getting everything done."

"The bells just *have* to be polished tonight, don't they?" Fischer said in jest.

"Someone's got to do them."

"Still trending up, aren't we?" Fischer said with an appreciative smiled. He was always amazed at the extra mile Jeannie would go for her job. "Hashtag, impressed."

"Ha," Jeannie said. "No change with Michael Chipparo, no word yet from District either, but I do have some good news. Someone wants to join the church. He just moved here, and works all day, so I set an appointment for tomorrow evening at 7:00. His last name is James. Hope that's okay."

"No problem," Fischer said.

Jeannie pointed to the office mailbox cubbyholes. "Oh, and there's a package for you over there."

Fischer went over and sifted through the letters and ads. *Strange parcel. Small, and a little lumpy. I don't remember ordering anything... and no return address.*

Luther followed Fischer into his office. Fischer sat down, turned on his computer, his green lowlight lawyer lamp, and queued up some music for a little mood ambience to get some late-night work done. *Read My Mind* by The Killers played. *Seems appropriate, Fischer silently joked to himself.* He looked out the window. Jeannie's van lights flipped on as she slowly pulled out of the parking lot. The music began to swell in the quietness of the dark church halls. Fischer harmonized with the lyrics when it crescendo. "...The stars are blazing like rebel diamonds, cut out of the sun... when you read my mind..." He took his letter opener and sliced open the side of the parcel and poured out the contents onto his desk.

Rev. Dr. Chase L. Fischer was stunned at what he saw lying in front of him. His face went ashen. He slowly stood, walked out of his office, down the hallway toward the nearby men's room. He looked in the mirror for a second and breathed in and out a few deep breaths. *Nope.* He dashed into the stall just in time to vomit. The old pizza and apple were notably not as tasty on the second pass.

Chapter 30

Tuesday, January 21st
9:16 A.M.

CHIEF TATUM SAT AT HIS office desk looking over the daily reports and briefings. He sifted through a few files and stood gazing at his bulletin board. His notes and pinned clippings to his wall mounted peg board ranged from Zodiac Killer newspaper titles, maps of attack locations, photographs of the victims, and other various paraphernalia. A knock at the door turned Tatum's head to see Detective George Greppin's tall dark 6'4" frame. "What can I do for you, George?"

"Morning, sir. I've gone through the donor list of the gala the other night. One name I think stands out more than any other. A guy by the name of Morgan Stern."

"Morgan Stern..." Tatum said pensively, turning back to his bulletin board. And what makes him so special?"

"Chief, best I can tell, he sold a tech start up, made it big, and was instrumental in making the gala event happen. He didn't just give to support it; he *made* it happen."

"Is that it?"

Detectives Jade and Praider arrived, one after the other, standing patiently outside the Chief's open doorframe.

"There's not a lot of information on the web about him," Greppin said. "Guys like Morgan Stern are either extremely well platformed, plastered all over social media, or they've whitewashed their past and don't want to be found, and there's usually a reason or two why they prefer extreme privacy. He's the latter, which raises more than an eyebrow for me."

Detective Jade boldly entered the room. "I might have something better than Morgan Stern."

Greppin and Tatum turned in mild surprise. "Feeling better than last we spoke, GJ?" Greppin asked.

"Maybe." She held up her assimilated notes and printout from the Truenativity.com website. "Listen to this," she said, and proceeded to update them on her research findings.

"El Nachash?" Tatum asked. "GJ, you know how many crazy churches there are in the greater Los Angeles area right?"

"Yes."

"And hokey websites pawning their wares of nonsense and garbage to the brainless and innocent. And you're all in on *this* one?" Greppin asked.

"Yes," Jade said more confidently. "Considering the greater context, his language, his mission, his messaging, I think this guy's incredibly plausible."

"Hold up," Praider said. "A new contender has arisen."

"What's this, now?" Tatum looked at him almost annoyed.

"The good doctor and I tracked down Christian, 'The Christmas Star Child,' yesterday, who we think in fact has actually been abducted for real this time."

"What?" Jade asked.

"How?" Greppin asked.

"By his real blood-related father," Praider said. "No way that should have happened with DCFS. No way. We got the name, Jim Latham, traced him back to a bogus street address. Dead end. No one there. *Something* shady is definitely going on."

"Does Fischer know why someone would want that kid though?" Tatum asked.

"Not yet. It's still just a theory, but I think it merits further investigating,"

Praider said.

Tatum paced back and forth thinking. "I don't know. All this is so thin, I'm tired of the guessing games. And I'm amazed none of you have mentioned *Pisces* which would be in tandem with the next target. You're all on to other things... Honestly, what's a wealthy philanthropist doing wasting his time on a monthly horror show like what we're watching unfold?" Tatum fired a look at Greppin. "Or a loony tuned dime a dozen internet preacher?" Jade equally received a skeptical blow. "And don't get me started on another Christmas baby, Praider." Justin Praider's head dropped to the floor. "And I'm still not convinced about the situation with Squirrel. Anything on his whereabouts yet?"

"I think I might be able to help with that," Fischer said somberly, as he stepped into the room. He tossed the opened parcel onto Chief Tatum's desk. Tatum's eyes took care of any inquisitive talking needed. "Go ahead, open it, Chief."

"How much of this conversation did you hear?" Tatum asked.

"Plenty," Fischer said emptily.

Chief Tatum hesitantly slid open the parcel. "Is that what I think it is?" Tatum said dumbfounded. "What kind of a sick bastard would—"

"Oh, my *Lord*," said Praider.

"Is that... Is that an ear?" Greppin asked, leaning forward over the desk.

"To be specific," Fischer said, taking out a pen and pointing with it through the clear zip-locked sandwich bag it rested in. "I think it's Squirrel's ear. It's bloody, but that appears to be his star-shaped earring."

"Oh no. Oh no. Oh no!" Jade said. "Oh... Squirrel..." She took a moment and then collected herself. "If he's a victim, does... Does that mean he's cleared? At least from working both sides?"

Greppin stepped closer. "I'm afraid not. I mean, it could be that he's in some insane hostage situation, but—"

"But what?" Jade asked.

"But," Fischer said, clearing his throat, "he could be being punished, as a sort of penalty as some failed acolyte, for whoever actually is kingpin behind all this."

"I can't even think about that," Jade said.

"If you can't think about that, then maybe you shouldn't be on this case," Chief Tatum thundered back.

"Sorry, I'm just not convinced, Chief," Jade said with a shrug of her shoulders.

"Oh, shoot, I almost forgot, that's not all," Fischer said. "This also came in the package." Fischer took out of his pocket a small, typed written note and carefully placed it on Tatum's desk.

Chapter 31

THE GROUP HOVERED OVER THE desk together to see the note which read:

He Knows The Way… to the next Café

Justin Praider's annoyance level began to ascend, evident in his tone. "What in the world? As far as serial killer brag notes goes, this wins the gold medal for ridiculousness. 'He knows the way, to the next café?' Seriously? I mean what? *Squirrel* knows the way?"

"See, Squirrel *could* be on the inside of this," Greppin said to Jade.

"All I know," Fischer said, "or at least what I'm pretty sure I know, is the man I saw at the house appeared to be the *same* man I saw at the aquarium, where Squirrel was last seen. And a guy like that would certainly be capable of doing something like this."

Praider looked at Jade. "Come to think of it, Squirrel also made the initial suggestion that the Aquarius murder could be at an aquarium… which it was…"

Jade shot him a dirty look, and whatever amount of Hispanic blood that coursed through her veins seasoned her eyes with extra spicy fire. "Don't," she said.

"What? I'm just saying…" Praider said holding up his palms.

Tatum picked up the phone on his desk and dialed an extension. "Get forensics… I want Chad Bostic up here… In my office… It's sensitive… Now, thanks." He hung up. "I want to see if forensics can tell us anything, up to and including if this is actually Squirrel's ear."

"What if the 'he' is not Squirrel?" Fischer said, deep in thought.

"What are you getting at now?" Jade asked.

"I've had a little more time to think about this note. I'm not sure about the café part, but the first part of the phrase is interesting, 'He knows the way,'" Fischer let the phrase hang in the air for a moment. "Look at the note. The word 'Way' is capitalized. What if *He* knows the Way, is talking about 'the Way of the Mazzaroth?"

"Are we back to that?" Greppin asked caustically. "Follow the money Fischer. Always follow the money. And my money's on Morgan Stern."

"It's obviously another taunting clue from this degenerate," Jade said. "Who else, Chase, I mean if the 'he' isn't Squirrel?"

"Well," Fischer said hesitantly. "Maybe it's someone we all know, someone famous."

"Get to your point, son," Tatum said.

Fischer struggled reluctantly before offering what he could only assume would be perceived as his next wild assertion. "Who else do we know who cuts off ears?"

The puzzled tension in the office slowly elevated until Jade fumbled out, "You don't mean… Van Gogh? *Vincent* Van Gogh?"

Fischer's face turned red. "I know it sounds crazy, and he cut his *own* ear off, but he also painted one of the most iconic paintings the world has ever known, and germane to our subject matter at hand."

"Starry Night," Tatum said introspectively, as if considering it seriously for the briefest of moments before exhaling his breath through his teeth like a train whistle. He shook his head violently. "Is this the best we've got?"

The proverbial seven-minute conversational lull arrived as painfully as it did silently for Fischer, waiting to hear what the consensus of the room was.

Praider couldn't take it anymore and broke the silence. "Okay, so, we're going to the nuclear option of speculation now, right? I mean, that is some serious second layer, Da Vinci Code 3D chess level stuff there, Fischer. *Come on.* Excuse me for being the conscience in the room. Chief, I've got an actual good lead, a woman by the name of Autumn Wildly. She filed a real report against this Jim Latham guy a few years back, a guy that may have actually abducted the boy. You know, *Chaplain* Fischer's last scheme of an idea. I'm going to try and track her down for some solid information." Praider stepped toward the door, pausing with a rollover glance at Fischer. "Dude, it's starting to get embarrassing." He walked out.

All eyes returned to Fischer, who uncomfortably adjusted his collar and tie. "I'm not saying there's some ancient cryptic code through Van Gogh's paintings." Fischer's eyes tilted up and back for a second of reconsideration. "Yeah, I'm not saying *that*, but I am submitting, based off of *this* evidence, that the killer might see something in Van Gogh's work, like he does in the Mazzaroth zodiac, and is acting in kind."

"And just what do you suggest we do about this, um, possibility?" Chief Tatum asked, arching his back and adjusting his belt fitting.

Fischer regained his poise. "I was thinking through this a bit last night, as you might suspect I was a tad apprehensive about suggesting this whole idea. I didn't sleep much as you might imagine. I have an old friend, an art expert I reached out to, that I want to track down. She might be of help. She's actually a curator at The Getty."

"Listen," Greppin said. "I'm gonna keep looking under the hood of Morgan Stern. I wanna find out a little more about this financial fat cat before I rule him out."

Morgan Stern... Intriguing name for a tech tycoon, Fischer thought to himself.

"Reach out to the FBI, just in case," Tatum said, "In fact, I'll set it up with my contacts in the bureau."

"Will do, Chief." Greppin exited just as Chad Bostic entered.

"You wanted me, Chief?" Bostic asked.

"Here, I need you to deal with this." Tatum put the clear zippy-bagged ear back into the parcel and handed it to Bostic. "Go on ahead, Chad. I'll catch up with you in a second. I want to give you as much of the details as I can, personally." Bostic left with the parcel.

Tatum looked back at his bulletin board for a bit and then turned over his shoulder to see Gemma Jade and Chase Fischer staring blankly at him.

"Well, what are you two still doing here? Don't you have a *date* at the museum?"

Detective Jade smirked. "You said it not me, Chief."

Fischer awkwardly chuckled. "I've actually already taken the liberty of setting up an appointment for us tomorrow."

Tatum shook his head. "I'll bet you did. You know, Fischer, all this concerns me. But most of all is, whoever sent that parcel to you knows who you are now—and where to find you. And don't think I haven't thought about your last name in conjunction with the next victim for *Pisces*, Fischer."

"Of course, Chief. I thought that too," Fischer said warily. *Holy cats, I totally didn't even think of that.* Fischer stepped out, a little more humbled than when he'd arrived.

Chapter 32

Wednesday, January 22nd
3:14 p.m.

FISCHER AND JADE RENDEZVOUSED IN the parking lot of the J Paul Getty Museum and strolled up toward its peaking grounds in the heart of Los Angeles. They paused in front of the brilliant green labyrinth bushes at the center of campus, flanked by ivory-like Lego-shaped mosaic looking buildings to their right, and an exquisitely constructed crescent-shaped building to their left.

"We've got a little time to kill. I have us set for a 3:30 appointment," Fischer said.

"Who is this again?" Jade asked as she lit up a cigarette.

"She's an old friend of mine I got to know from an art appreciation summer abroad program in Europe during our college days. Lori. Her goal was always to be a curator at a museum. Landing this gig at The Getty was a dream come true for her."

"Since we've got a moment, here." Jade gave Fischer her printed notes of TrueNativity.com. "I wanted you to see this."

Fischer scanned through it quickly. "This *is* bizarre. El Nachash? Sounds Hebraic."

"I was thinking," Jade said, "why would a church like this be doing outreach at an astronomy observatory?"

"*Exactly*," Fischer said. "Look at the star they used in their logo. I would think a 'ministry' like this, if it were legit, would probably identify with the star of David."

"The star of David has six points, right? Jade asked. Essentially one triangle inverted atop of another?"

"Right," Fischer said. "This one's a five-pointed star, but they've tilted it, positioning it more like a pentagram than a star of the nativity."

"I didn't even notice that before," Jade said.

"This has darkness all over it," Fischer said, analytically. He chose his next words with careful calculation. "Gemma, If I remember correctly, I hate to say it, but Squirrel's star earring was five pronged, too…"

Jade exhaled her smoke into Fischer's face. "I don't believe it, Chase."

Fischer coughed, waving his hand for a clean breath. "I'm sorry. I didn't mean to upset you again about that, but if there are dots to connect, we've got to at least ask the question, don't we?" He gently grasped Gemma's arm holding the cigarette.

Gemma froze. "What are you doing?"

Fischer smiled. "I've been thinking, March 5th is coming upon us real soon. Ash Wednesday, kicking off Lent. It would be a great time to, you know, get your ash in church, and kick this nasty little habit of yours," Fischer said riskily. He intimately removed the cigarette from her hand, dabbed it out and put it in a nearby waste bin.

"Get your *ash* in church?" Jade asked. "That has cringe all over it."

"There are a lot of corny-bad church puns out there, but there *are* some winners," Fischer doubled down. "That one's always made me laugh."

She gave him a skeptical glance.

Silence.

"Well, not laugh out loud, but quietly, to myself, in the private recesses of my m—"

"I see," Jade said. "A forty-day Lenten pact? Wow. I haven't done that since I was a good little Catholic school girl." Jade sucked in a deep inhale before she looked off into the view of the distant city and slowly let it out.

She turned back to Fischer. "I have a very needed long weekend coming up, starting tomorrow. Let me think on it and get back to you."

"I understand," Fischer said. "It's a pain of a commitment, but I do it every year. It's a great healthy spiritual exercise. We always have things we can work on, and when we make a sacrifice, as pathetically insignificant as it may seem to others, it's significant to us, and in those moments of 'suffering' going without, we reflect on Christ's greater sacrifice for us, which enhances the sweetness of the Easter celebration all the more when it rejoicingly arrives."

"Hmmm. I've never thought of it like that…" Gemma sighed in playful acquiescence. "Alright, *Pastor* Fischer, If I were to do this, what are you giving up? I'm not about to do this alone."

"Well, I really should cut back on my drinking. Fair enough?"

"Fair enough," Jade said.

Fischer offered forward his right pinky finger. "Pinky shake?"

Jade approvingly pinky-shook with Fischer. "Game *on*," she said.

Fischer couldn't help but allow his mind to wander a tad during the warm moment as their eyes locked with their fingers clinging snuggly together. *Could she be wife material?*

"*Chase*," a woman's voice yelled from across the way. Lori ran up and hugged Chase strongly. Lori's elfin squarish face was framed by a short brown wavy hairstyle and blue eyes, all naturally juxtaposed by her trim svelte figure. Her white *J. Paul Getty Museum* embroidered blouse top with charcoal business slacks rounded out her ensemble.

"Detective Gemma Jade, this is Lori Freitas," Fischer said. "Great to see you again, Lori. Honestly, we're not exactly sure why we're here. Just hoping you could possibly help us figure something out."

"Here," Lori said, giving Fischer a large artbook. "This is complimentary from our store, it contains most of Van Gogh's prominent works, just as a resource for you, but I understand time is of the essence," Lori said matter-of-factly. "I did a little extra research in response to your email prompting late last night. So, we have a religious psycho killer with an affinity for astronomy, who may be sending clues to you through Vincent Van Gogh's artwork, yes, I get those requests all the time."

Fischer shook his head self-consciously. "Sorry, I know it sounds ludicrous."

"But the guy we're after is probably somewhere on the crazy spectrum," Jade said.

"Obviously. Well, for starters, here," Lori handed them each a promo card for an event. "The Van Gogh Immersion experience is in town tonight. It's a special encore performance tour off its earlier success in recent years. You may want to check that out. It's exceptional to experience, but with your other endeavors, who knows. I wish I could go, but I have plans. Meanwhile, I'll share with you what I turned up from extra digging last night. From the little I know about the assailant you described, or his motivations, oddly enough I think there could be some explanations as to why he'd be so obsessed with him, that may intrigue you. Follow me…"

Chapter 33

FISCHER, GEMMA, AND LORI ALL stood in front of *Irises*, Vincent Van Gogh's iconic nature still, in the Gallery W204, West Pavilion of the Getty Center. The painting's thick textured blues and yellows of the flowers almost swayed in an imaginary breeze in front of them.

"The J. Paul Getty hasn't procured many of Van Gogh's works, but *Irises* would certainly be the most prominent. Tell me, how much do you know about Van Gogh?" Lori asked.

Fischer flittered his hand about in a brief attempt of recall from college art history courses. "Uh, master impressionist painter. Cut off his own ear, in response to some argument with a friend… He was committed to an insane asylum fo—"

"Hospital," Lori said. "Actually, he painted this piece here the very first week he was at Saint-Remy psychiatric hospital in southern France."

"Really? Wow," Gemma said.

Fischer soaked in the unique painting. "I'm basically like most people, familiar with a few details of his life and some of his major works, *The Starry Night*, in particular. I can't really say I know very much about the man or his provocations."

"Van Gogh suffered from epilepsy," Lori began. "Mental health assessment being what it was in the late 19th century, he often gets castigated as some insane type of lunatic artist, but he wrote tons of cogent letters to his brother, Theo, during that time. He was a bit of a tortured soul to be sure, but his breakdowns were more episodic than a constant plague."

"I see," Fischer said.

"What's more fascinating is he presumably took too much digitalis medicine which affected his sight, causing xanthopsia, a yellow vision, which serendipitously comes through in much of his work, including here," Lori motioned at *Irises* for a split second before returning focus to them.

"You may find this next bit very interesting, Chase. Van Gogh started out as a preacher in the Dutch Reformed Church."

"Huh," Fischer said in shock. "I had no idea."

"His family was quite devout, though his preaching time was short-lived. He ended up rejecting his faith, and for the most part became estranged from religion."

"But what about the astronomy side of him?" Gemma asked.

"Oh, he *loved* astronomy," Lori said. "To be honest it seemed he was quite fascinated by it. You know, *The Starry Night* was likely inspired by the Whirlpool Galaxy drawing by the mid 19th century astronomer, William Parsons. The one bears striking resemblance to the other. Van Gogh read about astronomers and even met with some of them. But, of more interest, particularly to the line you shared with me 'He knows the Way… to the next Café.'"

Gemma recoiled, elbowing chase in the side. "Police evidence, *Fischer*."

"You should talk," Fischer whispered back.

Lori tactfully moved forward, *"The Starry Night* is not Van Gogh's only nocturnal piece with stars. There is a trilogy."

Fischer and Gemma exchanged an enthusiastic glance with each other. "A trilogy?" Gemma asked.

"Yes," Lori said. "Here, look and see." She grabbed and flipped to the pages in the artbook. "His first was, you may find interesting, *Café Terrace at Night*. That same month he painted *Starry Night over the Rhone*, and then about a year later he concluded his nocturnal series with his quintessential masterpiece, *The Starry Night*. I was particularly thinking about what you said with the killer's comment about 'the Way,' being the annual Way of the zodiac. This one-year duration of Van Gogh's star themed paintings is intriguing."

"Are the stars depicted in *The Starry Night* accurate?" Fischer asked.

Lori smiled. "Van Gogh takes *some* artistic liberties, very few actually, but typically his astronomy is a spot-on match for the moment in time, which for *The Starry Night* was June 18th, 1889. I figured you'd ask that. Listen to this," she read aloud from the artbook. "This is Van Gogh writing to his brother about painting *The Starry Night*." Lori began.

"This morning, I saw the country from my window a long time before sunrise, with nothing but the morning star, which looked very big."

Lori looked back to Fischer and pointed to the image in the book. "The Morning Star is another name for Venus, which is the largest 'star' depicted in the center foreground. Cappella, Cassiopeia, Pegasus, they're all there accurately in place. The morning star was a big deal to Van Gogh, I wager it signaled the end of his nocturnal star trilogy, and a new beginning."

Chase Fischer thought for a while slowly spinning around. "Gemma, didn't Greppin say he was looking into a donor by the name of Morgan Stern?"

"Yeah, why?"

"It's just..." Fischer pondered, "Morgan Stern is *Auf Deutsch* for... Morning Star."

"That is weird," Lori said.

"Hmmmm, and what of the Café part?" Gemma asked.

Lori nodded, with bobbing brown hair, "Right, Vincent generally viewed the Café as his spiritual oasis, where people gathered, spent time, and laughed. He somewhat saw that as his own form of religion. And now, do I have permission to blow your mind?"

"You've already succeeded, but please continue," Gemma said, enjoying Lori's winsome demeanor.

"Flip to the *Café Terrace at Night* painting," Lori said.

Gemma turned to it as quickly as she could.

"Again," Lori said, "you'll find the stars in the painting are correct, it's Ursa Major, the Big Bear, his favorite constellation, but way more interesting is this entire painting actually contains a hidden image of the Last Supper."

"Of Christ?" Fischer asked in delight.

"Yeah," Lori said confidently. "Read again what he wrote about it to his brother, right there." She pointed to the quote in the book. "In a letter to his brother Theo about *Café Terrace at Night*, van Gogh expressed his 'tremendous need for, shall I say the word—for religion.' So, think about this; You have Vincent Van Gogh, a wandering star in the faith if you will, on the spectrum psychotically as well as a manic bi-polar, and perhaps among other things, viewing a Café as essentially his heavenly realm, and now we get to the juicy part..."

"Juicy?" Gemma said with increasing appetite.

Lori cleared her voice and spoke in a more hushed tone. "Some art historian scholars suspect there is also a darker ominous meaning to Van Gogh's starry nocturnal trilogy. Once again, thinking about the Morning Star, a new beginning, and the Way of the zodiac, he painted those three over the course of a year, and about a full year after his star paintings, he killed himself.

"What?" Gemma said in shock.

"Shot himself in the stomach." She flipped to *The Starry Night* page. "Here he brings the cypress tree—a frequent symbolic motif for death, much closer into the foreground, shooting up into the stars. And this quote of Van Gogh often gets cited in one of his letters to his brother..."

Lori looked up retrieving from memory and began,

"'If we take the train to get to Tarascon or Rouen, we take death to reach a star.' Interestingly, the church he paints in the scene, isn't actually in the view from his asylum window, which was his vantage point of the sky."

Gemma and Fischer cross-examined each other's eyes again.

"And," Lori forged on, "in *Café Terrace at Night*..." She flipped to that page again. "Optically, the scattered disks of the stars in the sky are mirrored in the elliptical tabletops below—tabletops thematic of a Last Supper, and a looming death, in the venue of 'heavenly café' of his imagination. There you see twelve people dining, and one in the center dressed in white, looking very much like a Christ figure." Lori marveled at the painting image on the book page and shook her head in wonderment. "He even has a subtle suggestive cross behind him."

"Wow, there's even a dark shadowy figure leaving from the side exit," Fischer said, pointing to the figure.

"*Judas?*" Gemma asked.

"Probably. Whew…" Fischer exhaled. *What to do with all of this?*

"Obviously," Lori said, "this is playing fast and loose with an iconic artist's interpretation, which many people do, but *if* someone is as disturbed as the person you described wanted to read wildly into it, that's what might jump out at me."

Detective Gemma Jade's phone rang giving each of them a start. Gemma looked at it. "It's Greppin, I better take it."

Jade walked discreetly away and answered. "Whatcha got, Grep?" she asked.

"Are you actually at the *Getty*? With Fischer?"

Reluctant silence screamed. Jade could almost hear Greppin roll his eyes in the tone of voice through his next question. "Well, did you guys *find* anything?" Greppin asked.

"Nothing you'd be too impressed with, at least I don't think. How about you?" Jade asked. Just then Jade's phone hummed a text. She looked. Chad Bostic.

FYI. Squirrel ear results in…

No extra intel from trace.

Any luck on your end?

Detective Jade double tasked reading Bostic's note and continued her chat with Greppin, speaking into her ear. "Best I can tell this Morgan Stern guy made his money in some type of marriage between technology, horticulture, big into some plant hybrids, artemisia absinthium, growth, watering systems, timing sequences etc..."

"That's really helpful, Greppin, thanks," Jade said sarcastically.

Greppin continued. "All I know is he did incredibly well in the agriculture community. *Incredibly* well. And the cannabis crowd loves him too, if you know what I'm saying."

"Is that so weird though?" Jade asked. "That someone like that would give to some lunar Gala at an aquarium?"

"Not in and of itself. But what if I told you he also gave a lot of money to that church website you mentioned?" Greppin asked.

"What was it, TrueNativity.com?" Jade said in shock. She looked back at Fischer. "Awesome. Thanks. I'll update Fischer. Gotta go." *Click.* Jade returned Bostic's text as she slowly walked back to Fischer and Lori.

> *Darn. I was hoping for something.*
> *Heading to a Van Gogh Immersion*
> *Experience tonight, trail oddly could*
> *be warming. Update the others.*

"Thank you, Lori, this was… illuminating, to say the least," Fischer said.

"My pleasure," Lori said. "I'm supposed to get running anyhow. My husband, Richard, set up his best idea of a date night for us. His beloved Gators are in town playing Michigan State in some rare midyear neutral site basketball tournament…" Lori sighed. "We have courtside seats. Tip off is in a little more than an hour. So I can't not go."

"Thanks again, Lori." Fischer gently hugged her and gave a quick thank you kiss on the cheek. "I've got an appointment tonight too, at church. And tell Richard I said, "Go Spartans!""

"It was a pleasure, Lori. You know your craft well," Gemma said, as the ladies shook hands, before Lori departed their company.

Gemma and Fischer stood together in front of Van Gogh's *Irises* with one last gaze of appreciation. She turned to him.

"Lots to think about. Hey, so Greppin said his Morgan Stern lead was a supporter for the TrueNativity.com church website too. You really need to research that more when you get a moment; you know, with your Bible mind."

Fischer snickered. "My *Bible* mind? Nice."

"Chase, you've got your thing tonight. I'm gonna check out that Van Gogh immersion experience, before my long weekend starts. We'll circle back and compare notes later next week. So, let's stay in touch." She began walking away.

"Be careful tonight," Chase said.

Jade stopped mid stride, turned and crisscrossed her arms with a smile.

"Yeah, okay, thanks, last I checked I was the only one of us carrying a gun," she said.

Fischer smiled and looked around briefly. *Stupid. Don't be stupid…*

"You know, The Getty is a pretty cool place. Could be nice to come back here with you sometime, spend a while, you know, when we're not stalking a serial killer and such."

"Wow. You really have a way with words don't you, Boomer. And you're a *preacher* you say?"

Fischer's mild laugh died out when he heard Gemma's next words.

"I don't think I'm a sidecar kind of girl."

"Understood," Fischer said sobering up as Detective Jade leisurely walked away from him.

She turned. "But I've recently wondered what it might be like to ride on the back of a Triumph Bonneville..." She gently raised her hand to her mouth, blew a kiss way up into the air, and shot it with her pointed pistol-hand as if shooting a clay skeet target out of the sky. She 'holstered' her hand pistol and proceeded toward the turn in the hallway.

"Extraordinary," Fischer said with an uncontrolled quiver streaking through his body. He glanced at the *Irises* painting, "There's beauty..." and returned to catch the last glimpse of her as she rounded the corner and out of view, "and then there's beauty."

Yet in that precious magical moment a seed of doubt somehow entered Rev. Dr. Chase Fischer's mind. An eerie unexplainable ominous feeling crept in. *Why do I get the feeling that may well have been the last time I ever lay eyes on her?*

Chapter 34

6:48 P.M.

FISCHER SAT AT HIS DESK in his office at Church of the Epiphany and turned on his computer. He pulled out the Van Gogh artbook Lori had given him from his messenger bag satchel and flipped through the pages. He admired the art for a bit and thought through the puzzling minutia of details Lori had shared. *A Hidden Last Supper? Death as a type of train to the stars... suicide. And a trilogy of Starry nights too... A severed ear, and a café as paradise... What a hot mess bag of 'clues' these are..."*

Fischer flipped a few more pages and turned his attention toward a sports website on the computer screen. *I wonder...* A few clicks later the screen read:

Michigan State 89, Florida 76. Final.

Fischer smiled with a soft shake of the head and chuckled to himself just as Jeannie poked her head through his office door.

"I'm putting on a pot of coffee, should I make it decaf?" Jeannie asked.

"You know, my dear, if I wanted to drink swill, I would," Fischer said in a weak attempt of a British accent, graduating his chuckle to a full-grown laugh.

"Jeannie cracked her knuckles playfully, "Would you like one lump or two with your swill, Boss?"

Fischer politely reverted to his normal voice. "Well played, Jeannie. Well played. Regular will be fine."

Fischer waited patiently for his appointment and checked the time. 6:57 P.M. He returned to *The Starry Night* painting image in the book. *Lori said the stars are astronomically correct. June 18, 1889. Venus... the morning star... and what was it? Pegasus, Cassiopeia, and... what was it? Cappella!* Fischer stared intently at the painting. "Wait a sec..."

He typed in the zodiac constellations star patterns into his internet search engine. Images. *Click.* He moved his cursor over the Aries prompt. *Click.* He stared at the screen in disbelief and back at *The Starry Night* painting in the book.

Fischer whipped back in his chair. "Aries." *I can't wait to tell Gemma.* Fischer's thoughts sputtered into speech as his excitement rose, and he traced his thoughts together. "Aries is the Ram... For the Mazzaroth story arc, it would be a *sacrificial* Ram... Right after Pisces. Come on Fischer, think..." *He knows the Way... the next Café?*

A *knock knock* sounded at his office door. "Pastor, Mr. James is here," Jeannie said, opening the door all the way and introducing him.

The potential new church member that walked in was a youngish looking Italian American man, at Fischer's best estimate. He appeared roughly in his upper twenties, clean shaven, khaki pants, and a collared dress shirt, mostly covered by a navy mechanics jacket.

"Actually, James is my *first* name, but you can call me Jim." He sat down across the desk from Fischer.

"Jim, I see," said Fischer. "Thanks, Jeannie."

"Door closed?" Jeannie queried.

"Sure," Fischer said without hesitating. Male visitors weren't usually a concern for him behind closed doors. She shut the door behind her.

"Well, hello. I understand you are looking for a church to join, or *this* church perhaps? I should tell you, there are a number of churches down this block, but ours is the best one," Fischer said lightheartedly.

Jim smiled with a little sweat beading up on his forehead. "Yes. I've heard you're an excellent Good Samaritan type of pastor."

Now there's a unique compliment, Fischer thought. He twisted in his chair over to his right side to retrieve some paperwork. "I usually keep some folders available for visitors, with new member information. It concisely provides a little bio section for you to fill out for our records, our most recent newsletter, a Time Talent & Treasure inventory, so we know which ministry you might be most suited to plug into should you desire. And a copy of the Church constitution… and our annual budget so as to be transparent about our accountability. Let's see…"

Fischer kept fumbling through paperwork on his busy cluttered side desk, stacked with books, print outs, documents, magazine journal articles and such.

"You know," James said, "they say a man's office desk is a snapshot of his mind. If it's orderly and organized, or messy and disorganized. One can tell a lot about a man."

Fischer sensed the tone of Jim's comment was seemingly intended to be snide, but he wasn't quite sure. It could be just a failed first attempt at humor on his part. Regardless, he was pretty used to dealing with petty comments from people. Besides, Fischer had learned the hard way on more than one occasion that his first impressions of people were usually wrong. No matter, Fischer victoriously found his new member folder packet and hoisted it up looking back at James. "Aha. Here it is."

Jim glared back at Fischer with darkening eyes. "No worries, Pastor," Jim said emotionlessly. "I'm pretty sure I'll be able to hold your complete and undivided attention."

He pulled out a small black shiny tipped gun from his jacket pocket and pointed it directly at Fischer.

Chapter 35

DETECTIVE JUSTIN PRAIDER PULLED HIS LAPD squad car to a stop and parked curbside, somewhere off Mulholland Drive near Downtown LA. He doubled-checked the street address with his computer screen, looking around the side of the block. "This is the place, alright."

The white etch-painted sign in the glass window said:

The Wiley Cat Café

"He knows the Way… to the next Café… hmmmm," Praider said to himself while stepping out into the street in his police uniform. The doorbell sensor chimed as Praider walked in prompting the hostess to come and greet him.

"Welcome. What can I get you?" The thirtyish hostess politely asked. She had long auburn hair, and oven-roasted almondy brown eyes. Praider couldn't help but notice her olive-skinned Italian features as he sized up the 5'6" petite frame of his newest interviewee. Her name tag read: *Autumn*.

"Latte?" she asked.

Praider looked around and saw the designated cat section behind a glass wall where people could enjoy a beverage and play with potential pet cats, seeking a forever home. The large feline-themed photographs and various sized carpet clawing posts rounded out the décor.

"Interesting place. I'm actually allergic to cats though," Praider said gruffly.

"I see, well you must love someone very much to come here to get them a pet."

"Not exactly. Um, Autumn, right?" Praider asked. "I'm glad I tracked you down. I have a few questions for you, if you don't mind. I think you might be able to help us."

"Oh, well, sure, I guess. What do you want to know?"

"I think I *will* take a black coffee, come to think of it," Praider said, suggestive of a looming lengthier conversation. After a quick transactional exchange, the steaming caffeinated drink soothed his scratchy throat.

Autumn led them to a small round table with two chairs, occupied by a midsized black and brown cat. "Scoot, Gizzy," she said.

Praider sat down. "We're trying to locate a young boy by the name of Christian. I think you might remember. You filled out a police report a few years back to protect him from his father. Let's start there…"

"Oh, absolutely," Autumn said, with immediate recall. "Christian was the sweetest baby, I remember. He had his mother's brilliant blue eyes. It was so awful what happened. I was really great friends with Christian's mother, Angela. We were childhood friends. High school, stayed in touch through college, marriage..."

Memory lane was proving to be mildly emotional for Autumn, Praider noticed, offering her a Wiley Cat Café napkin to dab her wetting eyes.

Autumn continued. "She wasn't, ya know, 'my person' necessarily, but when people get married, things evolve, focus shifts… priorities change. Truth be told, I never really liked the guy she ended up with, I hate to even say the word 'husband,' because it was so short lived. He doesn't deserve the title, you know?"

Praider jotted notes, while discreetly removing a lone cat hair from the surface of his coffee, hoping not to offend. "Was he abusive?"

Autumn's face portrayed a conflicted complex soul as she carefully began choosing her words. "No. Well, let me qualify that, I never witnessed any abuse, at least physically, at first."

"At *first*?" Praider asked.

"I mean he wasn't your stereotypical wife-beater personality. He took care of her, very well actually. He was military trained, strong, smart, had money, which he lavished on her and threw around town."

"Military and money don't always go together," Praider said quizzically. "Where did he get his money from?"

"Ex-military. He had a business. Something techy. Plants, computers, I don't really know."

Praider rubbed his eyes, a telltale sign his allergies were starting to get the best of him. "I see. What about the report you filed?"

"Right, well, they got pregnant. Great, right? Nope." Autumn began to work herself up in reminiscence. "If he was weird before, he got even weirder once she was pregnant, almost manic. Wild swings. Wanted her to call him... oh what *was* it... I dunno, some weird middle eastern camel jockey type name. El something... El..."

"El Nachash?" Praider asked.

"Oh yeah, I think that might have been it. I remember it sounded like 'cash', and he was doing well in business. That was the jokey play on words, I think. Wow. You're *good*." Autumn said, while sustaining her loquacious pace. "But then the baby was coming, original due date was mid-February, but he kept pushing for the child to be induced earlier. *Much* earlier. He said it was for her protection, not to carry to full term, but it was like an obsession for him. He pushed for the inducement, she refused, they fought, but he did it anyway, at home. And," Autumn said, breaking down, "she *died*."

"Forgive me," Praider said, venturing forward. "How did you know he forced the inducement?"

Autumn's head snapped up. "She called me, while it was happening in real time. They started it up at first while she was sleeping, but then baby was coming, she was in a panic."

"*They*?"

"One of their friend's, some science medical guy. And I think he helped with the agricultural side of the business. I don't even remember his name. I think he helped with the business a lot. But, of course, I haven't seen any of them in years now."

Praider wrote down as much of her words as he could before he came to his next question. "Does December 21, 2020, ring any bells for you?" Praider asked, managing to ward off a sneeze.

"Well, yeah. That was when Christian was actually born, tiniest little thing. So cute. I mean how could I forget? It was so sad, right around Christmas and everything. Oh Angela…" Autumn mused staring off into the foggy memories of time gone by.

"So, that's when you filed a report?" Praider asked.

"Listen," Autumn said, turning more intense. "I'm huge into child advocacy. *Huge*." She gently tapped the table in karate-chop fashion. "You'll be hard-pressed to find someone more passionate about the subject than me. I spoke up. I had to. That was, like, a triggered awakening for me. He snapped. I had specialized information. So yeah. I reported him. It was absolutely the right thing to do. No doubt. No way was he capable of caring for a child in the state he was. No way. Particularly after Angela died, and the *way* it happened. He wasn't close to behaving responsibly, let alone thinking clearly. I don't know how he stayed out of jail. Hard to prove, I guess, but the proper authorities at DCFS did seize the child. I was happy about that. It wasn't a safe long-term context for him, and they easily recognized that."

"Good for you," Praider said. "We *need* more people like you in this city." He quickly scribbled a few more notes. "Okay, curve ball question. Do you remember him doing anything with astronomy, or the stars?"

Autumn reflected for a second. "Wow. It's been a while, but yes. Moe had this telescope he loved. Some guys like football, or wall street. Moe had his telescope, and his business, and talked about both frequently. I mean, I was around less and less as their relationship devolved, but that's what I remember."

"Wait," Praider paused, "*Moe?*"

"Moe, yeah, Christian's dad. Angela's husband. Moe. Well, Morgan technically, Morgan Stern, but we called him Moe. Who'd you think I was talking about?"

Praider calculated through his notes and stewed for a moment. "Not… Jim? Christian's father?"

"*Jim?*" Autumn asked. "No, I filed a report against Moe." Autumn's almond eyes about swelled to chestnut size in a moment of seeming epiphany.

"Well, come to think of it, I do remember Angela saying Moe had legally changed his name to Morgan Stern. She called him James once, and so, I was like, who's *that*? So, she gave me the full story, something about wanting to reinvent himself after the military. So, Jim, Jimmy, that's a form of James I guess, but I only ever knew him as Moe."

Praider tried to hold his royal flush poker face hand as well as he could. "Autumn, this is incredibly important. Do you remember James', or Jim's last name?"

Autumn looked down with her hand to her forehead for a moment. She sifted her head side to side ever so delicately before coming up. "Wilthrop… Rathrop… Laden… She snapped her fingers in delight. *Latham.*

Chapter 36

CHASE FISCHER SAT IN HIS office chair behind his desk glaring at the gun-wielding lunatic across from him. He couldn't believe he was in this situation. *Don't panic. Throw him off his game plan and buy time.* "Read any good books lately?" Fischer asked. *Well done, Chase. Well done.*

"What? Shut up. I need you to—"

Fischer's desk phone *bleep bleeped* in the unique ring that cued him it was Jeannie's line from her office, not an outside caller. "Should I answer?" Fischer asked.

"I wouldn't," Jim said.

Bleep Bleep.

"It's Jeannie, my secretaries' ring. She knows we're in here. If I don't pick up, she'll *know* something's off."

"Get rid of her," Jim said, as menacingly as he could in a whisper through gritted teeth. "Or I may have to."

"Yes?" Fischer answered the phone, in a cracked voice, as he recognized his pulse was skyrocketing.

Jeannie spoke in her normal quiet voice into Fischer's ear. "I'm gonna run a few more copies and call it quits for the night. Okay?"

"Coffee? Sure," Fischer said. "Would you like one?" Fischer asked Jim.

Jim cocked back the hammer on his small gun with an ominous

click-click.

"I think that's just one coffee for me, Jeannie," Fischer said, trying to keep his cool.

Jim shook his head eerily back and forth cautioning Fischer and silently mouthed the words "end it."

"Actually, you know what," Fischer said. "I'll get it in a bit. You can head out. No worries. Just be sure to leave out the extras. You know how I love my coffee with *tons* of cream and sugar. Thanks."

Fischer hung up the phone feeling slightly better. He knew two things his assailant didn't. First, he and Jeannie had devised an emergency 'cream and sugar' code signal phrase years before, just for such an occasion as this, in the wake of all the church shootings across the nation. Jeannie knew full well Fischer always had his coffee black. *Always*. He couldn't believe he was actually employing their secret code-phrase in real life. The second ace up Fischer's sleeve was Jim had no idea Luther was lying at Fischer's feet out of sight under his desk. Pastor Fischer wasn't the only German Shepherd in the room. Fischer had heeded Chief Tatum's warning counsel wisely, knowing the killer potentially knew how to find him and Fischer took every extra precaution he could.

"Okay?" Fischer said, conferring with Jim. "So, what do you want?"

"I need you to come with me," Jim said nervously.

Fischer's experienced pastoral discernment sensed this was no hardened criminal, or poised thug. This was someone very uncomfortable with the situation, almost as much as Fischer himself.

"Nah," Fischer said.

"I *need* you to come with me, as recompense. For the scroll *must* continue to unfold. I have a sedative to make the trip more comfortable." Jim pulled out a syringe with what Fischer could only assume was a tranquilizer of some sort.

"I'll pass," Fischer said.

"El Nachash *says* you must," Jim said, altering his voice in a desperately demonic tone.

Fischer instantly connected the name to the TrueNativity.com website Jade had mentioned earlier. "I see. And *you* are this, El Nachash?"

"Yes, well. *Yes...*" Jim said, tripping over his words.

Fischer knew Jim was lying, as he looked nothing like the El Nachash man from the website print out Jade showed him. "And what does *that* mean?" Fischer asked.

"You have been given the name 'Christ' as a Christian... I'm sure you can figure it out," Jim said snidely.

Out through the side window Fischer and Jim both observed Jeannie come into view, get in her van, and drive away. Fischer remembered the pastor's office windows were tinted so they could see outside, but outsiders could not see in to protect the identity of church members who may want their privacy when meeting with the pastor. *Great. Dear Lord, she remembered the phrase, right? It was like five years ago, but please, call the cops. She remembered the phrase, right? And who's van is that in the parking lot? Must be Jim's.* Fischer's mind began to race through various scenarios of how this all might play out and remeasured his cavalier approach with Jim.

"I need you to stand and face the wall now," Jim said, rising from his chair.

Luther perched in position as Fischer held his collar, waiting at the ready, and still out of sight.

"*Seelsorge*," Fischer said collectedly.

"Huh?"

"It's what I do for a living. Seelsorge. It's an old German word for 'caretakers of souls.' And, Jim, I can see that your soul is conflicted. You're hurting greatly. You don't want to do this."

Jim's facial expression revealed to Fischer that something he said registered inside of him. Fischer could see Jim was starting to second guess himself. *Onward.* "It begins by putting the gun down," Fischer directed.

"I'm trapped," Jim said. "I can't turn back. I have to do this test. Mr. Fischer, you are half of the Pisces... I *have* to deliver. El Nachash will be very angry with me if I don't succeed. Very angry..."

"But this isn't you, what's your name, your *real* name?" Fischer asked softly.

"Tommy..." James said, with blank eyes.

"Tommy, it's spiritual triage," Fischer said.

Tommy lifted up the syringe in his left hand as the gun quivered in his right. "I have to. I'm sorry. I don't want to think what El Nachash would do if I *fail* him."

"Tommy, I assess where people are hurting and apply what aspect of God's Word might serve them best in the moment, either with the Gospel…" Fischer rose and walked toward the wall he was motioned to put his hands upon and did so. "Or when necessary, with the Law… *Now,* Luther!"

Chapter 37

DETECTIVE GEMMA JADE SAT IN her pearl white Ford Mustang outside a downtown LA warehouse deep in thought under her sunglasses. She fidgeted with a lone cigarette in her hand, sliding her fingers down each side, flipping it, and doing it over and again on the console. She shut off the engine, got out, and stood in her civilian clothes, blue jeans, and a Mellow Mushroom T-shirt.

She lit her cigarette and took one puff observing the Van Gogh Immersive Experience marketing signs in front of her. She took her sunglasses off in irritation. "Chase... You *stinker*," she sighed in mild frustration. She extinguished her mostly unsmoked cigarette and tossed it into a nearby trash can and walked inside the warehouse.

After a quick ticket exchange through the exhibit gate attendants, Jade was in the experience. Iconic Van Gogh images greeted her through the entry passageway. Massive cut outs, three dimensional pieces, designs, and set pieces came alive with motion, light, and sound. She turned the corner deeper into the immersion experience which lived up to its name.

Darkness encapsulated Jade at first until she rounded the next turn into a larger section of the warehouse. Erected corridors of artwork and paneling created a labyrinth maze effect for her to tour through. A decent sized crowd of people were scattered throughout, milling through the maze, reading, pointing at art pieces, and studying the exhibit. The darkness was accentuated by each panel and large rendition of art that glowed with translucent psychedelic colors. Soft melodious classical music steeped the room in a somber ambience.

As Jade began her walking tour, many of the panels which appeared to float in the darkness in front of her contained quotes of Van Gogh, large reproduced handwritten notes to Vincent's brother, Theo, referencing life, travels, his art, and philosophy. Jade quickly became impressed with how many of the accompanying art pieces Van Gogh had described in deep thoughtful literary format.

Jade slowly read each panel and meandered through until one of Van Gogh's quotes jumped out at her.

"In my picture of the Night café, I have tried to express the idea that the café is a place where one can destroy oneself, go mad or commit a crime. In short, I have tried ... to express the powers of darkness in a common tavern."

Jade scrutinized the piece of art, *The Night Café*, Van Gogh's infamously disturbing pool hall scene, with its clashing colors and drunkards scattered about the periphery of the frame, with various alcoholic drinks.

"Another ominous Van Gogh *Café* piece..." Jade wondered aloud, triggering the memory of the line that came with Squirrel's severed ear. "He knows the Way... to the next... *Café*..." A cutesy bohemian-looking exhibit attendant walked by as Jade seized her opportunity. Her name tag said 'Talitha' with a small caption underneath which read: *Did you Gogh to the Immersion Experience?* Jade took a stab. "Excuse me, Ta-*lee*-tha?"

"It's *Tal*-i-tha," the tall brunette thirty-something girl numbly sighed, as if she'd corrected a thousand people before.

"Could you tell me a little more about this *Night Cafe* piece, please?"

"Oh, sure. This is one of my favorites," she perked up. "It's set in Arles, France. Van Gogh even said it was one of the ugliest paintings he'd ever done. He's attempted to show the lowest edge of humanity, with visceral impact. He uses strong contrasting colors for tension, evoking human emotion. The sightlines and angles don't match up, which conjures the illusion to almost pull the viewer into the poolhall night café itself. The pool table is at rest, suggesting the night is late as the clock illustrates. The drunks are in an obvious late hour of the night stupor, with bottles of wine, beer, whisky and absinthe present. The yellow dark shadow under the pool t—"

"*Absinthe?*" Jade asked.

"Yeah. Van Gogh was *huge* into absinthe. A lot of the impressionists and artisans were at the time," Talitha said, innocently towering over Jade's shorter frame.

"It's just that it's an exceedingly rare drink of choice, isn't it?" Jade asked.

"Today, yeah, I suppose. Not so much then. In that pocket of time, it was all the rage. It had a lot of powerful hallucinogenic effects, but was outlawed in France for a long while, for such reasons. Van Gogh drank it a lot. It was one of his favorite drinks. It appears in his painted works with some frequency. In the *Night Café* here, look there in the lower left-hand corner, a carafe of absinthe. There's another painter, Henri de Toulouse-Lautrec, who painted a brilliantly colorful portrait of Van Gogh drinking absinthe. It was sort of the zeitgeist during that period."

"Did you say Van Gogh painted absinthe *frequently*?" Jade asked eagerly as her phone rang. She looked quickly. Praider. She answered it.

"Yeah, and probably even drank some *while* he painted," Talitha said. "Sorry, I gotta run, and check on a couple things, just look around, enjoy, there's more of that on the tour if you're into that kind of stuff." Talitha excused herself.

"Thanks," Jade said, "Hey, Praider. What's up?"

"A *lot*," Praider said excitedly. "So, get this, that lead I tracked down, from the old police report through DCFS, this Autumn gal... Turns out she runs and owns a *café,* which is interesting for a variety of reason, but even more so, she *knew* the child's father, Jim Latham, but by a different name. Morgan Stern. Sound familiar?"

"Na-*uh*," Jade said in shock.

"Wait for it, it gets better... he also uses a pseudonym... on a certain website... El Nachash."

"*What?*" Jade said, dumbfounded.

"Jim Latham, Morgan Stern, and El Nachash are all three, one in the *same* person. A bit of a bombshell you might say. Anyhow, I informed Greppin and Chief, but I thought you'd enjoy telling Fischer yourself. Great work, GJ. Where are you now? We've got a big strategy planning session coming up fast."

"I'm tracking down one last lead," Jade said. "Almost done." Jade turned the corner into the final room, a grand two-story high warehouse with surrounding images of Van Gogh's paintings. Her eyes landed on one particular image, freezing her in her tracks.

"Praider, I gotta go. I'll be in touch soon. I need to focus real quick, sorry, bye."

Click.

Jade stared in disbelief of the subject matter in front of her, dwarfed by the two-story image towering over her. "No *way*…"

Chapter 38

LUTHER LUNGED TOWARD HIS MASTER'S assaulter, channeling all the aggression of a werewolf. Tommy shrieked in surprise as Luther jumped up and bit his right arm holding the gun, but not before he jabbed the syringe of the tranquilizer into the back of Fischer's neck.

BLAM!

The piercingly loud sound of the fired gun went off immediately next to Fischer's right ear. The force of Luther, and the ear-piercing gunshot propelled all three of them to fall to their left. The gun fell and bounced back toward the center of the office room. Fischer fell hitting the left side of his head along the bookcase next to him. Luther pounced on top of Tommy.

Fischer could only watch in stunned shell shock from the floor. Luther went for the jugular, but Tommy fought him off with both arms and rolled side to side until he managed to curl onto his knees. Luther started working on his other arm as Tommy howled in pain. Tommy's thick jacket sleeves protected him, but only a bit. It wasn't a match for an angry German Shepherd's rapier sharp teeth, which ripped through the jacket sleeve, his shirt, and finally into his skin. Luther instinctively stood over the gun in the center of the room, as if he had been trained to do so. Tommy looked around for anything to use to defend himself. He quickly noticed a small wooden chair behind him in the corner of the room.

Fischer laid on the floor vexed in pain. He closed his eyes in concentrated focus. He sorted through his thoughts as quickly as he could. He could feel through the floor reverberations the struggle going on near him, though the violent ringing in his ears muted most of the sounds. *Come on Luther, get him...* The left side of Fischer's head throbbed in pain from the collision into the bookshelf. *Seemed like a glancing blow. Should be okay. Still, it didn't tickle.* Fischer rolled onto his back, bending the syringe at an angle causing a whole new element of agony. *Oh, Man, it's still in there... How much did he inject? Got to get it out...* Fischer tried to remove it while keeping an eye on Luther's battle. His hearing was slowly starting to return.

Tommy grabbed the small chair and swung it around. First, he tried to crash it over Luther's head, but Luther's nimble athletic agility outmatched Tommy's. Tommy quickly realized this, switching into a circus lion tamer defense mode with the chair. He kept looking around in the room for anything that might aid him. He noticed a closet door behind him. He speedily opened it recognizing it possessed plenty of space for the menacing dog attacking him. "Let's get you in here, puppy," Tommy said with eerie intensity.

Fischer could tell the mild numbing sensation of the tranquilizer was beginning to take effect. He'd had too much whisky a time or two before. He knew what it felt like to be buzzed, but this was a *completely* different experience. The drowsy blackness began to creep into the edges of his vision. Fischer attempted to grab the needle, but he struggled to reach it. *Why can't I get this? Starting to lose motor skills...* Fischer finally grabbed ahold of the syringe and yanked it out, sitting up with his back against the wall. He continued to watch in increasingly groggy detail the violent scene playing out in front of him. *Gotta stand up if I have any chance here.*

Tommy wildly screamed and thrust the chair at Luther, trying to gain a more advantageous position and corner him. Luther bit the bottom center rung of the chair and began a life and death tug of war. Tommy was able to leverage the clenching jaws of Luther, inch by inch, slowly but sufficiently to where Luther stood in front of the open closet door. Tommy charged forward shielded by the chair, backing Luther into the closet. He slammed shut the closet door, closing Luther within.

Tommy turned around in a drained huff. He assessed his wounds and caught eyes with Fischer who had just finished push-sliding his back up the wall with his legs. Fischer once again stood on his feet. Luther's barks grew louder. Fischer glanced down to the gun in the center of the office floor. Tommy glanced down at his gun and looked back at Fischer. Their eyes met across the room from each other. Fischer never dreamed he'd have an O.K. Corral moment in his life, but this was it.

Fischer felt like hell, but dug deep, recalling his old Wisconsin track coach's mantra barked at him every time his body wanted to quit at the end of an excruciating speed drill session on the track. *'This is the whole workout right here!'* This always seemed to push Fischer on for that last ounce of energy to force himself to the end. *Come on Chase, this is it...*

Fischer summoned every drop of energy and adrenaline and surged forward toward the gun on the floor. Immediately Tommy leapt in reaction towards the gun as well. The two collided as if at the bottom of a football scrum fighting over a fumbled ball. Fischer grabbed the gun, but Tommy's two meaty hands clamped around his. They rolled and struggled. Tommy pinched Fischer's hand and wrist then he started to bite Fischer's hand.

"Ahhhhhhhh!" Fischer screamed. "You rat *bastard*."

The gun dropped. The two wrestled a second more, but Fischer could feel the drugs taking more effect, though he still tried to fight. Fischer rolled over onto his back trying to extend his reach for the gun, but Tommy managed to snag it first and trundled atop of Fischer. *This is bad.*

Fischer clutched the gun in Tommy's hand and pulled it forward tussling more, figuring the closer their fight remained physically, the better chance he had. Fischer's eyes were blacking out more and more. Luther roared behind the closet door. Fischer yelled. Tommy yelled.

BLAM!

The last thing Fischer realized was the warm wet sensation of blood oozing across his torso.

Chapter 39

IN THE VAN GOGH IMMERSION Experience warehouse exhibit, Jade stood mesmerized by the gargantuan art image appearing before her. The painting title read: *Café Table with Absinthe*. Jade stepped back, as if assaulted by the two-story wall sized image all but screaming at her. The unusual green drink, captured in still life on a table next to a carafe, just like the *Café at Night* painting.

Jade spun around in the large warehouse room dizzy in thought, completely encapsulated by the surrounding four walls, floor, and ceiling all slowly transitioning through Van Gogh's major works, through motion, sound, lighting, and color. She took out her note pad to scribble a few notes.

As she thought, she observed small crowds and clusters of people milling about the room appreciating the art before them. One young ballerina woman danced in the corner as various backdrops changed, while her boyfriend snapped photos of her. Others sat on benches basking in the experience.

Jade wrote her thoughts down in phrases. *He knows the Way... to the next Café, Absinthe? Van Gogh's favorite drink of choice. Café Table with Absinthe. The Night Café (includes absinthe)* Jade bit the back of her pen, thinking long and hard before she wrote down her next word. *Bostic?*

The images around Gemma Jade kept swirling and evolving until a large portrait of Van Gogh stared back at her, a painting he did just after severing his own ear, with a blue hat, green coat, and the unmistakable white bandaging covering his right ear. Jade tapped the back of her pen on the pad for a moment and then wrote down her next thought. *Squirrel?*

A dark figured man with a slicked back ponytail spied Detective Jade slowly wandering about the large room. He stood behind a pillar. The tone of the room shifted to Van Gogh's nocturnal pieces. First the *Café Terrace at Night* gradually took over and occupied the entire room, beginning with the stars, and systematically filling in the colors and images of the street, the people, the tables, the yellows contrasted against the dark blues of the sky. The mood sounds pumping through the room fit the moment.

The man watched as Jade dialed her cell phone, listened, and spoke. The room now began its methodical shift to the next nocturnal painting, *Starry Night Over the Rhone*. The crowd of people verbally reacted with typical "ooohs" and "aaahs." Jade finished her phone conversation and hung up.

He cautiously crept toward her from behind. He drew closer until he said in uncomfortably close distance to Jade, "I've always loved Van Gogh. And I very much enjoy the fine art appreciation this good city of ours has to offer."

Jade looked over her shoulder at the man with the ponytail. "Sorry, do I know you?" she asked coldly.

"I don't believe we've met," the man said.

This was not the first time she'd been hit on by some weird art enthusiast. She steered the conversation with experienced poise. "Well, I was about to get going…"

The room began to transition once more to Van Gogh's magnus opus, *The Starry Night* ushering the crowd into as much a frenzy as an art exhibit can demand, with flash cameras, selfies, family's barking orders to gather into group shots, and cellphone videos.

"Oh?" the man said. "But this is the best part, *Starry Night*." He swooped his left arm out in front of Jade's view, pointing to the incredible art, drawing Jade's attention, and distracting her from his right arm. He pulled a syringe from his pocket and calculatedly put his arm around her. "And Venus… the rising *morning star*." He delivered the line with emphasis as he jammed a tranquilizer needle discreetly into the right side of Jade's neck, quickly pushing his thumb down, and completing the injection.

Jade stirred briefly, stumbling, as the man caught her balance. "Easy does it. Shhhh. It's a starry night night to you…"

Jade started to slump back losing consciousness. The last thing that registered for her was his parting line: "I am El Nachash, and I'm excited to meet you, my *Andromeda*." Jade could feel her eyes bulge wide when he identified himself but knew she had lost all control and functionality of her body before everything faded to black.

El Nachash carefully wrapped Jade's arm around his shoulder and hoisted her up into his arms. He headed toward the exit. A youngish male exhibit attendant approached him.

"Sir, is everything all right?"

"My wife is diabetic. Her blood sugar crashed, it's okay, happens from time to time, a little warm in here too. No worries. I'll get her out to the car, some cool air conditioning, and we've got some snacks out there."

"Are you sure?"

"I've got it. Thanks," El Nachash said in total control of the situation, as he was used to. He headed outside carrying Jade and made his way toward his sleek black Hummer in the parking lot. He looked around. No one in sight. He opened the back doors, laid her down gently inside, crawled in and pulled the doors shut.

Chapter 40

FISCHER BEGAN TO COME TO. The slow orientation of identity, time, and place reemerged in his still pulsating brain as he gradually regained consciousness. He remembered a warm wet sensation from before, but now it was different, higher. *Is someone soothing me? Kissing me? Gemma?* Luther's moist tongue lapped over Fischer's saliva-soaked face as his eyes opened splashing him back into reality. "Hey boy," Fischer said weakly.

"He's coming back," Jeannie's familiar voice said.

Fischer's thoughts came crashing back one at a time. *A man visited. Named Jim, but that wasn't his real name. Tommy. He was with El Nachash's 'True Nativity' cult. He had a gun.* "Ugh. My head..."

"Let's get him up."

Fischer recognized Greppin's deep bass voice immediately. Before Fischer knew it, he was sitting back in his cozy black office chair behind his desk. An EMT flashed a small light into Fischer's eyes, mildly blinding him for a moment.

"He's fine," the EMT said. "No cuts, wounds or blood loss here, no contusions, no signs of trauma at all. I'll double back in a bit, but, yeah, pretty much unscathed. Amazing." The EMT returned his attention to the others on the floor.

Fischer surveyed the room through blurry eyes. He saw Jeannie and

Detective Greppin, looking over him, Luther at his feet, and two more EMT's working on a very bloody Tommy on the office floor. *That's a lot of blood.* Fischer looked down at his clothes. *Yuck, I have a lot of blood.*

Blue and red flashing lights flickered through the windows causing Fischer to carefully swivel in his chair and look outside his window. Three cop cars somehow took a commanding presence of the whole church parking lot, lighting it up like Christmas.

Fischer turned back. "So… What *happened*?" He loosened his tie and took off his blood-stained dress shirt.

"You were lucky. And apparently you have an *incredible* secretary," Greppin said, jealously.

"Luck had nothing to do with it," Jeannie said. "You cued me with the 'cream and sugar' reference, so I knew something bad was about to go down."

"But you drove away," Fischer said inquisitively.

"Looked pretty convincing, didn't it?" Jeannie said with a couple quick-twitch eyebrow raises. "I just looped back around to the other end of the parking lot, made the 911 call, and came in the rear of the building. When I came to your office door, I could hear a struggle, but the cops obviously weren't here yet." Jeannie flashed a playfully skeptical glance at Greppin.

"Hey," Greppin lifted his hands innocently. "I think she should work for us."

"Jeannie served directly under an Admiral in the United States Navy. The LAPD would probably be a step down," Fischer said, cracking a smile.

"*Anyhow*," Greppin said, seizing control, "then what happened?"

"I could tell it was about to get out of hand, I opened the door, and, well, I did what any church secretary worth her salt would have done…"

"You *shot* him?" Fischer asked.

"I *shot* him," Jeannie said self-assuredly with a quick rock of her chin. "He was on top of you, pastor, holding a gun. I was well within my rights, officer. And I intentionally avoided all major organs."

"Well done," Greppin said, with sincerity. "We'll still have to sequester your firearm temporarily, you know… processing and reports."

"No problem, officer," Jeannie said winking at them. "I have more."

"I'll bet you do," Greppin said with a rare smile. "All right, this guy's gonna live, and that's great, cause we're gonna be asking him a *lot* of questions. Obviously, he's under arrest. It's gonna be a long fun week getting to know this guy after he's patched up…"

"One, two, *three*." The EMT's lifted and carried Tommy out on a stretcher. Greppin looked over the mess of a room that was Rev. Dr. Chase Fischer's office "Pastor Fischer, you've been through quite a lot, *again*. I'm making an executive decision. Rest up, heal up this weekend, focus on your Sunday services, and maybe come into the station Monday morning, but only if you're feeling up to it. We'll have a lot to discuss. GJ will be back in then too after her break. We can circle the wagons, make our plan, and go and stop this guy."

"Yeah… Fischer reflected. "It *was* disturbing, but what haunts me is that guy… Jim, James, Tommy, whomever he was, was in that 'True' Nativity cult group… He saw himself as some extension of this El Nachash guy. He wanted to take me *alive*… needed to, for 'the scroll' to unfold…"

"That *is* haunting," Greppin admitted.

"The worst part," Fischer continued, "he said I was 'half of Pisces.' Pisces, the pair of fish. It's next in this Mazzaroth murder sequence. Greppin… If I'm 'half of Pisces' who's the other half?

# # #

El Nachash sat in the passenger's seat of his Hummer as it pulled out of the warehouse parking lot into the busy evening traffic. He looked back at Detective Jade, unconscious in the rear of the vehicle. "Do you think she'll be out the whole way?" El Nachash asked with mild concern.

Chad Bostic glanced in the rear-view mirror at Jade and looked at El Nachash before refocusing on the road. "I made a strong dose this time. With her petite height and weight, she should be out for a real long time. No problem. But we can stop at my house in Glendale if needed before we head out to Antelope Valley."

"Excellent," El Nachash said. "The time continues to draw nigh."

"Any word on Pastor Fischer?" Bostic asked.

"I sense the fish may have squirmed off the hook," El Nachash said in disappointment. "My protégé did not call me as I specifically instructed him to do after he had him in hand. Hence, I fear he was unable to follow through."

"Then what next?" Bostic asked.

"I'll have to send him a message. I assure you; I can find another way to make him squirm. God will smite him…" El Nachash said with a sneer. "And I shall be his instrument."

Chapter 41

Monday, January 27th
10:35 A.M.

FISCHER HAD DONE AS DETECTIVE Greppin advised. A couple of down days rotating from his bed to his leather Lazy Boy, cuddled with Luther at his side was just what the doctor ordered. Fischer had somehow misplaced his cellphone, but temporarily being off grid was more of an unintended blessing than an annoyance for the time being. Fischer processed through the last few weeks as he wrote a powerfully well-crafted message and proclaimed it to his congregants over the weekend.

A little Sunday afternoon NFL playoff action with some takeout hot wings and a beer capped Fischer's weekend of convalesce. *Man, the Detroit Lions, out of nowhere this year.* He rose Monday morning, rejuvenated and ready to see Detective Gemma Jade and get to the bottom of this star-crossed killer insanity. But still no cellphone. *What the heck.* Fischer rode down to the LAPD station. *This whole chaplain thing is kind of growing on me.*

Detective Justin Praider escorted Fischer into the interrogation observation room. *Relieving to be on this side of the window.* Fischer could see Detective George Greppin had already begun the morning session with Tommy. Fischer was amazed Tommy was not still in the hospital. *Who had the better skill? The physician who patched him up, or Jeannie, who knew how and where to aim and avoid catastrophic damage?*

Chief Tatum sipped coffee, watching through the window as Greppin thundered away with his questions. Tatum turned and greeted Praider and Fischer. "Reverend. How'd you recover over the weekend?" Tatum asked.

"I'm feeling back, sir."

"Thanks for giving all the details to George the night you were attacked. He prepped early this morning for this from your report. It's been helpful, well done."

"Thanks."

"What do you suppose 'the recompense' meant?" Tatum asked.

"Not sure yet exactly," Fischer said with split mind. "Is Detective Jade here?"

"I haven't seen her this morning. I don't believe she's checked in yet." Tatum said, urgently turning back to the interrogation. He raised his hand to halt the chatter. "Hold on, Greppin's about to switch his tactic, by design. I don't want to miss this. We haven't gotten much of anything out of him yet using his real name, Tommy. George is about to address him as Jim now."

Through the window into the interrogation room, Fischer could see Greppin stood in extreme intimidating fashion over Tommy who appeared more than miserable. His eyes were watery and red from exhaustion. He stared down, zombie-like. A dull tremble quivered throughout his body, slumped over in a chair. Comparatively, Fischer satisfyingly recognized he had held his own in that room much better than Tommy was currently doing. Fischer listened intently.

"Okay, let's try it your way, *Jim*," Greppin said. "What were you doing at Pastor Fischer's church?"

Suddenly Tommy stopped trembling and looked up. He started to laugh faintly to himself, causing Greppin to scowl.

"You think this is funny?" Greppin asked. "Is it funny getting shot? Where'd you get the tranquilizer?"

Tommy looked directly into Greppin's eyes for the first time and laughed harder. "If only you knew."

"Where were you planning on taking Pastor Fischer?" Greppin asked.

Tommy became more serious and began muttering in a monotoned whisper.

Fischer leaned forward and concentrated hearing Tommy's voice, "...Eight, nine, ten, eleven, revelation...Eight, nine, ten, eleven, revelation...Eight, nine, ten, eleven, revelation..."

"Tell me about The True Nativity," Greppin asked annoyedly.

Tommy kept mumbling the same line over and over. "...Eight, nine, ten, eleven, revelation...Eight, nine, ten, eleven, revelation...Eight, nine, ten, eleven, revelation..."

"Who is El Nachash?" Greppin asked.

"...Eight, nine, ten, eleven, revelation...Eight, nine, ten, eleven, revelation...Eight, nine, ten, eleven, revelation..."

Greppin walked behind Tommy, and looked through the window to the team, mouthing the words: "I think we're done." Greppin passed off Tommy to another officer, and quickly joined up with Fischer, Tatum, and Praider.

"Whatcha think, Chief?" Greppin asked.

Tatum smiled. "I finally think it has *everything* to do with the zodiac."

"How so?" Praider asked.

Tatum counted with his fingers, "The zodiac so far has been Virgo, Libra, Scorpio, Sagittarius, Capricorn, Aquarius. If that's one through six, *and* he referenced our fine chaplain here as Pisces last night,"

"Seven," Greppin said.

"His pattern of 'eight, nine, ten, eleven, revelation' seemed to allude to the continued progression, if not culminating in some big revelation," Tatum said.

Fischer was lost in thought. *Where is Gemma? She should be here by now.*

"Fischer?" Praider asked. "What do you think?"

Praider's prompting jolted Fischer back to the moment at hand. "Um, possibly, sir. You might be right, but it's just that, technically it comes up short. If eight is Aries, that would mean Taurus and Gemini are nine and ten, and then Cancer. That's only eleven. He doesn't say 'twelve,' revelation."

Tatum shook his head. "Twelve would *be* the revelation."

"This guy is so specific with his clues, and the wording," Fischer said.

"It just stands out to me as odd."

"What's the twelfth sign?" Praider asked.

"Leo… the lion," Tatum said conclusively. "Yes, I suppose there is *that* slight sliver of a conundrum."

Fischer mused aloud. "And according to the stars, or rather, El Nachash's disturbed Mazzaroth interpretation of them, Leo would most likely be the Biblical Lion of Judah… slaying the hydra… the multi-headed hydra. It's another variant form of the Christ figure slaying the serpent."

Fischer put his hands and arms behind his head in surrender cobra formation, vexed in desperate thought. "It doesn't matter anymore," he said. "Gentlemen, we are *not* going to allow this to play out to the end. *Not* six more months. We can't. We won't." Fischer slammed his arm on the table. "I refuse to accept that. We are not going to even let this go one more time."

Fischer tapped his finger over his lips thinking intently. "A *multi-serpent-headed hydra*… Which raises the issue; how many people are working for this El Nachash anyway?"

Praider spoke up. "Funny you should phrase it that way. We were gonna have GJ tell you, but I discovered that amazingly, Jim Latham, Morgan Stern, and El Nachash are *all* the same person."

"You're kidding. Is that right?" Fischer asked, processing the information. "Yet my question still stands. How many heads to this hydra? How many are working for El Nachash? There was a white van in the church parking lot last night when I met with Tommy. It left late at night, but Tommy didn't drive away in it. Greppin had Tommy."

"So, who did?" Tatum asked.

Fischer couldn't stand it anymore. "And as for GJ. Guys, not to jump too quickly to conclusions, but where is she anyway? Should we be concerned?"

"Have you called her?" Greppin asked.

"No, I… didn't," Fischer said guiltily. "I seemed to have temporarily misplaced my phone."

Praider began calling her on his cell phone. "It's ringing… She's not picking up," he said, ear to phone. Chief, you want us to do a well-being check on her?"

Fischer gasped. "If they knew how to find *me*, presumably from the

Aquarius attack, where they may very well have gotten Squirrel, are we so recalcitrant to assume none of the rest of us there that night might also be susceptible, particularly if this Tommy guy said I was *half* of Pisces… could…" Fischer thought through everything. "Could she somehow be the other half?"

"Fischer makes a great point, sir. He's been right on all counts so far," Greppin said.

"As usual," Tatum said.

"I'll check GJ's apartment," Greppin said.

"Does your church have outside cameras?" Praider asked Fischer.

"As a matter of fact, it *does*," Fischer said.

"Let's see if we can't get some digits off that white van's plates."

Chapter 42

FISCHER TOSSED THE BALL AROUND with Luther a bit in his back yard then returned inside. He scrambled through his couch crevices and chair cushions a second time looking for his cellphone. *Where in the world are you?* He bounded up the stairs into his bedroom and sifted through his clothes strewn about. All his usual jacket and pant pockets came up empty. Fischer studied his closet, examining each article of clothing he could have possibly worn and left it in. *Nope. And I already looked at the office. Where are you? Gotta head over there and set up Praider with Jeannie.*

Fischer let Luther out the back door into the fenced backyard. "Luther, you hang outside for a while." Fischer felt guilty not playing with his dog more lately. The poor dog was always inside. "Back in a bit, boy." Fischer tossed Luther a milk bone and began his stroll to his office at the Church of the Epiphany.

A dull thunder rolled in the distance. *Rain? That'd be rare. We need it desperately in this drought though.*

By the time Fischer got to the church office, Praider had already introduced himself to Jeannie, who never failed to greet Fischer warmly. "Hi, Pastor. We're going through yesterday's footage, and will try our best on that white van," Jeannie said.

Praider's phone rang.

"You live for this military surveillance sort of thing, don't you, Jeannie?" Fischer asked. Jeannie offered her quintessential smile as Praider stepped aside for his call.

"Speaking of cellphones, have you seen mine, Jeannie?"

"Nope, sorry."

Praider walked back into Fischer's earshot. "Okay, thanks, Grep." He ended the call. "Jade's not at her place, neighbors say they haven't seen her car for a couple days."

Jeannie gave a look of maternal concern to Fischer. "Oh no, that's your officer friend from the hospital, right?"

"She was headed to this Van Gogh Immersion Experience thing last I knew," Fischer said. "She said she was looking forward to a long weekend. She could have driven away somewhere, right?" Fischer asked them unconvincingly.

Praider tapped his fingers on the office countertop in thought staring at Fischer. "But she didn't report for her shift. "You said she went to some art exhibit. Did anyone else know she went there?"

Fischer shook his head in thought. "Not that I know of."

"She'll turn up soon," Praider said with a twinge of false bravado in his voice.

"Who are you trying to convince?" Fischer asked.

Praider shrugged and returned his attention to Jeannie. "It's never good to assume anything. All right, Miss Jeannie, what do we have to work with?" They began scouring the computer screen video imagery.

Fischer headed to his office and stood in the room quietly for a moment. The blood stain in the center of the floor was inescapable. He closed the door, thinking through the previous violent event that had occurred there, and thanking God it hadn't ended disastrously different.

Fischer grabbed a few pieces of paper and covered the stain, so he didn't have to look at it anymore. *The building trustees will have their work cut out for them this week.*

Fischer sat at his desk and retraced his steps in his mind from the night before. He picked up the office phone on his desk and dialed his own cellphone number. Fischer's familiar ring tone sung out. "Where are you?"

Fischer stood up looking about and listened again, rounding his desk, and crouching down on the floor. He peered under a hollowed-out space under a set of bookshelves. "*There* you are." *Must have fallen out somehow during the tussle with Tommy.*

Fischer flattened his hand and inched it underneath, but his hand was too wide. He grabbed a ruler out of his office drawer and edged it out from under the shelving unit. "Finally."

He sat back down and examined his phone. Endorphins rushed through him as he realized a voicemail from Gemma awaited him. *Hmmm. Timestamped at 7:12 P.M. January 22. That was Wednesday night.*

Fischer tapped the icon and listened. "Chase. Gemma, I'm in the Van Gogh Experience... Listen, Chad Bostic in forensics texted me about Squirrel's ear earlier. So, I'm here, thinking about that, and Van Gogh's self-portrait of his own ear sliced off and, this... might be crazy, but I guess Van Gogh was apparently a huge *absinthe* drinker. It's in at least two of his paintings with the actual word 'café' in the title. Which is interesting with all the macabre stuff hovering around this subject matter from the whole 'He knows the Way to the next café' thing, and an ominous drink, connected to the thematic Last Supper death undertones drinking at the *Café Terrace at Night... Another* Café reference... Fischer, this might be really really dumb, but absinthe was Bostic's drink the night we all went to the Viper Room. And... I'm getting ahead of myself but Morgan Stern, Jim Latham, and El Nachash are evidently all the same person. Tech, business, and science... I really hesitate to say this, but could Bostic somehow be caught up in all this? His demonstrated acumen... it's kinda in his wheelhouse, right? Anyway, I wanted to tell you face to face, but I have a ton of thoughts spinning, so I wanted to share them with you as quickly as I could before I forgot any... That and... Yes, we'll have to do the Getty together sometime. She laughed. Alright, talk later, I'm being rude apparently and getting the stink eye from some people. *Bye.*"

Fischer popped up from his chair and sprang to his office door, flinging it open. "*Praider*, get in here."

Chapter 43

PRAIDER STOOD ALERT AS FISCHER quickly replayed the audio message from Jade. "She might really be on to something with all those Van Gogh connections," Fischer said. "Somehow it has to be all inter-related."

"Was that your big take away, Fischer? I don't get all that with the art obsession. You two *might* be right, but of greater concern is, A. You do realize she's making a speculative accusation against one of our own, *and* B. She said Bostic texted her yesterday, which solicits the question; did she text back? In other words, did he know where she'd be last night? Because *C*. She apparently never went home."

"We've got to find her," Fischer said desperately.

Praider put his hand on Fischer's shoulder. "Dr. Fischer, we've got to be *very* careful with this information, you understand me?" Praider asked. "Extremely careful. If Bostic isn't involved, or particularly if he is possibly involved, if this is handled wrong, things could get incredibly bad, incredibly fast, one way or another."

"Wait a minute," Fischer said. "The last thing Jade told me to do was check out that TrueNativity.com website, with my 'Bible mind,' to see if anything jumped out at me."

Fischer sat in his office chair, flipped on his computer, and surfed the website as fast as he could. He scrolled though the website remembering

Jade's request aloud. "With everything that's happened since, I guess I just forgot to look it over yet. Praider, if those three men are truly all one in the same, then Christian's life is in real danger. Not to mention Jade's."

Praider leaned in, pointing to the screen over Fischer's shoulder. "Look, there's a new video post…"

Fischer clicked on it and they watched. "That's *Christian*," Fischer said in terror motioning to the boy on screen.

A video showed an image of El Nachash speaking from a living room chair, with Christian playing on the floor in front of him, dressed in a Los Angeles Rams shirt.

"Hello, my faithful. This is a celebratory day. I am excited to introduce to you my Little Ram, and just in time for a New Moon restitution celebration, as we prepare him for his special welcoming ceremony. Long have I waited for this day, this moment in time to arrive, to share with you, and the world, my little Ram. Just as Abraham was so very proud of his son, Isaac, waiting so long for him to arrive by God's promise, I am all the prouder, and the wait just as untenable. Though, where he was called to show weakness, I have been called to demonstrate strength, for you and the *world*."

"Oh my, Lord. He's going to sacrifice him," Fischer said.

Praider turned to Fischer. "What? Why? How do you know?"

Fischer offered a weird glance to Praider. "Van Gogh told me."

"You're gonna have to explain," Praider said.

"Van Gogh's signature piece, *The Starry Night*, depicts the constellation Aries, which *is* the Ram… That was one of his little hints to us. And he's referring to him as his 'Little Ram." Praider, don't you remember your old Bible stories?"

"You'll have to refresh my memory on that one."

Fischer swiveled his chair and crossed his arms entering lecture mode. "Abraham was called by God to sacrifice his son, Isaac, but at the last second Abraham didn't have to, God was testing Abraham's faith… Abraham *proved* his faithfulness, and God spared his son, returning Isaac to him. Then the account says they sacrificed *specifically* a ram in Isaac's stead. But this whole, 'Where he, presumably like Abraham was called by God to be weak, but I am strong' stuff… This is pure evil."

Praider stood in the office in deep thought for a minute. "Fischer, keep researching this, see if you can dig up anymore details, times, locations, anything before we present this to the Chief. Jeannie managed to identify three letters off the white van from your church cameras, I'm gonna run those through the system. It will take a little longer, but that should be enough to track it down and put out an A.P.B. Meanwhile, don't say *a word* to anyone about Bostic, got it? That's a real longshot on Jade's part; we can't just throw accusations like that around on people in our department. That's a serious claim, if not libel. We'd have to be completely sure. I'm heading back into HQ. I'll be in touch." He left.

Fischer stood up to stretch, reflecting for a minute. He relaxed and hunched over his desk. He scrolled further through the website as he listened to Jade's message one more time. Her voice sounded even more tender and sweetly soothing as he anticipated the horror she might be enduring, or possibly already endured. *Absinthe?*

Fischer sat at his desk and researched absinthe. Phrases jumped out at him as he digested information. Van Gogh's drink of choice… dangerously addictive… psychoactive drug… hallucinogen… derived from the Latin: *artemisia absinthium*… wormwood… strong taste… easy to hide the flavor of poison…

Fischer stood and paced about his room, careful to avoid the paper covered bloodstains. His head raced and spun with information overload and too many looming questions to count. He sat down again at his desk, with both hands holding his head, trying to make sense of everything swirling about his mind.

Where Is Jade? Is she okay? Will I see her again? What about her voicemail? Are there more Van Gogh clues we missed? He knows the Way to the next Café… A heavenly Café? Absinthe? The Last Supper? Bostic? Squirrel? The Mazzaroth Pisces-Aries timeline? Christian? December 21, 2020? The 'Christmas' Star? Jim Latham? Morgan Stern? El Nachash? Tommy? The driver of the white van? Where to find them? How to stop them? What the hell is going on???

Fischer flailed his right arm across his desk in dramatic fashion causing several books, papers, and an old coffee mug full of pens to spill across the room and onto the floor. He breathed long and hard to catch his breath and calm down. He slowly began picking up his mess and sat down. His mug was broken. Fischer assessed whether it was repairable or not. *Nope.* He dumped it in the trash and stared back at his computer screen.

TheTrueNativity.com website stared back at him.

"*True* Nativity..." Fischer said, lacing the words with all the cynicism the world had to offer. *Nativity is the birth of Christ.* "Why call this the 'true' nativity?" Fischer deliberated aloud. "I've gotta meditate on this more."

And I know just the place.

A quick stroll down the hall and Fischer stood alone in the sanctuary. The scaping hammerbeam ceiling provided a classic gothic interior. The large deep sea blue two-story stained-glass windows created an aethereal doorway to heaven sensation. The antique windows, designed and brought over from Germany so many years before still echoed a more ancient, yet relevant story. The left side of the windows depicted scenes from the Old Testament, while the right shared images of the New Testament. The overwhelming central focal point that drew from both wings was the *Agnus Dei*, the lamb of God. The sacrificial lamb, or ram, typified in foreshadowing of the Old Testament, was ultimately fulfilled once and for all by Christ's sacrifice on the cross, delivering an eternal promise through his resurrection from the dead.

The light that shone through at this time of day was always mesmerizing for Fischer. He meditated in prayer as he saturated himself in the imagery once again. He lowered a kneeling bench in one of the long wooden pews and poised himself on his knees in prayer, looking up at the window. *Nativity is the birth of Christ... Christ is the lamb of God who takes away the sin of the world... Only by his sacrifice can people be saved... Why is sin so prevalent in the world? Why is this maniac doing all this? He knows the Way, to the Next café... the Café Terrace at night. Breaking bread and drink in fellowship... the Last Supper...*

Fischer looked up and studied the right side of the stained glass. A massive portion of the glass artwork was of the Last Supper; Jesus and his disciples, everyone drinking. *If El Nachash believes the true nativity is his son, and his little ram will be the sacrifice... then he sees himself as 'god.' His followers... recompense... a last supper... Absinthe... wormwood...*

Suddenly Fischer shot up in revelation. He grabbed a Bible sitting in the pew in front of him and searched for a reference in mind. He frantically flipped to the chapter and verse.

Fischer looked up in a scholarly studious trance. Everything started to become clear in a euphoric epiphany. The Way of the Mazzaroth, the unfolding of the scroll, the true nativity, The Christmas Star, the fish of Pisces representative of the God's people, a last supper, A New Moon celebration, Aries and Christian, sacrificial Ram, Van Gogh, the Stars, the café... even the role of absinthe. Finally... *Everything* made perfect sense.

Fischer whirled around and retrieved his cellphone from his pocket. He had to tell Praider and Greppin about his breakthrough. He had to tell Chief Tatum, *Dear God, there's got to be enough time to save Gemma.* Fischer's hands began to tremble with the information coursing through his brain, and the need to communicate it as fast as possible with precious life on the line.

As Fischer fumbled with his device the phone began to ring from an incoming call. Fischer recognized the number instantly. It was President Schumacher. *Now?* Fischer thought in fury.

Rev. Dr. Chase L. Fischer had been held in suspense of his future for too long, toyed with and mocked by the devil. His reputation had been unfairly tarnished through the entire scrutinized ordeal, examined under the microscope from the ecclesial hierarchy, while his character had been repeatedly attacked by social sideline snipers, shooting from the bell towers of his professional life. The phone kept *ringing*. The answer to Fischer's future career as an ordained minister awaited at the other end of the call. He took a long deep breath and clicked the green button.

"...Hello?"

Chapter 44

"PASTOR FISCHER?"

Fischer could hear President Harold Schumacher on the other end of the line, breathing in anticipation. *He's still calling me pastor. That's something at least.*

"Yes... Hello, President Schumacher?"

"Is this a good time, Chase? Do you have a moment?"

A splinter of lightning flashed outside which caught Fischer's eye through the stained glassed windows, followed by a grizzly thunder crash.

"Your timing is impeccable, sir," Fischer said.

"Good," Schumacher said. "Well, as you know I've been very busy tending to a billion ecclesial matters, on the local, national, and international level as well as in various public and private sectors..."

Enough bloviating. This is my life here. Get on with it. Chase thought to himself with a roll of his eyes.

"...But I have listened to many other bishops, their concerns, apprehensions and counsel pertaining to how to handle your, um, situational indiscretion."

The rain began to pour outside. *Great, I left poor Luther out in this.*

"Sir, with all due respect, I'm not sure it's fair to—

"The world isn't fair, Chase. Didn't your parents teach you that?

Neither is the Church. We don't operate in the realm of fairness. Gospel, grace, and mercy is when we get from God, that which we *don't* deserve..."

"Yes..." Fischer agreed cautiously.

"But we can't pass a blind eye to law, responsibility of actions, and truth either."

"*Truth?*" Fischer interjected with a slight elevation in his tone.

"The fact of the matter is, Chase, I've got, I mean that is, the presidium has right now a precursory straw poll seventy-five percent majority vote, in your favor to exonerate you from the situation."

"That's great," Fischer said relieved.

"I'm not done, son," Schumacher said admonishingly. "Remember, apparently, I need to remind you. You need *more* than a seventy-five percent majority vote, and I'm the tiebreaker. The official vote hasn't happened yet. That will take place tomorrow."

Oh, dear Lord, is he going to make me beg? Fischer didn't care to take a groveling approach, particularly when he knew he was innocent. He quickly switched his approach.

"Have you been lobbying against me?" Fischer asked directly. "Counting the votes you need beforehand and sending a message as you lord it over me?"

"I've done nothing of the sort," Schumacher said unconvincingly. "I've merely been doing my due diligence, as president, making sure everyone has all the information they need to make the best-informed decision they can when they vote. My daughter, Rosalynn, was *very* hurt by the whole thing, I'm sure you know."

"I see. Well, I'm sure the best construction was put on everything," Fischer said callously.

"There are days when I say, I can't believe I get paid to do my job, and then there are days when I say, 'you can't pay me *enough* to do this job," Schumacher said.

"And which day is this, Harry? It's as if you're willfully rooting for my defrocking," Fischer said sourly. He caught a little movement behind him, turned and saw Nancy, the church gossip, listening very carefully.

Fischer's eyes bored into her and she left in a startle. *How much did she hear?*

"Again, the official vote doesn't take place until tomorrow, but I just thought you might want to know where things stood, and to prepare you for what's about to happen."

"Is that all?" Fischer asked in irritation.

"All for now."

"It just seems odd how much enjoyment you seem to take out of this."

"There's no enjoyment here, Chase. Only disappointment."

"You got *that* right," Fischer fired back.

"I'll be in touch when all is decided and ratified and walk you through certain protocols, paperwork, and procedures," Schumacher said. There was a long silent pause.

"Goodbye, Chase."

The other end of the line went dead as Schumacher's words rang in Fischer's ear.

Goodbye, Chase... I can't believe this is happening.

Fischer collected and composed himself thinking through everything and headed back to the offices. *Ugh, Nancy.* The rain began to pick up, pounding on the building's exterior.

"Oh, Luther. Poor wet dog."

Fischer's walk turned into a trot as he neared Jeannie's desk.

"Is Nancy still here?" Fischer asked.

"She just rushed out, had some huge smile on her face when she said, 'bye' to me."

"Figures," Fischer muttered lost in thought. "I'll be right back."

He left the church of the Epiphany and entered the dark rain. Pastor Fischer had exited those doors thousands of times. But this departure felt very different this time.

Chapter 45

DETECTIVE JUSTIN PRAIDER TAPPED ON Detective George Greppin's cubicle frame in the LAPD headquarters. Phone calls and chatter buzzed around the space. "Grep, I've got some digits off that white van seen outside Fischer's church. Can you run it for me? I've got another, ah, little assignment I've got to check out real quick. Something one of my leads gave me is still bugging me."

Greppin took the slip of paper from Praider. "Sure thing."

Praider marched down to a private office, entered, and closed the blinds covering the clear glass. He searched through the office desk until he found the LAPD confidential photo directory. He quickly flipped through the pages, until he came to **Bostic, C.**

There was Chad Bostic's face. Praider took out his cellphone and photographed the image, carefully cropping out Bostic's credentials. He promptly walked out of the office and left the building. He crossed the busy street of traffic and sat down at a diner. He ordered a cup of coffee and took a deep breath. He looked over his shoulder. No recognizable faces from the department. He dialed his phone.

"Hello. Wiley Cat Café, how can I help you?"

"Hello, *Autumn*?"

"Yes?"

"This is Detective Justin Praider. We spoke a little while ago."

"Oh. Yes."

"Listen, you were very helpful the other day, and I had one more follow up question for you, if you don't mind..."

"Happy to help," Autumn said. "Shoot."

"You mentioned there was a guy, some friend of Moe's that showed up periodically. A science or some type of medicine guy, and such."

"Yeah, but I told you I don't remember his name. It's been so long."

"Right, but I wondered... Would you be able to recognize a photograph of him?" Praider asked.

"I dunno, maybe."

"I'll take a maybe. Is this a cellphone you're speaking on? "Uh-huh""Great, I'm gonna send you a pic. Hold on a sec." Praider searched through his phone, uploaded the pic, and clicked send, just as a waitress delivered his coffee in a ceramic cup and saucer. He carefully blew on it and took a sip, waiting in anticipation.

"Got it," Autumn said. "Okay... Lemme see... Wow. Yeah, wow, I think this is the guy."

"Are you sure?" Praider asked. "You have to be one hundred percent."

"Pretty sure. Again, it's been a while, I remember his hair darker, but yeah, I'd say, yeah. That's him."

"Thank you, once again. You've been very helpful. I would advise you to delete that image from your phone. I'll be in touch. Gotta run. Bye." Praider ended the call as abruptly as he did excitedly. He left a five-dollar bill next to his barely touched coffee still steaming on the table and darted back across the street hightailing it to Chief Tatum's office.

Tatum was on a call when Praider arrived outside his office. Praider respectfully eased his way in and with finger explosions of both hands signaled he had big news which trumped the importance of anything Tatum had going on at the moment.

"Hold on a minute," Tatum said. "I'm gonna have to call you back." He hung up the phone, annoyed. "This better be good, detective."

"Chief. I've got something you should know about. It's extremely sensitive." Praider closed the door. "It's Bostic, sir. Chad Bostic, in forensics.

I think he's involved in this whole zodiac killing spree. I have a witness who connects him with the strange details surrounding the forced induced birth of Christian, the Christmas Star baby kid, resulting in the death of the mother—"

"*What?*"

"That's not all. Fischer received a voicemail from Jade the night she went missing. In it she speculated Bostic is involved in her message to Dr. Fischer."

"I can contact Internal Affairs," Tatum said, perplexed.

Praider shook his head. "IAD? Sir, with all due respect, does GJ have the time it'll take to do that properly?"

Greppin tapped at the door. He opened it and entered as Tatum waved him in.

"Praider, Chief. I ran that plate on the white van of yours and got a hit. The owner is a one, get this, Wolfgang Manteuffel. A real mouthful of a name. I can have an A.P.B. put out in no time, just say the word."

Chapter 46

CHASE FISCHER WALKED BACK TO his home in the rain. His head spun with all the details of his life more than the leaves bustling around him in the wind gusts ever could. His umbrella shielded him slightly from the drops coming down. The weather was picking up, but Fischer's curiosity got the best of him. He opened his phone and touched the Facebook app. Nancy had already made a post which was getting a lot of traffic. Fischer read in horror:

It's a sad day for our Epiphany congregation, but we will be stronger for it... I hate to break the news, but the truth always comes out eventually. I have it on good authority that "pastor" Chase Fischer, will no longer be serving our parish. The sooner the better. Where there's smoke there's fire... #Defrocked

The number of likes was slowly elevating, which was alarming enough, but each line of the comment section hit like separate body blows.

Bout time...
He's too arrogant... Never liked him...
Wolf in sheep's clothing... IMHO
The audacity! Purge the evil among us...

Fischer tried to contain his fury and calculate through what an appropriate response might be. *Wow. Apparently, the commandment of not 'bearing false witness' has been suspended today... Any response on social media would just look too snarky and probably make matters worse. The record does need to be set straight as soon as possible, but what's the best way?*

A strong gust of wind blew Fischer's umbrella back, bending the metal irreparably. Fischer recognized immediately his cheap umbrella was a lost cause. The rain began picking up the pace, and so did Fischer's scurry back to his fading green and yellow house.

He rounded the corner looking for Luther in the backyard fenced area. No sight of him. *Odd. Must be hiding from the rain under a tree. Might as well snag the mail.* He snapped open his post box at the front of the drive, grabbed three envelopes out and scooted toward his garage door. The rain was starting to pelt. He typed in the code and the garage door slowly raised, clanging mechanical sounds and all. Fischer opened the side fence gate attached to the garage.

"*Luther*," Fischer yelled, and stepped inside the dry garage, soaked and sopping. He noticed two of the damp envelopes were usual bills, but the third was in emboldened type from **The California Highway Patrol**. *What's this?* Fischer quickly ripped it open, trying not to get it too wet. *A citation?* Fischer read the details and checked the date. He was guilty, running the red light, the day he chased after Christian being abducted from his home. *Honestly... Can't win for trying today... Luther should be here by now... Where is he?*

"Luther, Come on bo—"

Before Fischer could finish his phrase, something caught his eye. His front door was just barely visible from where he stood at the edge of the garage door out of the rain. It looked different. *Is that spray paint?* The dark blue painted words screamed vandalism to Fischer, but he couldn't read the message from his angle. He tossed down his things on the garage floor, walked out and stepped through the puddles, toward the porch to pull himself up and over. His last step in the muddy grass sucked his foot deeper than expected, soaking his shoe.

"*Gad.*"

He eventually managed to hoist himself over the rail onto the porch under the awning. The haunting black spray-painted words stung him like nothing ever before.

Andromeda is Ours.
Sirius-ly!
Much Restitution

An ominous smiley face was at the bottom of the words. *Andromeda? Another star constellation? What?* Fischer's mind flashed through thoughts as another thunder crash rolled through the sky. *And why spell Sirius that way? Sirius is the Dogstar... part of Canis Major... the dog star... Luther?*

"LUTHER?" Fischer hollered.

Fischer soaked in the words on his door one more time and hopped over the porch barrier back to the garage. He collected himself briefly and whizzed around the corner into the backyard.

Fischer scanned the grounds. He didn't see Luther anywhere. *Did they take him? How could they take him? Could whoever have driven the white van done something, taken him after what Luther did to that Tommy guy?*

"LUTHER!" Fischer barked one last time before turning back toward the garage and a hot shower. Something abnormal caught his eye. In the farthest corner of the yard under a bush was an unfamiliar mound.

Fischer slowly walked toward it. The mound became more and more familiar with each step closer.

"Oh no… Oh no… No… Please no…"

Fischer ran toward his best friend and once great German Shepherd.

"*Luther?* NOOOOO!"

Chapter 47

CHIEF TATUM STOOD OVER HIS desk addressing Praider and Greppin. His office door was shut. He spoke in a hushed voice. "Gentleman, if this is going to work it goes without saying, I need the *strictest* confidence from you two about what happens next."

"You have my word, Chief," Greppin said.

"Understood," said Praider.

"George. You have my authorization for S.W.A.T. The van was spotted at that *same* house in Glendale?" Tatum asked to reconfirm.

"It's the same house I checked with Fischer after the boy, Christian, went missing with his 'real' father," Praider said.

"The raid happens first strike, in the pre-dawn hours of the morning," Greppin said. "We'll be ready to hit 'em hard if need be."

"I don't have to tell you how important this one is," Tatum said. "Meanwhile, I'll be keeping Bostic busy on a special assignment through the night. God forbid, if he *is* involved, I don't want any interference from him. There's a lot of moving parts to this whole thing. I'm still doing some extra digging, and I'm trying to compartmentalize all this as best I can."

Tatum shook their hands. "Gentlemen, good luck."

"Let's do this," Praider said, with a testosterone-hyped glance at Greppin, causing a huge smile to flash across Greppin's face.

Greppin and Praider headed out and shut the door. Tatum looked over his bulletin board, studying the details once more and sat down at his desk. A knock at the door startled him. It was his middle-aged silver haired secretary. "What is it, Fran?"

"That information you requested about James Latham came in," Fran said.

"Tremendous. It pays to keep up relations with one's old Army buddies."

"If you say so," Fran said, handing the file to Tatum and leaving him to his solitude.

Chief Tatum opened the file and studied it for a while, pacing the room until he sat down in front of his computer. He hovered his mouse, opening his computer screen back to the TrueNativity.com website where he had been.

Tatum surfed through the web page a bit more clicking on different links and reading various articles. He refreshed the screen. To his delight a new live stream video link came up and would start momentarily. Tatum eagerly clicked the link and joined the queue. The numbers of followers soared into the tens of thousands as Tatum waited in anticipation. Finally, the video began.

El Nachash stood in full frame of the camera and spoke to his viewers. His hair flowed long, and his beard spread out. The lighting was dim, but his features were still readily visible.

"Salutations my fellow true believers. It is I, El Nachash. Our time is of the essence, the scroll is opening fast, and indeed already half-way revealed. The second half of the revelation is about to begin. You have been faithful with your following and your giving, and now it is time for us to gather together. A special ceremony is at hand this coming new moon. All true members of the church of the True Nativity are entreated to attend. The fulfillment of the truth is just about in our midst. You will not want to miss the ushering in of the full manifestation of this great event."

"What the *hell*?" Tatum asked himself as the video continued.

"You have followed the signs… You have observed the message… You know the next interval… And now you will know the way… Dear fellow church, let me tell you about our rendezvous for this most sacred ceremony. It is your destiny…"

Chief Tatum kept listening until the video live stream began wrapping up.

"Therefore come, and I shall lead you to the higher place. For a little while you will not see me, and then in a little while, you will." The live stream stopped. The website shut down.

"*What in the world?*" Tatum twisted in his chair in confusion. He thought for a moment and quickly scribbled down some notes on a yellow Post-it notepad and tucked it into his jacket pocket.

He quickly hopped on the phone and dialed. Chad Bostic picked up.

"Yes, sir?"

"Hey, Chad. How's my special project request coming along with the comparison and analysis?"

"Honestly, it's taking much longer than I expected. All this cross referencing. You sure you need all this done before tomorrow? *And* the paperwork? It's late. This is gonna take me all night."

"It's vitally important, Chad. A top priority of the strictest confidentiality. I have full confidence you can do it. This assignment is incredibly imperative to me, and time is of the essence. I'll tell you what, I'll even come down and keep you company, to help spur you along for a bit. You want a coffee?"

"Uh, sure," Bostic said in a surprised tone.

"I imagine you take it dark and bitter," Tatum said cryptically.

"Actually, yeah. Strong enough a spoon could stand up straight in it. How'd you know?"

"Just a hunch," Tatum said as he hung up the phone.

In the Forensic lab, Chad Bostic hung up the phone and immediately glided across the room on his rolling chair over to a drawer. He opened it. He checked the magazine in his gun. It was full. He cocked the top bullet into the chamber and laid it back down in the drawer. He picked up a tranquilizer syringe, filled it, and placed it in his lab coat pocket. He glided back to his station and continued his work.

Chapter 48

6:33 P.M.

BETRAYAL. REJECTION. HEARTBREAK. DEFEAT. DEVASTATION. Fischer had ticked off all these boxes of grief earlier in life. This manner of tragic loss was distinctive. There's no use comparing one's emotional pain to another's. One way or another, they all rip your heart out. It's only a question of how. Still, this felt different, Fischer supposed, as he trudged into the garage to fetch a shovel. This was unprecedentedly vindictive. He marched back to his dog. Luther was dead. His head, what was left of it, had been shot by what Fischer could only assume was one heck of a powerful gun.

The rain kept coming down blending in with the occasional somber tears that escaped past Fischer's defense mechanism of concealing his emotional pain. In this moment, he didn't care about Los Angeles city laws or county ordinances requiring citizens to not bury pets on residential property. All bets were off. The softened ground didn't put up much of a fight as his adrenaline kicked in. Fischer punished the earth making swift work of the task at hand. He carved out a four-foot-deep hole in record time.

"Goodbye, fella. Rest well…" Fischer heaved the last few crumbles of earth atop the grave, set a nearby stone in the center of the fresh soil mound, and plucked a single rose off his bushes, crowning the moment with a sliver of reverence. He tossed it over Luther's final resting place. Fischer went inside, threw his mud-soaked clothes in the laundry and took a long hot shower to rinse off the day.

In an hour Fischer was dry, though not feeling like a typical new man after bathing. He walked through the kitchen, barefoot in shorts and a t-shirt. He looked in the fridge, but nothing triggered his dormant appetite. He sauntered by his wet bar and stared at the tempting spirits looking back at him. *No...* Fischer thought, fighting the temptation.

Fischer opened his laptop and played a music loop. A compilation of *The Killer's* greatest hits. The somber ballad, *Be Still* played first, heightening the melancholy mood. He gave in and picked up a bottle of Jamison Irish Whisky and sat on the floor sipping straight out of the bottle. His room spun as he zig-zagged through various emotions. Each stage of grief lurked and rotated through the dark corners of Fischer's head. His mind raced. He didn't know how to make sense of everything, or what to do. He sang with the song.

"And when they drag you through the mud... Don't let it change what's in your blood..."

Fischer didn't know what next year might look like for him, or the next day for that matter. His phone rang. It was Jeannie. *Sorry, Jeannie, it's going to voicemail this time. Probably just about Nancy's post anyways. Oh well. I don't care anymore.*

The next emotion that splashed across Fischer's brain was that of a desperately confused version of guilt. He lowered the whisky bottle, savoring his current swig in his mouth, and remembered Gemma, and the nearing Lenten pact they made. And here he was, fast approaching a stupor, the likes of which he'd never known. He shot up and opened the front door, a little less stable in his stride than normal. He studied the spray-painted message again and took a photo of it. He sat down again on his living room floor near his bottle and opened his laptop. *Andromeda?* Fischer remembered how Perseus saved Andromeda in the ancient mythology story... *that's unsettling. Oh, God... Gemma... What are they going to do to you?*

Fischer never felt so helplessly powerless. He combed through different internet search engines. Fischer recalled the Mazzaroth murderer, El Nachash, or whoever he was, was currently still in the sequence of Pisces—the fish, two in number. Symbolic of the church, or at least El Nachash's "Church." Fischer was pretty sure what was soon to occur, but where? If Fischer was supposed to be one of the Pisces 'fish,' Gemma *had* to be the other in this sick plan now. Fischer looked up the decans of Pisces. Through all the previous events, research, and commotion he hadn't thought to do so yet.

He took another long shameful swig from his whisky bottle and continued to read in agony of the constellation patterns from which El Nachash was drawing his deviant plot.

The Decans of Pisces
1. The Band, holding up the Fishes, and held by the Lamb, its doubled end fast to the neck of Cetus, the Sea monster;
2. Cephus, a crowned king, holding a band and sceptre, with his foot planted on the polestar as the great victor and Lord;
3. Andromeda, a woman in chains, and threatened by the serpents of Medusa's head.

Fischer read on deeper into the night. His imagination, blended with alcohol and depression, getting the better of him. In another moment of weakness, he dared check what Nancy's post was doing. *Bad idea.* The proverbial mushroom cloud of its effect was blooming to full heights in the comment section. He clicked away and studied on, considering the potential fate of Gemma.

Andromeda, the beautiful woman, is representative of the church... She has fetters upon her wrists and ankles and fastened down so as to be unable to rise... This woman is the Decan... is the same as the Pisces sign... The change in image argues no change in the subject...

Fischer was just about halfway finished with his bottle of whisky, desperate in thought. *Andromeda is the potential bride of the Christ figure. If this El Nachash thinks he's some sort of new messianic persona...* A brief wave of self-awareness crossed Fischer's mind. *Oh, God. And who am I? Look at me... They better not do anything to her, but what can I do?* The Killers ballad had finished long ago. Their more anthemic *Dustland Fairytale* was playing now, channeling Fischer's depressed emotions up towards rage, with Gemma's potential peril at the forefront of his thoughts. He hit a crescendo when the song reached its bridge. He held up his bottle in toast-like fashion, sing-yelling out in harmony with the song lyrics, "Oh Cinderella don't you go to sleep… It's such a bitter form of refuge… Don't you know the kingdom's under siege… And everybody needs you… Is there still magic in the midnight sun? Or did you le—" Fischer's laptop died, leaving the drunk doctor of ancient history in silence to reflect on his decisions.

Fischer stood, barely. *Figures* he thought in annoyance. He slowly stumbled over to his composite photograph of all the pastors he'd graduated with from seminary. Too many faces already X'ed out. And now there would be one more. He grabbed his black permanent marker, uncapped the top and lurched forward to make it unofficially official. Before capitalizing on the thought, Fischer tripped over the foot of his chair, wickedly stubbing his toe, which started to bleed. He fell to the floor in pain and rolled on his back, nursing his sulk. *I can't do anything right anymore.*

As Fischer's thoughts flashed through a semantic field of which curse words to scream from his vast vocabulary, the front door handle began to turn. The door slowly creaked open.

Fischer considered being afraid for a split second then yelled out, assuming the worst of the mystery guest intruder. "Go on. You're back to finish me off. Go ahead and do it. Put me out of my misery."

The door swung wide, and Rev. Dr. Chase Fischer shivered in mortified shock at the person standing over him.

Chapter 49

DETECTIVE GEMMA JADE'S EYES OPENED. She was groggy as she lay in bed. The light was dim, but she could tell it was an unfamiliar bed. She slowly stirred, re-entering reality. She sat up and looked around. It was a small bedroom, simply decorated with bland eggshell paint, a single bed, a dresser, and a nightstand. Even a Motel 6 had pictures on the wall, for heaven's sake.

The small windows near the top of one of the walls let Jade know she was in a room of someone's semi-finished basement. The thin metal bars let her know she couldn't exit that way if she wanted. She stood and gazed out to see what view she could and discern where she might be. She could only see a wooden fence line and a couple small trees and bushes. Nothing more helped reveal her whereabouts.

She examined her room. Two doors. She opened the first one to her right. It was a small bathroom and a very welcomed sight. She enjoyed a few moments of freshening up and continued sleuthing. The big question was if the other door would open, or if she was locked inside. She reassessed her situation. Her shoes were near the bed. Her gun, nowhere to be found.

Jade pulled her hair back, took a deep breath, and walked closer to the door. She put her hand on the doorknob but froze as she heard sounds. It was a voice talking. Jade calculated as she listened. She quickly realized it was a voice coming from the sound of a television. She took a deep breath and turned the knob. It rotated all the way to the right and opened to her delight. She squinted through a sliver of a crack through the doorway frame but didn't see anyone.

She took one more deep breath and opened the door further. It was definitely a basement. The concrete floor was dirty, but not filthy. The foundational structure poles stood pillared in place; painted drab as could be. A small old couch and cheap coffee table were in the center of the room with an old nasty area rug sprawled out in weak effort to warm the space. The television blared as Jade examined her surroundings more. She stepped out into the room. Old boxes and cloth rags strewn about littered the place. It was an unfinished basement, slightly messy, but not horrible, and no pungent odor. She walked closer to the television and watched as a commercial flicked back to the current movie, *Papillon*.

"Where am I?" Jade whispered to herself, as she spied a couple more windows, similarly narrow and barred as her bedroom. A dank wooden staircase in the corner of the room led upward. As Jade considered heading that way, she heard another sound. A squeak from behind her. She turned instantly.

A different door slowly opened, mirroring the other side of the basement from the room she woke up in. Someone was coming. Jade scanned the room for anything to use as a weapon. Nothing. She stood in stunned disbelief when she saw the person walk in.

"*Squirrel*? Is that you?"

"*GJ*?" Squirrel said in equal surprise. "What are *you* doing here?"

"I'd *love* to know. What are you doing here? And where is *here*?"

"I wish I knew," Squirrel said. "Did you come from *that* room?" He pointed to the room Jade woke up in.

Jade nodded. "It's been locked since I've been here, and I haven't been here all that long. A couple days, I think. Who's doing this?"

"Whoever they are, they're smart. I've only seen one, the guy that…" Squirrel paused. He choked up.

"Your ear," Jade said tenderly.

He raised his hand to a gruesome dry crusty wound and did his best to compose himself.

"What the hell, you *know*?" he said. "I've only seen that guy that did this to me. He doesn't say much, but I gather there are others. I think I've heard their voices from upstairs, occasionally."

"Did he have a long black ponytail?" Jade asked, thinking through her last memories of her abductor at the Van Gogh immersion exhibit.

"No. My guy, the guy that cut me, is middle-aged, slightly balding, but a big tough dude."

"Where were you before?" Jade asked.

"No clue. Similar to this set up, kinda. This place is a bit better. I think they're one of the last people in the world with cable." He motioned to the wall-mounted television. "*Papillon*, I thought it fitting as a prisoner… They bring food periodically, and drinks. Mostly pizza, which is fine I guess, but you know… Same old stuff. And water. Could be worse. Obviously, the door to the basement is locked, and they have surveillance on us." Squirrel pointed to a couple video cameras. "I broke those, but there must be one or two others hidden somewhere. They only open the door with food when I'm sitting on the couch watching something or in the other room, far away from the doorway leading out. That must have been when they brought you down. What do you think? You've been out on the case longer than I. What's going on?"

Jade processed everything. The last night she'd seen Squirrel at the Aquarium, working with Fischer, Van Gogh, the Museum, the would-be slow unraveling of clues, crashing back into the frustration of the moment before her. "It's good to see you Squirrel," she said. "I'm so sorry about your ear." She gave him an awkward hug. "He sent a message to us with it, which led us to the Getty Museum an—"

"What?" Squirrel said in a crazed trance.

"It's a long story, Squirrel. I'm just glad you're *alive*. These people, El Nachash… Squirrel, I've got a lot to lay on you. These people are very dark—"

Squirrel touched the side of his head again. "You're telling me?"

"And we think it's building, culminating into some huge horrible climactic event, the likes of which we're not sure yet. But it's gonna be bad."

"And I think I know how," Squirrel said nervously. "Please tell me you guys found the cyanide already."

Jade involuntarily transitioned into her best doe in the headlights look. "*Cyanide?*"

Chapter 50

Tuesday, January 28th

THE WEE HOURS OF THE morning weighed heavily on the team in full on prep mode. The sun wasn't even thinking of peeking out over the San Gabriel Mountain range just yet. The S.W.A.T. division of the LAPD silently parked and scurried into position of the Glendale house.

The Glendale home was as secluded as could be in LA county, tucked away on the mountain side. It boasted plenty of high canopy trees and acreage to buffer from the other neighboring homes, as well as a protective fence line.

Detective George Greppin instructed orders soundlessly with his hands, directing the unit split in several groups. They slowly inched into place. Detective Justin Praider jetted up to the front door, gun drawn ready for action. He did one last reconnaissance about him. Sufficiently flanked, he motioned for the Halligan bar battering ram to breach the entrance. Two more officers sprinted up, one across from Praider, the other making swift work of the door.

"LAPD," Praider yelled.

BAM!

In no time Praider and several S.W.A.T. officers swarmed the place.

Greppin entered with his team, stealthily heading upstairs. Praider's squad spread throughout the sprawling labyrinth like downstairs. The outdoor S.W.A.T. unit encroached in from the rear of the homes' pool patio, and through a shed and tiki hut. They came up to the glass doors. The only sounds were a few random birds chirping.

Praider opened the glass doors letting some of them in.

A stocky butch blonde female S.W.A.T. approached Praider with her gun drawn. "No one outside on the premises, sir. No white van anywhere on the property. It's not in the garage either, we checked."

Greppin came back downstairs. "Nothing upstairs, Justin. Mostly empty rooms with a bed or two."

Praider looked around and saw one last door. "That only leaves the basement," Praider said.

Greppin examined the adjacent kitchen, opening and closing the fridge. "I don't think anyone lives here permanently. Hardly anything in here."

Praider took a couple guys and led the cautious charge into the basement. He flicked on the light and descended the stairs. It was quiet for a moment. Praider stayed at the base of the basement stairwell scanning the room. Greppin walked over to the top of the stairs, waiting in anticipation.

Praider looked up at Greppin. "*Grep.* You better get down here. You're not going to believe this…"

# # #

In the forensic lab, Chief Tatum received a text from Detective Greppin. *We're back at precinct HQ.*

Chief Tatum casually checked his text and looked up at Bostic. "You want another coffee, Chad?"

"No thanks, I'm good. Dragging, but good. Should be almost done with all of this. What'd you say all this extra legwork was for?"

Tatum hesitated slightly. "Again… It's a special project. I can't disclose that right now, but I can't thank you enough for your expediency and commitment."

"That's the job," Bostic said.

"You believe that, *right*?" Tatum asked, shifting tones. "Commitment... To protect and serve?"

"That's the LAPD motto, isn't it?"

"Isn't it, though," Tatum said smugly.

Greppin and Praider entered, catching Bostic off guard. They each carried a box.

"What are you guys doing here so early?" Bostic asked.

"Oh, we were hoping you could help us with something," Praider said, setting down a box in front of Bostic. He tossed out some thin green leafy plants. "I was thinking you might be able to tell me what this is?"

"What is *this*?" Bostic asked skeptically.

"Maybe I can help you, Bostic," Greppin said, asserting himself. He set down his box and picked up a jar of pale blue liquid. "I'll give you a hint, this substance has a bitter almond smell, but I don't think you want to drink it."

Bostic's eyes bounced back and forth in obvious thought. He was a brilliant thinker, but a lousy poker player. Panic surged in Bostic's eyes as he walked over to his desk.

"I have something to help explain..." Bostic said.

Bostic lunged toward his drawer and grabbed the tranquilizer from his lab coat pocket with his left hand.

Greppin, quick to respond, dashed forward and clamped a cuff on Bostic's left wrist. Greppin's eyes went wide. "Gun!"

Praider came crashing in like a linebacker as Bostic hoisted the gun in his right arm. Greppin yanked, slamming Bostic's arm down on the table.

BLAM! BLAM!

Bostic, Greppin, and Praider looked up as Chief Tatum crumbled to the floor holding his guts.

Chapter 51

A DARK FIGURE STOOD OVER Chase at the front door in a hooded navy rain slicker jacket.

"*AAAAHHHHH!*" Chase screamed.

The visitor slammed the door. "Chase. It's *me…*"

Rosalynn Schumacher stood over Chase with a familiar expression of concern on her face. She pulled down her hood and unzipped her jacket, gently laying it over a nearby chair. She wore dark charcoal plaid dress slacks, and a thin dark cowl-necked top with long sleeves.

"*Rosalynn?* You changed your hair."

Her silky scarlet hair still looked radiant. Chase had always liked that most about her appearance. It had always been long and flowing or sometimes pulled in a cute ponytail when they'd been together. She had it trimmed a lot shorter now with accenting highlights. Chase's former fiancée still looked amazing. Rosalynn possessed that type of rare natural beauty that had no need of make-up or enhancing cosmetic tricks. She could roll around in a muddy backyard football game and somehow come out looking like she belonged on the cover of a glamor magazine.

She crouched toward him. "You still hide your key in the same spot, Chase. It's kind of predictable. *Oh*, dear, you're bleeding. Let's get you cleaned up. She looked about the general state of the room and picked up an empty whisky bottle laying sideways on the floor.

"Tea?" she asked rhetorically.

Within minutes Rosalynn soon had a kettle of water heating over the stove and scurried through the medicine cabinet for band aids and ointment.

Chase patched himself up, downed some Tylenol and ice water, and gathered himself on the couch. It was time to address the proverbial elephant in the living room. "So, Roz, thanks for all this, but… what are you *doing* here?"

Rosalynn sat down on an adjacent chair, sipping a mug of hot tea, and offered one to Chase, who quickly accepted. "I hear you've been having a rough go of it lately."

"You don't know the *half* of it," he said guardedly. *Tread lightly, Chase.* Whatever he shared with her could instantly get back to her father and be used against him. And he didn't feel he had the stomach to start making himself vulnerable to her again.

"What's with the graffiti on your door?" A serious tone took over her voice. "Chase, is everything okay?"

"Probably just some pranksters. They can be real ornery around here sometimes." *Please don't ask me about Luther. I just don't have the stamina right now. Everything's too raw.*

"I've been working on myself, after everything, last year, how we ended and all. I remembered a phrase I've heard you quote a time or two. I think it's from C.S. Lewis? 'Forgiveness is a beautiful concept, until we have someone to forgive,' or something to that effect."

"Yes…" Chase agreed curiously.

"Look, Chase. You *hurt* me, at least I thought so. I realize now not everything that happened was as it seemed or even accurate… And then I hurt *you*… with that other guy."

"Bad," Chase looked down in aggravation.

"Yes, bad. I cheated… on you… in retaliation, based off what I later learned was a lie about you. It was foolish. It was reactionary, and I understand that now and—"

Chase raised a hushing hand for her to stop.

"Please just listen." Rosalynn took a deep breath. "I want to say, for what it's worth… I forgive you… And that… *I'm* sorry."

Rosalynn's words washed over Chase like a soothing salve. He had been misunderstood, judged by the public, and hurting for much too long. The pain stung more than he ever cared to reveal to anyone. But somehow, amazingly, inexplicably, and serendipitously in this moment, her words made that suffering cease. Chase tried to muster an appropriate response, but all he could come up with was.

"Ditto."

Rosalynn seemed taken aback slightly, then Chase could tell she read the sincerity in his eyes and heart.

She let out a constrained chortle. "Unbelievable. *Ditto*? You, Rev. Dr. Chase Fischer, who are so eloquent in speech… At a loss for words…" Rosalynn delivered in equal surprise and amusement. "Well, I should probably be going. I'll get out of your… space." She looked around the place one final time. "Goodbye, Chasey." She stood near him, leaned over and kissed him on the forehead.

"Goodbye, Rosalynn," Fischer said almost inaudibly as she walked toward the door. "And thank you." Then an epiphany hit him. Fischer's head shot up. "Actually, Rosalynn, if you wouldn't mind…" She stopped in the opened door frame staring back at him. "Now that we have this new understanding. Do you think I could ask you for one *small* favor?"

Chapter 52

AFTER A LONG BODILY HYGIENE clean up session, Fischer arrived at the LAPD station late morning. His belly was filled with a garbage omelet from his last few eggs and whatever leftovers he found in his fridge. He walked in with a humble, yet hopeful revitalized swagger. He went up to the officer on duty at the greeting counter. "Morning, I'm here to see Chief Tatum."

The younger Asian male officer with round glasses and black hair jerked uncomfortably. "I'm sorry sir, that will not be possible."

"*Believe* me, he'll want to see me," Fischer said.

"I'm sorry, sir."

"I don't think you understand. I'm Dr. Fischer. I've been working on a very difficult and important case with his department as a Chaplain liaison for a while now. This is *serious*." Fischer was losing his patience, batting both hands on the countertop.

"Fischer," Praider said from the other end of the room, "come with me."

Praider guided Fischer back to the interrogation observation room. He was intensely quiet during their brisk walk. Through the two-way mirror, Fischer saw Greppin grilling Chad Bostic.

"Oh, *wow*. You've got Bostic in custody already?" Fischer asked. "What's he saying?"

Praider looked at the floor and back to Fischer with steel eyes he'd not seen from Praider before. "Fischer, he shot the Chief last night."

Fischer's heart sank. "Oh, Lord, *no*."

"He's alive, barely, but it doesn't look good. The Chief wanted things kept quiet, for obvious reasons, and he kept Bostic occupied away from the raid we did on the Glendale house, where we found—"

"*Gemma*? I mean, officer Jade. Did you find her?" Fischer asked with no fear of the concerned tone in his voice.

Praider shook his head. "Unfortunately, no, but we did find cyanide. Lots and lots of cyanide. And *plants* if you can believe that. It was a botanist's paradise in the basement."

"Actually, Justin… I can believe it. It makes perfect sense to me."

"It *does*?"

"I'll fill you all in, but I wanna hear this," Fischer said turning his attention toward Greppin's work inside the interrogation room.

Fischer and Praider watched through the glass as Greppin worked away at Bostic.

"How long were you on El Nachash's payroll?" Greppin asked. "Or should I say, Jim Latham's? Or should I say Morgan Stern's?" Greppin snarled. "Yep, we know it all. You're just gonna use your friends and co-workers as pawns in your sick silly games?" Greppin slammed his fist on the table.

Bostic only offered a stoic inhuman smile. "I have no friends here. I have no co-workers. My peers are those who know what the truth of the heavenly scroll declares."

"Oh, my word," Fischer said looking through the two-way mirror window. "This guy's in *deep*."

"And for a long time," Praider said to Fischer.

"*Enough*," Greppin shouted, pushing Bostic's chair back with his powerful leg. "You sold us out—for money. Plain and simple. There's no truth in what you're doing, what you've done. There's no honor there. Did you cut off Squirrel's ear? Where is he? Where is GJ? What did you do to them?"

Bostic spoke with a coolness in his voice. "I merely performed my role and responsibility, in service and sacrifice. What happens to whom is not for me to decide, but for the One called higher than me."

Fischer walked into the interrogation room with Greppin and Bostic as Greppin continued berating him on his tirade. "What's the cyanide for, Chad?" Greppin asked.

"You'll know soon enough. All will be revealed in due time," Bostic said.

"Tell me," Fischer asked, "how long have you been preparing for your church's 'last supper?'"

Greppin gave a perplexed look. Bostic froze. Fischer pushed his point. "That's what you're planning isn't it? A special last supper moment for your church, where they—"

"You think you're so smart, you arrogant prick," Bostic said with a snide cackle. "You think you know the truth to the mysteriousness of the universe and pass it off so *cavalierly*. You have no idea, no *iota* of what I know, who I am, and who El Nachash is, or *will* be for that matter."

Fischer could feel the blood rushing to his face. "If you've hurt her…"

"You disgust me," Greppin said. "Chad Bostic, I'll be adding a few more charges to your arrest record. You're going away for a long time, *Friendo*." Greppin leaned in uncomfortably close to Bostic's face. "And believe me, if I weren't a police officer, I'd beat the living snot out of you right now."

"I'm not," Fischer said coolly, and for the first time in his life, Fischer clenched his fist, recoiled, and cold-cocked another person in the face. Fischer's powerful right cross stunned all three of them.

After the moment of shock wore off, Praider came into the room.

Bostic looked up with a bloody split lip. "That was a sucker punch."

"Fitting," Fischer said, rubbing his knuckles mildly. "You're a *sucker* for believing all the drivel you're spewing out."

"Get him outta here, Praider," Greppin said.

"With pleasure," Praider said, clamping the handcuffs closed extra tight. He walked Bostic out.

Greppin looked over Fischer in a new light and snickered through a Cheshire Cat-like grin.

"What?"

"I didn't think Christians, or especially pastors, could act like that, all angry and stuff."

Fischer beamed. "Not anger, Grep. Righteous indignation."

Greppin giggled softly in a brief lighthearted moment. "What about the whole 'what would Jesus do' thing?"

Fischer leaned back against the table; arms folded. "It's important to remember, when people pose the question, 'what would Jesus do?' in a sort of challenge to Christian conduct, I like to remind them—flipping tables and whipping wolves in sheep's clothing out of the temple *is* in the realm of possibilities," Fischer smiled back a mile wide grin.

The mood turned serious again. "Last Supper?" Greppin asked searchingly.

"George, I've got a lot to tell you…"

Chapter 53

FISCHER SAT DOWN IN THE conference room with Praider and Greppin. Greppin slid a file across the table to Fischer. "Fischer, before we start, here. This was on the Chief's desk. I honestly can't believe he managed to acquire this, but we're fortunate he did, and you may find it very helpful."

Fischer raced through the classified document on Latham. "Wow. That explains a lot."

Greppin shifted in his seat with pad and pen at the ready. "Okay, lay it on us. What have you got?"

"I suppose we should begin from the top," Fischer said, as if preparing for a long university lecture in front of his students. "We know the alleged Zodiac Mazzaroth killer, El Nachash, a.k.a. Morgan Stern, a.k.a. Jim Latham has been behind all this. What else do we know about him?"

Praider raised a finger, in semi-student mode. "He's incredibly dangerous, aided by a mercenary type of guy, by the name of Wolfgang Manteuffel."

"And lest we forget Chad Bostic, on the payroll this whole *freaking* time," Greppin said.

Fischer snarled his face and shook his head in disgust. "So, *they* have been meticulously conspiring to commit these murders in a specific time sequenced pattern, as unfolding by the zodiacal seasons." Fischer counted slowly with his fingers. "The Virgo killing of Shelly Davidson, the Libra

Scales killing of the crucified man, Scorpio and the old man at the Viper Room, Sagittarius and the arrow-impaled woman, Capricorn and the goat head masked man... and of course the attempt of Aquarius at the Aquarium of the Pacific on Clare Nelson-Frost. Gentlemen, he's half-way to completing his masterpiece."

Praider stood and paced a bit. "There's been this whole braggadocios business talk of the scroll unfolding, but he's gone offline. His website's gone dark. He very obviously can't help mocking and bragging but certainly doesn't *want* us to stop him."

Fischer stood excitedly facing Praider. "He's married Mazzaroth astrology to his own unique prophecy. Through a healthy dose of hubris and some delusion of grandeur for good measure, you have a perfect cocktail of dangerous fundamentalism. El Nachash is in no poverty of self-confidence."

"Hence his outrageous trail of clues," Praider said. "The Van Gogh thing was particularly ludicrous."

"Yet he gave us so much with that," Fischer said. "His Van Gogh references were the most enlightening, all things considered."

"How so?" Greppin asked, listening intently and scribbling notes.

Fischer turned toward Greppin. "The star allusions were easy enough surface references, but the layers beneath take some examination. The affinity with absinthe, the hidden Last Supper imagery, the dark appreciation for a higher celestial café all points to..." Fischer looked back and forth at the two detectives waiting to see if their internal lightbulb's flicker. *Not yet.* "The cyanide," Fischer said.

"The cyanide?" Both Praider and Greppin asked in unison.

"Specifically, drinking it," Fischer said. "Are you ready for the kicker?" He asked with a knowing professorial grin. "We weren't hearing Tommy's confession correctly."

"The 'nine, ten, eleven, revelation,' thing?" Greppin asked.

"No. The 'eight, nine, ten, eleven, revelation,' thing, Greppin." Fischer said. "He kept repeating it over and over, but I think our listening loop was off on his cycle."

Praider hunched over the table. "Huh?"

Fischer flashed his iconic know-it-all smile again. "It sounds a lot different when you say, 'Revelation eight: nine, ten, eleven,' wouldn't you say?" Fischer asked.

"Holy smokes," Praider said. "What does *that* verse say?" Praider asked.

"Way ahead of you. Listen to this" Fischer said, pulling up his Bible app on his phone. "Oh, and keep in mind, absinthe is rooted in what is commonly referred to as *wormwood*."

And the third part of the creatures which were in the sea, and had life, died; and the third part of the ships were destroyed. And the third angel sounded, and there fell a great star from heaven, burning as it were a lamp, and it fell upon the third part of the rivers, and upon the fountains of waters; And the name of the star is called Wormwood: and the third part of the waters became wormwood; and many men died of the waters, because they were made bitter.

Fischer finished reading and looked up to see how Praider and Greppin were processing everything, then gently forged forward. "He needed someone like Bostic, with his expertise to pull off something like this, particularly with a strong enough lethal poison, like cyanide. I believe they're going to gather their unassuming 'church' together and have them drink to their unbeknownst death in some celebratory Last Supper fashion."

"Bostic made it and arranged the whole thing, bankrolled by 'Morgan Stern's' money," Greppin said in revulsion, shaking his head. "This is like the David Koresh Branch Davidians type stuff."

"I was thinking more like Jonestown," Praider said. "I researched a bit after we found the cyanide. The effects of potassium cyanide and sodium cyanide are identical, and it can work fast. Symptoms of poisoning typically occur within a few *minutes* of ingesting the substance. The person loses consciousness, and brain death eventually follows. There're usually some wicked convulsions and eventual death by cerebral hypoxia. This waxes heavily of the whole Jim Jones's 'drinking the Kool-aid' cult crap."

"*Exactly*," Fischer said. "And there's no telling how many people could potentially be in jeopardy. This El Nachash guy sees this whole network as his church—to destroy. Pisces, the two fish symbol represents God's people in the Mazzaroth, and it's next. We know he zeroed in on me as one of the fish, and now they've got Gemma, which they referred to as 'Andromeda,' the woman in chains which *is* a decan of Pisces."

"Hold up. *When* did they do this?" Praider asked.

"They spray-painted it on the front door of my house… right before they killed my dog."

"Damn. He gone and went personal," Greppin said. "Wait. Obviously, all this is very fascinating, but what about the child, Christian? How does he fit into all this?" Greppin asked.

"Fischer and I figured that out already," Praider said. "Aries is the sacrificial ram in the Mazzaroth, which comes right after Pisces. We saw the video. It was open-sourced right there on his 'TrueNativity' website. He spelled it out for us, taunting us actually, calling his long sought-after son, his 'Little Ram.' Referencing Abraham almost sacrificing his son, Isaac, but a ram taking his place…"

Fischer smiled in validation.

"So," Greppin said processing everything. "It's not an ideal timeframe for GJ, but we should have until at least February 18th to prepare before he acts again, right? That's the date of Pisces clicking over, and Aries another month after that."

"Unfortunately, I think not," Fischer said. "El Nachash referenced the 'New Moon' in his last video I saw. And 'restitution.'"

"So?"

"So, that was the other word spraypainted on my door." Fischer said. "In large words, 'Much restitution.' It makes perfect sense. The darkest skies, and hence the brightest stars, are always around the new moon, when the moon rises and sets with the sun. So, the moon is not in the night-time sky, which is ideal for stargazers. And new moon celebrations are also an ancient Biblical observance, which plays right into this guy's wheelhouse of celestial observation. The New Testament even references it. The celebration of the new moon has always had great prophetic significance for Israel as the bride of Yahweh, and it was an appointed time of His choosing to give prophetic revelation to His people of His purposes for them… I think he's going to kill them off as restitution."

"Restitution for what?" Praider asked.

"From us preventing the death of Clare, the Aquarius victim? I don't know," Fischer guessed. "We stopped Aquarius from happening, at least in his mind. Who can really make sense of all this insanity?"

"Oh, man," Greppin said. "Don't tell me... When's the next new moon?"

"January 29th," Fischer said in deep concern.

A shock of panic splashed across Praider's face. "We don't have much time."

"I know, I just," Fischer choked back some welled-up emotion in his throat. "I just really *really* hope it's not too late for Gemma. The message in the Zodiac is told from the standpoint of a 'wedding' as the bridegroom comes out of his chambers and runs his course... The fundamental message to all humanity written in the stars at creation is that of a 'groom' coming forth, paying the ultimate price for his bride with his life, and redeeming her from death, and ruling together in the Kingdom. But this guy's twisting the whole thing."

"Twisting it into what?" Greppin asked.

Fischer looked hauntingly at Greppin and then at Praider, more serious than he'd ever been in his life. "He sees himself as the coming true Messiah."

Chapter 54

Wednesday, January 28th

FISCHER SPENT THE NEXT MORNING wallowing in worry. With all his learned wisdom and everything he knew, he still felt helpless, powerless if they couldn't figure out where El Nachash would be. Each passing minute was that much closer to the new moon and the fate of Gemma, not to mention the other church member victims unwittingly involved. Fischer couldn't just sit around. He had to do something. He needed to at least talk to someone that understood and maybe figure something more out. Fischer's vexation continued until a comforting idea occurred to him.

Fischer drove to Zhou Ming's house. It seemed like he had just been there and met him as he parked in front of the now familiar charming home with the brick driveway. He knocked on the door. *Please be here.* He heard movement on the other side of the door. *Yes.* Within no time Mr. Zhou's friendly face greeted him and they were once again sitting on his couch sipping steaming hot tea and catching up on the zodiac killer events.

"And now she's missing, Joe, and we haven't been able to help, at all," Fischer said, setting down his cup and leaning back against the couch.

"If I know Gemma, and I *do* very well," Mr. Zhou said, "she is tough, she is smart, she is strong. I believe she will rise from this, *stronger* somehow.

Still, it is very concerning, not to mention upsetting. Tell me, what more have you learned about who is doing all this?"

"We think we understand the 'who.' It's a complex multi-persona individual. He's incredibly wealthy, well connected, super savvy, and very dangerous. And he doesn't work alone."

"Not to mention being off the deep end of extreme fundamentalism."

"*You're* telling me. If David Koresh had some cosmic bastard lovechild with Jim Jones, that's essentially who we're dealing with here. Which is also the 'what,' and 'why' of this whole thing I suppose."

"And you think the 'when' is this next New Moon right around the corner?"

"He all but spelled it out on his website. As you recall, he *loves* to taunt."

"You just need the 'where' and it all comes together?"

Fischer sat up in extreme attention. "It has to, Joe. We have to stop him… I have to find her."

"Wait here," Mr. Zhou said, walking out of the room. "I have something you may want."

Mr. Zhou walked back carrying a small black duffel bag. He sat down, unzipped it, and pulled out an aged white garment. Fischer had never seen one up close but was pretty sure what it was.

"If this man loves to flaunt his work as much as you've said, I suspect something will arise before it's too late. Something will turn up, and you'll need to be prepared. You have already been in danger, and will only continue to be, how and whenever the rest of this eventually plays out. *This* is a bullet proof vest. It's old, like me, but it still works… I think. Here, you take it."

Fischer reached out and held the vest. It was lighter than he'd expected. There were two old bullet indentations in it already.

"What are these? Were you shot wearing this?"

"Those are stories from another time," Mr. Zhou said with an enigmatic smile.

"Well, thank you, I guess," Fischer said.

"I'm not done. Here," Mr. Zhou held out a gun. "I hope you don't need it, but just in case. You know how to use one?"

"Um…" Fischer hesitated.

Mr. Zhou rolled his eyes and commenced with a brief tutorial of the magazine, the bullets, the safety, and how to hold it when aiming and firing.

"Your generation is so afraid of guns. Again, this is just a precaution, but… I sense this thing is far from over for you. I'm too old. Find her, Chase."

Fischer walked out with his new tattered duffel bag. He shook Joe's hand, but Joe pulled him in for a hug.

"*Find* her."

Fischer stuffed the bag into his black leather saddlebag and zoomed off, deep in apprehensive thought. He was well outside his wheelhouse of expertise, and he knew it. He arrived home with no dog to greet him. He shut the garage door and played around with his new items in the duffel bag. He tried on the vest. It seemed to fit, though the zippers were difficult to adjust. He carefully tampered with the gun, just to reassure himself once more and gain confidence with the weapon. It didn't work.

Fischer flashed the weapon to the left and to the right, aiming and preparing for what an altercation might seem like. Nothing felt comfortable. He hated the entire sensation and concept of it all. *This isn't my weapon.*

Fischer couldn't eat. His appetite was lost. The night's darkness rolled in like an unwelcome stranger invading his personal space, reminding him the new moon was that much closer, forcing him to deal with it. He walked over to the church gazing up at the night sky and the stars. It was a spectacular view. After a deep inhale of the early evening air, he entered the church sanctuary.

It was pitch black. Only the faint half-light of the streetlamps and starlight fought through the stained glass, offering a dim setting for prayer. Fischer knelt at the railing near the altar and exercised the only weapon he was comfortable wielding, prayer. He laid all his concerns out… *Rosalynn Schumacher… the Praesidium's vote… The congregation of Epiphany to see and know the truth… Shelly Davidson's family…* the *other victims' families… Michael… Christian… Squirrel… Gemma… All the other poor souls caught up in the madness of this situation…* Fischer choked over another jagged pill of a thought to digest. He shuffled uncomfortably. Rev. Dr. Chase L. Fischer struggled praying for his enemies just as much as the next person. With sour-patch kid candy-like stinging in his glands, he managed to pray for his adversaries; "For Tommy… Bostic… Manteuffel… for El N—Morg—

no… For Jim Latham… Lord… I place it all before you…"

Fischer cycled through his mental catalogue over and over, and in his deep meditation, another name surfaced, he'd realized he'd mistakenly left out. *Tatum*…

Chapter 55

Thursday, January 29th

FISCHER AWOKE THE NEXT MORNING, not well rested. Despite his best efforts to sleep in, he couldn't ignore the rising sun and the gloomy day awaiting him. His knees were still sore from the night before as he waited for his coffee to finish percolating. He felt a twinge of peace but still waited for some sort of realization to kick in or an idea of how he might be used in this whole mess. He knew the dreaded Praesidium vote would occur later that day. As he poured his 'Jamaican Me Crazy' roast into his mug, and burnt his tongue on his first sip, an ironic thought crossed over his mind. *I better check on Chief Tatum, while I'm still officially a man of the cloth, and unofficially an honorary chaplain for the LAPD.*

    Two hours later Fischer arrived at the downtown hospital in full black clerical and suit. He figured it would be more challenging to gain access to the Chief's high-profile status than most hospital visitations he'd done. Thanks to the newer COVID 19 protocols, he had become accustomed to being treated as a second-class citizen in the medical world, as opposed to the esteemed visitation privileges he had enjoyed in previous years.

    Thankfully Detective Praider was there. Praider cleared Fischer with no problems and in no time the two stood in the small private room over

Chief Tatum. A respirator was in function with a breathing tube inserted through Chief Tatum's mouth and down into his chest cavity.

Fischer listened somberly to the various beeps and suction noises as Praider began rambling with an update. "He's been in and out a few times, the last few days, but not very lucid. His wife's been here in and out most of the time, too. She'll probably be back any time. It's not looking good. They did a lot of surgery, three different times, apparently. They had real trouble stopping the bleeding."

Fischer was working up a question in his mind when Praider's cell phone rang.

"Lemme take this," Praider said as he stepped out of the room.

Fischer looked over the once proud-standing Chief, laying injured and weak on the bed in front of him. He sat down beside him just as a woman walked in who Fischer could only assume was Mrs. Tatum. She had dark hair, with just a touch of sliver protruding at the roots, but presented herself in an elegant manner, notwithstanding the gravity of the condition of her husband. She carried a charcoal blazer across her arm.

"Hello. And you are?" she asked.

Fischer immediately stood up and extended a polite hand. "Hello. Pastor Fischer. Mrs. Tatum, I presume?"

She nodded slowly. "Yes," she said, not looking at Fischer anymore. She only had eyes for her husband.

Fischer was used to uniquely awkward moments of health crisis in people's lives and continued. "I've gotten to know your husband fairly well this last month. I've been... assisting with this zodiac ca—"

"Did you know that Chad Bostic?" she asked, her question laced with venom. "Did you work with him?"

Chief Tatum stirred at the sound of his wife's voice. His eyes popped open and flickered.

The moment subsided and Fischer responded in a soft, gentle manner. "No, I didn't really know him all that well, just bumped into him a few times," he said.

"It's sickening. Just *sickening* that someone on his own staff would do this. Absolutely *appalling*." She noticed the Chief stirring. "Hi, Honey."

She made eye contact with him and touched his cheek. "Can you hear me?"

Chief Tatum blinked intentionally.

Praider returned to the room. "Great news. We've been able to locate a large residence in Antelope Valley, some palatial estate outside of Lancaster. The owner's name is listed as Morgan Stern. Old satellite imagery shows a lot of activity in and out of it, including Wolfgang Manteuffel's white van. This is where that New Moon thing *has* to be going down, at his very own home church," Praider said. "Chief, we're gonna get this guy for ya, and put an end to this whole thing. Ma'am, believe me, the LAPD is gonna go to *war* on this guy. It's on."

Chief Tatum's eyes went wide.

"Can I come?" Fischer asked.

"Pastor," Praider said. "This isn't a ride-along situation. We don't know what to expect. This guy's got *resources*. Best to leave it to the experts." He bolted from the room and looked back through the doorway. "Don't worry, Chase. When we find GJ, I'll make sure you'll be the first to know." He tapped the side of the doorframe with two quick pats, and he was gone.

Fischer acquiesced in frustration, dropping his head, but understood. *I get it. Stay in your lane, Bro.* He looked back at the Tatums' tender moment.

The Chief pointed to his jacket.

"What is it dear?"

He blinked fast twice and passed out again.

"Two blinks means yes," Mrs. Tatum explained to Fischer. "We've managed to work out that system in the brief moments he's come to. He's been lucid so preciously little."

"Was he motioning for his jacket?" Fischer asked.

"I don't know, maybe."

"Was that the jacket he had on when," Fischer paused a second trying as best he could not to be insensitive. "When he was shot?"

"Yes," Mrs. Tatum said, looking over her husband in a trancelike state. "They gave me his personal effects early today." She snapped to, composing herself. "Pastor, does the Tree of Yeshua mean anything to you? Or the New Golgotha?"

"*Excuse* me?" Fischer asked confusedly.

"The officer said your name was Chase, right?"

"Yes, Pastor Chase Fischer."

"It's just that, the orderly gave me his things, and I went through them. There was this little note in one of his pockets." She looked through the jacket. "Here it is."

Mrs. Tatum retrieved it and handed it to Fischer. Fischer took the small yellow Post-it note, unfolded it, and read the words.

Chase The Tree of Yeshua
New Golgotha?

"What is this?" Fischer asked.

"I have no idea," said Mrs. Tatum. "I saw it earlier. I didn't think much of it. I think I've been in shock, processing everything…"

"Of course," Fischer said.

"I guess I thought it was some motivational proverb or something, as in Chase 'after' the Tree of Yeshua… Jesus maybe? But that would be odd for him. And the other word…"

Fischer recognized his cue. "Ah, Golgotha means 'the place of the skull." And yes, Yeshua is Jesus, the tree of Jesus, where he died on Calvary's hill, the mount of Golgotha." Fischer thought for a moment. "Mrs. Tatum, as I said, I've been working with your husband. I think he might have been planning to give this to me. But why?"

"Your guess is as good as mine," she said.

"Unfortunately, I need to get going, Mrs. Tatum," Fischer said, searching through his pockets until he found what he was looking for. "Here, take my card. If your husband wakes up and is at all communicative with his eyes, please call me at this number immediately."

Chapter 56

FISCHER OPENED HIS GARAGE DOOR to create some fresh air before beginning his work on the Triumph. He tuned in the classic rock station on his old radio atop his wooden worktable and rolled up his sleeves. Journey's *Don't Stop Believin* blared. He looked at his bike. His project was a job he didn't want to do. He picked up his wrench and savored one last moment before committing to the task. The sun was just beginning to fight its daily losing battle with dusk, bleeding its colors into the horizon of yet another glorious Southern California evening. Fischer meticulously began detaching the side car from the Bonnie. *I guess it's solo time.* Fischer's thoughts of Praider and Greppin going after El Nachash's estate kept him preoccupied mentally. Fischer's cell phone rang. He turned down the radio.

"Hello?"

"Pastor Chase, it's Mrs. Tatum. He's awake."

"Ok. Great," Fischer said. "Ask him if that Post-it note of his was a message from El Nachash."

"What?"

"El Nachash," Fischer said with careful articulation over the phone. "Just do it, trust me."

"Okay, I did…He blinked twice."

"Excellent… Ask him if he thinks that's where he'll be next."

"One second... Ah, yes. That's two more blinks. Yes."

"Mrs. Tatum. Thank you. That is very helpful, I gotta go and think through this. Prayers to you for him right now... okay. Bye bye." Fischer hung up.

Fischer looked out at the sky, and back to his red motorbike. He turned up the radio again and returned to his zone of thought. Springsteen's *Dancing in the Dark* played.

Fischer hummed along and mouthed the words as he worked and thought. Springsteen ended and the Radio DJ came on. "That was another greatest hit from the one and only legend, The Boss, never gets old. Next up, U2's *Still Haven't Found What I'm Looking For*, from the iconic Joshua Tree album."

Fischer kept working away, his ratchet wrench flipped back and forth like a metronome matching the melody.

"The Joshua Tree album... U2's pièce de résistance...," Fischer said in slight marvel.

Fischer slowed his wrench work, distracted in deep thought. *El Nachash always picks a distinct matching location for his targets... The tree of Jesus... The Tree of Yeshua... The Joshua Tree... National Park? Interesting... What about the New Golgotha?* He dropped his wrench in horrified shock. Fischer had rock climbed all over the SoCal region, including Joshua Tree National Park, which has a lot of distinct rock formations to explore—including Skull Rock. *Could that be the New Golgotha?*

Fischer fastened the last bolt and his bike's transformation was complete. The red Triumph Bonneville looked different without its sidecar. It suggested a new sleek maneuverability. Fischer trembled with his new revelation. He looked out the window. Dusk would be giving way to night rapidly. The night of the new moon awaited. Joshua Tree National Park on this night would be incredible for stargazing. Precious little time was left. *I Can't be right... The whole LAPD team is dialed in and focused up on the estate in Antelope Valley of the Mojave Desert...But if I'm right... I have to act fast.* He opened his saddlebag and pulled out the gun Zhou gave him and looked it over, refamiliarizing himself with it. *Oh, Lord, do I have to do this, there's virtually no time left.* Nausea began to percolate in his belly.

Fischer's cellphone rang again. He didn't notice the battery was running extremely low, mostly because it was President Schumacher's number calling. He answered. "Hello?"

"Chase? President Schumacher."

"Yes." Fischer's pulse and breathing was already throbbing at a rapid rate. Schumacher's voice gave it a pump of nitro. He tapped the speaker option on his phone and laid it on his motorcycle seat and kept examining the gun.

"I wanted to inform you that the council of presidents cast their votes late this afternoon on your status..." Schumacher let the moment linger. He enjoyed every torturous second he could inflict until he said, "You've been cleared. There were a few dissenters, but... my Rosalynn reached out to me. She spoke on your behalf, and, uh, explained a little bit more of the whole situation to me. So, as a result, I didn't end up voting against you either. This of course means you are *exonerated*. I'll send out all the proper notifications to the powers that be and make sure they understand you retain your status as a pastor in the church body and done so in good standing. God's blessings to you son, I can't imagine this was easy for you."

"Thank you, sir," Fischer said, sucking in sweet oxygen. "That is great news. I appreciate your words very much."

"All right, well, don't go off and get in anymore trouble again too soon," Schumacher said with strained humor.

Fischer click-slammed the small magazine into his gun. "No worries there, sir."

"Christ be with you," Schumacher said, and hung up.

"And also with you." Fischer looked out the garage door. It'd be dark soon enough. He had a bit of a drive to Joshua Tree National Park if he was going to do it, but there was one quick stop on the way that made sense. He tossed his ratchet wrench in the tool chest and, zipped tight his café racer leather jacket, packed up his saddlebag items and fired up the engine. *That sound never gets old.* A few revs got his adrenaline pumping, and off he went.

A brief drive brought him to a painfully familiar spot.

Astrology & More
Emporium

Fischer cut the engine. He took off his helmet, shook his head, and headed in.

"Maren, I take it you remember me? I really need your help," Fischer said. "Again… it's an emergency."

After a quick transaction Fischer ran back to his bike and fastened another small bag with his new purchase into the other side of his saddlebags and sped away. Fischer roared down the 210, pulsating in fear and second guessing himself as he eventually neared the outskirts of Joshua Tree National Park. The seemingly quick trip brought every thought imaginable racing through his mind, culminating in *I hope I'm not too late for you, Gemma… I can't believe I'm going to do this... Dang it, I have to get a message to the guys. No direct lines to Praider or Greppin… Jeannie it is.*

Fischer pulled over to the side of the highway and speed dialed Jeannie. It rang.

"Pick up, Jeannie, pick up… I know you're watching some Star Trek marathon or something."

Jeannie's voicemail answered and prompted with a *beep*.

"Jeannie, it's Pastor. Please call the LAPD asap! I'm headed to Joshua Tree National Park, Skull Rock, it's the 'Tree of Yeshua,' the 'New Golgotha.' Get this to Detective George Greppin, or Justin Praider. Please, *hurry*."

Fischer looked at his phone. It was dead. *Oh, man. How much of that got through? Can't worry, there's no time.* He zipped up his phone in his jacket pocket and rode off into the sunset approaching a park entrance. He needed a focus-inducing confidence booster and turned on his playlist radio in his helmet. *The Killers? No… Not for a ride like this into Joshua Tree at sunset…* there was only one song that came to mind… U2's *Where The Streets Have No Name* soon built its swelling hymnlike anthem, coursing through Rev. Dr. Chase L. Fischer's helmet radio, and into his soul. He prayed he wasn't too late to meet his imminent moment.

Chapter 57

FISCHER CUT THE HEADLIGHT TO his Triumph Bonneville. He stared at the one-mile marker on the dusty winding road leading to Skull Rock inside Joshua Tree National Park. He hit the kill switch stopping the engine, took off his helmet, and listened. The park was as quiet as a priest's prayer on Good Friday. The night sky was way past sundown and popped brilliantly with stars offering an ominous half-light. *I'll give El Nachash that... It certainly is a perfect night for stargazing.*

Now came the guessing part. Fischer wondered how close to venture toward Skull Rock before stashing his bike and heading in the rest of the way on foot. He couldn't risk being spotted early. Fischer was well outside his comfort zone. He knew he didn't have much going for him as he quickly approched the presumed menacing ordeal. The element of surprise and his wits were about it. *Offroad time.*

Fischer started up the engine and lights again, stealthily heading off the road into the desert. Skull Rock was immediately off the main road. He figured a quarter mile deep from the road and a half mile back should be enough space to buffer him from the site, no matter how many people had gathered there. Fischer carefully navigated through the jagged terrain. *I knew I should have gone with the Triumph Scrambler. Right Chase, for all my nocturnal vigilante needs, which are never.* Fischer's internal attempt for levity failed. He was scared beyond his mind. His pulse began to pound with each bike length that inched nearer to his objective.

Fischer finally drew as close as he dared to Skull Rock with his light on and the engine rumbling. He powered down the bike and hopped off. He grabbed his stowed items from the saddlebags and began double-timing it as best he could toward the periphery of the gathering site. *Would anyone be there?* Fischer's physical shape and stamina were just a twinge past prime. His old running days for the Wisconsin Badgers told him he could close this distance in under five minutes, easy.

Fischer huffed closer, wondering what time it was and if or when help could possibly arrive. *The phone's dead, no way of knowing. It's already super late. Great.* Running alone, in the dark of night, in a desert toward a perilous situation, he never felt more alone.

Fischer heard a low murmur coming from a dim firelight in front of him. The environmental topography was perfect for sneaking up on unassuming people. Large rocks everywhere provided ample hiding spots. The shroud of night blessed him in a natural cloak. Though Fischer was utterly cognizant of the equal curse that came with darkness. Every step presented the hazardous risk of potentially bad footing, or ensuing catastrophic injury, particularly if any climbing should be necessary.

Fischer stopped for a moment and slipped on his special protective rock-climbing gloves. He was aware the Joshua Tree terrain was particularly arid and prone to slice up the hands of unassuming novice climbers or sightseers. He pulled the special gloves on tight as his fingers poked through the hollowed-out tops. With these gloves on his fingertips, he could still feel the sensation of the rocks and be able to pinch into tiny crevices to support himself if need be.

The murmuring grew louder as Fischer treaded closer and caught his first glimpse of the gathering. Hundreds of people had brought tents and set up a small camp. Their dull tiki torch lights provided an eerie ambience through the low-lit night smoke haze. *This whole insanity is one effigy away from their own Burning Man festival. These poor souls have no idea what's in store for them.* Fischer stared in amazement. The clientele base he saw had painted themselves, and were drinking and laughing into hedonistic intoxication, following a cultist egomaniac. *They pride themselves as freethinkers yet follow so blindly.* They danced and nibbled on food and discussed the evening before them. Fischer barely managed to make out a few broken words listening as they looked up and made commentary of the starfield in the sky.

"I can't believe they confiscated our phones for event access," a female voice said.

"Doesn't matter. This will be epic, *historically* epic," said a male voice.

No, that can't be. Fischer recognized in horror the voices he overheard. It was Nate Maddix and Chelsea Ferguson embedded within their amiable tribe. *So, this is their amazing new church... How do these young minds get so easily seduced? Lord, have mercy.*

Fischer felt the sand and rocks surrounding him that had still been warm from the day in the desert sun but were now past cool and well into cold. He shivered, unsure if the night temperature or the McCabe spectacle were to blame. He continued to scan. *No Gemma... No El Nachash... Gotta get closer.*

Fischer silently walked further. After a long while he noticed a shadowed figure to his far right approaching the gathering. He dropped to the ground out of view. He heard a brusque male voice bark an instruction. "It's *time*. We begin the gathering now."

What time is it anyway? One o'clock? Two o'clock? The painfully slow-moving mass began shuffling to Fischer's right toward the large rock formations. Even though Fischer viewed everything from a distance, he knew they were all painstakingly headed near the base of Skull Rock, maneuvering through the rock formations and narrow paths.

An exhausting hour or so later the few hundred people had finally entrenched themselves in the Skull Rock base area. There were mostly torches for light, but a few scattered flashlights peppered about aided the masses. Fischer retained his shadowy camouflage in the rocky pathways but felt more confident as he edged close. *Even if I'm spotted, they'll probably just think I'm part of their group.* Fischer snuck in behind a large rock facing directly across from Skull Rock. Then he saw something that shook his innards.

Down at the base of Skull Rock a long table had been set up holding hundreds of small white disposable cups, already meticulously filled with what looked like a blue liquid. A few large jugs sat idly by. *It's a sure bet those aren't filled with water. Oh, God.* Fischer heard the now familiar gruff voice of Wolfgang Manteuffel begin barking instructions. Fischer turned his attention toward the direction the voice was coming from. Fischer saw Manteuffel walk away from a white van into the middle of the people. *Holy cats, That's the white van. Do they have Gemma in there?*

"Faithful people, shut off your lights,' Manteuffel said. "Extinguish your flames and be settled. Do you want to see the scroll further opened?"

Fischer slyly scurried over to the lonely van, separated from the crowd and Manteuffel by about thirty yards. He slowly looked through the tiny, opened shaft of the small back door window. To his amazement, Christian Chipparo sat safely playing video games, eating Doritos chips, and slurping soda. His eyes didn't even glance over or break concentration from his game. Fischer tugged gently at the back door handle. *Locked. Figures.*

Fischer scanned the interior. Tons of tools, ropes, buckets, were strewn about. *If only I could get some*—He stopped mid thought when he looked down. *Eureka!*

A bucket on the roadside of the van near him held hammers, a hacksaw, a bolt cutter, large screwdrivers, a mallet, and other odds and ends as a makeshift toolchest. Fischer instinctively grabbed the bolt cutters.

Mantueffel's voice thundered again over the crowd. "Do you want El Nachash to appear?"

Fischer had to deliberate in an instant. *Okay, break Christian out and send him running down the dark road in the desert alone, no... and I can't risk loud noises and blowing my cover just yet... He's safe for the moment, all things considered. Hang tight, Christian, I'll get you outta here as soon as I can.*

Fischer dashed back to the high rock facing Skull Rock.

The crowd swelled in wonderment and excitement, as if a rock performer was about to come on stage. Their soft whispers began to rise with cries and wild cheers of "Yes" and "Yeah," and some random mountain man of a cowboy screamed a powerful "*Yeehaw,*" which jazzed the crowd even more.

"Then put out your lights," Manteuffel said. "For El Nachash will be your light tonight, and always."

The lights of the crowd slowly died down as did their voices. "I give you... El *Nachash,* in the flesh..."

Atop of Skull Rock a massive light turned on streaking straight up into the sky. From the looks of it, Fischer reckoned it was a portable super flashlight with a rim about the circumference of a large bowling ball. Its spotlight was powerful and intensely blinding up close with a direct look.

A figure stood behind the light, clicked a dimming effect, and then stepped over the softer vertical spotlight and stood before it. He looked down from his rocky perch upon the people.

The crowd screamed in a fanfare of pandemonium. Fischer listened intently. He'd been in front of a crowd plenty of times in his life. Some of the multitude seemed genuine, others drunk, and still others responded in almost a mocking, yet curious tone. *El Nachash is a performer... and he knows how to play to the crowd.*

El Nachash's sinister voice spewed out his first words. "My faithful... are you ready to see the scroll unfold?" The euphoric screams gave him the answer he wanted. His voice ascended into an altered state of demonic twang. "Are you ready to enter *my tabernacle*?" They roared again. "Then look *up.*" He turned off his powerful vertical light as everyone's eyes adjusted.

Oh, Lord. Fischer knew he had to act swiftly.

Chapter 58

GEORGE GREPPIN SAT IN HIS LAPD-issued SUV some distance down the road from the incredibly well-lit El Nachash estate, on the outskirts of Lancaster, Antelope Valley. He spoke into his commlink radio while looking through infrared binoculars. "Alright, Praider, you guys ready?"

In a nearby military issued style Humvee Praider clicked on his mic. "Affirmative Greppin. Recon showed there's tunnels all throughout the underneath of this place. If there's a huge gathering of people on campus here for some mass scale massacre attempt, I'm guessing they'd be down there."

"Tough to say, they could be anywhere," Greppin said over the com. "No way of telling for sure until we go in. This guy's got money, and with that kind of coin, I'd imagine he'll have some unique toys to defend himself. Be on the ready."

"Copy," Praider said. "Red Team Leader; are you in position at the field tunnel hatch?"

"Standing by," Praider's radio crackled back.

"Green Team Leader; do you have the rear flank?" He asked.

His radio crackled again with a different voice. "In position, sir."

"Sniper, where are you?" Praider asked.

"Check. I'm on the side of the property at the rim of the tree line. I can see activity from the front and rear of this place."

"And I've got Silver Team charging the front gate, Greppin," Praider said.

"Remember guys, this one's for Chief Tatum," Greppin said. "Okay... move out, *go go go*."

At Greppin's command the three teams simultaneously went into action. The Red Team blew off the doors of the field hatch to the tunnel system and dropped into action. The Green Team coordinated a rear tactical assault approach from the back of the property. Praider and the Silver Team barreled through the front gates with a military issued style Humvee and deployed two vanloads of officers swarming the front of the property.

The Red team stealthily slithered through the tunnel system, lights blaring, and guns drawn. The tunnels were clean with cement floors, and a few offshoot rooms. They methodically cleared them one by one.

Half of the Green Team in the rear of the property went to the back door, sprawling out in tactical fashion. The other half of the unit scoped out a large two-story storage unit adjacent to the house. Vehicles, agricultural equipment, and tools were in plain sight.

Praider charged the front door with his Silver unit. "LAPD, *open* up."

BAM!

The battering ram did its job as the Silver team forced their way in easily. They quickly overran the inhabitants. Art decorations adorned the palatial interior. Several Van Gogh replica pieces hung among the numerous marble statues, ostentatious wall mounted sconces, and Persian rugs. The whole place reeked of money, spent with cheap taste.

Outside, the Green Team Leader looked through the back glass door when he heard the growling. He twitched his head to the left and yelled an alert to his team. "*Dogs*."

Two attack pit bulls came barreling toward the Green team but dropped to the ground almost as fast as they came into view.

BLAM... BLAM...

"I hear gunfire," Greppin bleeped over the radio commlink.

"Two dogs down. All clear," the sniper said, crackling over the radio.

"Green Team thanks you," Greppin said.

Red Team Leader's voice came over the radio. "Red Team In the tunnel continuing search. What would a cult leader plan to do with this kind of layout?"

Greppin held his commlink up to his mouth. "Going off past examples, I'd say staying hidden under the radar, and maintaining an easily defendable homestand would probably be his top priorities," Greppin said.

"But there's no *sign* of them," Red Leader said.

Detective Praider cleared the rest of the home with Silver Team, then noticed one last door. He warily approached when it suddenly burst open.

"*Red Team, Red Team,*" the Red Team Leader screamed, with hands raised, as Praider's squad pulled back their aim and eased off their trigger fingers.

The Green Team began coming in the home's rear glass double doors.

"Nothing in the tunnels?" Praider asked the Red Team. They shook their heads. "And you?" Praider looked over the Green Team.

"Nope."

Praider looked around and then noticed a trap door beneath him. He looked at the Red Team Leader. "Did you see this hatch from where you were in the tunnels?"

"No. That's most likely an independent shaft from what we saw."

"Greppin," Praider said into his shoulder commlink. "A whole lot of nothing in here, but one more basement to search, apparently."

"Do it," Greppin ordered back.

Praider ripped back the hatch and descended the rickety wooden staircase. A couple of Silver Team officers immediately followed.

"Looks empty. I've got a large room, simple tv and couch set up," Praider reported via commlink. "And two closed doors. Going left first."

"Ugh, what's that smell?" Praider asked one of his men.

Praider kicked down the flimsy wooden door to the left and entered. "Nothing but a small empty bedroom."

"Justin... You said there were *two* doors?" Greppin's voice squawked back.

"On it." Praider said leaving the space and heading over to the door on the right. He took a long deep breath and kicked down the door as his two Silver Team members flanked his sides. Praider stood in the doorway and scanned the empty room. The bed had been slept in. A nightstand lamp laid broken on the ground. The room offered no other inklings of information.

"Just another small bedr—wait, hold up." Praider noticed something on the floor of the far side of the bed. "It looks like there's chains on the floor… Oh, Lord," Praider said.

"Praider, whatcha got?" Greppin asked via his commlink.

"We've got a body."

Chapter 59

EL NACHASH REACHED HIS EUPHORIC moment, standing atop Skull Rock preaching to his church.

"Tonight... *Tonight,* we finally gather at the Tree of Yeshua, and the *New* Golgotha. We come together to celebrate. For the church, *our* church, is now assembled on this night. It is your time to inherit the eternal promises as the Mazzaroth declares.

"The Mazzaroth, God's celestial zodiac map for his Hebrew people, painted in the sky from ancient of days, has always been and continues to be a sign for us and to us. And it has been ordained to arrive and reveal itself at such a time as this. The Psalmist declares, 'When I consider Thy heavens, the work of Thy fingers, The moon and the stars, which Thou hast *ordained...*' My friends, when God ordains things, they are made to proclaim. And so they *do.*"

Rev. Dr. Chase L. Fischer, well hidden in the rock cleft, listened to El Nachash's delusion of grandeur, equally trembling from disgust and the frigid night air. The tip of his nose began to chill. He rubbed it briefly for a little friction heat and began to carefully creep down, while intensely remaining focused on the charade at hand. *Now's my best chance.*

El Nacash swelled with self-importance as each new sentence spewed forth. "The heavenly scroll tells the story God desperately wants you to know... It depicts the preparation of the bridegroom coming forth from his chamber, to join his true church and ultimately vanquish the foe. The first half of the scroll is already complete, as the stars continue to move forth in their season... But who *is* this bridegroom coming forth from his chamber? This beautiful story God wants you to know has been maligned, adulterated, and perverted, over two millennia by the anti-Christ and his minions. You may *think* you know the messianic figure. You may *think* you know the anti-Christ, but you have been lied to for ages by that which portends itself as God's representative."

Sweat dripped down from El Nachash's forehead. He dapped it quickly before resuming his soliloquy. "There is an image of a false Messiah, which has been venerated for far too long, haunting us for thousands of years, forcing humanity into suppression and death, and forcing the masses to worship this image. The abomination of desolation has been committed for far too long. This propaganda is so extensive, twisted, and complex it has deceived all of mankind until now. My friends, no more. In this late hour, God has raised men of understanding..."

Hidden within the shadows and on the move, Fischer shook his head in repugnance. *Oh, I'll bet he has. My gosh, does this guy have verbal incontinence, or what?*

"So, I stand before you now," El Nachash said. "And I ask... Will you *listen*?"

The crowd looking up at El Nachash responded with affirmative cheering and applause to El Nachash's delight.

"This man, the anti-Christ, is not a future political leader... he has already come. Mankind began inventing myths and legends of godmen to fulfill the prophecies in the heavenly Scroll and religions were formed about these myths and legends. The Greeks, the Romans, and the Christians. You have been told that Jesus of Nazareth is the Messiah, but you have been told this ancient lie from the Church of Christianity... and I have news for you tonight. That. Is. Blasphemy."

Fischer's eyes widened and felt a hot streak of disgust shoot through his body. The audible heresy was too much for him. *Good grief, speak of the devil, and he's just condemned himself...*

"But as Jesus' own father had him put to death, and a fact spun to great deception, so too, another god, your truer and greater God will put to death a son to restore all things, *tonight*. A fulfilling little Ram will take its rightful place in sacrifice. This young blood will finally be spilt at the New Golgotha, at the Tree of Yeshua, and once and for all make the final covenant, and make right what once went wrong."

Oh, man. Christian... El Nachash, you sick bastard.

El Nachash's voice elevated to a near yelling of every sentence. "This will restore back to Yeshua the message that he authored in his creation, A *Solar* Messiah, which illuminates the heavenly scroll for you and me for the true message. Sun worship in its highest form. This message is universal for all people, corrupted since the tower of Babel. This is why every pagan solar messiah since is only a mere demi-god... a human attempt at fulfilling the heavenly scroll story. Only true prophets..." El Nachash caught his breath, soaking in the moment.

Like you I suppose El Nachash? Fischer's thoughts raced with sarcasm.

"Only true prophets understand the message in the stars as foretelling of the true coming Messiah. The false prophets hinted that the message in the stars was speaking of their pagan king Jesus of Nazareth. To worship Jesus as the Son of God is false son worship of the highest form. Christianity so willingly changed the holy day for Jesus, this fallen morning star, and replaced it with new rituals, and abolished the law—all of it is corrupted. This lie has been winning the battle long enough. But I, Yeshua, your Messiah returns to destroy the false image—the false messiah—and put an end to the mystery religion of Babylon known as Christianity."

Well, you've really outdone yourself here, El Nachash... This is high form rocket science folly. Fischer sensed the tone in El Nachash's voice lower again and figured he was mercifully near conclusion of his speech, but quickly realized he was wrong, and rolled his eyes.

El Nacash taught as he spoke. "Pisces, Aries, Taurus, Gemini, Cancer, will continue to churn the prophetic tale; the church born, the slain sacrifice, the Judgement, the Messiah and his anti-Christ twin, the waiting Church resting securely. And, of course, Leo, the true Lion of Judah arising to rule *forever*." El Nachash raised his fists in triumph. The crowd cheered, as he played to them all the more. "Yet would you *believe* there are those who work against the unveiling of the scroll?"

"*Booo…*" the crowd hollered.

"And what do we do with enemies of God's message? You see all those smaller palm sized rocks easily in the grasp of your hands… To prepare I ask you to each pick one up. In a little bit, I will bring out my Little Ram… For the church can only be born through the death of another… And I have a special libation for us to all partake together. 'And do not let anyone judge you by what you eat or drink, or with regard to a religious festival, *a New Moon celebration* or a Sabbath day. These are a shadow of the things that were to come; the reality, however, is found in…'" El Nachash cackled. "Me… But first, a lesson. Let me tell you the tale about the fate of Andromeda…"

Chapter 60

DETECTIVE JUSTIN PRAIDER DASHED AROUND the bedframe and assessed the figure laying on the ground. "I think… I think it's…"

The body lay face down. Praider gently rolled the body over. There was just enough room between the side of the bed and the wall. Praider looked at the face and knew immediately who it was. "It's Squirrel… I found *Squirrel*, Greppin," he screamed into the commlink.

"*And?*" Greppin asked over the radio.

Praider assessed the room. "Looks like there was a violent struggle here… He's not responding. Oh, man. He's gone, Grep."

In the LAPD squad car, Detective George Greppin's head dropped, then suddenly lurched up hearing a commotion over the commlink, with guys shouting.

Squirrel began twitching and coughing. His face was bloody, grotesquely swollen, and bruised. Agony vividly oozed out of every pore of his body.

"Squirrel. *Squirrel*. It's me, it's Praider, Justin Praider. You're okay, we're here, LAPD is here."

Squirrel moaned as his broken body convulsed.

"Greppin," Praider said. "He's back, Squirrel's alive, I repeat, Squirrel is *alive*. Get a medic in here, *stat*."

Squirrel coughed up a pulpy concoction of blood and phlegm and faintly tried to speak. "Help…"

Praider tried his best to console him in the awful situation. "Yeah, we're here to help, Squirrel. We're gonna help you real quick,"

"I… I tried to help… GJ," Squirrel said through a garbled mess.

"GJ?" Praider asked, zeroing in. "Yeah, where's GJ? What did they do? What did you do? How'd you help her?"

"Chains…" Squirrel gasped for breath in between word bits. "I… tried… stop them…an…"

"We're *losing* him here, Greppin, we're losing him!" Praider yelled.

An LAPD medic barged in, set his kit on the bed and went to work. Praider held Squirrel's head and assisted with directions. Chest compressions began, as more EMTs entered and took over the situation.

Praider stood over his friend and got out of the way as a stretcher came in. The rhythm of counting and chest compressions paused. They strapped Squirrel to the board and hauled him out and up the stairs.

Justin Praider looked around the dark basement one more time in solitude. After a few somber moments passed, he found himself standing near the coffee table and wall-mounted television. Detective George Greppin walked down the steps.

Praider looked into Greppin's eyes. "I don't know if he's gonna make it."

Greppin let out a long breath. "I was at the ambulance when they got Squirrel in there. The EMTs confirmed his heart stopped. They were hooking up the paddles and had to go. They said he was brave, but… it didn't look good. Didn't think they had enough time to get to the hospital for surgery."

Praider sulked in defeat, lowering his head. "We were too late." He stomped the center of the coffee table, snapping it in the center, looked at the television and with a loud guttural cry, punched it in the center of the screen causing a spiderweb crack pattern throughout the glass.

"Clam down," Greppin said. "Did you get anything out of him before he lost consciousness?"

Praider collected himself briefly with a few deep breaths. "Jade. He mentioned GJ. They tried to chain her up or something I guess, the sickos.

And I think he tried to stop them, help her maybe… But I gather we're witnessing how that played out."

"Indeed," Greppin said.

"Where do we go from here? How the hell do we find her or stop this guy?" Praider picked up and threw the remote control over the sofa and across the room.

"Praider…"

"I'm gonna need a hot second here, George. I just lost one of my guys, right here in my hands." Praider stared at his palms in front of him.

The Silver Team leader trotted down the steps into the basement. "Detective Praider?"

Greppin waved him off. "Hold on. We need a minute here."

"Sorry, but dispatch messaged in from headquarters… It was for Detective Praider… There's some secretary that wants to talk to him."

Praider did his best to pull himself together as Greppin shot an irritated glance back at the Silver team leader. "Oh, *great*, that's rich. That's all we need right now," Greppin said hotly.

"She says it's urgent," the Silver Team leader insisted.

"I don't wanna talk to anyone right now," Praider said, before his index finger shot up in the air as a thought surfaced. "Wait a minute… Is it a *church* secretary?"

Chapter 61

EL NACHASH CONTINUED TO PLAY the crowd like a lyre. "I have a teaser for you. Behold, Andromeda, the woman in chains under the sign of Pisces." He turned his powerful flashlight to his left spotting it atop another nearby adjacent rock formation.

Fischer turned to his right just in time to see Gemma illuminated in the beam of light. She still wore her now dusty jeans and shirt. She was bound in chains with her mouth gagged. Fischer had to bury his feral emotions pleading to rage forth. *Hold it together, Chase, don't blow your cover now.*

El Nachash smiled as the people continued picking up rocks and stones. They began judging the distance to the innocent target, that was Gemma. The crowd bore into her with a mob mentality level of animosity.

"*Now,*" El Nachash cried with adrenaline pumping.

"*WAIT!*" A booming voice from the crowd cautioned. A hooded and cloaked individual stood up in the middle of the throng with outstretched arms. The crowd paused.

The spotlight shifted from Gemma onto the cloaked man who stepped up on a slightly elevated rock across from El Nachash. "Oh, great teacher, as one of your strongest followers, I beg you consider a suggestion on behalf of your people. It seems it would be a great shame to endure the poverty of fine beverage while we seek to enjoy this delicious moment of exacting revenge... We see your libation is poised, as you mentioned. Might I be so bold to propose a toast, *on the rocks* as it were, for Andromeda's farewell?"

El Nachash hesitated slightly in consideration and then sniggered in amusement at the request. "Yes," El Nachash said. "That will work... I've been reading the stars, but you have read my mind. Wolf?" he asked. "What say we get the night festivities going a little early?" El Nachash moved the spotlight through the sea of people, finding Wolfgang Manteuffel, waving his hand, and emerging from the fringe of the crowd. He walked near the table of filled cups and began handing them out. The spotlight stayed on him as the people came forward.

Manteuffel shouted instructions. "*No one* drinks alone. We wait to drink together. We *wait* to drink communally in unison," he said in raised voice as he meticulously monitored handing out the drinks for a few minutes.

Fischer seized the diversionary crack of an opportunity and crept in darkness up the backside rock wall to where Gemma was located. The large rocks were child's play for his experienced self, scurrying up and over them. *Not much time.* He drew close to Gemma, still enshrouded in darkness as the spotlight remained on Manteuffel's table of cups. Fischer grabbed Gemma's shoulder and turned her toward him. Her eyes were misty. The panic, real. Her usual bravado had understandably faded from her, leaving her feeling like a shaky doe. Fischer pulled off her mouth gag.

Gemma breathed deep into the refreshing cool night desert air as Fischer hugged her, cradling her head in his arms. "Chase?" she whispered. "What are you doing here? I didn't think I'd s—"

"No time," Fischer said. "Turn." He whipped out the bolt cutters and snipped apart the chains around her legs, and then her hands. "Thank God these chains aren't the super *thick* kind. Hurry, Christian is in the white van down there. You'll have to break him out, quietly if you can. There are some tools in a bucket next to it. I'll make a distraction for you. Get him out and hide him. On the other side of the road, as far away from all this madness as you can... I've gotta get back down there, fast."

"Chase? What are you going to do?" Gemma asked in disbelief.

Fischer looked at her with a knowing smile. "There's only one way I know how to battle lies... With the truth."

They gently began their ninja-like descent down the back of the rocks.

El Nachash looked over the horde and was pleased as he roared over them. "We will finally celebrate a covenant bond in unity." He noticed the cloaked man discreetly walking up in the dim light and retrieve his cup and returned to his small perch where he spoke from earlier.

The cloaked stranger began speaking again. "Oh, great teacher, I am as ready as the next to expel the wicked from among us," he said, gesturing toward the dark shadowing section of rocks where Andromeda was chained. "But before we join in communal love, I have just one more question I was hoping you could instruct us with… Your son, our sacrificial little Ram, to rectify all this as you say, was born December twenty-first, 2020, correct?"

"Yes," El Nachash said, laced with confusion. "How did—"

"But *why* not September twenty-third, 2017? That *is* the better date for a more accurate sign in the heavens of a messianic birth. If we are becoming the true church under you, we *should* have a sacrificial lamb born on that day, to die for us and breathe life into our new church, should we not? Your Lamb, seems more of a conveniently contrived date, to exploit the masses, *inauthentically*."

"*No*," El Nachash said with a violent burst. "That is not what has been revealed."

"Yet it was readily evident to all… Any *great* theological astronomer like yourself would know that September 23, 2017, was an astronomical phenomenon like no other, particularly related to the birth of a son, in fact *the* Son of God to die for his people."

"Of course," El Nachash said cautiously.

The cloaked man grew in confidence. "You know full well that on *that* day, a fascinating celestial spectacle took place in the heavens which had never occurred. The Sun, the moon, and the stars aligned in perfect agreement with the Revelation 12 prophecy… about a woman clothed with the sun, with the moon under her feet and a crown of twelve stars on her head, pregnant and about to give birth. And of course, Virgo, during *that* day was clothed with the sun… Only until a solar eclipse occurred, revealing the kingly planet Jupiter which had been within the window of the 'womb of Virgo' amazingly for the nine previous months, and passed through exactly at that time, just as the moon appeared under Virgo's feet."

The cloaked man sensed he had rattled El Nachash and pressed on. "So, if as you say, Jesus of Nazareth *is* indeed a false messiah, an anti-Christ even, and Christianity a fraudulent tale, then what of the previous prophecies?"

El Nachash sneered in rage. "*Wolf?* It's time. Bring out my Little Lamb."

Wolfgang departed the company heading for the van.

El Nachash returned his attention back to the cloaked man, in rage. "I have an *earlier* authority. Now, who are you?"

The cloaked man forged forward. "Excellent. How early? King Josiah did away with idolatrous priests who burned incense on the high places of the cities of Judah and Jerusalem, to Baal, to the sun and moon, to the *constellations*, and to all the host of heaven. And earlier than that, God spoke through Moses when he said, 'when you look up to the sky and see the sun, the moon and the stars—all the heavenly array—do not be enticed into bowing down to them and worshiping things the Lord your God has apportioned to all the nations under heaven?'"

The cloaked man recognized the crowd shifted uncomfortably as they swayed back and forth, listening to the delivery of the eloquent speech before them.

"*Silence*," screamed El Nachash. "I have received special revelation from on high. And you try to quote the Book to me? 'For the wrath of God is revealed from heaven against all ungodliness and unrighteousness of men, who by their unrighteousness suppress the truth. For what can be known about God is plain to them, because God has *shown* it to them.'" El Nachash pointed up to the sky. "My friendly followers, it is *all* in the stars above us."

The cloaked man yelled back. "*Suppressing* the truth? You left out the best part of that passage from Romans, '…and claiming to be wise, they became *fools*.' The cloaked man pulled back his hood, revealing his identity.

Rev. Dr. Chase L. Fischer stood in the midst of the madness. His mind flashed through several thoughts as he riskily revealed his identity and exposed his position. The stakes were now raised to their highest level. He spied Chelsea. *Can't let her or anyone drink this poison… would Gemma have enough time to get away… or break Christian out to safety… not to mention himself and how all this might play out…* The nerves in Fischer's legs began to subtly shake uncontrollably under the pressure.

"*Samaritan*," El Nachash said sinisterly through gritted yellowish teeth. "Oh, you are good…"

Fischer turned toward the crowd, while pointing at El Nachash. "He induced his wife into labor, *killing* her in the process, to bring forth his son on a specific day for your manufactured sensationalized obsession. A contrived evil for his infanticidal desires, and ludicrous quest of destroying Christendom or *anything* decent in this world."

El Nachash shrieked the most demonic howl Fischer had ever heard in his life. "*No*. Christianity is only about deception. '…And I saw a star that had fallen from heaven to earth, and it was given the key to the pit of the Abyss.' Jesus *is* the morning star who fell from heaven… and his minions like you have distorted the truth hence forth."

"Your hubris amazes even me," Fischer said. "But I shouldn't be surprised, Lucifer became so impressed with his own beauty, intelligence, power, and position that he began to desire for himself the honor and glory that belonged to God alone."

Wolfgang Mantueffel ran back to the outer rim of the people, desperate and out of breath. He looked up toward EL Nachash. "The boy, he's *gone*."

El Nachash shone his light onto Manteuffel's confused face, then bounced it up toward Gemma's rock perch where only broken chains remained. El Nachash flashed it back toward Fischer as he slowly watched his dream crumble and desperately ordered his dreadful decree. "Everyone sup our drink together, *now*."

"Dear people," Fischer spoke back, "I *plead* with you, please hear me now, the only deceiver here is this self-appointed 'El Nachash,' which literally translates from the Hebrew as *the snake god*. And his alias, Morgan Stern? It's German for *morning star*… Fischer stared directly into the light. "But your real name is Jimmy… Jim Latham. And the only truth about you is you're nothing more than a dimwitted self-absorbed, messianic-complexed Scripture slashing, pulpit pirate."

"*Drink!*" El Nachash yelled in a borderline temper tantrum.

"You *first*," Fischer snapped back. "He won't, my friends. He's mixed a toxic potion of death for you, a cup of wrath… and to put this all to an end,

I think it would be fitting to remember the last decan in the last sign of the Mazzaroth is *Crater*—the Cup of Wrath. Let us pour out the cup of wrath... Here's to you, *Jimmy*."

Fischer held up his cup toward Jim Latham in mocking toast fashion. "Salude! To *our* health." Fischer poured out the poison potion onto the rocky earth.

One by one the mass of people began pouring out their cups, as the action went viral.

Latham howled. "NOOOOOO! WOLF! *Kill* him!"

Manteuffel immediately shifted from shock to attack mode. He fought through the crowd of people toward Fischer. Fischer quickly jerked out his gun from beneath the cloak Maren had given him. *Oh my God...*

Fischer trembled as he squeezed the metal trigger. **BLAM!** And for the first time in his life, he knew what it felt like to fire a gun.

Chapter 62

FISCHER'S ARM WAS RAISED VERTICAL in the air; the bullet sped toward the stars. His hope of inciting chaos worked to great effect. The throng of people screamed at the sound of gunfire in their proximity. They frantically scurried in every direction, but the large rock formations only provided two main possibilities for exit. The once tranquil gathering now had more pandemonium than a freshly kicked ant pile, just as Fischer hoped. The table still holding the extra jugs of cyanide drink tipped over and spilled out in the stampede. *Excellent.*

Fischer jumped off his small rock perch with a flap of his cloak and became lost in the fray. He ran in the opposite direction from Wolfgang Manteuffel. Jim Latham's powerful flashlight beamed about but only caught fleeting confusion in his attempt to find Fischer.

Fischer, safely shadowed for a moment, bumped into Chelsea. He grabbed her by both shoulders. "Chelsea, get out of here, as far away as you can, they're trying to kill all of you. Go. *Run.*"

Fischer watched her run away like a frightened deer through the rock corridor, but he knew Gemma was most likely in the other direction. Fischer calculated through the options for his next move. *Gemma must have gotten Christian out of the van... Where exactly are they? Do I head for my bike? What are these poor people going to do? Two madmen on the loose. I can't just run away now… The sun should be popping up sometime soon, not as easy to hide… Gotta find Gemma.*

Jim Latham reluctantly turned his spotlight toward his pathway down from Skull Rock. He moved as swiftly as he could and marched to his van. Manteuffel met him there.

"I lost him in the frenzy," Manteuffel said in annoyance.

Latham opened a long compartment in the back of the van. He hauled up his sniper rifle with infrared scope. "*I'll* find him," Latham said mechanically, loading a fresh magazine. He stepped out and looked through the lens, which created an incredible level of visibility in the dark. He scanned around and could easily see people from his crowd still moving and hiding in a panic.

Fischer hiked down the edge of the road away from the rear side of the van. *It'd make the most sense if Gemma had headed this way.* Fischer peeked out from a rock. The van was almost one hundred yards away and the back door still closed. *Please, God, I hope she got him far enough away in time.* He dashed across the road near a large rock to hide behind. *She did, she's a professional. I know she—*

CRACK!

A loud sound exploded near Fischer's head, just in time for him to see a small section of the rock disintegrate into powder. *Holy cats…* Fischer dropped down. *They're shooting at me.*

Fischer heard a low ghoulish howl in the distance he could only assume was Latham's.

"Wolf, he's that way."

Fischer knew it wouldn't take long for them to run down an empty road toward him. They could close on him in less than thirty seconds. *No time to think. Gotta Run.*

Fischer scrambled deeper into the Joshua Tree National Park, and the vast rocky desert terrain. He easily moved from rock to rock, down paths, and crevices through a geological labyrinth of boulders. Rock-climbing had always been a zealous passion of Fischer's since his first visit to the Badlands of South Dakota as a kid on a family vacation. Every experience and iota of skill had to be channeled here, now.

Another violent sound *CRACKED* nearby Fischer, which crystallized a chunk of rock, and signaled a second rifle bullet had narrowly missed him. *How can this guy see me? Keep moving.* A thought ripped across Fischer's soul. Of the fight or flight options, Fischer was much more comfortable in 'flight' mode. *Can I fight back? I can't actually shoot a gun at another human being, can I?*

Latham's yelling broke into Fischer's cloud of thought.

"Fischer... I'm going to do to you the same thing I did to your dog."

BLAM! BLAM! Fischer lowered his gun, after firing back in the general direction of the voice. *Question answered... Stupid, Chase. Keep moving... That only gives away my position...*

Fischer kept slipping through corridors and rocky slopes in a desperate game of cat and mouse for what seemed like ages. *Gotta head East. Get this guy behind me.* He finally came to an incredible hiding spot catching his breath and listened. He hid for a long while secluded, for what felt like an eternity. *Will they give up chasing me? What time is it? It's Gotta be morning soon... The horizon's getting brighter. I'll lose the cover of darkness. And the coolness of the night. So thirsty... Where's Manteuffel?*

Jim Latham spied Fischer through his infra-red scope of his rifle. Fischer was still, crouching at rest. "Perfect," Latham said quietly to himself, aiming carefully. He lined up Fischer's head in his sights. "Yes..." He made one last calculated click adjustment for distance. Latham looked through the scope one more time. The Good Samaritan was as good as gone.

The first ray beams of dawn burst over the rock mound behind Fischer. The powerful sunlight stunned Latham with a stinging blindness as he aimed through his infrared scope, just about ready to fire. Latham screamed in agony. The irony all too palpable.

"AHHHHHH!"

Latham fired anyway. Another near miss bullet whizzed past Fischer, prompting him to go on the move again.

Latham looked up into the eastern blood-orange sunrise. Fischer was nowhere to be seen.

"*Blast* it," Latham said.

Fischer's mind raced as he kept displacing from one footing to another.

His stamina, while superb, was beginning to show signs of fatigue. His long cloak which had been keeping him warm had to go. *I have to move quicker.* After another jagged twist and turn through treacherous footing, he came to a decently steep embankment that sloped beside a shallow curved ravine. Fischer spotted some larger boulders perfect for more hiding further up the embankment and across the ravine ledge. *If I can just get up and over that* Fischer thought, preparing to sprint up the angled landscape.

With his gun still drawn, Fischer surveyed the approach aptly, save the tiniest of pebbles. Fischer sprinted up, maintaining momentum to near the top and jumped over the ravine. His calculated jaunt instantly twisted into a slip, as a pebble snuck underfoot. Fischer's gun flew forward and over the small cliff in front of him into the blind side of the ravine. Fischer slid down sideways scraping his legs and fell roughly eight feet down into the tight ravine. He managed to land on dirt and avoid the large rock near him. The lightning pain streaking from the bottom of his left leg confirmed one of his bigger fears. His ankle was sprained. Bad.

Fischer lay still, his ankle swelling more with each passing second. He looked down both directions of the ravine. One direction he could see about twenty yards, the other only about five. *My gun must be down that way. Can't stay here... Oh, no...* Fischer heard footsteps. Someone was about to turn the corner. Fischer picked up a couple small baseball sized rocks. *This is it...*

Wolfgang Manteuffel's frame turned the corner down the far end of the ravine. Their eyes locked. Manteuffel sneered and pulled out a large fat knife, the kind Fischer had only seen in Rambo movies. *Jesus...* Manteuffel began rushing toward him. *Please help me.*

Chapter 63

FISCHER THREW HIS FIRST OF two rocks at Manteuffel a bit prematurely, but he couldn't risk waiting too long. The rock fell short only slightly causing Manteuffel to flinch before he regained his speed.

Fischer waited another eternal second as Manteuffel neared closer. Fischer flung his second and final rock with hydraulic adrenaline. Manteuffel slowed but batted Fischer's best effort away like a father eluding a young son's wiffle ball pitch. Manteuffel kept coming. His knife only got bigger with each step closer. Fischer couldn't scream. He'd lost his breath long ago. Fischer helplessly crossed his arms bracing for impact.

BLAM!

Fischer's body contorted a massive twitch or two, and he was sure he was in shock. That was the only explanation of why he didn't feel Manteuffel's gunshot. Then he remembered. *Manteuffel didn't have a gun drawn.* Fischer quickly composed himself and looked up.

Wolfgang Manteuffel laid on his stomach, face down. His body quivered slightly. He was suffering. Fischer looked behind him. Gemma stood; pistol aimed past him toward Manteuffel. She lowered it.

"*Gemma?* How did you find me?"

Gemma came over to Fischer and assessed his injury. "Well, it wasn't easy, but all the yelling and gunfire may have helped."

Fischer enjoyed the briefest second of levity before the peril they were in came punishingly back. The psychopath sniper, Jim Latham, was still stalking them, and Gemma's gunshot, while rejoicingly opportune, broadcasted their location.

Christian poked his head around the blind side of the curve where Gemma had come from.

"Oh, thank goodness. You have Christian," Fischer said. "Here, get this on him." Fischer unzipped his bullet proof vest but struggled on the ground.

"Let's get you up," Gemma said, yanking Fischer's underarm.

"*Ahhhh*." Fischer stood and hobbled over to Christian slowly, with Gemma's assistance. "Christian, it's Pastor Fischer. Do you remember me? From Church?"

Christian nodded.

"Do you like superheroes, Christian?" Fischer asked.

Christian nodded again, with the tiniest of smiles.

Fischer handed him the vest so he could touch it. "Here, this is a *special* coat. Like a superhero's coat, it's going to keep you safe." Fischer watched as Detective Jade nonchalantly tucked the gun in her waistband centered in the small of her back, like she'd done a thousand times before, and wrapped up Christian in the bullet proof vest and picked him up.

"Nice. Magnum P.I. style."

"Huh?"

"Nothing."

"You okay to walk?" Gemma asked.

"I *have* to be," Fischer said.

They cut through the rock path and continued speaking in hushed tones.

"My motorcycle is about a half mile on the far side from the skull rock."

"We're *at least* a half mile from that on *this* side of the road though," Gemma said. She hesitated in thought for a second. "There's the other vehicles of the campers."

"They've gotta be long gone by now, don't you think?"

"Probably. Who knows. Your bike's probably our best option."

The three of them blazed their way further through the rocky land. They came to the base of another large boulder formation. Fischer, limping badly, pointed with his arm in the general direction of his Triumph Bonneville.

"It's that way. If we can ju—"

"*Fischer,*" a voice yelled. "It's over."

Fischer's spine shivered from the nape of his neck to his tailbone. He recognized the insidious voice.

Fischer and Gemma immediately examined their surroundings. They both saw him at the same time. About thirty yards away, Jim Latham had his rifle aimed directly at them.

Fischer assessed the situation. *Gemma has the gun… but she's holding Christian with both hands…*

"You're right, Jim. It *is* over," Fischer said. "Your followers have left. Your henchman is dead. Your 'prophecy,' falsified. It's over."

"On the contrary," Latham said. "You concluded the Revelation 12 passage too soon. Don't you remember? It says, 'Then another sign appeared in heaven: an enormous red dragon with seven heads and ten horns and seven crowns on its heads. Its tail swept a third of the stars out of the sky and flung them to the earth.' I need you to climb to the top of those rocks behind you. For you will be flung to the earth. The prophecy is true… and the mindless multitudes will still follow. Now *climb*."

Gemma stared at Lathem coldly, holding his child.

"You're *not* going to do this," she said defiantly.

Latham pivoted his frame viper-quick and fired his rifle, hitting a large rock mound beside them. Christian screamed.

"You're really going for father of the year, aren't you?" Fischer asked.

Latham sneered. "Abraham took his son to the top of the mountain, at God's bidding, with the promise his descendants would be greater than the stars in heaven. So, it begins again as the scroll unfolds. Many will see and fear."

Chapter 64

LATHAM DIRECTED THE GROUP AS the four of them converged at the top of a large rock mound. Latham guarded Fischer, Gemma, and Christian at gunpoint with his firearm at the ready. "Give me the boy," Latham said.

Gemma glared a look of disdain at him, crinkling one side of her upper lip. "No."

"*Now*," Latham said, doubling down.

"Jim," Fischer said with his hands raised innocently. "You don't want to do this. Your real name is James Latham. I know who you are." Fischer took a deep breath knowing the risk he was about to take. "I *know* who you are… Our police Chief managed to pull your file. I've seen it. Your *military* file, the counseling report… I know what that priest did to you…"

"Shut up," Latham said with a pained inflection.

"It was wrong," Fischer said, pressing the matter. "For years, it was wrong what he did to you."

"I said shut up. *Stop* it," Latham hissed, working himself up more. The veins in his forehead bulged like earthworms ready to surface after a fresh rain.

"*Chase?*" Gemma asked in a soft quizzical manner.

"It wasn't your fault, James," Fischer said.

Latham absorbed the words.

"It wasn't your—"

"I was *chosen*..." Latham said.

"Unfairly," Fischer said.

"I was chosen for a *higher* purpose. For something of which you can't possibly understand. Now give me the boy," Latham said, shifting his attention toward Gemma and extending his hand.

Gemma hesitated, gripping Christian tighter.

"*Do* it," Latham said.

"No," Fischer said.

"Chase," Gemma said, calmingly. "It'll be ok. You've got my *back*, right?"

Gemma turned her back inching toward Fischer for a moment, while still holding Christian.

"Ah, right," Fischer said, recognizing how brilliant she was, and never more appreciative of Tom Selleck. He quickly and discreetly grabbed the handgun from Gemma's waistband and tucked it away out of view from Latham.

Gemma crept closer to Latham, unwrapped Christian from the bullet proof vest, and began placing him in Latham's arms.

"No. Stop. Set him down," Latham said.

Gemma ignored him, getting intimately close placing the child in his arms and grabbing Latham's gun. They began to scuffle allowing Christian to drop between the two of them and promptly scoot in terror in a hiding crevice close by. Latham's struggle with Gemma was brief as he twisted and yanked his rifle powerfully back and forth, shaking her. He kneed her in the gut as his rifle flew a few yards away from them.

Gemma, briefly stunned, lunged toward Latham. He kicked her as hard as he could in the guts again. Gemma dropped to her knees and rolled over on her side in anguish.

Latham grabbed Gemma's hair by the scruff and cocked back his fist ready to pummel her.

BLAM!

Fischer aimed the pistol directly at Latham and hobbled closer. "Not so fast, Snaky. Let go of her." Fischer shook the gun near Latham's face. "*Release* her." Fischer pulled back the hammer on the gun, which finally convinced Latham to let go.

"Sit down," Fischer said.

Latham sat as Gemma slowly crawled as far away in the direction Christian had fled.

Fischer leaned in closer to Latham. He shoved Latham's shoulder with the back side of his foot. Each of Fischer's words grew more heated than the next. "You are so hell bent on harming... Hurting... Destroying... You're blind in your personal vendetta of rage. Everyone wants to act in violence sometimes, you know that? Even Christians... Even *Pastors*."

"*Chase?*" Gemma asked weakly.

Fischer's handgun trembled with emotion. "I'd love to retaliate. I'd love to go to town on you. For all the senseless destruction you've caused. But you know what? That's not the way, that's certainly not God's way, even the way declared in the stars above. Vengeance is not mine. It's the Lord's."

Fischer calmed down, controlling his voice and temper more with each passing breath. "You had something awful happen to you. I hear you. I get that. We all have been wounded in different ways. But Christianity is not to blame... The Church is not to blame. The ultimate message is not about eye for an eye revenge... Christendom is about... *forgiveness*. Grace... Fischer lowered the weapon.

Fischer looked at Latham's broken face and eyes. Suddenly it was just two men talking, like a pastoral counseling session Fischer had done countless times before. Fischer extended his hand. "The whole message is about the Gospel..."

Latham bowed his head discreetly placing his right hand under his shirt.

"You're right, Samaritan. Vengeance is God's... And that's who. I. *Am*." Latham pulled out a concealed knife and slashed Fischer's right arm.

Fischer dropped his gun in a panic to stop the bleeding. Latham picked up the gun with nimble quickness in his left hand and stood up.

Fischer held his right arm, bleeding from a knife slash, again. *Dang it, that's twice.*

Latham sneered. "I think it's *high* time this little gathering came to an end." He walked Fischer over to the edge of the rock cliff. Fischer looked down assessing the steep jagged fall, then back at Gemma.

Latham closed in on Fischer, double-fisted with weapons and full of frenzy. "*Jump.*"

Fischer looked tenderly at Detective Gemma Jade. "Goodbye." Rev. Dr. Chase L. Fischer took one last breath, turned, and jumped off the side of the rock wall. The last thing Fischer heard was Gemma's scream.

Chapter 65

DETECTIVE GEMMA JADE WATCHED IN horror as Latham turned back with a relieved smile on his face. His grin instantly faded to an ashen frown when his eyes met Gemma's. Gemma had picked up Latham's rifle and currently had it pointed directly at him. "I think Pastor Fischer meant to say, 'It's all about *Law* and Gospel.'"

She cocked the rifle.

BLAM!

Latham's left hand holding his gun burst apart. He squealed in anguish for a moment. Latham examined the small pulpy stump where his hand once was and covered it under his right arm, which still held his blade. He stepped closer to Gemma, with blood streaking down his shirt. Gemma cocked and pulled the trigger of the rifle again.

Click.

Latham jogged forward faster, galvanized in wrath as his eyes zeroed in on her. "You *witch.*"

Gemma held the rifle up crossways to defend herself.

Latham entered his attack stance, instinctive muscle memory from his military training. He swung back and forth as Gemma did her best to block and defend, from his glancing blows and slashes.

Latham's blood continued to spurt as he danced with Gemma around the rocky top of the formation. He wiped his arm on his pant leg and pinched it under his right arm again, breathing heavily.

Latham summoned his strength and pounced forward. Gemma masterfully blocked again with the rifle, but Latham's momentum and weight overpowered her. Suddenly Gemma was on her back fighting for everything. Both her hands held back Latham's one good hand holding the knife. She clasped her hands around his wrist as the toothed blade inched forward closer to her face.

"I can feel you weakening…" Latham said. "You can't keep this up forever."

Tears began to swell in Gemma's eyes. It was evident to each of them that his words rang true. Latham's blood mixed with the dirt on Gemma's clothes.

Gemma glanced over at Christian, still watching in a small rock crevice, terrified out of his mind. Her life flashed before her. Latham's blade was an inch away from her throat.

"*Stop*," Christian yelled.

Latham heard the voice of his son which shook him momentarily. He paused and looked at Christian. "Shut up, you little *snot*."

He turned back at Gemma, ready to finish her off.

A long shadow crossed over the back of Latham and then upon Gemma's face. Latham turned in surprise.

Chase Fischer stood over them with a football-sized rock and slammed it on top of Jim Latham's head. Latham fell sideways, entirely knocked out. Blood sprinkled from his head.

"I think he's gonna be out for a long time," Fischer said.

"Chase? I thought… you were *gone*."

Fischer helped pull Gemma up into a sitting position and sat down beside her.

Fischer enjoyed the moment for all it was worth. "I'm known to be rather agile from time to time… What can I say, I like rock-climbing a lot, and my fingers are like little vice-grips. When he had me there at the edge, I looked down and saw a small ledge with a few tree branches protruding and what I thought was a possible holding point I could make work. For the record, I did *almost* slip. It wasn't the easiest move I've ever done, particularly with a bum ankle and a sliced arm. But it was definitely one of my top ten... meh, top five *riskiest* rock-climbing moves ever."

Fischer smiled at Gemma, relieved of the outcome, and then his heart sank.

"Oh, my. Where's Christian?"

Gemma stood up and brushed herself off as best she could. "He's an amazing little trooper. He's ok. He's right over there." Gemma pointed to the small crevice Christian hid in. "Come on out, Buddy. It's going to be alright," Gemma said sweetly.

"I don't *think* so," a sinister voice said from behind them.

Fischer and Gemma looked behind them.

Wolfgang Manteuffel came up over the rock mound crest, staggering in blood-soaked clothes, and still holding his survival hunting knife. His voice sounded like Satan himself. "I most certainly don't think everything is going to be *alright*."

Fischer, still near Jim Latham, turned his head and assessed the situation. *Oh, come on.*

He quickly scanned the ground. Latham's knife was still there, though much smaller than Manteuffel's. *Two against one, but we're all injured.* Fischer picked up the knife. Fischer barely had a puncher's chance, and he knew it. "Gemma, get behind me."

Gemma picked up a small rock and gingerly stepped back toward Fischer, keeping her eye trained on Manteuffel.

"You ruined *everything*," Manteuffle said. "Everything. All that *work*. Gone."

Fischer's heart began beating hard. Harder and faster. It seemed like he could almost hear it pounding louder and louder as they slowly stalked each other in a circling turn. *Is that my heart thumping so loud?*

Fischer turned behind him and saw an LAPD chopper hovering in the air closing in on them fast. *Jeannie must have gotten my message through. Yes! Always trending up...*

Gemma waved both arms as the helicopter zoomed in closer.

"It doesn't have to end like this, Wolf," Fischer said.

The helicopter side compartment door opened. Justin Praider had a sniper rifle aimed, adjusting for a potential shot.

A booming voice came over an amplified loudspeaker from the chopper. "This is the LAPD. Drop your weapon."

Manteuffel looked at Latham on the ground, bleeding from the head. "What did you do? *What* did you do?"

Wolfgang Manteuffel threw his knife at Fischer. Fischer swerved slightly and barely managed to avoid the flying blade.

Praider fired a round. He missed as the rock powder puffed up near Manteuffel's feet. Manteuffel ran toward the edge of the cliff. "This was the year of El Nachash… It *still* is," Manteuffel hissed. "You have no idea what you've done, or the cup of venom wrath that will now pour down upon you. *Mark* my words."

Manteuffel jumped off the rock mound. He bellowed out a violent cry which faded down the fall until it was no more.

Fischer looked up at Praider in the helicopter and signaled to him a reassuring salute wave. Fischer turned and saw Gemma pick up Christian and begin walking toward him. Fischer staggered toward them until they drew close to each other.

Fischer wrapped his arm around Gemma and tucked her head underneath his chin. Gemma consoled Christian and pointed out the stream of police cars and paramedics with flashing lights, flickering like a parade down the road coming toward them.

Fischer could feel Gemma breathe in a deep rich breath of the crisp comforting morning air as her lungs inhaled.

"I just have one question for you," Fischer said. "Are you still planning on giving up smoking for Lent?"

Gemma started laughing. "Oh… that *hurts*." Gemma adjusted Christian at her side and held her ribcage. "That hurts a lot," she said in a half-laugh, half-cry funny-boned voice.

Epilogue

Easter Sunday, April 20th

REV. DR. CHASE L. FISCHER stepped into the pulpit of the Church of the Epiphany, bursting full of people. "Grace, mercy, and peace be to you from God the Father, and our Lord and Savior, Jesus Christ…"

Fischer began preaching a sermon about the incomprehensible joys of the empty tomb and triumphing over death on the Last Day. He had practiced, processed, and word-smithed his message so much, his entire delivery was memorized. His amount of preparation provided him the luxury many skilled thespians enjoy; to orate live in front of an audience while simultaneously thinking clearly of other topics while the familiar words flowed faultlessly from his mouth. It was enough to make the great Church father, John Chrysostom proud, he supposed.

As Fischer preached his homily, his eyes kept landing on face after face of people who had been intimately touched by a recent death. Mrs. Tatum, listened attentively on one side of the congregation, wearing a dark lavender dress, and dabbing an occasional tear from her eye. She was actively coming to terms with becoming a recent widow as Chief Tatum had sadly succumbed to his wounds. Squirrel, freshly recovered from recent surgery, accompanied her.

Fischer continued scanning the faces as he spoke good news. Michael Chipparo, who had successfully come out of his coma stronger than ever, bounced Christian on his knee, midway on the other side of the packed gathering. Jeannie assembled with her fellow bell choir associates in a reserved section of the transepts. The self-proclaimed bellringing 'Ding-a-lings,' waited for their next moment to accompany the service with music and chime.

In the back, officers Justin Praider and George Greppin stood at the perimeter of the overflow section in their Sunday best. They absorbed the message with one eye and ear, while instinctively standing sentinel over the large crowd at their newfound friend's parish.

In the front row sat Detective Gemma Jade, with a mesmerizing East to West smile. She rocked a lovely saffron yellow dress with an adorable Easter hat decorated with light purple bows pinned in her freshly trimmed pixie cut hair style.

Fischer couldn't help but think that in a moment's notice, her radiant ensemble could almost double as a Kentucky Derby attendant, whilst sipping a mint julep if need be. All he knew was he held the winning ticket with her by his side. He was full of hope and continued preaching the same.

"I believe in the resurrection of the body… Whose body are we talking about when we confess that in the creed? If you think it's Christ's, you'd be incorrect. We've already proclaimed *His* resurrection during the second article of the creed, after the part about suffering under Pontius Pilate, crucified, died, and buried, his descent into hell, and *rising* on the third day… No, my friends. When we confess 'I believe in the resurrection of the body' we are stating that because of our faith, we believe our *own* bodies will rise on the last day. And that *exclusive* message is the unique hope I have to share with you today, and every day. For we are Easter people…"

The service concluded with an exquisite brass rendition of 'I Know that My Redeemer Lives.' The full voiced throng impressively sang in four-part harmony, as Fischer guided Jeannie and the choir down the center aisle, recessing out the rear led by an acolyte and crucifer.

Pastor Fischer stood in the receiving line and began engaging the barrage of greetings and salutations. Greppin and Praider came through first.

"Great message, Chappy," Praider said.

"Chappy, eh?"

"That's Praider's way of saying, if you want to continue serving as our Chaplain, we'd be more than willing to bump you up from honorary status to full-fledged," Greppin said with a wink.

"That's a serious offer from *Chief* Greppin," Praider added.

"Chief? Congratulations, I hadn't heard," Fischer said shaking Greppin's hand. Fischer could feel a level of respect delivered through Greppin's intense grip.

"And to think, just four short months ago you were about ready to arrest me on the spot right here," Fischer said with a laugh.

"Oh, I haven't forgotten," Greppin said, cracking a smile. He picked up one of Fischer's business cards from the welcome stand nearby, winked at Fischer and walked away.

District President Michael Walton sauntered up and put his hands on both sides of Fischer's shoulders. "Attaboy, Chase. Incredible day. *Incredible* service. You had them captivated at every word. It was impressive. Keep it up, son."

After a short sea of greetings and excitable families with children seeking Easter brunch and jellybeans, Mrs. Tatum approached. She said nothing. She didn't have to. With intense sincerity she leaned in, hugged Fischer, and kissed him on the cheek. Squirrel, sporting some new mild facial scars, shook Fischer's hand.

"Peace be with you," Fischer said.

Squirrel extended his arm and assisted Mrs. Tatum on as Fischer marveled at the transitions of life before him. Squirrel walked with a cane, nobly so. Fischer soon turned back to the line and found another welcomed couple, Lori and Richard Freitas.

"Great to see you guys," Fischer said.

"Wouldn't miss it for the world," Lori said with a hug.

"I certainly need hope, particularly after the way my Gators bowed out early of the Big Dance Tourney, *again*," Richard said.

Fischer couldn't help but toy with him. "You *might* need a new team, that or I'll expect to see you here for refueling hope every Sunday."

They congratulated Fischer and swept by. Next in line was a middle-aged couple with their grown daughter. Fischer recognized them immediately. "Charlie and Benita Ferguson. Awesome to see you back. Happy Easter to you." They shook hands. "And Chelsea."

Chelsea popped out from behind her parents in line.

"Where's uh, what's his name?" Fischer asked.

"He was a *loser*. You were right," Chelsea said with a smirk.

"My father always had a great line," Fischer said, "'self-discovery is the best teacher,'"

"Isn't it though," Chelsea agreed with a hug. "We're back. You'll be seeing a lot more of us from now on."

"Awesome. Blessings, guys," Fischer enjoyed every interaction. *So cool they're back in the fold. Amazing how these things work out.* Fischer turned again, caught up in surprise as his right leg was latched on to by Christian.

"Hey there, Little Guy," Fischer picked up Christian.

"I've got him," Michael said, taking Christian back in his arms. "Sorry about that."

"No worries."

"He's doing pretty well, all things considered. Counseling has been amazing," Michael said. "Best money I've ever spent."

"Great," Fischer said, as he noticed Michael holding the hand of a young woman he'd not had the pleasure of meeting before.

"And crazy thing, let me introduce you to Autumn. Turns out, she was good friends with Christian's birth mother. She's been a godsend as I've been working through everything. And get this, she owns a cat café and runs it all by herself. Who *knew*?"

"Is that right," Fischer said, shaking Autumn's hand, but not for too long, as Fischer's eye caught Gemma's next in line.

"And Miss Gemma Jade," Fischer said endearingly greeting her.

"Gemma Jade? *Cool* name," Autumn said as they departed.

"I've got my mother to thank for that," Gemma said.

Fischer watched as Michael, Christian, and Autumn sauntered off into the festivities, effervescently enjoying each other's company. *Extraordinary...* He eagerly turned his attention back to Gemma.

"You look *brilliant*," Fischer said.

"I bet you say that to all the LAPD detectives that show up to church."

"Yeah, that thought wasn't the first one that came to mind when Greppin first darkened these doors."

Gemma stepped in close and hugged Chase for a long moment. "I think I can live with being the exclusive recipient of that compliment," Gemma said.

They continued their tender embrace. Gemma wore the same perfume Fischer had only caught brief whiffs of before. He was delighted to finally breathe in her scent, as his face brushed past her hair.

"*You* were brilliant," Gemma said. "This whole morning has been tremendous. Seriously."

"Thank you."

"I'll see ya tonight," Gemma said, crisply pinching Fischer's hand in hers and made her way out. Fischer finished basking in the morning celebration and mingled in the merriment of the congregant members until the last worshiper had departed for home.

Fischer waltzed into his homey office, set a couple envelopes on his office desk and jotted down a few notes to follow up on later. He opened his right desk drawer for a pen and discovered it was filled to the brim near overflow with black licorice jellybeans.

"Jeannie," Fischer said in a snicker. *It never gets old working with her.*

Fischer flicked off the lights and began his well accustomed stroll home to the light-yellow cape house with green trim.

Fischer entered his front door and hurriedly followed whimpering noises to a small cage in the living room. "Alright, hold on."

Fischer opened the small cage and let out a small Border Collie puppy rich with quintessential black and white markings. Fischer rushed him outside for a tug of war and a chase. A thick ham sandwich and a well-deserved nap later, Fischer arose feeling invigorated.

He walked past his wet bar. *Not yet...* He picked up his laptop and scrolled through a few news outlets and couldn't help himself to pop in on a few social media platforms. Nancy had a post that was gaining traction.

Great Easter message this morning. I so love our little cloister of

Epiphany. He is Risen! #Blessed

Fischer could only shake his head in amusement. *And wonders never cease.* Fischer looked at the time, popped up and sprang into action in the kitchen. He grabbed a bottle of red wine, and a prepackaged charcuterie board with a wide variety of assortments. He headed toward the garage and opened it in time to see Gemma pulling up in her mustang.

He smiled watching her park and get out of the car in her jacket and jeans as he loaded up his saddlebags on his Triumph Bonneville, sans sidecar.

His Border Collie pup ran out into the garage and greeted Gemma with rambunctious enthusiasm.

"Oh my, and who is *this*?" Gemma asked.

"This is Chemnitz."

Gemma knelt down and let Chemnitz sniff her hand. "Wow… Just, *wow*." She started to pick him up.

"Careful," Fischer said, "I almost named him Puddles… You ready?"

Gemma smiled and nodded. "Uh-huh."

In no time Fischer's Bonneville roared over the San Gabriel Mountain crest. Gemma was clung snug to Fischer, arms wrapped around him as they zipped through the winding curves enjoying the beautiful Spring foliage blooming everywhere it could. Fischer glanced in his mirror and could see the sun beginning to lean in for a kiss of the Pacific.

The two headed for a remote park in the desert outside of the bright lights of LA. After finding a secluded spot, Fischer parked and rolled out a small blanket for a cozy late evening picnic. Gemma opened the charcuterie as Fischer uncorked the bottle of wine.

"No whisky to break your fast?" Gemma asked.

"I decided to go with a Robert Mondavi Red, but it *is* the bourbon barrel aged version," Fischer said with a sparkle.

"Nice."

"No celebratory cigarette?" Fischer asked, toying back.

"I think you'll be proud of me. I think I'm done with them. I really didn't miss them nearly as much as I thought I would…"

"Cool," Fischer said.

"But I did acquire a celebratory cigar." Gemma whipped out a stogie and lighter.

"Don't tell me. A Swisher Sweet?" Fischer ribbed as he poured two glasses of wine.

"Oh, no, no. *This* is a Cuban."

Fischer and Gemma nibbled, sipped, and puffed their way into the night as the stars slowly came out one by one.

"So, you really said '*Law* and Gospel' to him right before you blew his hand off?" Fischer asked.

"It just came out," Gemma said with a giggle. "I wanted to say something cleverer like 'I can't read your palm anymore, but I can see a lot of bars in your future,' but I only thought of it after the fact."

"Yeah, getting those great one-liners out in real time at the proper moment is a thing, isn't it?" Fischer asked.

Gemma looked up to the stars. "I was actually thinking recently about the whole theme of this wild episode. The promised hero, crushing the head of the serpent and all. And it was crazy, because in the end, you actually hit El Nachash, 'the snake god' on his *head* with a rock."

"Well, that's not all that surprising," Fischer said. "After all, I *am* a Leo."

Fischer's line sank in for Gemma until she laughed so hard, she snorted. "*Now* you tell me your sign?" She playfully hit his shoulder.

Gemma took another puff of her Cuban and offered it to Chase, as she sipped another taste of wine. Her phone chimed. "Hold on. It's my sister."

"You have a sister?" Fischer asked.

"Yeah, Bella."

"Bella Jade… the beautiful stone," Fischer said contemplating the name's meaning as he blew out a puff of smoke toward the heavens.

"Easy," Gemma said as she read through her text message.

"Huh… Looks like big sis is in some big legal trouble," she said.

"Oh?"

"Well, she is a lawyer, so par for the course, but this sounds different. Hmmm. I'll call her tomorrow."

"You sure?"

"Yeah."

"Deal," Fischer said laying down on his back and looking up at the night sky. Gemma laid down on her back next to him, their heads touching each other.

"So, the Mazzaroth. Do you really think God has a message for us, written up there in the stars?" Gemma asked.

Fischer took a long deep breath in and sighed. "If we believe that God created the universe, *with* intention, it's compelling to consider. From the naked eye, we know the stars are still in place compared to their earliest approximate referent points dating back to the dawn of creation. The Bible certainly condemns *astrology* but does offer a sliver of compliment to the idea of a backdropped salvation epic, and definitely of a redeemer that speaks through all locations, tribes, and tongues. As the psalmist describes the firmament, 'Day unto day uttereth speech, and night unto night showeth knowledge. There is no speech nor language, where their voice is not heard. Their line is gone out through all the earth, and their words to the end of the world. In them hath he set a tabernacle for the sun.'"

Fischer leaned up on his elbow. "Without question, the patriarchs told the ancient Gospel story, and without written language, it's quite plausible they used the stars to help them tell it, as a primitive celestial storytelling aid, literally assisting them connecting the dots. And it's *further* possible a later secularized world would only continue to blur the lines of those ancient stories. It's fascinating when you take everything into consideration. I do think there's *something* there. I suppose at the end of the day, if the Mazzaroth causes people to look up at the stars of God's creation, ponder a bigger meaning of a Gospel salvation story, that He has to communicate to them… of a redeeming savior… and we're all covered by his redeeming blood… I'd say that's a win…"

"*And* they twinkle," Gemma said. "Just like your eyes." Fischer's heart warmed like the sun in the chilled evening light. "I bet you say that to all the pastor/professors of ancient history you bring out into the desert…"

Gemma laughed. "I don't know," Fischer said. "I suppose I can live with being the exclusive recipient of that compliment."

On the outskirts of Fischer's periphery vision, a shooting star bulleted toward the horizon line.

"Oh, did you see that, Chase!" Gemma said, pointing her arm. "Yes, but if I'm being honest, something better has caught my eye…"

Gemma turned warmly back toward Fischer. After the briefest of awkward silences, he slowly leaned in for a long-awaited kiss. Their bodies quivered and coiled into a passionate embrace under the stars, which idly watched on, just as they had done since the origin of time.

The End

In Gratitude to

Castle Bridge Media, for providing a home for Rev. Dr. Chase Fischer.

In Churl Yo & Jason Henderson, for catching the vision and seeing what this could be.

Robert Wilson, for tirelessly helping to navigate the literary minefield.

Kara Eichinger, the love of my life—my sounding board and a constant, supportive joy with whom to share ideas.

Troy Ernst, for always answering "emergency" phone calls with sage forensic science advice.

Paul L. Maier, for inspiring me through a lifetime of quiet mentorship.

Howie Klausner, for big ideas and literary sword-sharpening.

My dachshund, Doppelbock, who keeps me company during the wee early morning hour writing sessions.

Friends, loved ones, & supporters too numerous to list, many of whom are inspirations within these pages.

and Jesus, for everything— The last shall be first.

About the Author

ERIC T. EICHINGER IS AN ordained minister, professor, and accomplished author who writes at the intersection of ancient mystery and modern suspense. Drawing on years of theological training, pastoral experience, and rigorous research, Eichinger brings profound depth, rapier wit, and intellectual precision to the thriller genre. His previous works are best known for casting theological light into human darkness with captivating technique. In *Blood of the Mazzaroth*, Eichinger delivers a high-stakes theological thriller that challenges readers to question power, prophecy, and the hidden forces shaping history. The sacred and the secular dance in a tightly paced narrative that feels both timeless and urgently contemporary. Eichinger lives and works in the greater Los Angeles area with his family.

Other books by Eric T. Eichinger include:
The Final Race
Lord of Legends
Faith by Numbers

CASTLE BRIDGE MEDIA RECOMMENDS...

If you liked this book, you might also enjoy reading the following titles from Castle Bridge Media available on Amazon or by order at your favorite book store:

The 23rd Hero
By Rebecca Anne Nguyen

ANIMAL CHARMER
By Rain Nox
Animal Charmer
Magic & Melody

Austinites
By In Churl Yo

Bloodsucker City
By Jim Towns

SOUL CATCHER
By Don Sawyer
The Burning Gem
The Tunnels of Buda

THE CASTLE OF HORROR ANTHOLOGY SERIES
Volume 1
Volume 2: Holiday Horrors
Volume 3: Scary Summer Stories
Volume 4: Women Running From Houses
Volume 5: Thinly Veiled: The 70s
Volume 6: Femme Fatales*
Volume 7: Love Gone Wrong
Volume 8: Thinly Veiled: The 80s
Volume 9: Young Adult
Volume 10: Thinly Veiled: Saturday Mournings
Volume 11: Revenge
Volume 12: Ripped From The Headlines
Edited By Jason Henderson and In Churl Yo
*Edited By P.J. Hoover

Child of Dark Water
By E.G. Rand

Castle of Horror Podcast Book of Great Horror: Our Favorites, Top Tens and Bizarre Pleasures
Edited By Jason Henderson

Cherry Dark
By R.L. Wilburn

Dream State
By Martin Ott

Dominic
By Lee Guzman

FRENCH DECEPTION
By Janice Nagourney
A Forgery in Paris
A Forgery in Lyon
A Forgery in Marseille

FuturePast Sci-Fi Anthology
Edited by In Churl Yo

GLAZIER'S GAP
Ghosts of the Forbidden
By Leanna Renee Hieber

Hellfall
By Jay Gould

Isonation
By In Churl Yo

JAYU CITY CHRONICLES
By Chris M. Arnone
The Hermes Protocol
Necropolis Alpha

Junk Film: Why Bad Movies Matter
By Katharine Coldiron

Nightwalkers: Gothic Horror Movies
By Bruce Lanier Wright

MID-LIFE CRISIS THRILLERS
18 Miles From Town
By Jason Henderson
Lost Angel
By Sam Knight

Ties That Kill
By Deven Greene

THE PATH
By David Bowles
The Blue-Spangled Blue
The Deepest Green

Strange Shape of Love
By Herta Feely

SURF MYSTIC
By Peyton Douglas
Night of the Book Man
Dark of the Curl

The Thing That Happened When We Were Little
By Caroline Kelly Franklin

Tick Town
By Christopher A. Micklos

Yesterday's Tomorrows: The Golden Age of Science Fiction Movies
By Bruce Lanier Wright

Please remember to leave us your reviews on Amazon and Goodreads!

THANK YOU FOR SUPPORTING INDEPENDENT PUBLISHERS AND AUTHORS!
castlebridgemedia.com

www.ingramcontent.com/pod-product-compliance
Lightning Source LLC
LaVergne TN
LVHW091719070526
838199LV00050B/2457